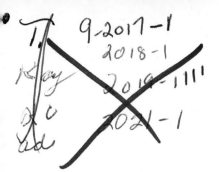

T. 9-2017-1
2018-1
Kay 2019-1111
DC 2021-1
ad

W9-BFE-567

BLOWOUT

ALSO BY CATHERINE COULTER

THE FBI THRILLERS

Blindside (2003)
Eleventh Hour (2002)
Hemlock Bay (2001)
Riptide (2000)
The Edge (1999)
The Target (1998)
The Maze (1997)
The Cove (1996)

BLOWOUT

An FBI Thriller

Catherine Coulter

Doubleday Large Print Home Library Edition

G. P. PUTNAM'S SONS ・ NEW YORK

⑪P

G. P. Putnam's Sons
Publishers Since 1838
a member of
Penguin Group (USA) Inc.
375 Hudson Street
New York, NY 10014

ISBN 0-7394-4363-1

Printed in the United States of America

This Large Print Book carries the
Seal of Approval of N.A.V.H.

To my doctor in the house:
You are an incredible man.

CATHERINE

BLOWOUT

CHAPTER
1

Pocono Mountains
Near Blessed Creek, Pennsylvania
Friday evening

It was darker than Savich was used to, what with no city lights within fifty miles. The moon was a sharp sickle, cutting in and out of bloated black clouds. He rolled down the window and sniffed the air. Snow was coming, he thought, lots of it, more than enough to build a snowman with Sherlock and Sean in the morning; then the three of them could tramp through the beautiful woods filled with spruce and pine to Lake Klister.

Savich started singing one of his favorite

country-western songs, written by his friend James Quinlan, as he drove the straight road with snowcapped boulders and stands of thick trees on his left and a guardrail on his right. *"A blameless life ain't no fun at all. I robbed that bank, laughin' till my belly hurt, till I—"*

When there was a sudden pop, loud as a shotgun blast, he flung himself to the side in automatic reaction. The pop was followed by the hard slap of rubber against the asphalt. A blowout, a damned blowout. The Subaru's steering wheel jerked in his hands as the car's back end lurched wildly to his left. He gently eased the car into the skid and let up on the accelerator, but the Subaru's momentum lunged it into a snowbank. Despite his seatbelt, his head slammed against the steering wheel, stunning him for a moment. Then everything was quiet. Savich raised his head, shook it, hoped he hadn't hurt himself, and slowly climbed out of the car. The back driver's-side tire had blown.

All in all, he preferred the snowbank to going through the guardrail. He buttoned up his coat, wrapped his scarf tight about his neck, and cleared snow from beneath the left front wheel. Satisfied, he climbed back in and put the gear in reverse. The Subaru hardly hesitated, just backed right out, leaning heavily to the left. Savich climbed out again and collected the spare tire and jack. He called Sherlock, told her what had happened, told her he'd be about twenty minutes late.

The grocery bag from Lew's Friendly Staples, in the small town of Blessed Creek, had spilled over. Lew's Staples, he thought, was really for tourists; Lew was expensive, but his little store was open nearly 24/7 and that was what counted for everyone from out of town, that and the fact that the cabin where he, Sherlock, and Sean were staying for a long weekend was only ten miles away. He picked up a bunch of wizened carrots off the passenger-side floor, for the snowman's nose. The quart of two-percent milk for Sean hadn't burst open, unlike the lovely big watermelon, an unexpected find in the middle of January, in a nearly empty produce bin in a grocery store the size of his dining room. It had splatted open, drenching the microwave-popcorn box.

He wasn't about to clean it up now, but it didn't look too bad, maybe even most of it salvageable. As he jacked up the rear end of the car, he thought the watermelon looked rather like the cabin they had borrowed from Savich's boss, Jimmy Maitland, who regularly loaned it out to his friends and his college sons—it had taken them two hours of scrubbing before the cabin was habitable again.

It didn't take him long to change the tire. He was fastening down the last lug nut when he heard something. He turned to see a woman burst out of the trees twenty feet ahead of him, running directly at him, waving her arms wildly, screaming something he couldn't understand. Her hair was long, dark, and straight, flying back as she ran. Her face was stark white beneath the pale sickle of moon that suddenly shone down through the dark heavy clouds.

She was still screaming when she reached him, her breath hitching. Words he couldn't understand bulleted out of her mouth.

He was on his feet in an instant. "It's all right. It's okay, you've found me. I'm an FBI agent. It will be all right." He left his SIG in his belt harness for now. She was so terrified she was heaving, speaking fast and high, hysteria smearing her words like thick grease. "The man, he's in the house! He's trying to kill me. Oh God, *help me!*"

She threw herself against him. Savich was startled for just a moment, then he took her arms and gently drew her close, patting her back. She wasn't wearing a coat, not even a sweater, only what appeared to be a light summer dress, with thin straps. "It's all right," he said against her hair. A young woman, not more than thirty, he thought, but so frightened she would collapse if she didn't calm down. He tried to soothe her, but it wasn't working. She kept saying over and over again, her voice breaking, her terror slamming him in the face, "The man, he's in the house, he's trying to kill me. You've got to help me!"

The same words, over and over, nothing specific, no names, nothing more than what she'd said since she'd run out of the woods. Her voice was hoarse now, but her hysteria kept building. Her eyes were dark, wild and terrified.

He clasped her face between his hands and looked right in her face. "Listen to me. I'm a cop. You're going to be all right. I'll protect you. Just tell me, where do you live?"

"Over there." She threw a wild hand in the direction off to their left.

"All right, is the man still there?"

"Yes, yes, he's there, he wants to kill me."

"It's okay, just hold yourself together. I'm going to call the sheriff."

"*No,* please, please, help me now, you've got to, take me back to the house, the man's there, please! Help me!"

"Why do you want to go back there if someone is trying to kill you?"

"Please, you've got to take me back. You've got to get him, stop him. Please!"

Savich drew back, held her arms in his hands and stared down into her white face. Her eyes were very dark, and her face was so white he thought she was going into shock. "The sheriff," he said, but she jerked away from him and began running away, off the main road.

He caught her in an instant. She fought, sobbing, the wild frenzy bubbling out of her, until he said, "All right. I'll take you back home. You can trust me. No, don't try to move. But it would be stupid for me to go there with you alone. I'm calling for help."

He held her by one arm, pulled out his cell and punched in 911. She made no move to get away. She stood docile and quiet beside him, saying nothing. The phone didn't work. But that made no sense. He'd spoken to Sherlock just a half hour before, calling from the very same spot. He tried again. The cell was dead as those shriveled carrots he'd just bought. It made no sense. He tried one final time. Nothing. What was he to do? "My cell doesn't work. It doesn't make sense."

"You've got to help me." He looked down into her white face. There was no choice. He could haul her into the car and drive to the sheriff's office, but he knew in his gut that she'd fight him like a madwoman. He saw her urgency, her fear, pumping off her in vicious waves. "Listen to me. I'll take you back to the house. It will be all right. Come back to the car with me."

He put the groceries back in the bag and moved the bag to the backseat. He picked up the watermelon and heaved it into the trees, then helped her into the car and fastened her seatbelt. She whispered thank you a dozen times, maybe more, over and over. In that moment, there was no doubt in his mind that someone was trying to hurt her. He shook his head at the vagaries of fate. All he'd wanted was a nice long weekend where he could go for walks in the woods with his wife and his son, teaching him how to tell a spruce from a pine, and now he was back on the job. He turned the heater on high, but she didn't seem to notice. She didn't even seem to be cold.

"Where do you live?"

She pointed to a side road, up off the main road, to the right. "Up there, please hurry. He's going to kill me, he's waiting, he'll—"

Savich turned onto Clayton Road, narrow, but nicely paved. "This is the way?"

She nodded. "Please, hurry, hurry—" She was heaving for breath, gasping. He drove in the middle of the road. Snow was piled up around them.

He drove around a corner to see a large house on a gentle rise to the left, lights shining from the windows on the first floor.

"That's it, yes, that's my house, please hurry, please God, you have to hurry—"

"Yes, we're here. I want you to stay here—"

But she was out the door, running to the front door, shouting over her shoulder, "Hurry, hurry, hurry! You've got to stop him!"

Savich pulled out his SIG, caught up with

her, and grabbed her arm. "Slow down. This man—do you know him?"

She said nothing, wildly shook her head, sending her hair flying, and kept repeating, "Hurry, hurry!"

The front door was unlocked. Savich held her behind him as he opened the door, swinging his gun from side to side. He saw nothing, heard nothing.

He nearly lost her as she tried to jerk free, but he held her, saying, "Where's the living room?"

She seemed more terrified now than before, her pupils wildly dilated, and she was sobbing, incapable of speech. She pointed to the right.

"All right, it's okay, we're going in the living room." He moved slowly, carefully, fanning his SIG in every direction.

There was no sign of anyone. Nothing. It seemed to be an empty house except for the two of them.

There was a lovely fire burning in the fireplace, so she couldn't have been gone long. It was warm in the large room, even cozy, with all the lamps lit against the blackness and the bitter cold outside.

"Listen to me," he said, easing her down

onto the sofa. "No, don't say anything, just listen. I want you to stay right here, do you understand?"

Her mouth was working, and he was afraid she was going to fold in on herself, but she slowly nodded.

"Don't move. I mean it. I want you safe, so don't move from this sofa. I'm going to search the house. If you see anyone or hear anyone, yell as loudly as you can, all right?"

Again, she nodded.

Savich looked back at her once again before he left the living room. She was sitting frozen, her hands on her knees, looking straight ahead at nothing in particular. One of the thin straps of her summer dress had fallen off her shoulder. Summer dress?

The house was large, one room opening into the next. Every single light was on, and why was that? Who would want to hide in a lighted room? He walked through the dining room and into the large kitchen, then into a mudroom. From the right side of the wide hallway, he looked through a library, a study, a half bath, and a small sitting room that looked like an old-fashioned woman's space, with a small writing desk, a plush love seat, and a lovely Persian carpet on the wood floor. There were lots of file cabinets in the room, and an old typewriter.

There was no one lurking anywhere. He checked every inch of the first floor.

The man, the killer, whoever he was, was gone, and that made sense, of course. She'd escaped him to find help. The man knew that and had run himself. Savich walked quickly back to the living room. She was sitting right where he'd left her, her hands still on her knees, still staring, this time into the fire-place.

"There's no one here, at least on the first floor. The man probably ran away when you escaped. Now, you've got to tell me more. Who is this man? Do you know him? Why is he trying to kill you? Are you certain it's not a burglar, and you surprised him? He tried to kill you and you ran? Was he chasing you?"

She didn't make a sound. Slowly, she turned to look up at him. Then she looked up at the ceiling.

It was then he saw the wedding ring on her finger. Where was her husband? "You've got to talk to me, Mrs.—?"

She kept looking upward. Savich frowned as he looked up at the ceiling as well. It was a good nine, ten feet up, with handsome old-fashioned dark molding.

Suddenly, a noise sounded overhead, a thump of sorts, solid, loud, like a man's heavy footsteps, or perhaps a piece of furniture someone had knocked over. But how had she known even before he'd heard anything?

Savich felt a spurt of fear so strong his breath caught in his throat. He brought up the SIG and stared upward at that ceiling. There was nothing more, of course, no sound of anything. He was disgusted with himself. What had he been expecting?

He was getting himself steady again, drawing deep breaths, when there was another noise, but not a thump this time, he didn't know what it was.

All he knew was that someone was right above their heads.

His mouth was bone dry when he said, "Is the man up there?"

Her lips worked, but nothing came out but gasping breaths, full of fear too deep to understand.

"You stay here," he said. "Do you understand me? That's right, don't move. I'm going to take a look up there."

Savich walked to the wide staircase. Why were there no lights on upstairs? He climbed the stairs, his SIG held firm and steady, pausing every couple of steps to listen.

There it was, another sound. He was pissed now. Someone was playing games, the sorts of games that reminded him a bit of the most horrific criminal he'd ever run into, Tammy Tuttle, a nightmare that still haunted him when his brain shut off enough to let it in. But it wasn't Tammy up here. Thank the good Lord she was long dead.

The steps weren't carpeted, just bare solid oak, beautifully finished, and his footsteps echoed loud in the silent air. He felt the weight of each step, sure his feet were sinking just a bit into the heavy planks.

He reached the top of the stairs and paused a moment to listen. He didn't hear anything. He felt along the wall until he found a light switch. He flicked it on and the long corridor lit up. Here the floor was carpeted with thick old broadloom. He went into room after room, all bedrooms, most looking long empty, except for a well-used boy's room with posters of old rock groups on every wall, all sorts of toys and games covering the surfaces. There weren't any clothes strewn about and the bed was made. There was an old signed football from the unde-feated 1972 Dolphins sitting in the middle of it. At the end of the corridor there was a huge master suite, the bed made, the whole space neat as a pin. He opened a closet to find a pair of jeans and a sweatshirt lying on the floor, and a pair of women's boots, one lying atop the other. He went into each of the five old-fashioned bathrooms, searched more closets than he cared to count, and finally he eased into a den of sorts, the walls covered with prints of London and Paris. There was no big media center, just a TV on a stand in the corner and what looked like a *TV Guide* lying precariously on top, a pool table, sev-eral easy chairs, and one ratty leather sofa that looked like it had been used for at least two generations.

There was only silence, thick and dead.

Whatever they had heard, no, *whom*ever they had heard, was gone. Savich felt help-less, something he hated. He wondered if the man who'd made these noises had sim-ply slipped out of one of the upstairs win-dows. Savich walked slowly back along the corridor, alert, his SIG steady in his hand. Suddenly he felt something, something that was close, something right behind him. Savich froze for an instant, then quickly, crouching low, he whirled around, his SIG up. No one was there, not even a dust mote, but the odd thing was that there was a heaviness in the air itself, as if something should be there, as if perhaps it was, just invisible to him. He shook his head at himself.

He had no idea what was really going on. The only one who could clear things up was the woman downstairs, seated on that flowered sofa, staring into the fireplace, wearing a dress more suited to summer than this bone-cold winter night. He could give her tea, calm her down, get her talking, convince her to let him take her to the sheriff.

He'd nearly reached the stairs when he heard another noise. It was above him.

CHAPTER

2

An attic. He'd heard the creak of footsteps overhead, as if someone were walking from one board to the next, carefully, slowly, so as not to fall, trying to move as quietly as he could. Savich got his brain focused and calm. So some fool was in the attic, trying to scare the bejesus out of him. The same fool he and the woman had heard before. He hadn't gone out a window after all.

Angry now, Savich forced himself to stillness. He kept staring upward, waiting for another footstep to pinpoint where the man was, but there was nothing, only the quiet of an empty house.

He saw the attic pull cord nicely camouflaged against a window, down at the end of the long hallway. He trotted to it, unlooped it, and pulled it down. The stairs slipped smoothly down from the ceiling, their lowest rung touching the hallway carpet.

Darkness poured down. He pulled out his Swiss Army knife with its penlight and switched it on. It was better than nothing, though not much.

He climbed the stairs, every sense heightened. He kept his feet firmly planted on the wooden ladder when his head and chest cleared the attic opening and looked around him as far as the meager light from the penlight would penetrate. It was black as Sean's pirate eye patch, with no windows to let in the moonlight. He remained on the ladder, unwilling to climb all the way into the attic. It was too dark and he knew himself vulnerable, even with his SIG. He continued to flash the penlight around him, but its range was so limited, he couldn't make out anything more than ten feet away.

Finally, he spoke. "Is anyone up here?"

There was no sound, not a whisper of a sound. The air itself seemed old and dead, like breathing inside a mausoleum. He circled the penlight again.

He stopped once again, listened. "Is anyone up here?"

There was nothing, not even the scurrying of a mouse to disturb the thick layer of dust that was part of the air itself.

Suddenly, there was a loud whooshing sound, like something was sucking up all the air in its path. It seemed to come from all around him. It was something large, something black, moving like a dozen flapping wings, and it slammed hard into him, hurtling him backward. He lost his balance and fell back down through the opening, his feet not finding purchase on the ladder. He landed on his back on the carpet. He lay there just a moment, his brain stunned into inaction, wondering what damage he'd done to his body.

He had to get it together. Whoever had struck him could strike him again in the next instant. He aimed his SIG upward and listened, but he heard nothing at all from the black hole above his head. Slowly, still listening, he rolled to a sitting position and queried his body. He was aware of the lights around him, steady and bright. He seemed to be all right. He slowly rose, stretched, and stared up again into that black hole, wondering what had hit him. If not a person, and he was pretty sure it hadn't been a man, then there were few logical choices. Bats, he thought, he'd probably disturbed a whole lot of bats. What would bats be doing in a beautiful house like this one? For the life of him he couldn't think of anything else it could have been. And maybe the bats had made the noise. Perhaps bats were common up in the Poconos, particularly in the winter, when the cold drove them inside, to places where it was dark and warm.

Enough was enough. He strode to the top of the stairs, paused one final time, listening, fingers tightly wrapped around his SIG.

He had to get her to talk to him, had to calm her, it was the only thing left to do. He took the stairs two at a time and rushed into the living room, his mouth opening to tell her he hadn't found anything.

The living room was empty.

He pulled out his cell phone, dialed Sherlock before he realized it hadn't worked the last time he'd used it. But she answered immediately.

"Dillon? What's up? You having problems with the car?"

"Sherlock, I'm glad I reached you. The last

time I tried to use the cell, it was dead. Something's happened."

A brief pause, a touch of panic in her voice, then, "Are you all right?"

"Yes, I promise, but something's happened."

"Tell me." As quickly as he could, he took her through it. When he told her about something knocking him out of the attic, he kept his voice as calm as he could.

"She's gone. I imagine she's run away again. She was so terrified, so hysterical, that I couldn't get anything out of her. We've got to find her. I don't know if she's still in danger, but she believes she is. It's cold outside and she didn't have on a coat, she wasn't even wearing a sweater. She could freeze to death."

"Dillon, I think you should go to the sheriff's office in Blessed Creek. I remember passing it, right there in the middle of Main Street. I'll be there with Sean as soon as I can. I'm going to call the sheriff, ask him to meet us at his office. You be careful, Dillon, drive slow and careful, keep your eyes open for that woman. Don't worry. We'll get this all figured out. I love you." He could hear Sean singing away in the background. Now, that sounded normal. He smiled.

Ten minutes later, Sherlock climbed out of Jimmy Maitland's old jeep, which he left at the cabin for his boys' use. She was worried about Dillon, feeling more scared than usual, perhaps because they were on vacation and this was so unexpected. With Sean asleep in the backseat, snoring little puffs of cold air, she could let the worry show on her face. She stood a moment, looking into the sheriff's small office, with its single light shining in the wide front windows. She saw an older man with a thick shock of white hair, fiddling with a coffeemaker. Good, he had to be the sheriff. He'd taken her seriously.

Sheriff Doozer Harms stood in the middle of his office, his back to his coffeepot, his arms crossed over his beefy chest as he watched a man pull up behind the woman's jeep. The man opened the jeep's passenger side, unfastened the child's car seat strap, and lifted out a sleeping boy. They all huddled close, then turned, as one, toward his office.

The man pulled his I.D. out even as he stepped into the office. "Sheriff Harms? I'm Agent Dillon Savich, FBI, and this is my wife,

Agent Lacey Sherlock. We have a problem and we need to move quickly. My wife is the one who called you."

"Yes, she did," said Sheriff Harms as he looked them over. Well, well, two FBI agents, and they were husband and wife, even had a little kid. What was this all about? Agent Sherlock had told him only that her husband had something important to tell him. Doozer wished he was finishing the Bud Light he'd left on top of the TV, and began tapping his foot.

He'd been the sheriff of Blessed Creek for nearly thirty-two years. He figured he'd heard every tourist problem anyone could think of, even if the tourists were FBI agents. But he knew the importance of being polite, knew how to listen even if he was thinking about how much he'd like to be home watching the 76ers.

He shook hands all around, patted the little boy's head, and pulled out two chairs. "What seems to be the problem, Agent Savich? Your wife said it was urgent that you see me."

"It's a woman, Sheriff, she ran out in front of my car, waving her arms, hysterical, yelling that a man was trying to kill her."

Sheriff Harms didn't say a word, just leaned a bit closer, his eyes on Savich's face. He hadn't heard anything like this before. "Where is she, Agent Savich? This woman?"

Savich told him what had happened, including the bats that had knocked him off the attic ladder and onto the second-floor corridor.

"Bats," the sheriff said, then nodded for him to continue.

"It's the only logical explanation I can come up with. We've got to hurry, Sheriff. You need to get your deputies together so we can search around the house. She ran away again, and I'm very worried for her safety. She believes a man is trying to kill her, and whatever's going on, something's just not right."

"I can see that you're worried, Agent Savich. You spoke of driving her back to her home. Where was her home?"

Savich was ready to throw Sheriff Harms through the front window. Time was not on their side. She was out there on this dark night, it was cold, and she had been so disturbed he knew she'd do something stupid. He could see her huddling in the thick trees, shuddering with cold, crying, her hysteria building until maybe the man would find her. Or maybe she'd just die of fright without his help.

"She lives in a big house on Clayton Road. We have to hurry, Sheriff," Savich said, rising. "It's about a fifteen-minute drive."

"Just a moment, Agent Savich. You said she was gone when you came back downstairs?"

"Yes, I'd left her in the living room, told her not to move an inch. I was coming back down to give her some hot tea, hoping to calm her down, to get some sense out of her."

"She didn't tell you who this man was who was trying to kill her?"

Savich shook his head. Sherlock said, "If my husband says this woman is in danger, Sheriff, she's in danger. Do you think we can get out to that house, begin a search for her?"

"You said it's a big house on Clayton Road?"

Savich wanted to coldcock the old guy, but since this was a local situation, no matter he was at the center of it, he held to his patience. "Yes, on top of a small rise on the left side of Clayton Road; it's a narrow road off

Route 85. All the downstairs lights are on, so it's like a beacon."

Sheriff Harms began fiddling with a tooth-chewed pencil on top of his desk. "Would you say it's no more than a half mile off Route 85 on Clayton Road?"

"That's right. Maybe twelve, fifteen minutes from Blessed Creek. Look, Sheriff, time is running down. If I have to call in the Philadelphia Field Office to get some action, I will, but it will take time. I don't think this woman has much of that left. We've got to get out to that house and find her."

Sheriff Harms slowly rose, leaned forward, his palms flat on the desktop. "You're talking about the Barrister place, Agent Savich. Biggest house around these parts, you're right about that. You said the woman lived there?"

"Yes, of course, she lived there. It's a lovely house, really big, but nice and warm, cozy. There was a fire burning in the living room fireplace. No one was there, no husband, no help, no one. I searched the place top to bottom."

"After the bats knocked you out of the attic, you came back downstairs? And she was gone?"

"Yes. Maybe she heard me crashing out of the attic and it terrified her. She must have run outside to hide in the woods."

"What did the woman look like, Agent Savich?" Sheriff Harms spoke slowly, his faded blue eyes intent on Savich's face.

"She was about thirty, thin. Her hair was long, straight, dark, parted in the middle. I don't remember her eye color, but her face was very pale. She wasn't dressed for winter, I can tell you that, which is part of why I'm concerned."

Sheriff Harms said, "That was an excellent description, Agent Savich. Now, we can go out to the Barrister place and look around. We can shine big lights all through the woods, make a lot of racket—but the thing is, that'd be a waste of time."

"I don't see how, Sheriff."

"Well, the fact is, Agent Savich, the Barrister house has been abandoned for well nigh thirty years now. There's no one there, hasn't been for half my lifetime."

Sherlock said, frowning, "Thirty years? You're saying that no one's lived there for that long a time?"

"Yep. I know the Barristers still own the

place, since the taxes are paid on it every year, but they all left."

"No," Savich said, rising, leaning over the sheriff's desk. "No. You're thinking of a different house. Look, Sheriff, I didn't dream this. The woman was as real as you are. I've described her to you. We've got to go out there; we've got to find her and help her." He turned on his heel, said over his shoulder, "Sherlock, I want you to take Sean back to the cabin and wait for me. I don't know how long I'll be."

"You want me to come with you, Agent Savich?"

"That would be up to you, now wouldn't it, Sheriff?"

Sherlock stood by the front door of the sheriff's office, rocking Sean, who was bundled up in his winter jacket and gloves. "Why don't we all go?"

All of them piled into the sheriff's big black SUV. Ten minutes later, without Savich saying anything, the sheriff pulled off of Route 85 onto Clayton Road. It was dark and cold, the black clouds thick overhead. There was the smell of snow in the air, not rain. Savich supposed he expected the woman to come running out on the road again, waving her arms madly—wearing that skimpy dress. She could freeze to death. She could be dead already. The man could have been hiding outside, at a safe distance, watching to see what would happen. If so, he could have seen her run outside, and followed her.

He didn't believe for a minute that the Barrister house, the one Sheriff Harms said was deserted and abandoned, was the house he'd been inside.

"We should see the house any minute now," the sheriff said. It seemed to Savich that there were more ruts in the road than he remembered, the asphalt crumbling in many places, as if it hadn't been tended in a very long time. No, he was wrong, he was misremembering. That beautiful big lighted house would come into view at any moment. Yes, there, another hundred feet and the small rise appeared, on the left, and on top of the rise was the house, trees closing in around it from all sides. He didn't remember the trees being so close.

There were no lights shining out of the first floor of the house now, none at all. It looked like a huge black hulk, crouched atop that rise. Someone had come back and turned the lights off, or the power. A small voice in the back of his brain asked why.

"This is the Barrister house," Sheriff Harms said, as he pulled to a stop in front of the big, dark house. "Is this the place where you brought the young woman, Agent Savich?"

Savich didn't say anything. He pulled on his leather gloves as he slowly got out of the SUV and walked to the front of the house. He paused a moment, unwilling to accept what he was seeing. He walked up the wide wooden stairs that led to the covered porch which extended the full width of the front of the house.

Suddenly the moon came out from behind the black clouds, and he saw the house clearly for the first time.

It was the same house he'd been inside an hour before, but it wasn't, not really. This house looked deserted, dilapidated, as if it had been neglected for many years. Trees pressed in toward the house, some of their branches whipping against upstairs windows. There were boards nailed over downstairs windows, broken glass scattered on the porch. There was even graffiti on the wall next to the front door.

The house was dead, had been dead for a

very long time. His heart pounded as he looked at the front door that was barely hanging onto its hinges, studied it, and accepted what he saw because there was simply no choice. He closed his eyes a moment, seeing the woman clearly in his mind's eye, realizing how very pretty she'd been, not having noticed it at first because she'd been so frightened.

He turned and walked back to the car.

Sheriff Harms said as he turned on the engine, "Her name was Samantha Barrister. She was murdered here back in August of 1973."

"I want to see a photo of her," Savich said.

Sherlock took his hand, held it tight.

Two hours later, Sherlock awoke to find Dillon standing by the bedroom window, staring out at the falling snow.

She got up and walked to him, and wrapped her arms around his back.

"Did I wake you?"

"No. You're thinking about her, aren't you, still trying to find logical reasons for what happened."

"There aren't any. It's driving me nuts. Even

though I've been over and over it, I guess I can't get around the fact that I've experienced something, well, I guess you'd have to call it otherworldly."

She kissed his shoulder. "Then perhaps it's time to simply accept it."

"But the reasonable part of my brain doesn't want to." He turned and pulled her into his arms, buried his face in her hair.

"There's another thing, Sherlock, something I just remembered. I called you when I had the blowout. It wasn't ten minutes later that she came running out of the woods. I insisted on calling for help, but I couldn't get through on the cell phone. But then later, at the house, after she was gone, I called you and it worked just fine again."

She held him more tightly. "It's possible the signal was better there." She paused a moment, touched her fingertips to his jaw. "I just remembered something else, Dillon."

He wasn't going to like this, he knew he wasn't.

"You called me at about eight o'clock."

"Yes, that's right."

"The second time you called me, it was only about a quarter after eight."

He sucked in his breath. "No," he said, "no,

that's just not possible. That would mean that all of what happened—no, that's ridiculous. I spent a lot of time with her, even more time just searching that house. No, I can't accept that all that happened in fifteen minutes."

"Maybe we're both wrong about the time. That's the most reasonable explanation." She hugged him again, touched her fingertips to his cheek. "It's very late. It's snowing. Sean will be up and raring to go in less than four hours. We'll have time to discuss this tomorrow; you can decide what to do then.

"There's a reason she came to you, Dillon. You'll have to act. But sleep is the best thing for you now."

He came back to bed, held her close against him, and prepared to stew about it until morning. He knew he would have to investigate what happened to this woman, even if he never convinced himself that what had happened was real. But he didn't lie there staring at the dark ceiling as he fully expected. He fell into a dreamless sleep in three minutes.

At six-thirty Saturday morning, Savich's cell phone played the opening of *Chariots of Fire*.

His first thoughts were of Samantha Barrister and the strange events she'd put him through.

"Savich." He listened a moment, then looked over at Sherlock, who whispered urgently, "What's wrong? What's happened?"

Savich flipped off his cell phone, then turned on the bedside lamp. "Mr. Maitland is sending a helicopter to take us back to Washington."

Sherlock said, "Goodness, it's something that big? Something so big we can't even build one snowman with Sean?"

"Yeah. You're not going to believe this."

CHAPTER

3

Supreme Court Building
First Street N.E.
and East Capitol Street
Washington, D.C.
Late Friday night

Associate Justice Stewart Quinn Califano
stepped out of the underground garage, bent
his head against the cold wind blowing in his
face, and walked around to the front of the
Supreme Court Building. He paused to look
up at the sixteen marble columns at the west
entrance that supported the famous pedi-
ment and the words incised on the architrave
above: *Equal Justice Under Law.* He loved

the neoclassical style of this magnificent building, one that would be his home until he shucked off his mortal coil, or retired, something he couldn't begin to imagine. Every time he entered, it was like walking into a Greek temple. Once inside, he greeted the three guards at the west entrance security checkpoint, making a point to ask about their wives, Amanda, Georgia, and Tommie, passed through the airport-like security gate, and stepped into the main corridor of the Great Hall. He paused a moment to give a little salute to the closed-circuit TV camera, not three feet above his head, and made his way through the Hall, his footsteps echoing loudly on the marble floors. He was well aware that every guard on duty tonight already knew he was here, alerted since he entered the garage. Not a single one would be surprised at his presence close on to midnight, even on a bone-cold Friday night in January. It was his habit to come here at all hours.

He paused a moment, as he always did, to admire the monolithic marble columns that rose to a coffered ceiling. The first time he'd visited the Supreme Court Building he'd been twenty-two years old, in his first year at Harvard Law School, and he'd stood there staring at the Great Hall's incredible beauty and opulent detail, its acres of creamy Alabama marble.

The guards never dared ask him why he came long after closing hours. Truth be told, this was his refuge, a place he found utterly and completely private in the hours when most everyone was safely home. He could come here and be certain no one was listening or looking, the one place where he was safe from prying eyes, endless conversations, endless wrangling, and Eliza, he thought, smiling.

He quickened his pace, giving the Court Chamber at the end of the Great Hall only a cursory look. He walked to the right and paused in front of his chambers, his footsteps echoing loudly. He looked back at the romantic gloom and saw the shifting movements of the guards in their rubber-soled shoes. His hand was already on the doorknob, his eyes on the personalized placard that had been placed there seventeen years before, when he realized he would prefer to be in the library tonight. His inner office would feel too close, too full of recent conversations with Eliza, Fleurette, and Danny, his law clerks, and the tears of one of his secretaries, Mary, who was retiring come March.

Justice Califano turned and walked quickly to the elevators that took him to the third floor and the 500,000-volume library. He heaved a deep satisfied breath as he entered the main reading room. He loved this place, with its hand-carved oak-paneled walls, its soul-deep warmth that came not from the oak and mahogany but from all the books that surrounded him. Here there were no cameras, no electronic eyes to monitor his activities. He took off his coat, his cashmere scarf, and his leather gloves and laid them on a chair at his favorite study table. He took his time adjusting the old-fashioned lighting fixture. He paused a moment and looked toward the beautiful arches. He sat down, leaned back in his chair, and thought about *Jackson v. Texas*, a death penalty case the four liberal justices had voted to hear that was coming up on Tuesday. They wanted to revisit the *Stanford v. Kentucky* case of 1989 that allowed by a five-to-four decision the execution of juvenile offenders age sixteen and over. They were hoping to swing him and Justice Elizabeth Xavier-Foxx over to their side to gain a plurality and do away with the death penalty for all minors. It probably wasn't the best case to push into the court, Stewart thought, since the sixteen-year-old boy had committed three particularly heinous murders. He was, according to his father during his original trial, a psychopath, exhibiting all the classic symptoms from the time he was eight years old. The father had tried to have him committed, but the boy was charming and intelligent, and the psychiatrists and social workers had failed to see through it. Then came the murders. Now he faced a death sentence in Bluff, Texas.

Stewart was interested in hearing the lawyers' arguments about what had changed since 1989, both for and against. He hoped they would cover new ground, but chances weren't good. Though he wasn't certain which way he'd vote, he knew he was leaning toward the exclusion of all juveniles from death penalty eligibility, although by the time a juvenile offender actually faced the lethal injection, he'd be at least forty years old.

He stroked the soft leather arms of his chair, the one he'd first sat in when he'd walked into the library right after his confirmation. It was, he thought, rather cool to be

one of the Supremes, so charmingly mis-
leading, since all of them were grandparents.
It was time, he thought, time to make decisions, time to stop thinking about upcoming
cases. His hand shook slightly as he pulled
the sheaf of papers from his breast pocket
and smoothed them out on the shiny table.
He began to read.

He paused a moment, looked up. He
thought he'd heard footsteps. It was the
guards, making their rounds, he thought, and
went back to his reading. Since 9/11, the
number of guards protecting both the building and the personnel had been tripled, and
more sophisticated equipment had been in-
stalled, but not in the library, thank God.

He read what he'd written earlier in the day,
felt a shot of renewed anger, then paused
yet again. More footsteps, soft, but closer.
And moving slowly, very slowly. He didn't
know any of the guards to tiptoe around. It
was probably someone new come up here to
check on him, to make sure everything was
all right.

He swiveled in his chair and looked toward
the darkness. Then he looked through the
row of arches. Finally, he turned to look toward the open library doorway. In all direc-

tions he saw only midnight shadows surrounding the small circle of light he'd provided for himself. Suddenly, he felt afraid.

He heard a voice, a deep voice, close yet somehow muffled, whispering something. To him? He half rose in his chair, his hands on the arms.

"Who's there?"

Was that his voice, that thin whisper layered with fear?

There was dead silence, but it was no longer comforting. He called out louder, "Who's there? Say something or I'll call the guard."

Califano stood, reached for his coat, only to remember he didn't have his cell phone. He looked toward the internal call phone on the wall not ten feet away from him. Guards could be here in a matter of seconds.

He wasn't a coward, but it didn't matter. Fear had him by the throat, hurling him into a race toward that phone, his hand outstretched when something thin and sharp went around his neck. "Now, isn't this nice?" a voice whispered against his ear.

Califano pulled at the wire. Tight, so tight. He couldn't breathe, even though his shirt collar was between the wire and his skin.

The low quiet voice said near his left ear, "Now, this won't get it done, will it?" Something struck him on the head. Pain and white lights fired through his brain, and he felt himself falling. His hands fell away and his shirt collar was ripped downward, exposing his bare skin.

He was hurled to his knees, his attacker behind him. He felt the wire digging into his flesh, felt the welling sticky blood, felt such pain he wept. The wire loosened a bit and somehow he managed to get his fingers beneath it, and that low, intimate voice laughed. "Well now, a fighter, are you?"

Slowly, inexorably, the wire tightened, sliced right through his fingers. His brain was crystal clear in that instant when he knew he would die if he didn't do something. Now. The wire cut smoothly into the bones of his fingers, and his brain exploded with pain. Still, he managed to push outward enough to scream. It wasn't loud, but surely a guard would hear him, hear that strange sound and come running.

"That was pathetic, Mr. Justice, but I think that's enough now."

Had he heard that voice before, or was it the intimacy of death making the voice sound familiar? The wire jerked tighter. The explosion of agony made tears spurt from his eyes. He felt the wire cut through the last of his finger bones. It was inside his throat now, and soon it would cut all the way through his neck. He couldn't breathe now, couldn't think.

The god-awful pain was easing, his brain was blurring, his thoughts breaking apart, scattering, but amazingly, his last thought before death was, *I would vote the death penalty for that psychopath boy.*

When the wire loosened and was pulled back up over his head, Justice Stewart Quinn Califano fell over onto the floor of the Supreme Court library, the quiet air now filled with the smells of death's final insults.

CHAPTER
4

Washington, D.C.
Saturday morning

Callie Markham put one boot in front of the other, bent her head into the wind and the lightly blowing snow, wished she was roasting herself under an electric blanket, and kept walking. One foot in front of the other.

Her teeth were ready to chatter, and her toes were wet despite her expensive leather boots and the lovely thick wool ski socks Jonah the jerk had given her for Christmas. Okay, she'd been stupid to walk the eight blocks, but she was still so angry that she'd chosen not to drive or take a cab. She'd intended to walk off her mad before she sat down at the breakfast table with her mother and stepfather. Now she rather thought the mad was the only thing keeping her going. It was cold and getting even colder, if that was possible.

It was just after nine o'clock, enough time for them to catch up on everything. Maybe she'd even tell them about the jerk Jonah Blazer, a journalist for *The New York Times.* She really didn't want to admit that she'd been so wrong about him, but of course if they asked, she'd have to tell them about that lying moron.

Everywhere she looked, the feathering snow was stark white, soft and romantic in spite of the cold wind. She wondered how long it would stay so achingly clean. But she didn't want to freeze to death in a winter wonderland. She finally turned the corner onto Beckhurst Lane, old, rich, and beautiful, its big houses set way back from the quiet, tree-lined street.

She came to an abrupt halt. There were three strange cars, mongrels all, at odds with the Beemers and Benzes and the occasional sexy Jaguar. These sedans were pedestrian, nondescript, and they'd been parked here awhile, given the amount of snow on their hoods. What was this? She paused a moment, frowning, watching the silent snow cascade like lace from the leaden sky.

Oh good heavens, was she ever slow. They were cop cars, and that meant something was wrong. She ran to the front door, nearly tripping, and panting because she was so scared. She tried to find her keys in her leather bag, but her hands were cold and shaking and she couldn't find them. She pounded on the front door. "Let me in! Somebody, let me in!"

She heard footsteps coming, not her mother's light high-heeled step. The door swung open. A woman in a black pantsuit stood there. "Yes? May I help you?"

"I'm Callie Markham, Mrs. Califano's daughter. What's going on here? Who are you? Oh God, has something happened to my mother?"

A man's voice called out, "She's the daughter? Bring her in here, Nancy."

It was then that Callie heard a woman weeping, quietly, hopelessly. It was her mother.

Callie ran into the living room, only to stop

cold. There were three men there, two in dark suits, the third in a leather jacket, white shirt, black tie, and black slacks, black half boots on his feet. Mr. Leather Jacket rose from where he'd been sitting close to her mother, and walked to her. He was a big guy, tall and tough-looking, out of place in this soft cream-and-blue room. The two suits with him didn't look all that tame either, but their clothes didn't fit as well as his. "Ms. Markham?"

"Yes. What's going on here? Who are you?" She tried to get around him, to go to her mother, but he blocked her path. "Just a moment, ma'am. You're Mrs. Califano's daughter, the one who is supposed to be in New York?"

"Yes, yes, I came back early because I found my boyfriend in bed with another woman, if you can believe that. Now move, before I deck you."

The man smiled down at her, and even though it was the meanest excuse for a smile she'd ever seen, there was also a bit of humor in it.

"Excuse me?"

She shoved hard against his chest. "Move, dammit!"

Margaret Califano raised her head. Her face was ravaged, eyes swollen, her mascara smeared around her eyes.

"Callie? Please, Detective Raven, it's my daughter. She's not here to hurt me."

"Mama? What's going on here? Why would anyone want to hurt you?"

She watched her mother rise and weave a bit until she steadied herself. Her strong, self-assured mother looked fragile, terrifyingly fragile. She held out her hand, her mouth worked, but nothing came out. She sent a look toward the man, fanned her hands out in front of her, and fell back onto the sofa, her face in her hands.

Detective Raven. Of course the man was a cop.

He said, "I'm very sorry, Ms. Markham, but it's your stepfather. He's dead."

She slowly turned to face Detective Raven again. "That is ridiculous. It's a beautiful Saturday morning, and here you are saying things like that? What kind of a sadistic creep are you?" She tried to shove him away, but he didn't move.

He said, "Look, Ms. Markham, I'm sorry I didn't ease into it better, but I'm telling the truth. Someone murdered your stepfather last night. I'm very sorry."

Callie was shaking her head, back and forth, unable to accept what the words meant. "I want to talk to my mother. Go away, all of you. Mama? What happened? Was there an accident?"

"No, Callie," Margaret whispered, her breath only a whisper against Callie's cheek when she held her tight, "no accident. What Detective Raven said is true. Stewart is dead. Someone murdered him in the Supreme Court library last night."

Callie still couldn't accept what she was hearing. "A Supreme Court Justice doesn't get killed in the library, for God's sake. It can't happen. All of you must be wrong about this."

"I'll agree it's a shock, Ms. Markham," Detective Raven said, "but we're not wrong."

She shook her head as she said, "All right, all right, who killed him? How? Why? I know that he enjoyed visiting the Supreme Court Building after hours, that he liked the solitude and the privacy, but what was he doing there last night, for heaven's sake?"

Detective Raven said, "We don't know much of anything yet. An FBI forensic team is at the Supreme Court Building, along with about six of our guys and a gazillion or so Feds. Judge Califano was garroted. We don't know who did this as yet, but we will find out, Ms. Markham.

"The media will have found out about this by now, even though we laid down a temporary blackout until we got security under control and reached your mother. The media have as many grubs as we do. I expect both the print media and TV reporters to roll up here any moment. I'm to get the two of you down to the Daly Building before the vultures light and start coming down the chimney."

"I can handle the media. I don't think my mother is up for going anywhere."

"Ms. Markham, it would be better than being barricaded in here with the media pounding on the windows, using bullhorns to ask you how you feel."

But Callie, now stroking her weeping mother's back, said to him, barely above a whisper, "He's dead? Stewart is really dead?"

"Yes. I'm sorry."

She stared over at him, through him really, he thought, trying to make sense of the situation. She said, "No, don't say anything more. All right, tell me this. Where were the guards? There are a zillion guards in that building. They're sharp, they're smart, and my stepfather knew most of them. They wouldn't hesitate an instant if someone dangerous broke in. They'd shoot him dead. And the whole building is monitored."

"I'll tell you everything we know, Ms. Markham, but let's get out of here first. Trust me on this, neither the FBI nor the local cops nor the Justice Department want you hounded by the press right now. Please come, we've got to go."

Callie stared up at him. "Who are you, exactly, besides a big mean guy and a snappy dresser?"

"I'm Detective Ben Raven, Washington Metro." He flipped out his badge. She studied it. "You can check out Officer Kreider and Detectives Boaz and LeBeau later." Come on, let's get out of here. Captain Halloway said the FBI is bringing in one of their hotshots. The guy was out of town, probably off skiing somewhere. He'll be meeting us at the Daly Building. Of course Director Mueller and Deputy Assistant Director James Maitland will be in charge of the investigation." He held out his hand to her. "This FBI hotshot they're bringing in will probably want to lay you out on a rack, and find out everything you don't even realize you know."

"I see. You've already pounded the grieving widow and now you're ready to move on to the daughter."

"Yes. Actually, you're his stepdaughter, aren't you?"

Callie rose, in his face now. "And your point would be?"

"Just trying to be accurate, Ms. Markham. In my line of work, accuracy is important."

"Accuracy is important in mine too, Detective Raven, but I try not to be a moron about it."

He couldn't find another lick of patience. "We must leave now." He knew she was angry, for her mother, he imagined. He'd seen her eyes go glassy there for a while, and he'd worried she'd collapse along with her mother. But he wasn't worried now. She was ready to do battle, ready to chew some nails. He had a feeling that nails were a staple in her daily diet.

Margaret Califano was no help at all. It took both Officer Kreider and Callie to get her into her lovely dark blue cashmere coat, to pull boots on her feet, and to work the gloves onto her hands. She was weeping silently, not fighting them, but not helping either. And Callie kept thinking, *Stewart is dead. Someone murdered him.* How could this happen?

The three men stood there, of no use at all, uncomfortable but stoic, until she was ready.

Callie and Officer Kreider half-carried her mother to the four-door white Crown Victoria, the last car in line. Detective Raven helped them into the backseat after sweeping away a box of Kleenex, an empty pizza box, and a stuffed dog with a dangling left ear.

He got in next to her, crowding her over, and closed the door. "Bobby, we're ready."

"Was that close or what?" Detective Bobby LeBeau said. "Here are the vultures now. Nancy's going to follow in her car, and Ray will bring yours in, Ben."

Bobby pulled out onto the snow-covered road as the first of the media vans was searching the street for the right house.

Ben smacked him on the shoulder. "Go, Bobby."

Callie said quietly to Detective Raven, "How did the killer manage to get into the building, much less up to the third-floor library?"

He frowned at her and grabbed the chicken stick above the passenger window when the car started sliding on the slick road. "Before we get to that, do you know, personally, what Justice Califano was doing at the library last night, Ms. Markham?" To her surprise, he pulled his PDA from his pocket and waited, the small stylus poised.

"I have no idea. I told you he liked to spend time there, to be alone, I suppose, study briefs, review opinions, whatever. If he went for a specific reason last night, I don't know what it was. May I ask why it didn't occur to any of you to call me?"

"Your mother didn't know your hotel in New York. We didn't try your place because your mother didn't think you were there."

"All right. I answered your question, now answer mine. How did the killer manage to get to my stepfather?"

She felt her mother flinch. She was listening. Callie hoped that Detective Raven— what kind of name was that?—had something to tell them. He didn't answer her immediately because he was looking out the back window to see if any of the media were following. He turned back and said, "All we know so far is that we have one guard, Henry

Biggs, who's in the hospital unconscious because someone whacked him on the head when he went out for a smoke, took his clothes and waltzed right into the building. When Officer Biggs regains consciousness, and the doctors aren't saying yet if he'll make it, then we'll find out all the details. The guards didn't pay much attention, probably because the killer looked enough like Henry Biggs in size. So that means the uniform fit him well enough.

"The FBI forensic teams are superb. You can bet they will come up with some evidence. It's rare that a murderer leaves a pristine crime scene."

"The man who killed my stepfather must have followed him around," Callie said, "learned his routine, hung around the Supreme Court Building, learned the guards' routines. Someone had to have seen him, noticed him. Wait, there's closed-circuit TV in the building. The cameras would show him, wouldn't they?"

"Yeah, we're already checking the security tapes to see if the killer shows us any features we can use to identify him. The guy had to have visited the building several times, probably in one of the tours. Maybe we'll see him."

Callie was stroking her mother's gloved hands, staring through the windshield at the soft snow. "So that leaves us right now with no obvious motive, and a guard in the hospital with a cracked skull, still unconscious so we can't talk to him. What does he look like?"

"The Supreme Court marshal told us that Biggs is tall, beefy through the chest, a white guy, around fifty. So our guy can't be that far off in appearance. I assume you got home before midnight last night, Ms. Markham?"

"Why yes I did. And isn't this just lovely. I'm a suspect."

"It's my job, ma'am. I'm just doing my job."

Again, Callie wanted to smile, but didn't. "Do you know," she said slowly, turning to look out the car window, "I can accept that he's dead, intellectually." But there was nothing intellectual about how devastated her mother was. She supposed that it would hit her soon, but for now, she had to protect her mother. It gave her mind focus.

Margaret said, not looking up from Callie's shoulder, "Callie wasn't supposed to be home until tomorrow, Detective. We were having a surprise birthday party for her."

"Thank you, Mrs. Califano. How old are you tomorrow, Ms. Markham?"

"Twenty-eight, Detective Raven. How old are you on your next birthday?"

"Thirty-two on March twentieth."

Margaret raised her head. "My daughter wouldn't kill anyone, Detective."

Callie said, "Well, the thing is, Mom, if I'd had a gun last night, I might have shot that jerk Jonah. As for the bimbo he was with, I thought about drop-kicking her out the window."

Ben grinned, couldn't help himself. He was suddenly thrown against the door. Bobby was slipping and sliding all over the street, which was, thankfully, empty. Only cops and idiots would be out in this. It was only another mile or so to the Daly Building. He watched a big black SUV slide very gracefully across the road into a fire hydrant, barely missing an old Caddy. It was a strange moment, he thought, sitting next to this woman, her grief palpable, her life as she'd known it gone in a flash.

"Yes, Detective Raven, I got home about eleven o'clock last night. Delta Shuttle from

La Guardia into Reagan. It never even occurred to me to stay in New York."

He would check that she'd been on board
that Delta flight from New York City in any
case.

CHAPTER

5

The Henry J. Daly Building
Metropolitan Police Headquarters
Judiciary Square

Captain Halloway met them inside the imposing granite entrance of the station house, surrounded by several of his men. He was very solicitous with Margaret Califano and Callie, and said in a low voice to Detective Raven, "Ben, I just got a call from Deputy Assistant Director Jimmy Maitland. Those two agents were brought back from the Pocono Mountains by helicopter. They're on their way over here to speak to Mrs. Califano. And we've got a safe house to take them to for the next couple of days."

They walked through the security checkpoint into the station. It was warm inside and thick with the smells of sweat, wet wool, coffee, and an occasional whiff of forbidden cigarette smoke. Ben said to Captain Halloway as he warmed his hands, "I guess since a Justice of the Supreme Court is high up in the federal food chain, we'll have to get used to the Feds. I wonder if these FBI hotshots will be neck stompers."

"Maitland said these two don't waste their time on dickhead power plays.'

"Hello, Detective Raven. Good to see you again."

Ben Raven was grinning even before he saw Dillon Savich, Sherlock at his side, come through the security checkpoint. "Well, I know them, sir. Would you believe this? As I live and breathe, it's the wild man and his keeper. He's a lot like you were, Captain, in the bad old days."

"Hi, Ben," Savich said, and shook his hand. "Captain Halloway, this is my keeper, Agent Sherlock."

Ben became serious after he'd made introductions to everyone. "And last, this is

Callie Markham, Justice Califano's step-daughter."

Margaret Califano stared at Sherlock. "I've never seen such beautiful hair. How do you get all those curls?"

Savich laughed, relieved that the widow could be distracted, if only for a moment. "It takes her hours, ma'am. I beg her to come to bed, but she'll call out that she's got one more roller to go."

Sherlock poked her husband's arm, then took Margaret's hand. "You're very nice to notice, Mrs. Califano. We're sorry about your loss, ma'am, Ms. Markham. We're here to help in any way we can. And we will find the person responsible, you can take that to the bank. We know it's a really bad time for you, and everyone at the Bureau thinks it's best if you guys were protected for a couple of days. That means keeping you out of the media feeding frenzy that's already started. In a couple of days, we'll set up a press conference if you wish and you can say your piece."

"Justice," Callie said. "You're promising my mother justice."

"Yes, it's not enough, but it's all we can offer. Mr. Miles Kettering has loaned us his lovely house in Colfax, Virginia. You won't be disturbed by the media. We will have agents there, available to you if the need arises. We'll have agents screen your phone calls and forward important ones to Colfax." Sherlock didn't add that both she and Dillon had buckets full of questions, and this, along with their safety, was one of the main reasons everyone at the Bureau wanted Mrs. Califano isolated for a while. Having the daughter with Mrs. Califano was a bonus.

"Why, Agent Savich, would someone kill my husband?"

He heard the bewilderment in Mrs. Califano's voice, saw it in her ravaged face. "We don't know yet, but we'll find out."

Sherlock said, "I'll send some agents to pack clothes for the both of you. Ms. Markham, it would be best if you remained with your mother. I imagine the media have found out about you and are camped out right now at your apartment."

"All right." Callie saw that her mother was staring at the two FBI agents—no, she was staring through them, obviously over-whelmed. Her eyes were vacant. Sherlock realized it at the same moment. She and Cal-lie each took one of her arms, and half carried her over to a bench. "You sit down, Mrs. Califano. I don't want you to worry about anything right now. Your daughter will stay with you."

Margaret raised her head. "But he's dead, my husband is dead. Gone. And there wasn't any warning, nothing at all."

"I know. Put your head down, ma'am, and breathe nice slow deep breaths. Just like that." Sherlock nodded to Callie. "You try not to worry either. Take care of your mother. Once you're moved into the Kettering house, we'll come and talk."

Margaret whispered something to her daughter.

Callie said, "My mother would really like a cup of tea."

"No problem," said Captain Halloway. "If your mother is up to it, we'll go upstairs to my office. It's nice and quiet and warm."

He took Margaret Califano's arm and led her to the elevator.

"I'll be up in a moment, Mother." Callie turned to Sherlock. "I've never seen her like this before in my life."

Sherlock said, looking at Margaret Califano as the elevator doors slid shut, "It's tough for a child to see a parent fall apart like that,

I know. And how are you holding up, Ms. Markham?"

"Call me Callie. I'm not in shock yet, but my mom's awfully close. Thank you, Agent Sherlock, for getting the house for my mother. But really, I don't need to go to this house in Colfax. My mother has four very close women friends who will stick close to her if you let them, provide her all the support she'll need. They'll be a real comfort to her.

"I think it would be better that I stay here, keep busy, work with you to find out who killed my stepfather. Of course I'll stay at a hotel, maybe under a different name, so the media won't bother me."

"No way, Ms. Markham," Detective Raven said. He'd been speaking to Savich, and he spoke without even looking at her.

"My mother needs protection and comfort and support, I don't. Actually, I think I'd like to have the media find me."

Ben said, "Nobody but an idiot wants to deal with the media."

Callie drew a deep breath, fanned her hands in front of her. "I thought you would have known. The thing is, I'm one of them."

"What does that mean?"

"It means, Detective Raven, that you know

I was Justice Califano's stepdaughter, but you haven't bothered to check out what I do for a living. I'm an investigative reporter for *The Washington Post.* I'm one of the vultures."

"Well, sh—" He wanted to curse big time, but didn't.

"So some would say," she agreed, "what almost came out of your mouth. Nice save."

"So you caught a reporter jerk in bed with another reporter jerk and you're the third reporter in this triad?"

"Hey, another good save. You didn't call me a jerk."

"The boot doesn't fit just yet. Damn, what are we going to do with you? Why don't we go sit down in one our primo interview rooms?"

Callie looked him up and down. "As long as it's warm. My feet are wet. Yes, all right, let's go talk. But I want some tea before you sweat me."

Savich laughed. Officer Nancy Kreider said, "Personally, I'd kill for some coffee."

"That would be okay, too," Callie said, then felt a rush of misery. She cleared her throat, aware that they were all looking at her. "The thing is my stepfather believed coffee is the first cousin to evil tobacco and wouldn't let it through the front door. I once brought a thermos of coffee to their house, had to swig it on the sly."

Officer Kreider patted her arm. "I'll send someone to get us coffee and bring it to the interview room."

Sherlock pulled two teabags out of her purse. "Dillon wouldn't exactly call coffee a first cousin to evil tobacco, but close enough. Could we have some hot water?"

Callie walked down a corridor of dirty linoleum, the color of lettuce, streaks of muddy water making puddles here and there where the linoleum had caved in, thinking that a Justice of the Supreme Court of the United States of America had been strangled, and they were talking about coffee. There weren't a whole lot of people around, cops or otherwise. She thought this was odd until she realized it was Saturday morning.

The small interview room was warm, if nothing else. There were half a dozen chairs and a single scarred table. The walls were painted the same lettuce color as the linoleum in the corridor. Callie thought if she were a criminal, she'd confess, just to get out of this room.

She shrugged out of her coat, sat down, and slipped her boots off so her socks could dry out.

No one said anything until the coffee and hot water for the tea arrived.

Callie looked from Detective Raven, who'd taken off his leather jacket, to the special agents. Officer Kreider sat against the wall, saying nothing. "I was on the debate team in high school. I had quite an edge because my stepfather taught me. My mother wasn't married to him then, but they'd been seeing each other for at least six months as I remember. He was brilliant, I recognized that even as a self-absorbed teenager. I told him once when he demolished me in an argument that he could probably convince a fencepost to tango." The instant the words were out of her mouth, Callie burst into tears. Sherlock handed her a Kleenex. She hiccuped, then managed to get herself under control.

Ben Raven rolled up his shirtsleeves as he said, "How long was it before your mother married Judge Califano?"

She took a slow sip of the strong black coffee until she was sure she wouldn't lose it again. "She didn't marry him until I went to

Bryn Mawr. She took a long time deciding, I guess, for the simple reason that she was and is very rich. Even a Justice of the Supreme Court could have been interested in her money."

"And the other reason?"

"You're fast, Agent Sherlock. My aunt Marie, her sister, married a second time only to have her new husband sexually abuse her twelve-year-old daughter, my cousin, Moira. I've never asked her, but I think that was the other big reason why she waited."

"So," Ben said, "she waited until you were out of the house."

"She was careful," Callie said. "My mom's always been very careful with me. So, no matter how much she believed in her second husband, I guess she wouldn't take a chance."

"Is she that careful about everything?"

"She's brilliant herself, Agent Savich. She came from a rich family, it's true, but she didn't sit back and let servants pop peeled grapes into her mouth. She started her own business, and now she owns four high-end boutiques in the metropolitan area, all of them doing quite well indeed. I think she's a little too driven, but that's just the way she is.

To answer your question, she's careful about money. She has hers and, I suppose, my stepfather kept his own accounts. She earns the money, and she's always protected it. That, and her reputation, it's very important to her, and it's not got anything to do with her family name. It's because of her own pride in what she's accomplished, in what she is. I liked to see the two of them debate something, anything." A sob caught in her throat again, and she stared down at her feet. "Yeah, she's careful about everything."

Savich took a sip of tea before saying, "What did your stepfather think about her financial attitudes? The separate accounts and all that? Since he was an older man, wouldn't he have expected joint accounts, expect perhaps to manage his wife's money?"

Callie shrugged. "I wasn't at home enough to form an opinion. When I visited, neither of them ever raised any contentious subjects. I remember only one real argument I walked in on and that was five years ago."

"Do you remember what the argument was about?" Sherlock said.

"She was angry about something he'd done, something she'd found out about. I don't know what it was, but my mom was nearly in orbit. Then they both saw me and clamped a lid on it. Again, this was five years ago, hardly relevant to anything."

Detective Raven said, "Are you aware if your stepfather was ever involved with anyone other than your mother? Did he ever make a pass at you?"

She shook her head at him. "That's such a strange question to ask about my stepfather. He simply wasn't like that."

Savich said, "So, from what you heard five years ago, do you think your mom was winning the argument?"

"This is quite a round robin you've got going here, and all of you fall into it so smoothly. My mother could argue with the devil, Agent Savich. If she and my stepfather ever got into it other than that one time, my nickel would be on her, mainly for persistence. She's strong, my mother. This horrible murder has flattened her, but she'll rebound, you'll see."

Sherlock asked, "Do you think she loved her husband?"

"Yes, I believe it. As I said, around me, they rarely argued, never questioned what the other chose to do. When they were alone?

Sure, why not? I assume all married folk argue from time to time. Why all these questions? Do you think my mother killed him?"

Savich said, "Of course not. All these questions help us get a handle on how Justice Califano lived his life, how he dealt with the people close to him. The more we know, the faster we'll find your stepfather's killer. Do you know of any possible enemies Justice Califano had? Anyone he disliked?"

She thought a moment, cupping her hand around the still-warm coffee cup. "There were a number of politicians he didn't care for, and there were some lawyers he believed were scum, but who doesn't? Anyone close to him—sorry, but I can't think of anyone right now."

"How was your relationship with your stepfather recently?" Detective Raven asked.

"It was fine. The truth is I was well aware of who my stepfather was—impossible not to realize that your mother's husband is a Justice of the Supreme Court of the United States. Everyone who knew was completely bowled over—there are a lot of sycophants out there—but truth be told, he was just my stepfather, nothing more, nothing less."

"You said you admired his brilliance."

"Detective Raven, he could have chewed you up for breakfast and still enjoyed his croissant."

Officer Kreider laughed, then coughed into her hand. "Sorry, the coffee went down the wrong way."

"I did some debating in college myself." Was there a bit of a snit in Detective Raven's voice?

Sherlock said, "Ms. Markham—"

"Please call me Callie since I have this feeling we're going to get quite chummy."

"That's fine. Call me Sherlock. My husband is Dillon."

"You two are married?"

"Nearly forever," Savich said. "Ever since she shot me dead in Hogan's Alley. That's a dummy town down at Quantico that has the world's highest crime rate. Agents-in-training catch bad guys there. She caught me and brought me down."

"And my name is Ben," said Detective Raven. He eyed Callie a moment, saw that she seemed to have it together, but that could change. "Now, Callie, when did you last see Justice Califano?"

"Last weekend, our usual Saturday-morning brunch." Her voice caught and she fell silent. She swallowed. "I was coming over this morning for brunch. It was a surprise since they thought I was in New York."

"What did he think of this Jonah character you were hanging out with?"

"The Jonah character happens to be on staff at *The New York Times,* Detective Raven. My stepfather once said he only had to read the first two lines of Jonah's supposed hard news, and the bias smacked him in the face. But he also said if anyone wanted to have objective news, he'd have to go to Mars. There was no such thing here on earth. The truth was, he thought Jonah Blazer was an opportunist. I did hear him say that once when he didn't know I was listening."

Savich said, "And what did your stepfather think of your reporting, Callie?"

"As I said, my stepfather was a very smart man. When one of my investigative pieces impressed him, and it did happen twice, he told me. Otherwise, he stayed out of it. We made a deal after I started with *The Washington Post*—get that look off your face, Detective Raven, he didn't help me get the job at the *Post*. I got it on my own merits." She paused, drew in a deep breath. "Okay, they probably hoped I'd dish up insider news to them on the Supreme Court, but I never did. I never would. It worked well."

"I thought it was going to be 'Ben.'"

"Not when you're obnoxious. Just get that look off your face, he did not get me my job."

Sherlock raised a hand. "All right, children, enough insults. Now, Callie, what did your mom think of this reporter in New York?"

"She despised him, although she tried hard not to show it."

Ben said, "So your mom and your stepfather couldn't stand this guy and yet you still had him on your A list?"

"I'm young. I'm stupid. I thought Jonah was a deep thinker."

"You're not that young," Ben said.

"Thank you for the diplomatic correction."

"Hey, it's why I'll never be the police commissioner. And about your reporter—after all this deep thinking, it turns out he was just horny like most of the guys on the planet."

"That's exactly right, Detective Raven."

Sherlock said, "Why the strong emotion on their parts? Did they think you were going to marry the guy?"

Callie frowned down at the dregs in the bottom of her coffee cup, then leaned down to pull her boots back on. When she sat up again, she said, "You know, I really don't know why she couldn't stand him. I asked her once, but she slicked right out of answering. As for my stepfather, he never really said anything about Jonah other than that one comment I overheard."

Savich said, "All right. If everyone is done for now, I think it's a good idea for Captain Halloway to get you and your mom to Colfax."

Sherlock nodded. "Thank you very much, Callie, for your assistance. If you think of anything that might help, call us immediately. I know this is very difficult for you, but I have a favor to ask. Please don't report this to your newspaper or give anyone an exclusive. We really need to get a handle on all of this, and it would be helpful if you could hang back, help us keep the lid on things."

"I would never do that." Callie thought for a minute. "I'll bet my editor, Jed Coombes, is jumping up and down with excitement. But I'll deal with him. I'll drop out of sight for a while. I just hope he won't fire me."

"Nah, he'll keep thinking he can talk you around," Ben said.

"At least until the funeral," Sherlock said. "That'll be toward the end of next week."

Callie stared at her. "The funeral. I hadn't thought about that. I need to take care of things. My mother's friends can help me." She wrapped her scarf around her neck and headed for the door.

"Your coat, Callie," Ben said. "You forgot your coat."

CHAPTER 6

The flamboyant white marble columns of the Supreme Court Building were festooned with both yellow police tape and blue FBI tape. Savich thought it looked rather like a madly decorated Greek mausoleum. The first of the forensic teams had already come and gone. Marshal Alice Halpern, flanked by two Supreme Court police officers, was first to greet them. She seemed alternatively reserved, shocked, and defensive. Savich wondered if Marshal Halpern would be forced to resign. Already she was being beaten up by politicians and the media for allowing a Supreme Court Justice to be killed on their turf. Given the large security budget, the criticism was fierce and continuous.

The snow was still coming down, thin and floaty as a bride's veil. The wind was quiet, but as the afternoon wore on, Savich knew the temperature would drop. He stood with Sherlock and Detective Ben Raven in the third-floor library, their voices lowered out of some strange sense of reverence.

Savich slipped his cell back into his jacket pocket and looked at the two of them. "The President, the FBI director, and the Attorney General announced the death of Justice Stewart Quinn Califano to the world a few minutes ago. As you can imagine, the media are in full twenty-four-hour-coverage mode. We got Mrs. Califano out just in time. This is going to be a huge investigation, bigger than anything we've been involved with, coordinated by the FBI, under the control of the FBI, but with the help of Washington Metro. I've been assigned to report directly to my boss, DAD Maitland, and you'll be the point person at Metro, Ben. It'll be your job to keep all the Metro brass in the loop, all the way up to Police Commissioner Holt. Metro will have its own group interfacing with ours. You need any assistance at all, you let me know. Our first big meeting is this afternoon at FBI headquarters. Sherlock, you've been study-ing the room. What do you think?"

Sherlock pointed to the chair at the end of the beautifully carved table. "He took off his coat, pulled off his gloves, unwound his cashmere scarf, and neatly laid the lot on the back of this chair. He's sitting in the next chair, at ease since he's comfortable here. He's alone, but protected. What are there—a dozen guards patrolling the building on a Friday night? And a sophisticated communi-cation system connecting everything in the building."

"So he's not at all worried about being alone," Ben said.

"Right. Okay. It seems strange to me that a Justice would spend his whole week here and then come in on a Friday night for the fun of it. So he's obviously here for a reason. Maybe he's got some papers to review, something he doesn't want to commit to his computer or share with his wife, and we know he was a computer buff. What he wants is privacy. So what are these papers? He pulls them out of his coat since he didn't bring his briefcase—"

"Unless the killer took the briefcase," Ben said.

"The guards said he didn't have one," Savich said. "Said he pulled out a sheaf of papers along with other stuff to go through security. He didn't have to do this, naturally, but it was one of his habits. So he's sitting here reading, relaxed, and then he hears something."

"Yes," Sherlock said. "He hears something, and it pulls him out of his reading. He looks up, maybe he calls out, then maybe he's suddenly scared, wants to call for help. He gets out of the chair to use the wall phone."

Savich picked it up. "Since there was no warning, no fight, it was probably at that moment that his killer came up behind him and looped the garrote around his neck."

Sherlock said, "And it was a man. The M.E. says there's no way a woman could have gotten the leverage to do the job. Remember, he had to loosen the loop at some point to get the shirt collar out of the way, and he had to be strong."

Savich said, "There were two cuts on the Justice's neck, which means the killer started pulling it tight but Califano's shirt was in the way. And so he loosened it, gave the Justice a chance to slip his fingers underneath it, and then he finished it off."

Sherlock said, "The pressure was so great, the wire so sharp, that it cut right through the bones of his fingers. The killer must have worn gloves. This was brutal, almost gleefully brutal."

Ben said, "Why do you say that?"

Sherlock shook her head. "I don't know, really, it just feels that way to me."

Ben said, "I wonder if Justice Califano knew who the man was. I wonder if the man said anything to him before he choked him to death, or did he come up behind him and do the job without a word."

Sherlock said, her head cocked to one side, "I think this guy talked to Justice Califano, taunted him after he had that wire around his neck, after he was sure he had control. We've got a good-sized ego here. This is a guy who's full of himself, strong enough to take down a man like Califano, a good-sized, fit man for his age.

"The guy took huge risks here, knocking out that guard, coming back into the building wearing the guard's clothes, assuming he'd blend in so he could roam free in the building. Since it was late at night, there was a good chance he could slip up to the third-floor library unnoticed, unless one of the other guards spoke directly to him."

Ben stared at the two of them. "You know what, guys? There were far easier ways to do this if all he wanted was to kill Justice Califano. Why would he choose to kill him right here in the Supreme Court Building, ostensibly terrorist-proof, heavily guarded? Was he making a point? Is he just crazy? Sherlock said the murderer was gleefully brutal. This guy sounds like a professional, but he didn't behave like one."

"If he is a professional," Sherlock said, "there must be a huge paycheck at the end of it."

Savich said quietly. "And if he is a professional, he enjoys his work. Could be the money's secondary."

"Again," Sherlock said, "we get back to Ben's point. Why take all those unnecessary risks to murder Justice Califano?"

"If we find that out, we've got him," Savich said.

Ben looked from one to the other and back again, his eyes finally resting on Savich's face. "Maybe it was some sort of test, some sort of a challenge."

"Maybe," Savich said. "But it could also

have been someone who hated Justice Cal-ifano's guts to such an extent that he wanted not only to hurt him badly before he killed him, he also wanted to humiliate him, and maybe the Supreme Court itself, and that's why he chose to do it here."

Sherlock lightly touched her fingers to the glossy library table, the rich wood glowing in the dim early afternoon light. "I think the killer had to be a professional. Otherwise, if it was someone who knew him, someone who hated him deeply, then I'll bet he would have been smart and gotten him someplace pri-vate and killed him with as little risk as pos-sible."

"So this was for enjoyment because it's the way the guy gets his jollies," Ben said. "For Feds," he continued after a moment, looking back and forth between them as they both nodded, "you guys are making some sense. So you're thinking professional regardless of the risks he took?"

Sherlock nodded. "We'll check on the whereabouts of all the professional assas-sins with anything like this M.O.—using a garrote, liking big risks. Think that might track?"

"Yeah, I do," said Ben. "No terrorists at all in this scenario then."

Savich said, "We'll cover all the bases. The CIA is already deep into it. So far, there's nothing, and no one has claimed any responsibility. Revenge sounds good to me, something up close and personal."

"Not a random madman or an extremist of some persuasion?"

"Could be, but it doesn't feel right."

As they walked from the Supreme Court Building on East Capitol Street, Ben said, "You want to know the truth about something? If someone wants you dead, you're dead. You can have the Praetorian Guard, motion sensors, a gazillion alarm systems, it wouldn't matter."

Savich said, "You're right, of course, but no one is willing to accept that. Now, we've got a murdered Supreme Court Justice, so that means endless and exhaustive media attention from every talking head who's ever been a cop, or just thinks he's smart, and the President will likely get twice-a-day briefings on our progress. Everyone will focus on the murder for maybe a day and a half, then turn their attention to who the President will nominate to take Justice Califano's place on the Court.

"In the meantime, we'll have unlimited resources, both federal and local, and huge expectations to live up to."

Sherlock said, "It all comes down to the fact that our Justice Califano made a big-time enemy, so this gives us another starting place, the money behind the murder."

"So alibis don't mean diddly squat," Ben said, "if this big-time enemy didn't want to get blood on his own hands."

"That's about it." Savich yawned. He was tired to his bones what with staying up half the night thinking about what happened in that house in the Poconos and getting called so early on Saturday morning to come back to Washington. He wondered if his father, FBI agent Buck Savich, had enjoyed sleeping in on a Saturday morning sometimes, at least once a decade.

Saturday afternoon

Jed Coombes, editor for *The Washington Post* and Callie's boss, could hardly contain himself. "What the hell do you mean you're not coming in? Look here, Callie, I know it's Saturday, I know you're supposed to be in New York, but you're back home now. I know the Justice was related to you, but that's exactly why we really need you here—"

Callie held the phone to her ear but tuned him out. Jed always used six sentences to say what he could say in one. He was understandably pissed, since he saw her as his direct pipeline to the background on the story, and she let him rant, even toss in condolences when a tug of his long-forgotten manners kicked in. She waited for him to run down, like a wind-up toy. He said the words Pulitzer Prize at least three times. Finally, he was reduced to panting a bit because he hadn't taken a single breath in his entire rant.

"I understand, Jed," she said at last, "but the bottom line is that it was my stepfather, and my mother needs me. It doesn't matter that I'm a reporter, I will not go against the FBI on this, and I've promised them I'd stay away from work for a while. Surely you don't want to see this case compromised because I shot off my mouth."

"It's not my job to care about the FBI's case. It's my job to run a newspaper."

She smiled into her cell. "I'll speak to you

again after the funeral, Jed. My mom's in pretty bad shape, as you can imagine. I don't know when I'll be back."

"Callie, why don't you speak to your mom, get me some personal stuff here—"

"No, Jed."

She heard some ripe curses, then a deep sigh. "You'll let me know the instant you have all the funeral details? Regardless of the specifics, you can be sure there'll be a big service, probably with the President and everyone in line to be President. They'll be up there saying how great a man Califano was even if they might have hated him. Come on, Callie, there's a lot going on that has nothing to do with the investigation."

"Okay, Jed, you've got a point on that one. The instant things get nailed down, I'll call you."

"But—"

"I don't even know when the M.E. will release my stepfather's body." She swallowed, tears pooled in her eyes.

"Callie, you there? What's wrong?"

"Nothing, Jed. Look, I've got to go now. I'll probably see you at the funeral. Thanks for authorizing a week's leave of absence."

"I don't know, Callie, you're a big part of

the team here and you've got to realize that—"

Callie shut off her cell and slipped it back into her pocket. It began ringing within three seconds. She turned it off. She wondered what Jed Coombes would do if someone in his own family was murdered. He was such a news junkie, such a hard-ass when it came to getting a story, he'd probably give himself an exclusive.

CHAPTER
7

The Kettering home
Colfax, Virginia

Callie walked into the living room of the lovely Colonial house in Colfax where she and her mother were stashed. One of her mother's oldest friends, Anna Clifford, was with her. Poor Anna had a son in jail for dealing cocaine. Her other two children, however, were upright citizens and gainfully employed. Her husband was a quiet man who owned a large Virginia construction company. Anna was speaking quietly to her mother, holding her hand. Callie paused a moment, then went on upstairs. She'd gotten her clothes hung in the closet when she heard the front doorbell, then Anna's voice, and her mother's.

It was agents Savich and Sherlock, and Detective Raven. She imagined they'd be regulars in her daily life until this was over.

She pulled on jeans and a fleece sweatshirt and went down into the kitchen to make coffee and tea for Agent Savich and her mother. She found some croissants on the counter, stuck them in the oven to heat up, and stood there in the bright kitchen, watching the snow sheet down outside the window.

When she carried the big silver tray into the living room, her mother was weeping, Detective Raven looked acutely uncomfortable, and Agent Sherlock was gently stroking her mother's arm.

Callie had never in her life seen her mother so wrecked. She looked up then, and gently pulled away from Anna Clifford and Agent Sherlock. She tried a smile. It wasn't much of one, but it was a start. "Callie, I would love some tea and then—and then we need to talk."

Her voice was suddenly calm. Callie smiled at her mother, served everyone, then sat down with her own cup of coffee. She realized soon enough that Agent Savich and Agent Sherlock were taking time with their coffee and tea, nibbling on the croissants, giving her mother time to collect herself. Detective Raven, however, seemed impatient, prickling with nervous energy. She watched him pick up his second croissant. He looked over at her and grinned. "It's true, you know, that all we ever have at the station is jelly donuts, all sugar and lard, not like the pure butter that holds these delicious things together."

Margaret Califano said, "Everyone is acting normally, and I suppose that's a relief. Do you worry about your cholesterol, Detective Raven?"

"I'm genetically blessed, Mrs. Califano."

"You're also very young."

Callie looked at his long solid athlete's body and laughed. "Yeah, I bet you just gorge yourself on donuts."

Margaret sipped her oolong tea, shuddering at the delicious dark flavor.

Savich said, "I'm sorry we have to ask you questions at a time like this, Mrs. Califano, but a murder investigation requires it. Do you feel up to talking to us now?"

"Yes, Agent Savich, of course."

He said, "Did your husband behave differently in the days before he was killed? Did he seem concerned about something or someone?"

"No, he was the same as always, even yesterday. At least I didn't notice anything different. Oh God, maybe there was something that I simply didn't see because I was in a rush to get to one of my stores."

"No, Mrs. Califano, don't blame yourself. I need you here with me, now."

Margaret drew a deep breath. "Yes, of course you're right. I'm sorry."

"It's all right. Now, did your husband tell you why he was going to the Supreme Court Building last night?"

"No, he didn't. And I didn't ask. Everyone knew he went there whenever the spirit moved him. Even Anna knew, didn't you?"

Anna nodded. "Oh yes. It was Stewart's refuge."

Margaret said, "He told me once that it was the only place he could hear himself think." Her voice quavered. She quickly lowered her head and sipped more tea. Then she straightened her shoulders. "If he was studying something specific, I don't know what it would have been. Perhaps in their weekly Friday meeting, a minority of Justices wanted to grant a cert. that Stewart didn't believed warranted a hearing."

"A cert.?" Savich's eyebrow went up.

"I'm sorry. A cert., as it's called, stands for *certiorari*. It's a formal request that the Court hear a case. If four Justices vote to grant the petition, then the case is scheduled for argument. If the four votes aren't there, the cert. is denied." She studied the dark stain of tea in the bottom of her cup. "As I said, it's possible. As to anything else on his mind, I couldn't say. When he walked through the front door, he might be brooding, but he wouldn't speak of it, if it was work-related."

"Were you and Justice Califano having any personal problems, Mrs. Califano?"

Callie hissed quietly through her teeth, but Margaret merely patted her arm. "No, Agent Savich, no problems. Yes, we disagreed sometimes like every married couple does, but in the nine years we've been married, I've never thought about killing him. Surely you don't think our personal life had anything to do with this. Terrorists, or some sort of extremists, must have killed Stewart."

Sherlock said, "Did he express any concerns about terrorists?"

"No, he didn't. Stewart was quite moderate, not at all controversial. To the best of my knowledge he didn't overly offend either side. That's why it would be so strange if some sort of fringe madman did kill him. Why, for heaven's sake? Why not Chief Justice Abrams? Why not Justice Alto-Thorpe, who's far to the left, or Justice Alden Spiros, who's far to the right? Both held very strong opinions on all the hot-button issues, like abortion, the death penalty, affirmative action, that sort of thing. That makes more sense, doesn't it?"

"Perhaps it does," Savich said.

Ben Raven said, "Did he ever speak to you about someone he was having a conflict with? Someone he didn't approve of? Someone who hated him?"

"Detective Raven, Stewart was a very private man. His best friend was Justice Sumner Wallace. Perhaps he would know if there was something troubling Stewart or if he was having a major problem with someone, particularly someone out of his past." She fanned her hands in front of her. "Everyone pictures the Justices sitting around a big mahogany table, wearing their robes, sober and stately, spouting big words and discussing esoteric legal precedents. The truth is they spend very little time together. They usually work alone, reading, or meeting with their law clerks.

"Their weekly meetings are Wednesday and Friday, and it always sounded to me like it was all business. That doesn't mean, naturally, that they don't argue and yell and be furious with each other when they're in conference. No one but the Justices are allowed in that conference room on Fridays, so they can be rancorous without fear of anyone gossiping or leaking information to the media.

"Politics plays a bigger role than Stewart liked. Every Justice has an agenda very strongly colored by his or her political beliefs, more so now than say thirty years ago, before Watergate.

"Stewart would laugh about some of the really nasty comments everyone knew would not be written down. There's still a tinge of sexism among some of the Justices—remember we're talking about nine people who are all from the older generation—even though the men try to control their feelings, for example, if one of the female Justices has disagreed strongly with them. Also, both Democrat and Republican Justices have historically selected men as law clerks. Even today, out of the thirty-six law clerks, only ten are women. Stewart had two female law clerks.

"Now, if you want the raw truth about the Justices, you go to the law clerks. They're the ones who really keep the Court running. They write opinions, lobby the Justices about cases they care about, and so much more. The clerks know about most everything going on in that faux Greek temple— that's what I call it." She paused, looked blindly at Savich. "I still can't believe anyone would want to kill my husband, actually take the life of a Supreme Court Justice. It simply makes no sense. It's got to be a madman, it's got to be."

Savich said, "Perhaps. Mrs. Califano, everyone who is as successful as your husband makes enemies along the way. Before President Reagan appointed him to the Supreme Court in 1987, Justice Califano was the Deputy Attorney General, the Attorney General, and an Associate Justice of the Superior Court, all of New York. He was a judge of the United States Court of Appeals for the First Circuit. He was sixty-four years old, and that means a long professional life, more than long enough to make enemies. Please think, Mrs. Califano."

"He did have a long professional life, Agent Savich. Do you think an enemy would wait that long before exacting revenge? I can't think that's very likely."

Ben said, "When I was a rookie, ma'am, my trainer was shot by a man he'd put away twenty years before. There's no statute of limitations on revenge."

"No, I suppose you're right. But it's rather frightening to think that decisions you made years ago could come back and kill you. No, I really can't think of anyone, at least he never mentioned anyone he was worried about."

"What was your husband's relationship with his senior law clerk?"

"That would be Eliza Vickers, graduated the top of her class at Harvard Law School. I've met her, of course, spoken to her at social functions and occasionally on the phone. Stewart said she's an emotional liberal, from a social welfare point of view, but a firm legal conservative, is horrified at the thought of social engineering. He liked that. She's smart, well organized, and the other two law clerks are under her control. He has three clerks, not four like most of the Justices. Stewart admired her and trusted her, I believe. I liked her too. Unlike most law clerks who spend only a year working for a Justice, she was in her second year with him."

Ben said, "I wonder what will happen to the three of them now?"

Margaret shrugged.

"Three more lawyers will be turned loose on society a little early," Sherlock said. "That's a thought to curl your toes."

Margaret smiled, just for a brief moment.

Sherlock said, "With your permission, Mrs. Califano, we would like to go through your address book as well as Justice Califano's to compile a list of your friends and anyone with whom your husband had ongoing contact."

"Certainly." She looked down at the delicate Rolex on her right wrist. "Janette, Bitsy, and Juliette should be here soon. Anna, you did call them, didn't you?"

Anna nodded, and went with Margaret to get her address book.

Thirty minutes later, Callie walked agents Sherlock and Savich and Detective Raven to the front door. "Are you going to see the other Justices now?"

"Yes, they knew Justice Califano best. And the law clerks, naturally. We need all the information on him they can provide us. We need to form a clear picture of your stepfather, what he was really like—his likes, dislikes, people who rubbed him the wrong way and vice versa, and especially, if his behavior was different in any way on Friday."

When they reached the door, Callie looked straight at Ben Raven and said, "You're going to split up, right?" At their nods, Callie said, "I've known the Justices since I was sixteen years old, and I know more about the law clerks than my mom. For example, Eliza is a major league ballbuster. She ruled my stepfather's chambers with an iron fist. Why don't I go with Detective Raven? I can fill him in, maybe give him an introduction that will help you guys."

Savich shook his head. "No, Ms. Markham, that isn't possible. We would certainly like to hear everything you know about any of them, but you cannot be a part of the official investigation."

She dug in her heels. "Look, Agent Savich, I want to help. I'm not about to go running to the *Post* with a big inside story. Stewart was prissy, he was rather rigid, and he could never tell a joke right, but he was a good man, and he had a brilliant legal mind. The thought that someone murdered him enrages me."

"Forget it, Ms. Markham," Ben said. "Go home and have a cup of tea. Write your gossip columns."

"I don't write gossip columns, you jerk." She paused, pointed a teacher's finger at him. "Let me put it this way, Detective, agents, either you let me help or I might go back to work, all the way back. I already have lots of good inside information, enough for the first page, don't you agree?"

"That's blackmail," Sherlock said, eyebrow arched, and gave Callie a look of respect. "That's ugly."

"I know, Sherlock, but please listen to me. I'm not stupid, and I know these people, and I know how to keep my mouth shut. I'm only pushy when I'm in my reporter mode, and even that could be useful. I took time off from the *Post*, much to my editor's annoyance. Please, let me help."

Ben said, "I could put you in jail for the attempted blackmail, Ms. Markham. Give it up.

You're not a cop, you don't know anything. We're the professionals, let us do our job."

Callie struck a pose, tapped her fingertips against her chin. "Hmm, you know, I can see the headline right now in my head. *FBI and Metro Police Flummoxed.* If you don't let me work with you, I will investigate on my own. My mother, our friends, the Justices, the clerks, they will talk to me, more easily than they'll talk to you.

"Use some brain cells here, Detective Raven. Do you think they're more likely to tell a cop what's going on, or me, someone they know, someone they trust?"

"Has anyone ever decked you, Ms. Markham?"

She gave him a cocky grin. "There have been those who've tried. Don't you even think about it, Detective." She looked him up and down. "I could take you down without breaking a sweat."

"All right, enough," Savich said. He turned to Sherlock, who was eyeing Callie with amusement.

Callie, scenting victory, pushed hard. "Actually I have a black belt in karate. I can take care of myself. I could probably protect Detective Raven too, if it came down to it. The only one I'd be worried about in this group is Agent Sherlock."

Savich laughed. "You're probably right about that." He heaved a sigh. "There are going to be lots and lots of interviews happening during the next three days. Probably a good fifty agents and local police working the case. What's one reporter added to the mix? Ben, would you mind keeping Ms. Markham in tow?"

"Yes, I mind," Ben Raven said. "I'm not going to be saddled with a reporter—a *reporter*—Savich. For God's sake, not even your garden-variety sort of reporter, but an investigative reporter who thinks she's smart and in reality doesn't know squat.

"As for you, Ms. Markham, and your big mouth, if you could take me down, I'd hang it up, leave the force, go find me an isolated cabin in Montana. Savich, you're worried about blackmail, you take her with you. No damned way is she getting within six feet of me and any suspect. It ain't going to happen."

CHAPTER

8

Callie Markham said to Detective Ben Raven as he drove to Justice Sumner Wallace's house in Chevy Chase, "Okay, now I'm going to come through as promised. Here's something I doubt you could have found out. My mother told you that Stewart's best friend on the court was Justice Sumner Wallace. Maybe that was true at one time, but not recently. This may shock you, but Justice Wallace has a bit of a reputation with women. I think he was inappropriate with my mother and that Stewart was aware of it. He wasn't happy with his old golf buddy."

Ben was shocked and he tried not to show it, but Callie laughed. "I know, it just doesn't fit the image. Now, I guess Mom didn't real-ize my stepfather knew. She likes to keep the peace, so she wouldn't have said any-thing, just ignored it, or handled it herself if it got bad."

Ben was still trying to come to grips with something he never would have imagined. "So this Justice of the Supreme Court of the United States, this guy who's older than my dad, was putting the moves on your mother? Are you absolutely sure about this?"

"Yes. Listen up. Justice Wallace is about sixty-five, not yet ready for the grave, De-tective Raven. My mom was talking on the phone about him once to one of her friends, Bitsy, I think it was. Mom only smiled, and said now wasn't he a frisky one. I think she knew I was listening, and so she finished her call up fast."

"You were eavesdropping?"

"Sure. It's my stock in trade. She never said a thing to me, but she did acknowledge me after she hung up the phone, so I'm sure she knew I was there. Right about that time, Stewart stopped speaking with Justice Wal-lace."

"So, not only is he old, he's married, and he was lusting after your mother?"

"My mom is very pretty, Detective Raven. I'm not surprised that any man would be interested in her. I'm more shocked that he would actually act on it."

"I didn't mean to insult your mother, it was the incredulity speaking. When did this happen?" Before she could answer, Ben's cell phone rang. He listened for some time, frowned, and punched off. "That was Savich. He spoke to the medical examiner, Dr. Conrad. He said TV vans are all around the morgue, but he's trying to keep a lid on things. He's threatened to lock any of the staff who dares whisper a word to anyone, including spouses, in the morgue freezer. Also, something unexpected. Dr. Conrad said Justice Califano had about six months to live. It appears he had pancreatic cancer. He doesn't think Justice Califano knew it yet, since he'd probably not had any pain. Said he'd only lost about six months of life, and even with that, this cancer can be really bad once it gets rolling."

"Oh no," Callie said. "Oh no. Stewart was damned either way. I guess I'm glad he didn't know. Can you imagine what it would be like to know you were dying of cancer, that you'd be gone in six months?"

"Agents will be speaking to his doctors, see if he did know, but kept it to himself."

Callie leaned her head against the seat back. "Poor poor Stewart." She started crying, silently, tears rolling down her face. The dreadful irony of it. It was like losing him all over again.

Ben Raven looked around at the TV vans in front of Justice Sumner Wallace's 1960s single-level home, and the three cars parked at the curb. "I wonder where the federal marshals are. Would you look at all the media." He pulled his white Ford Crown Victoria, sedate on the outside, lots of muscle under the hood, in front of the house. Reporters jumped out of the cars and ran toward them.

Ben ignored them, looked over at the sprawling brick-and-wood house set back in the woods. "Even if you yelled, the neighbors wouldn't hear you. It feels like we're in the sticks somewhere, not in a corner of Chevy Chase."

Ben and Callie climbed out of the car, trudged through the snow-covered sidewalk toward the front door, still ignoring the reporters. By the time they were halfway up the walk, the reporters had swarmed. Ben didn't stop walking, just pulled out his badge, held it high, waved it in their faces, and shouted, "We have no comment at this time. We don't have any news for you."

The snow had thickened a bit. Callie kept her head down, hoping none of the reporters would recognize her.

It was not to be. "Hey, Markham, what are you doing here? I know Justice Califano was your uncle or something, but how come you get to go in with the cop?"

"Hey, sorry, Markham, but can you tell us—"

"What idiots," she said under her breath, but at least two reporters caught her words. She continued to ignore all of them as best she could, just as Detective Raven did. The microphones were no longer in her face for the simple reason that Ben gave them all a look that could kill. That backed them up a foot, but no more.

"Why don't you threaten them with your gun?"

"Doesn't work. I tried it once, but as I recall, they laughed at me. You don't make a threat unless you can back it up. That's what my dad always said."

"Your dad was a cop?"

"Oh yeah. Now he's private. He's a riot, finds humor in every case he takes. Once he was dealing with a real badass, but he told me how the guy broke out in hives whenever he visited his mother. He's very successful. My father, not the badass."

She blinked up at him and smiled, despite herself. She tuned out the reporters' yells behind them. "I remember a lot of laughter, too, when my dad was alive. You're lucky, Ben."

"That depends. How would you like to have four siblings, all of them older than you, all of them obnoxious and nosy, always in your business, always trying to set you up with blind dates? I've had dreams of being an only child, like you."

She laughed. "None of us are ever satisfied with what we've got. Like you've got this slight curl in your hair that's real sexy, and you wear it a little on the long side that makes it even sexier, while I have this straight-as-a-board hair—"

His hair was sexy? Because he wore it too long? "I suppose you're fishing for a compliment, aren't you? However, since you're perfectly able to see yourself in a mirror and know—well, never mind that. Nearly there, just keep walking."

A TV reporter who'd had to wait for his cameraman to catch up to him yelled, "Hey, Callie, how do you feel about your stepfather being murdered in the Supreme Court?"

Callie stopped in her tracks. "That's just too much." She took a step toward the reporter, ready to do battle.

Ben grabbed her arm, said close to her ear, "Just be quiet. You're already a story to them by yourself. Ignore them, keep your head down. In a minute we'll be inside."

Ben rang the doorbell and called out, "It's Detective Ben Raven of the Metro Police. Please let us in."

Ben knew they were being closely observed, and he held his badge to the peephole. Three shouted questions later, the door finally cracked open, and Ben was eyeball to eyeball with a federal marshal. They exchanged badges without saying a word.

Callie said, "We wondered where you were." She saw another federal marshal standing behind him, and an older woman with a tired face peering over his shoulder. "Come in quickly, Detective Raven, Miss, before those jackasses try to knock you down to try to get to Justice Wallace," said Federal Marshal Ted Ricks. The federal marshal behind Ricks cracked his knuckles. "Yeah, hurry it up."

Ricks said, "They've been lurking for about two hours now. We figured inside was the most useful place to be." He grinned. "And the warmest."

The older woman stepped up. "Justice Wallace thought to speak to them, but he decided he prefers a more dignified setting. We're locked up tight in here, prisoners in our own home. My husband is in his study."

Ben introduced himself to her when the two federal marshals stepped out of the way. Naturally Mrs. Wallace knew Callie. Ben said quickly, "Ms. Markham isn't working for the *Post* on this, ma'am. She's along to help."

"I'm sorry about your stepfather, Callie," Mrs. Wallace said. "Very sorry for all of us really, especially poor Sumner, who's naturally devastated." Callie could only nod and took her hands. There was strength and comfort in them. Mrs. Wallace was wearing old black wool pants, a baggy Redskins sweatshirt, and house slippers. Whenever Callie had seen her before, she'd been dressed to the teeth, an elegant, well-coiffed woman who knew her own worth. But now all she looked was exhausted. Callie knew that Beth Wallace and her mother got along well, although Callie didn't know how close they were. It was Callie who remembered to take off her coat and wipe her boots on the small rug inside the front door. Ben followed her lead. Callie hung up their coats in the front closet. Mrs. Wallace gestured down the hallway. "Both of you, come along now." The federal marshals remained by the front door, Ricks looking out the peephole at the reporters milling around.

Mrs. Wallace led them down a long hallway. Every wall, every surface, was covered with Art Deco art and artifacts from the 1930s. Their footsteps sounded loud on the oak floors, echoing up to the twelve-foot ceiling.

"Sumner is devastated by this," Mrs. Wallace said again, as if there were simply no other words available to her, "as you can well imagine." She paused a moment, drew herself up, knocked on a door at the end of the hall, and immediately opened it.

The room was dark. Mrs. Wallace sighed, walked into the gloom, and turned on a lamp. It sent out a circle of stark light, and in the center of that circle sat an older man on a small sofa, perfectly upright, his hands clasped between his legs, eyes staring straight ahead.

"Justice Wallace," Ben said as he walked to the man, his badge out. "I'm Detective Ben Raven from the Metro Police. I'd like to speak to you, sir."

Justice Wallace slowly turned his head to look up at Ben. Then he looked beyond him to Callie. "Callie? What are you doing here? Why are you with this police officer?"

"I'm not here as a reporter, sir. I'm here as part of my stepfather's family."

Slowly, Justice Wallace rose, walked to Callie, and took her in his arms. She was nearly as tall as he was. He felt strong as an ox, she thought as she hugged him tightly. "Stewart was a fine man, a fine Justice," he said, his voice choking. "Dear God, I will miss him." He hugged her more tightly.

Callie wanted to cry; it was odd, but what held her back was the thought that this man had actually made a pass at her mother, the wife of another Justice who was supposed to be his best friend. So she merely comforted him as best she could, wondering if he was bitterly sorry now for what he'd done.

After a few more moments, Justice Wallace straightened. His shoulders went back. His bearing was once again that of a Justice of the Supreme Court, strong and in control.

He turned to Ben. "Won't you sit down, Detective? Beth, would you please get us coffee?"

Callie didn't want any coffee, but Mrs. Wallace had already turned away.

"Why are you here, Detective? Where is the FBI? As you saw, we already have two federal marshals to guard us. From a murder attempt or to protect us from the media, I don't know. Do you?"

"I would say both, sir," Ben said. "As for the FBI, they'll be here to talk to you, Justice Wallace. I'm part of the team put together by the Bureau. I really appreciate you seeing me. If you don't mind, sir, any information you could give me about Justice Califano would be helpful."

Justice Wallace sighed. "So many guards, so much security assigned to keep us safe. How could this have happened? In the Supreme Court Building, the bedrock of the rule of law in our nation, the symbol of freedom and balance in our government?"

Now that was eloquent, Ben thought, a lot

more statesmanlike than hitting on Margaret Califano. Ben decided there was no reason for him not to tell him. "It appears that the killer knew one of the guards would go outside for a smoke. He hit him on the head, took his uniform, and came right back in. It was after midnight, quiet, and unfortunately he succeeded." It was a lousy excuse, Ben knew, but it was the truth. "Justice Wallace, I understand you were Justice Califano's closest friend. Did you notice anything different about him on Friday? Or during the past week? Did Justice Califano appear distracted, perhaps worried about something?"

"No, not at all. Stewart appeared the same as always on Friday, and throughout the week as well. I knew he didn't want to revisit the death penalty in the upcoming case, but then again, neither did I."

"Why would that be, sir?"

"He believed it wasn't a good case for the anti-death-penalty people to use since this sixteen-year-old boy had murdered three people in a particularly brutal manner. Still, he hadn't made up his mind about overturning the ruling they'd made in 1989. The liberal Justices wanted to swing him around to their way of thinking to gain a plurality. There was lots of maneuvering. I don't know what Stewart would have ended up deciding to do."

"But you don't believe he was in the Supreme Court Library to think about this particular case?"

"It's possible. Whenever Stewart wanted to be alone to think, to study a case or a contentious issue like this one, he went to the library. He simply felt an affinity for it. He enjoyed being among those thousands of books that give us the roots of what we are as a people. They helped focus his mind, he said, on the meaning of his work."

"Do you have any idea who could have killed him?"

Justice Wallace began rubbing his hands together, like Lady MacBeth, Callie thought, and wasn't that a strange image to appear in her mind? He said finally, his voice slow and thoughtful, very much like a Justice rendering an opinion, "No, there was no one, either in his past or in the present, that I know of."

"Do you know of anything on a more personal level that was bothering Justice Califano? Some disagreement he'd recently had? Some argument?"

"No, naturally not. Stewart was very well

liked. He was happily married. He had a stepdaughter everybody likes." He sent something close to a smile in Callie's direction.

"You were his best friend, sir?"

"For many years. We both went to Harvard Law. In those years, we drank too much, spent too much time in clubs." He fell silent, sighed.

For the good old days? Ben had to remind himself that the Justices of the Supreme Court had once been young and that meant doing stupid things, but it was still tough to believe. Justice Wallace was one of the Supremes, so high up he could call the President by his first name.

It was time to move on, time to go to the meat of the matter. He thought of what Savich had said to him. "Remember, Ben, any of the Justices could probably have you taken out and shot, so be diplomatic, be respectful." Well, this wasn't going to be respectful at all. Ben could almost hear the firing squad readying their rifles, but he formed the words in his mind and managed to get them out of his mouth. "Would you tell me, sir, whether you've been personally involved with Margaret Califano?"

Justice Wallace's eyes flashed. What? Rage? Embarrassment? No, not embarrassment, but what? Astonishment that he'd been observed and was being called on it? That was probably it. His face paled a bit as he drew in a long, slow breath. Ben prepared himself to be lambasted, possibly threatened. He was aware that Callie was staring intently at Justice Wallace.

But all the Justice said was, "That's ridiculous."

"Yes, of course it's ridiculous," said Mrs. Wallace from the door. "How dare you, young man, intimate such a thing? You are speaking to a Justice of the Supreme Court of the United States."

Ben wanted to apologize, but he held himself still. He looked briefly at Callie. She was still staring at Justice Wallace's face, not moving.

Beth Wallace wasn't through. "The thought that Sumner would ever do anything like that, it's nonsense. Both Stewart and Margaret were our friends, both of them. It is also an insult to me, Detective. My husband is faithful to me, always has been. And to ask such a thing at this time, in the context of Stewart's death—it's reprehensible." The silver tray she carried trembled in her hands. Callie quickly jumped to her feet and took the tray.

Ben wished Mrs. Wallace could have remained out of sight for two minutes more. Well, damn. Her timing couldn't have been worse. And that was all he was going to get—a denial. He nodded as he said, "Please let me apologize to both of you. There are some questions a policeman is forced to ask even though he doesn't want to. To return to Justice Califano's professional career. Can you think of anyone who hated Justice Califano enough to kill him?"

"Of course not," Justice Wallace said without hesitation. "If there were ever such a question, any threatening correspondence, for example, it was forwarded to the FBI immediately. They always follow through on such things. Of all the Justices, Stewart was least likely to receive hate mail. Realize, Detective, that the nine of us spend most of our time in the Supreme Court Building. We're not out haranguing defense lawyers or sentencing criminals, haven't been for many years."

There was a moment of tense silence, then

Justice Wallace said, "You don't believe this was a terrorist act, do you, Detective?"

"I don't know, sir. And since we don't know, that's why you have two federal marshals assigned to guard you. They will remain until we've solved this case. Now, sir, for our information, and with my apologies, would you please tell me where you were last night?"

Justice Wallace raised an eyebrow and said, "Both my wife and I were home last night, playing bridge with our next-door neighbors, the Blairs. They left at around midnight. Isn't that right, Beth?"

Beth Wallace nodded. "Then we went to bed." She looked down at the beautiful silver coffeepot no one had touched. "It does occur to me to mention Eliza Vickers. She was Stewart's senior law clerk. She isn't a very nice woman."

Justice Wallace frowned at his wife. "There's nothing to say about her, Beth." When she attempted to open her mouth again, he said over her, "Eliza is one of the most effective law clerks at the Court. She was always locking horns with Stewart, always debating, especially when she really cared about something. She would nearly hold him prisoner in his office when she wanted to bring him around to her way of thinking." He sighed. "She was with him nearly a year and a half. He could speak of nothing but keeping her on with him beyond two years, something that's very rare."

Beth Wallace said, venom in her voice, "She disliked him, I know it for a fact."

Now this exchange was peculiar, Callie thought. She said, "Mrs. Wallace, why do you think that?"

"It's nonsense," Justice Wallace said, before his wife could speak. "You rarely visited the Court. How would you know?"

"Tai Curtis, one of your own law clerks, told me, Sumner."

Justice Wallace looked embarrassed, but he managed a dry laugh, waved his hand in dismissal. "Ah, Tai dislikes her because she's a better law clerk than he is. Forget her, Beth."

Mrs. Wallace looked at the coffeepot. She said nothing more.

They took a respectful leave of Justice Sumner Wallace and his wife, and shook hands with the federal marshals who were still standing near the front door. Ben was already plotting when he could speak to Mrs. Wallace alone. The reporters were still outside when they left, shouting questions, but all they got for it was a quickly pressed-together snowball that Callie hurled at one of the reporters. She hit him in the head.

"I always say to make use of what's available to you," Ben said. "Not a bad shot."

Callie gave a quick bow to the laughing reporters, and got into the car. "Where are we going now?" She was staring through the veil of snow at the face of Bob Simpson of Fox, a man she'd turned down some months before, which hadn't made him very happy. She gave him a little finger wave. "Others will come to interview Justice Wallace?"

"Oh yeah," he said, carefully easing the Crown Vic onto the street.

Callie hung on to the chicken strap, and watched the world slide by. Fortunately there weren't many cars out, Washingtonians evidently living up to their reputations for self-preservation.

"I'm taking you back to Colfax. Then I'm going to the Hoover Building. We're having our first big organizational meeting. I've never been involved in something this explosive, but—"

He shut up like a spigot.

"But what?"

"You're a civilian, Callie. You shouldn't even be in this car with me."

"Get a grip here, Detective Raven—"

"Ben," he said mildly. "You don't want to be formal after you've told me I have sexy hair."

She wasn't even tempted to laugh. "Ben, we've already been through this with Agent Savich. Get used to it. It doesn't matter that you have sexy hair. I want to go with you to this meeting."

He turned the Crown Vic toward Virginia.

Ben waited until Callie stomped into the Kettering house before he headed back to the Hoover Building. He wondered if Savich would ever tell her the main reason he'd let a civilian tag along on an official investigation was that, bottom line, he believed her threat to investigate on her own, and he knew that might put her in the sights of the murderer. He wanted her to keep safe. So, on top of everything else, Ben was a bodyguard for a big-mouthed reporter.

CHAPTER
9

Bethesda Naval Hospital
Maryland

Savich looked down at the flaccid skin and grayish pallor of Supreme Court Police Officer Henry Biggs. His head was wrapped in a wide white bandage. Savich knew he was fifty, married, with three grown children. He was a man with a long stable career, a man who, unfortunately, hadn't kicked the smoking habit. He was lying perfectly still on his back, an IV drip in his arm, his eyes closed, his breathing a bit labored. He looked pretty bad, but Savich could see the rise and fall of his chest through the heating bag they'd put him in to regulate his temperature after he'd been left outside in the snow for so long. He could have frozen to death. Then his eyelashes fluttered as he became aware someone was there. He slowly opened his eyes. From behind Savich, Dr. Faraday said, "Mr. Biggs, two FBI agents are here to speak to you, but only for a moment. Do you feel up to it?"

"Track the bastard down," Officer Biggs whispered. "Fry him."

Sherlock touched her fingertips to his forearm. "You can count on that, Officer Biggs. We'll fry him to a crisp."

Officer Biggs tried to smile, but couldn't quite manage it. "You FBI?"

"Yes, sir," Sherlock said. "Both of us. We'd like to go over what happened to you, have you give us every detail you can remember. If you become too tired, we'll let you rest. But we do need your help as quickly as we can get it, Officer." She heard the doctor move restlessly behind her. She turned, gave him a sunny smile, and said, "We're not going to put him on the rack. When he tires, Doctor, we will go. May we ask you to leave now?"

No one, Savich thought, bucked Sherlock when she used that sweet iron voice.

Officer Biggs studied Savich for a moment. "You heading this investigation, Agent Savich?"

"The FBI is heading it, Officer Biggs."

"So the marshal of the Supreme Court Police isn't coordinating everything?"

How could Biggs ever have thought that, Savich wondered. "Marshal Alice Halpern and her people will be involved, certainly. You're really a lucky man, Officer Biggs. One of your friends, Officer Clendenning, wondered about you, and went looking. The man who struck you down had thrown a tarp over you, left you right there beside the wall."

"And nobody realized when he came in that he wasn't me."

Savich said, "No, but we're still speaking to all of the officers on that shift. Maybe someone noticed something, felt something wasn't right. By the time the alarm was raised, the killer was gone.

"All right now, Officer Biggs." Savich leaned close to his gray face, where so much pain and rage flickered in his faded eyes. "I need you to think back to this past week, particularly yesterday. Did you notice anyone who seemed to be hanging around, watching, waiting, perhaps leaving, then returning, anyone who didn't look right, who gave you pause?"

Officer Biggs closed his eyes. Slowly, he shook his head. "We've got a residential neighborhood not a block behind us, and there are people hanging around all the time. I didn't notice anyone in particular, and they'd be more noticeable at night when I'm on duty."

"I want you to think about this after we leave. If you recall anything, call us. Now, sir, it's a quarter of twelve last night. You haven't had a smoke for two hours. You're antsy, hurting. You want to skip this break since you're trying to stop, but you had an argument with your wife, and it's eating at you. You don't want to go outside because it's cold and beginning to snow, but you've got to have that cigarette. Tell us exactly what you did."

"How did you know about that fight with my wife?"

"She told us," Sherlock said. "She's really worried about you. She wants you to forgive her."

Those pain-faded eyes burned a bit. "It

was about our oldest son. It doesn't seem like much now. But she really made me mad," said Officer Biggs. "Okay, so, I have my area, right there on the first floor, through the Great Hall and into the courtroom. I keep watch, always listen for any noise that shouldn't be there, make my rounds, watch and listen. Dear God, Justice Califano is dead, he's dead, such a nice man, and it's all my fault."

Sherlock put her hand on his forearm again and left it there. "Did you see Justice Califano come in?"

"No, but I heard some of the guys talking. Justice Califano was a regular, coming in at all hours of the evening. It was kind of a joke, you know? We'd lay bets on when he'd come in, laugh about fights with his old lady, about her driving him off."

"But you have no idea why he came in last night?"

"A couple of the guys were talking—something Justice Califano said at the entrance, something about having a lot to think about. But no one knew for sure. Jerry Quincy thought it could be about that death penalty case they were hearing on Tuesday. That sixteen-year-old kid killing three people. Of course he isn't sixteen now, he's closer to thirty. Jerry saw him head up to the library. That was one of his favorite places. It's really beautiful up there, all those arches, all those books."

Savich paused when Officer Biggs closed his eyes, licked his dry lips. He watched Sherlock lightly stroke the man's forearm, soothing him.

"Anyway, it was about a quarter of twelve, like you said, Agent Savich, and I was ready to chew off my elbows I wanted a smoke so bad. So I tell my supervisor, that's Mrs. Parks, and she tells me to step out and do the deed. I get my coat and gloves out of the locker—we're down in the basement, you know?"

"Yes, we know."

"And I went out from there, out the side door that's next to the information desk. There's lots of construction going on, and it looked like an unfinished Hollywood set out there, what with the piles of raw wood, the row of Porta Potties, temporary construction buildings, all covered with a sprinkling of white. It was pretty, but cold, real cold. Not much wind, which was good. I lit up. Ah— you can't imagine how deep I sucked it in, the taste got me over my anger at Glyna." He paused, and Savich imagined he was remembering the feeling of drawing that smoke deep into his lungs.

"I was standing there, leaning my shoulder against the wall, thinking about stuff, you know? My son is in law school, but he's having some trouble with it, and the fight with Glyna—then I heard something, something I shouldn't have heard. We're trained, you know, to tell sounds apart, to know which ones are the usual sounds of the building or the wind, which ones shouldn't be there, even the sound of someone or something brushing against all that marble. I swear I can hear someone running a finger over the marble, you get real sensitive to stuff like that. Anyway, I was reaching for my gun as I turned, and something crashed down on my head. I was gone, Agent Savich. Just gone. I don't even remember hitting the ground. I woke up here with a nurse leaning over me."

"That's excellent, Officer Biggs. Now, relax and think back again. You're smoking, thinking about your son. Then you hear something. What is it exactly?"

"Like someone was there, behind one of the temporary buildings, real close, not more

BLOWOUT   129

than a half dozen feet away. I remember thinking, now what the hell is that? I even called out, 'Who's there?'"

"The sound was only six feet away?"

"Not more than ten feet, that's for sure. You saw the construction there, right? Nearly right against the building. Yeah, real close."

"How long was it after you heard the noise that you were struck on the head?"

"Not more than a couple of seconds. Like I said, I turned really fast when I heard it, came right to attention, you know? Drew my gun and everything. And just when I turned, I got smashed on the back of my head."

Sherlock said, "Do you think there were two people there, Officer Biggs? One to distract you, make you turn toward the noise, the other person behind you?"

The man's eyes closed again. Savich said, "That's right, try to feel it again, try to remember exactly what you were thinking, hearing. Okay, you're standing there, Officer Biggs, you're alert, you're listening. You're at attention."

In a defeated voice filled with despair, Officer Biggs whispered, "Now that I really concentrate on it, I think it was one guy, Agent Savich. Maybe he tossed something to make me look in one direction, to distract me."

Sherlock stroked her fingers down to close them over his hand.

"I think I would have felt it if there'd been two of them—I've got real good instincts for stuff like that, real sharp senses. But he still got me, still laid me flat."

"Thank you, Officer Biggs. We'll be speaking to you again, but not until you're feeling better. You rest. You've given us excellent information."

"Did Marshal Halpern know anything? What does she think of all this?"

Sherlock said, "She hopes that you're better soon. She asked us to tell you she'll be coming to see you shortly. Special Agent Frank Halley is speaking with her now. She'll let you know if she has any other ideas about this."

"She's been a good boss, doesn't take grief from any of the guards. I hope she doesn't fire my ass."

Sherlock nodded to the guard stationed outside Officer Biggs's room. She said as they walked down the quiet hospital corridor, "He'll have to live with this for the rest of his life."

"Yes. And I'll bet you he'll never smoke another cigarette."

They passed Glyna Biggs in the waiting
room, nodded to her, tried to look reassuring,
and continued on their way.

"Now," Savich said, "it's back to headquarters. I have no doubt that Agent Frank
Halley will be ready to take my head off for
being assigned over him on this."

They left the huge complex, heads down
against the blowing snow, and walked to the
parking lot. Once in his Porsche, Savich
turned the heater on high. Sherlock said, as
she pulled off her gloves, "Frank will get over
it. It's what Director Mueller wants." She
grinned, patted his arm. "I'll tell him that
we're the best. Then you can invite him to
the gym."

Savich grinned at her, controlled a sudden
skid in the snow that would have slid them
into a fire hydrant. "The thing is, Frank is
good. I'm counting on him for his input. But
he's old school, believes in rank and senior-
ity, regardless."

Sherlock eyed an SUV negotiating a corner
some twenty feet ahead of them, and
thought about the turf wars. Most of the old
guard had retired in recent years. Under the

leadership of Director Mueller, the FBI had reevaluated, reassigned, and refocused itself, placing anti-terrorism and homeland security squarely at the top of its priorities. All agencies had been ordered by the President to communicate, to work together and share information—a concept that was finally catching on. But there were egos and old rivalries at play, so the going could still be tough.

Director Mueller was overseeing this extraordinary case himself, with his second in command, Jimmy Maitland, who was Savich's boss. Both would keep the waters calm, at least on the surface.

CHAPTER 10

Hoover Building

"I'd like to know why the hell you're heading this investigation, Savich."

Reassured by Frank's show of consistency, Savich said easily, "I'm not. Director Mueller and DAD Jimmy Maitland are. I'm lower down on the chain."

Neither Director Mueller nor Jimmy Maitland was there as yet, so Frank Halley could vent. Frank had collared Savich the moment he and Sherlock had walked into the large conference room on the fifth floor, blocked him off from the other fifty or so agents who stood around in groups. The large room was buzzing with conversation before the meeting, about the dozens of interviews that had already been conducted during the past nine hours, the newest available reports.

"Yeah, so you say, but not as low as the rest of us. You're the one handing out interview assignments, speaking to Officer Biggs, coordinating the whole direction we take. Why have I been passed over?"

No, Sherlock thought, there was no shortage of egos and turf, not in any organization in the world. Given the sheer size and bureaucracy of the FBI, they weren't doing so badly, really. She patted Frank's arm. "Dillon's doing the major interviews because he's the best, Frank. If you've got a problem, take it up with the director. Otherwise, I'd suggest you get a grip and pull your nose back in joint, or I'll have to haul you down to the gym and wipe up the mat with you."

It was hard, even for a veteran of nearly twenty years, to be mad enough to want to tear a strip off Sherlock. He grinned down at her, this small faerie with her marvelous curling red hair, and he just couldn't help himself. "You're half my size. You really think you could take me?"

"Curious, are you? We'll have to give it a try

sometime." She gave him her brightest smile. "Now, listen up. You really want to do all the paperwork, interface with the media? That's nuts. You're vital to this investigation, Frank. Get in the field, that's where you're best, that's where the action is. It's where we're going to try to spend most of our time."

But he still couldn't let go of it. "It isn't right, Savich. It should have come directly down to me, I'm the next in command. This should be my deal."

Sherlock, who'd turned to speak to another agent, said from just behind Frank's left elbow, "It's whoever's deal Director Mueller wants it to be. You've got to hang it up, Frank."

Frank waved his hand. "Boy, the first thing I'd do is wipe up the floor with Marshal Halpern at the Supreme Court. Actually when I was interviewing her, it was hard not to do a slam dunk with her head. Can you imagine? One of her own police—that idiot Officer Biggs—going out for a smoke, letting himself get taken down like that, like an agent right out of the academy."

"That's the truth," Sherlock said and imagined that Marshal Halpern was probably so defensive when Frank went after her that he didn't get anything useful out of her.

"Ah," Savich said. "Here are the bosses. Let's get ourselves seated. We've got lots to talk about, lots of plans to make."

Frank didn't want to sit down, didn't want to do anything but break both of Savich's arms, but in a moment of stark clarity, he knew he'd have to fall into line. He'd been raised in the Bureau to do just that. But it was very hard for him this time. A Justice murdered in the Supreme Court library, it was an incredible thing to happen. The Supreme Court, that prissy Greek temple sitting on the crest of Capitol Hill, was supposedly one of the most easily secured buildings in Washington. Here he was, Special Agent Frank Halley, one of the top guys in the Criminal Investigation Division, and yet Director Mueller had placed Savich, with his dinky computer-based unit, over him.

"Director Mueller."

Everyone settled in and listened to the FBI director fill them in on what had been happening in the executive wing, Congress, and the media. He closed by saying, "We have the resources to find the person or persons responsible for this heinous crime. I have

confidence in all of you. We are the best police force in the world." He looked around
the room for questions, then turned the
meeting over to Jimmy Maitland. Maitland
was brief, reminding them how critical this
investigation was to the nation and the Bureau. "Justice Califano was murdered right
under the noses of the Supreme Court Police. Fair or unfair, it doesn't matter, we're on
the hot seat with them since we're Federal,
too. All of us are painted with the same
brush. Let's get this nailed down, boys and
girls." He introduced Savich as the person
who would be heading up the operation.

Savich walked to the lectern and adjusted
the mike, since he was about five inches
taller than his boss.

He looked out over the fifty-odd agents,
the representatives from the CIA, the Secret
Service, and Homeland Security. "Everyone's greatest fear is that Justice Califano's
murder might have been committed by a terrorist. Both Homeland Security and the CIA
are covering every aspect of this possibility,
calling on every government to provide any
intelligence that might point in that direction.

"However, we're all inclined to think this
wasn't a terrorist act for several reasons.

There has been no such intelligence, no hint that any group was thinking along these lines. No terrorist organization has taken credit. The murder does not fit the profile of any known foreign-based terrorist group. While it's true that a home-grown terrorist, such as a political extremist or a deranged individual, could be expected to go for a high-profile assassination, you have to wonder why such a murderer would not have gone after the Chief Justice himself. That would have created even more chaos, more publicity, worldwide.

"So why would a terrorist of any sort select Justice Califano to murder? What kind of statement was he hoping to make? Justice Califano's opinions were considered mostly centrist. Well, let me qualify that. Like some of the other Justices, his opinions could go to the right or the left, depending on the specific issue. For example, he was basically conservative on affirmative action, but he voted for the most sweeping definition of sexual harassment in the workplace. But there are Justices who are far more polarized on issues. Justice Califano doesn't fit the bill as a prime target.

"Don't forget, the murderer followed an extremely high-risk script. He actually struck down a Supreme Court police officer, he took his uniform and entered the building itself. Even in some fundamentalist mind, this was a huge risk. And then garroting Justice Califano and slipping away? That was not the act of a bomber, or a shooter in a crowd. That was the act of a single man, done in a very personal way.

"The chances are greater, as many of you have already concluded, that this murder was personal. It was up close and hands-on. Revenge, possibly. Justice Stewart Califano served as a DA, an Assistant Attorney General, and the Attorney General before he was named an Associate Justice of the New York Court of Appeals in 1979. He prosecuted drug dealers, mobsters—people who could have spent twenty years in jail planning to murder him. We will scour every high-profile case he was involved in throughout those years.

"At the same time, we can't afford to take the chance that the murder wasn't the work of terrorists or a madman for the simple reason that Justice Califano's murder could be the opening assault with more to come. Extra security has been provided, not only to the Justices, but to a number of elected federal officials as well. As you know, federal marshals accompany the Justices only when they travel. They have temporarily extended their protection to twenty-four/seven.

"All of you, many through painful experience, know that the media will be following all these directives right along with us. When they find out which of you are involved in the case, they'll hound you. We will expect your usual professionalism. You will refer all press questions to DAD Maitland for official comment.

"We've got all of Justice Califano's phone logs and contacts, his computers, both from his chambers and his home, and those of his law clerks and secretaries. We have a list of all pending cases that the Supreme Court will be hearing, also cases handed down in the past years in which Justice Califano played a critical role in reversing decisions such as those involving race, abortion, individual death penalty cases, and the like. The list is daunting, but we'll take them on.

"Investigation of the crime scene itself and preliminary interviews are already ongoing, as you know. We have divided you into twelve teams of four agents each. Ollie

Hamish will be posting your names and handing out assignments to each team, hoping to key in to the strengths and experience of the members. We are fortunate to have the teams made up of agents from a wide variety of FBI divisions and units assigned to us. It is true what Director Mueller said. We are the best police force and intelligence community in the world, and we will solve this and do it quickly.

"By the way, you will have a unique resource available to you from my own unit that is new to many of you. We have developed a number of computer programs that allow us to combine data-mining capability with an artificial intelligence engine—we call the program MAX, after my laptop. We have found it extremely useful to us, though we haven't made it available this broadly before, or in a case of this importance.

"I've assigned agents Drucker, Bruner, and Hart to instruct you about its capabilities. Some of you will be asked to work with them on this project. All of you will have the benefit of any information MAX provides. If you haven't worked with these agents before, I'll tell you they're excellent detail people. They share with MAX an uncanny ability to help you when everything starts to look like chaos."

Savich paused. "Now, before we split up, I'd like to hear ideas about directions any of you want to take that we haven't covered."

The agents were eager for open discussion, which quickly turned to the crime scene photos Savich had tacked to a large bulletin board. The meeting continued long after Maitland had left. Pots of coffee were consumed, and the snow blanketed the windows despite the warmth of the room. When sandwiches and pizzas were delivered from the cafeteria upstairs, everyone took a break.

Frank Halley saw Savich talking to a man he didn't recognize, a big guy, a sharp dresser, standing near the door with his arms crossed over his chest. He was dressed in black slacks, white shirt, black tie, and black leather jacket. He looked like a smart-ass wiseguy with that hard face of his. Frank walked over and put himself in the guy's face.

"And who the hell are you?"

"I'm Detective Benjamin Raven, Metro Police."

Frank turned on Savich. "What's a local cop doing here, Savich?"

"It so happens that the Supreme Court Building is in the Washington, D.C., jurisdiction, Frank. We're leading the investigation, but Detective Raven is our local liaison with the police commissioner at the Henry J. Daly Building."

Frank gave Ben one final look, then took himself off to the table where there were still two unopened pizza boxes.

Savich said, "Don't mind Frank. He's a good agent, just protective of the Bureau and somewhat territorial. Now, how did you manage to ditch Ms. Markham? I would have sworn she'd have been hanging on to your coattails to get herself in here."

Ben ran his fingers through his thick hair, causing it to stand on end. "I didn't ditch her until she was safe back at the house in Colfax. I'm lucky she didn't follow me in. I'll bet she could have talked her way past the guards."

Savich laughed. "She seems like a pistol, Ben, smart and insightful."

"Well, maybe. Who knows? All I know so far is that she's a pain in the butt. She wanted to smack a reporter at Justice Wallace's house. Can you believe that? She's one of them."

"Yes, well, don't forget, Justice Califano was her stepfather, and the shoe's on the other foot now. But the thing is, she's on the inside. Use her, get her talking. I'll bet she knows things she can't even put together right now, things that are in her brain waiting for you to get them out."

"Actually, she's already started to earn her keep." And then he told Savich about Justice Sumner Wallace hitting on Margaret Califano. "Doesn't that boggle the mind? The guy's a grandfather."

Savich said, "This is going to take some thought. You're right, Callie did good, give her a medal. I guess after she told you that, you can trust her not to feed stuff to the *Post*."

"Okay, yeah, so she's a straight shooter, at least so far. Like I said, I dropped her off at the Kettering home before I drove back in. Nearly landed myself in a ditch a couple of times. The roads are a mess."

"The snow's supposed to lighten up tonight, be gone by tomorrow. Hopefully it won't freeze, the ice would really make it tough for us to get around."

"At least the pizza's pretty good here."

"Yeah, agents are often stuck here for

meals during an investigation, so the cafeteria keeps the food coming, about anything you like. The only section Sherlock doesn't approve of is the Mexican wagon. Ah, I see Agent Halley looking over here at you again. He's not a happy camper since he thinks Director Mueller should have appointed him to run the show, so ignore the attitude."

"Not a problem. Everyone at Metro is hyped about this. I'm lucky to be heading up the field assignments. I've got maybe a dozen cops ready to do whatever you need."

"I'll give you the assignments, don't worry."

"Oh, by the way, Savich, I meant to ask you. How is Sheriff Kettering doing?"

Savich gave him a big smile. "That's how we met, isn't it? They've moved back to Jessborough, Tennessee. Miles is building a new helicopter facility there, and Katie's the sheriff of Jessborough again."

Ben shook his head. "Talk about a pistol, that sheriff sure qualifies."

"Do keep our own pistol in the loop. I don't want Callie calling me at midnight, frothing at the mouth. And thank her for the information about Justice Wallace. It sure opens up some interesting possibilities."

"Yeah, it sure does. Did I remember to thank you for sticking me with her?"

"No, come to think of it, I don't think you thanked me at all. There's a couple of slices of vegetarian pizza left. Why don't you tell me all the details of your interview with Justice and Mrs. Wallace while we chow down."

CHAPTER

11

She ran right in front of him, her long straight hair flying, frantically waving her arms, her eyes wild. He could tell she was yelling, but he couldn't hear her voice even though she was right in front of him, yelling in his face. She was close, so close, and he could feel her terror as though it were his own.

And then he was in that lovely big house on the rise, all the lights on, looking back to see her sitting on the living room sofa, rocking back and forth, her thick veil of hair hiding her profile, the fire blazing behind her in the fireplace. He looked up at the ceiling when he heard a noise, the sound of quiet footsteps overhead.

Then he was climbing slowly up the ladder into the attic, every sense on full alert, but there wasn't a man there. Something flew at him, hard and fast, swooping like a bat, or something else, something his brain couldn't accept, and slammed him back through the ceiling door, knocking the breath out of him.

Savich jerked awake, wheezing, heart pounding so hard he thought he was dying. He couldn't breathe, couldn't do anything but sit there trying to suck in air.

"Dillon? Are you all right? You're here with me. It's okay now, you were having a nightmare."

He still couldn't talk. He felt her hands rubbing his chest, his arms. "Samantha Barrister," he managed at last. "I saw her, felt her right here, in my face. And then I was back in the house, going up those ladder steps after I heard the footsteps overhead. That bat, or whatever it was, knocked me back down to the corridor floor."

"It's all right now, you're awake. Come here." She pushed him back down, her palm rubbed over his chest, felt his pounding heart. She turned and pressed herself over him, kissed his neck, and whispered, "It will be all right. You probably had the nightmare because you can't deal with Samantha's murder right now. What happened to Samantha was thirty years ago, Dillon. It has to wait. Let it go for now." She continued to rub her palm over his chest until she felt his heart slow and his breathing steady.

"I saw her in the road, Sherlock, saw her terror, I knew she was screaming, but I couldn't hear her. Then she was right here, probably yelling for me to help her to stop him, only I couldn't hear her."

Sherlock was silent for a moment. He could practically hear her thinking. "Perhaps she was, for you. I said it had been thirty years, but the fact is, Samantha came to you—just you—in the Poconos. Maybe something's happened to make her frantic, to make her come here to Washington. Something bad."

"What could it be? Now, after thirty years? And what can I do about it? I can't leave Washington and go ghost chasing right now."

She kissed his nose, his mouth, his throat. "We could call the closest field office to do some checking."

He thought about that a moment, then

shook his head. "No, this is personal. I want to deal with it, I have to deal with it, no one else. I know it sounds weird, but I know she wants me to be the one."

"All right then. When MAX is freed up, we can put him on it. He can scour databases, find out about the Barrister family, see what happened to her son and her husband."

"But it's going to be days before we can free MAX up to do that."

"I know, but I think Samantha will understand."

She felt a measure of calm flow through him. He turned on his side and drew her close. He said against her left temple, "Do you know something?"

She shook her head against his. Her curly hair brushed against his ear.

"Some people would think I've flipped out over this, want me to lie down on a shrink's couch."

"You're the sanest person I've ever known. If I ever doubt you about anything, I'll stretch out on a shrink's couch myself." She kissed him hard on the mouth, and eased down to tuck her head against his neck. "It's nearly three o'clock. Sean will give us until seven o'clock. Let's use the time wisely. We've got to sleep."

When he fell asleep, Samantha Barrister wasn't with him.

Washington, D.C.
Sunday

Ben Raven flipped the channel on his TV from national to local news while he ate his bowl of Wheaties. It was his mom's favorite cereal, and she'd fed it to him every morning, which explained, he supposed, a great deal. Director Mueller's face was everywhere on TV, as well as sound bites from the Attorney General, the President, even the Director of Homeland Security. Anyone the media could get to, which was just about every politician inside the Beltway. And they all had something important to say. The politicians and the talking heads led the charge, blaming the FBI, the Supreme Court Police, even the President for not providing the nation with enough security from terrorists. Of course Director Mueller laid out why he didn't believe terrorists were responsible, but no one liked that. It had to be either a terrorist or a madman, like the Washington snipers of a few years ago, that was the theory everyone wanted to run with.

Not even a day had passed since Justice Califano's murder before speculation began on who would be on the President's short list for appointment to the Supreme Court to take Justice Califano's place.

Ben put his cereal bowl in the sink and filled it with water. He had thirty-five minutes to pick up Callie Markham, and then they were off to interview Justice Elizabeth Xavier-Foxx, one of two female Justices on the High Court.

When he pulled his Crown Vic in front of the Kettering house in Colfax, he saw Callie Markham looking out at him through one of the living room windows. She had the door open when he was still a good six feet away.

"It stopped snowing. Is it icy?"

"Nope, it isn't bad at all. I gather you're ready to hit the road?"

"Oh yeah, but you said you wanted to speak to Mom some more. Oh, Ben, here are our guards, federal marshals Dennis Morgan and Howie Bentley. Gentlemen, Detective Ben Raven from Metro."

He shook hands with the federal marshals,

asked if they'd seen any reporters, to which they said all had been quiet, thank God. Screened condolence calls were coming through for Mrs. Califano, so many of them that her four women friends, who seemed to be here all the time since she'd moved in, were assisting her in dealing with them.

Things sounded under control. Ben wiped his boots off on the front step, and followed Callie into the warm living room. A restful house, he thought, full of light and high ceilings. He'd lived in condos all his adult life after graduating from the police academy, and he liked the space, the openness of the house.

"Mrs. Califano," he said, stepping into the living room.

There were four women seated with her, all of them about the same age, all wearing subdued colors, all of their attention on the new widow who'd just hung up the phone. When he spoke, they looked up at him.

Ben said, "I hope you're all right."

She nodded. "It's difficult, Detective, but yes."

He nodded toward the phone on the end table beside her.

"Another condolence call?"

"Yes, so many people, so kind. You remember Anna Clifford?"

Ben nodded to the woman he'd seen briefly yesterday. The other women, waiting to be introduced, inclined graceful heads as Callie called out their names. "Janette Weaverton, Bitsy St. Pierre, and Juliette Trevor." Elegant names all, rich names, trust-fund money kind of names. He'd met all sorts in his nine years on the force, but working primarily in the bowels of D.C., it wasn't often he met society types.

They were gracious and attentive, and clearly concerned about Mrs. Califano. The team already had their addresses and phone numbers. He wasn't certain yet if he would be the one interviewing them and their families. He asked to speak to Mrs. Califano alone. Callie gave him a look, but ushered the four women out of the living room.

Ben sat down beside Mrs. Califano. He looked for several moments at her beautiful profile, similar to Callie's, he realized, with her clean, straight nose and high cheekbones. He supposed he could understand Justice Wallace being attracted to her even though she was his mom's age, and when he thought of his mom, he thought of Wheaties and big laughter, not sex, for God's sake.

"There are a whole lot of people working around the clock to find out who killed your husband, Mrs. Califano."

"Yes, I would imagine so." Her voice was quite without emotion, as if she'd simply put a cork in the bottle.

"When Justice Califano went to the Supreme Court Building on Friday night, he said he had something to think about. Please, try to remember, Mrs. Califano. What could it have been? Did you have an argument? Was he worried about some business deal? Something like that?"

She sighed, clasped her hands in her lap. She was very pale. "I've already told you three or four times that I can't think of anything other than that case coming up, the death penalty case in Texas. Also, before you ask again, we didn't have an argument Friday evening. Sure, we fought occasionally. All couples do, Detective. Aren't you married?"

"No, ma'am."

"You should be. You're old enough."

"The guards at the Supreme Court thought Justice Califano seemed preoccupied Friday night, something weighing heavily on his mind." This was a stretch, but worth a try. "You were closer to him than anyone in the world. What was eating at him, ma'am? Please, think."

She sighed again, fanned her hands in front of her. "Oh, all right. I knew he was upset at Sumner Wallace for, well, for being inappropriate with me, but you already know that, Detective. Yes, my daughter told me that she'd passed it on to you when you were going to interview Justice Wallace. I hope it won't come out since it has nothing to do with anything, but now I suppose you want to know the rest of it. My husband knew about what Sumner had done as well because I myself told him just last week. He was singing Sumner's praises about something. I just couldn't bear the hypocrisy of it, so I told him what Sumner had tried with me."

"How did he take it?"

"He was angry, as you'd expect. I don't know if he confronted Sumner about it since he never mentioned it to me again, which surprised me. But I wasn't about to bring it up. Was he thinking about that on Friday night? I don't know, Detective Raven."

"Justice Sumner Wallace denied this, ma'am."

"Well, naturally. Wouldn't you?"

"I suppose I would. His wife did as well."

She shook her head. "Poor Beth. She puts up with a lot from Sumner, and has all their married life. How was he dealing with this?"

"Not well, neither of them were. Two federal marshals were there in the house with them, reassuring I'm sure, but still an invasion of their privacy, and a constant reminder that they might be in danger. Also, since reporters were camped out in their front yard, they felt like prisoners."

"I so wish Callie weren't a reporter," she said. "Doing that to people when they're in such obvious distress, and then trying to justify it with that idiotic refrain they so quickly toss out—'the public's right to know.' It's only an excuse, of course."

Since he agreed with that assessment wholeheartedly, he nodded. "Let me ask you this, Mrs. Califano. Sumner Wallace is not only of an age when he should be settled, he's a Justice of the Supreme Court. This reputation you're attributing to him, it seems so unexpected and surprising, so very incompatible with what he's supposed to be—

a reasoned brilliant legal mind, deciding huge issues for our country."

"Yes, I suppose it would come as an unpleasant surprise, but the fact remains he's still a man, a man who's carried on a number of affairs all his adult life. In my experience, particularly in politics, it's not at all uncommon for men who hold a great deal of power to exploit the women who are drawn to it."

Ben couldn't disagree with that, too much evidence to the contrary. He wanted to point out that Justice Wallace also had six grandchildren, but he kept his mouth shut.

"You had no hint that your husband might confront him on Friday, Mrs. Califano?"

"No, no hint at all, like I've already told you, Detective. No, wait a moment. Now that I think about it, I did hear Stewart on the phone—not on Friday, but last Wednesday, I think. He wasn't happy. On the other hand, he wasn't screaming either. Whether or not he was speaking to Sumner, I can't say."

"What did you hear your husband say?"

She was quiet a moment, hands clenching and unclenching in her lap.

"Something about 'You will stop this immediately, do you hear me?'—along those lines. That's all I really remember, Detective. His voice, as I said, wasn't particularly angry."

"Did he pause then? For the other person to answer him?"

"Yes, I believe he did. Then he sort of nodded into the phone, didn't say anything more, and hung up. When he turned to see me standing there, he shrugged. 'Nothing to worry about. It's done,' that's what he said. I suppose he wanted to cut off any questions from me, and it did. In many ways, Stewart was a very private man. His first wife had died some years ago, you knew that, and in the intervening years before we met and eventually married, he became used to being alone, to keeping his own counsel. That isn't a good thing, Detective. People shouldn't be alone.

"Get married, Detective. It's healthy to have another person in your life, someone so close they can feel what you're thinking." And she burst into tears.

Ben didn't know what to do.

CHAPTER 12

Close to a minute later, Ben still didn't know what to do. He said finally, "I'm going to catch the monster who killed him, ma'am. I promise you that. Thank you for speaking to me. You remembered more, as I'd hoped you would. And thank you for telling me about Justice Wallace."

She wiped her eyes, tried a smile. "It can have no possible relevance to any of this, but you appear to want to know about all the skeletons in the closet."

"Yes, ma'am."

When he came out into the entry hall a few minutes later, he nodded to the four women as they went back into the living room to rejoin Margaret Califano. Callie was standing in the hall, looking ready to leap at his throat. He splayed his fingers in front of him. "You ready?"

She waved toward the living room. "What, you're not going to arrest any of those five killers?"

"Not your mom. We'll see about the other four ladies. Hey, that was pretty funny, Callie."

Federal Marshal Dennis Morgan caught a laugh, turning it quickly into a cough behind his hand.

"Yeah, right. You ready?" She was nearly dancing from foot to foot, wanting so badly to leave. He nodded toward the living room. "I'll tell you, Callie, all of them look suspicious to me, look like they're hiding something. Do you think I should go back in there and grill each one of them in turn, privately?"

"Har har," Callie said. "Let's go."

He nodded to the federal marshals and ushered her outside. He said, "Isn't it amazing what money can do? My mom is about their age, but believe me, she looks like she lives on a different planet. She's cushy, her hair is always frazzled, and she has the biggest smile east of the Mississippi."

She punched him in the arm. "You snob.

Their smiles are as big as your mom's. I've known them all my life. So they're not cushy. That just means that they take care of themselves. They work out. Money doesn't play a big part in looking good. Hey, maybe you should get your mom to work out, she'll be healthier for it."

He took her arm when one of her boots went out from under her. He couldn't imagine his mother walking on a treadmill or pumping iron in a gym. But now that he thought about it, she and his dad had begun walking together in the evenings, quite a lot, in fact. He said, "Careful, this drive isn't for wusses."

"I wish I could have been at your meeting at the Hoover Building yesterday afternoon."

"A reporter in the Hoover Building? Are you nuts? They would have locked you in a detention cell if you'd managed to sneak in. They would have turned you over to Big Matron Bubba, and she'd have strip-searched you and taken the fillings out of your teeth. The good Lord knows what would have happened to you then."

She couldn't hold back the laugh, but sobered immediately. She pulled her hat down over her ears because the temperature was sitting about three degrees above freezing. "I'll just bet there were hardly any women included, were there? All you machos, sitting there preening, believing it's up to you to solve all the world's problems—"

"You're being sexist, Ms. Markham." His voice was perfectly easy and mild, although he was tempted to let her slide around on the driveway on her own. "Maybe if I don't support you, you'll go right down on your butt. Of course, the macho is here to haul you back up." Then, of all things, he found himself looking at her butt, realized hers was an excellent butt, and looked away quickly.

But she saw it in his eyes and arched an eyebrow. "I believe that's approval I see. Well, now, let me say that you've got a very fine butt, too, Detective Raven. When I don't want to kick it, I admire it. Now, so you can get your mind onto other things, let me ask you how many female agents were important enough to be included in the meeting?"

"As I recall, more than a dozen of the special agents present were female. Your point?"

"That's a start, pathetic though it be." She stared at his Crown Vic, and said nothing more.

"When I'm able to get rid of you later, why don't you shovel the driveway? Or you could arrange to have some macho guys come here and do it for you. You wouldn't want any of your mother's lovely rich friends to break their necks, now would you?"

She looked thoughtful for a moment, then frowned up at him. "Well, of course not. That's a good use for macho guys."

He'd hoped she'd take the bait, but she'd turned it around on him. Well done, dammit. "All right. You were bragging about how helpful you'd be, so tell me about the four women."

"Well, they and their families have always been in my life. The only person I don't like is Juliette Trevor's son. He's a spoiled trust-fund baby, and really smart. That combination always irritated me. No, I didn't sleep with him, but it wasn't for his lack of trying. I remember Mrs. Trevor gave me a Hermès scarf from Paris when I graduated high school. Wasn't that nice?"

"What's the big deal about a Hermès scarf?"

"They're very expensive, and so beautiful they make you weep."

"Yeah, right, I can see myself crying over a scarf." He gave her a look. "Only a woman."

When he started the car, she said pleasantly, "Did I mention that you're a pretty sharp dresser? Maybe you'd like to hear about the shoes I bought to go with the Hermès scarf?"

He groaned, rolled his eyes. "All right, I can see where this is all going."

"Probably so. I've always felt sorry for guys. Even though you obviously know how to dress, are doubtless well aware of the effect you have on the female population, you still don't have the gift of the shoe-shopping gene. No man alive has it that I've ever seen. That's the gene that forces a credit card right out of your wallet when you pass a neat pair of shoes, no matter how many are already in your closet. No, all guys have is the Home Depot hardwired into your brains. It's really sad." She turned the heater on full blast.

He laughed at her. "Another good use for macho guys—fixing toilets."

"All right, you got me fair and square. Tell me everything that happened yesterday."

To his surprise, he did. She asked questions, grew thoughtful. She said finally, "The pancreatic cancer, that will come out soon, won't it?"

"Oh yes, too many people know. Everyone likes to talk, everyone. No exceptions to that, unfortunately."

She felt tears sting her eyes. Her stepfather would have died in any case. But he would have had six more months to live. Perhaps he would have had a chance, with new drugs discovered every day—

"I read up on pancreatic cancer. It's a killer, so don't go there, Callie. Someone brutally murdered him, that's our only concern. Whatever fate would have dealt him we have no control over."

"My editor called again last night, on my cell, thank God. If he'd called the house, I would have freaked. I hate leaks, I really do, and if Jed Coombes had gotten the Kettering house number, I'd be doomed."

"What has he offered you to feed them information?"

"The inside track to a Pulitzer Prize."

He whistled. "Hard to turn down."

"Don't worry, I'll earn one on my own. I nearly got one last year, it was that close." She held up two fingers, nearly touching.

"What did you do?" He was driving very

carefully even though there weren't many cars on the road, the sun was bright overhead, and the snow was melting. But the occasional pockets of slush could take a car into a ditch with no warning.

"I have snitches, like you cops do. One of them tipped me off that a child pornography ring was operating out of the Barrington Hotel right here in Washington. I broke the story."

He jerked the steering wheel in his surprise and nearly sent them into a telephone pole. It was dicey for a moment until he got the car straight again. "You were the one who broke the Cadillac Ring story?"

At her nod, he could only stare at her. "I'll tell you, Callie, you had a lot of people pissed off at your paper about that. We already had undercover guys in there gathering evidence, then you had to move in with your battering ram. Lucky for the good guys we were nearly ready to close them down."

"Yeah, sure you were," she said, eyes narrowed. "I heard about an undercover operation, but I didn't see anything coming out of your efforts. I got all the evidence for you, Detective Raven. Oh yeah, you guys did a great job—once I cracked it."

Well, okay, she had done a lot and she had given them a day's warning, he'd hand her that. And she had uncovered more evidence than they had, dammit. He decided to give the devil her due. "Well, maybe you did okay. It was federal racketeering for the bastards. The Attorney General brought them all down. There were big names among their clients, lots of money."

"It was the children that got to me. They were stolen from all over the world. They weren't physically hurt, actually, they were just prisoners with anything they wanted—so long as they did exactly what they were told."

"They were all returned to their families."

"Yes, but their lives will be messed up in the short term at the very least. Poor kids."

"All right, so why didn't you pull a Pulitzer?"

"Olsen Tynes at *The New York Times* broke that big political scandal about Governor Welles in Louisiana. Since the *Times* is Northern liberal, and the governor was Southern conservative, they poured every-thing into nailing him."

"So you're telling me you're philosophical about that?"

"What do you want me to do? Go blow up *The New York Times*?"

"The least you could have done was not date that moron *New York Times* reporter you caught in bed with another woman. Me, I'd have gotten right in this Tynes guy's face, made sure he knew who should have carried off the prize."

She grinned at him. "Thank you, Detective Raven. I feel all sorts of warm and breathy getting advice from such an alpha male."

"Breathy?"

"Do you know, I'm beginning to think you're becoming resigned to me hanging around you."

"Not in this lifetime. Well, you're not as bad as I thought you'd be. Look, now we're heading into the hills of Virginia, horse country, that's where Justice Xavier-Foxx lives. I can't imagine how she can help us, but who knows?"

"Did you know Justice Holmes said the nine Justices were like nine scorpions trapped in a bottle?"

He grinned at her, shrugged. "Well, all the Justices are in the same small area for hours on end. Maybe she heard something, saw something. I will live in hope until the contrary is shoved in my face. Did Holmes really say that?"

She nodded. "Okay, let me fill you in. As you know, she'll go down in the history books as the first black woman appointed to the Supreme Court. She was at the top of her class at Stanford, law review, all extremely accomplished for a black woman back in the sixties—pretty remarkable. She wanted to clerk for Justice Raines, a noted conservative on the Court. She was recommended by two top Federal Appeals Court judges, none of which mattered since only men were taken by both parties, and still are, for the most part. You'll appreciate this—she has three women law clerks out of ten in the total count of thirty-six.

"She's much like my stepfather, usually votes conservative—pro death penalty and against attempts to increase prisoners' rights. Like him she can go the other way as well—she's very much a proponent of women's rights, rabidly against sexual discrimination, and pro abortion, except partial birth abortion, which she is very much against.

"Her husband trains horses, races them, has quite a stud program. She uses a hyphenated name—Elizabeth Xavier-Foxx. It's interesting, isn't it, how the two women Justices have kept their maiden names? I guess it gives them more heft, like they really were somebody before they got married.

"Even though she's black and a woman, there were attempts to derail her confirmation, the excuse being that there was lots of money on her husband's side, with perhaps the taint of corruption."

"What was the accusation? That she'd be influenced unduly whenever there was a case about federal horse racketeering?"

Callie laughed. "Nah, it was just politics as usual."

"What do you know about her confirmation?"

"Well, after some huffs and puffs because she wasn't staunchly pro abortion all the way, and she was—gasp—pro death penalty, the Senate confirmed her. They knew it was an historic moment. No one was willing to try to shoot her down. She's expecting us?"

"Oh yeah. Do you like her?"

"Yes, I do. She's got lots of class; her husband stands behind her like this huge silent power, as if daring anyone to come after her.

I personally don't believe he's guilty of anything other than not being a Democrat."

"But if he had been, then the Republicans would have blown a fit."

"True. Ain't politics fun?" She grinned over at his profile.

"Yeah, right."

"Savich," she said, then frowned, paused.

He arched an eyebrow.

"He's cute. Whenever I see him, I think of that actor James Denton."

Ben rolled his eyes. "I'll be sure to tell him that, it'll make his day."

"As for his butt—"

"Get yourself together, Ms. Markham. We're here at Foxx Farm. Oh yeah, happy birthday."

She gave him a perfectly blank look.

"You're twenty-eight today."

"Oh my, imagine that. Yeah, I guess you're right. I forgot. Isn't that something? Thank you."

CHAPTER
13

Summerton, Virginia

Foxx Farm was huge, judging by the miles of white fence that bordered it, a score of white paddocks, rolling hills and forests. There was a huge barn, two big stables, all dusted white with snow, looking still and impossibly beautiful on a Sunday morning. It looked magical to Ben, and utterly alien.

A lone media van idled outside a gated entrance.

When Ben pulled up to the intercom, a reporter jumped out of the van and ran over.

"Hey, you FBI? Can you get us in? They won't even let us through the gate."

"Sorry," Ben said. "Why don't you head back to Washington? I hear it's really pretty about now, a nice Sunday morning. You can go to a park for a picnic."

"That's what we told him," said a tall man in a thick black wool coat, a federal marshal's hat on his head. He stood behind the gated driveway, his arms crossed over his chest. Good, they were here protecting Justice Xavier-Foxx. "We figure as long as the media is camped out all over the place, ain't no assassin going to get to the Justice. All we've got to do is protect her from these baboons."

"Probably true," Ben said as he handed over his badge. "We're here to interview the Justice."

The federal marshal studied the badge, raised an eyebrow, but didn't say anything. "Go on through. I'll keep this charming gentleman out here."

"Hey, you're Callie Markham, *The Washington Post.* What are you doing here? What—"

The gate buzzed open, and Ben gave a small wave to the guy. He ran back toward the van, trying to make it through the open gate after him, despite the fact that two federal marshals were standing in front of the gate, guns at their belts, legs spread. They could hear him shouting after them, probably something about the freedom of the press. The gate closed smoothly behind them. Still, the guy stood there, shaking his fist at the exhaust of the Crown Vic.

Ben parked in front of a sprawling white one-story house with a porch all along the front. He could imagine sitting on this porch in the summer, maybe drinking a beer, listening to his hair grow. Justice Xavier-Foxx answered the front door herself, greeted them politely, gave a cursory look at Ben's I.D., then ushered them into a long narrow entrance hall, where they removed their coats and scarves. Then she led them into the living room. Ben sighed with pleasure as he paused in the arched doorway. It was a long, deep room with a very old floor-to-ceiling stone fireplace, beamed ceilings, lots of homey, oversized furniture that looked like you'd sink to China when you sat down, and Persian carpets scattered over the shining wide oak-planked floor.

"You have a beautiful home, ma'am."

"Thank you. Callie, what a pleasure to see you. I'm so very sorry about Stewart." She pulled Callie into her deep bosom and patted the back of her head. Callie nearly burst into tears. It was close, but she held it in. She felt Justice Xavier-Foxx's steady strong heartbeat, felt the warmth from her solid body, breathed in her rose scent. She was well into her sixties now, but solid and fit, her hair flat against her head, in her signature tight thick chignon. Callie slowly pulled back in her arms and looked into her beautiful dark eyes, liquid with tears.

"Thank you," she said, and knew tears were thick in her own voice. "It's difficult."

"I know. It is for all of us. This has been such a shock, such a terrible thing. Come along and sit down. We'll all talk, try to figure something out about this madness."

She gave them mugs of coffee and pointed to a tray. Ben saw a covered plate on the tray beside the coffee. The Justice made no move to uncover it. It had been a long time since his bowl of Wheaties.

"You're not an FBI agent. That surprises me, Detective Raven."

"I'm with Washington, D.C., Metro, working with the FBI. What we need, ma'am, is as much information as you can give us about Justice Califano—his daily routine, his likes, dislikes, how he related to other Justices, and other staff, anything you can think of."

She sat back and crossed her legs. She took a sip of coffee. "We are a conservative Court, Detective, six to three is the normal voting pattern. However, depending on the case, Stewart and I are the ones who will swing toward the liberal side. There are three Justices who make up the core of the liberal wing—Justice Alto-Thorpe, Justice Bloomberg, and Justice Samuels. Justice Samuels is eighty-two, swears he won't retire because the President would appoint another conservative. Frankly, he's getting senile, plus he has a heart condition. Once a law clerk found a *Playboy* magazine sitting on top of his desk, which has led to a good deal of awe and admiration among the law clerks. I'm telling you about Justice Samuels because he openly detested Stewart's stand on many issues. He was always accusing him of being a Neanderthal in a black robe, which gave everyone a big laugh, including Stewart.

"On the conservative side are Chief Justice Abrams, Justice Spiros, Justice Gutierrez, Justice Wallace, Justice Califano, and me, although again, Stewart and I were the

ones most often seduced by the Dark Side."
This was said with a chuckle, and both Ben
and Callie laughed.

Ben said, "It sounds like there's constant
maneuvering, ma'am."

"Oh yes, always. However, regardless of
our political leanings, all of us love to delve
into arguments; we love to dissect words,
how and why they're being used, the legal
underpinnings and rationales. We're accused of spending most of our time studying the nuances of our navels, and perhaps
this is true, in part. We spend hours alone.
There is voluminous reading, studying, and
just plain thinking time. We have only two
formal meetings a week, Wednesday and
Friday. Much of our communication is done
through various sorts of memos, my own
personal favorite being the 'I Join' memo.
This means, simply, that one Justice is noti-
fying another Justice that he or she is willing
to come onboard in a particular case. Naturally it isn't usually that clean-cut, but it sig-
nals the beginning of negotiations.

"We try to be pleasant to each other, but
when there are contentious cases, it can get
loud and argumentative. Everyone has an
agenda; there are shenanigans pulled by all

the Justices, like adjusting parts of a majority opinion without telling anyone. Since there is so much paper flowing in and out of our chambers, it's up to the law clerks to carefully read all the decisions.

"As for Stewart, he was considered a centrist, which annoyed both sides. He enjoyed being courted, as I suppose I do, because we were able, many times, to bring more compromise to a majority decision.

"Stewart had a keen mind, a way of pulling arguments apart that showed both strengths and weaknesses. But he had certain core beliefs that wouldn't ever change. He was a good man." She lowered her head, looking at her clasped hands in her lap.

Ben said, "You told us about Justice Samuels. Are there any other Justices who didn't particularly care for Justice Califano?"

Justice Xavier-Foxx laughed. "Justice Lydia Alto-Thorpe. She's a dyed-in-the-wool ideologue, Detective. She was happy as a clam in the very liberal Brennan court. She was always pushing her agenda. Unfortunately, Lydia has little grace or tact, so she tends to raise hackles rather than gain consensus for what she wants. She sulks, Detective Raven. She's very protective of the

Court, and all its rules and formality, its sacred majesty. When you speak to her, I imagine she will be very angry that this has happened. When she's angry, she demonstrates a remarkable vocal range.

"She disliked Justice Califano more than any other Justice. Stewart made the mistake a long time ago of laughing at her. She never forgot. It didn't matter that he sometimes voted with her, unlike Abrams, Spiros, Wallace, and Gutierrez. The other Justices liked Stewart and respected him."

Ben took a sip of the sinfully rich coffee. "Justice Califano was in the Supreme Court Library on Friday night, near midnight, something obviously on his mind, something that made him want to be alone, to think. Can you think of anything in particular that was bothering him?"

Justice Xavier-Foxx frowned, looking down at her brown suede flats. "You know, Stewart was somewhat distracted, I remember thinking that during our Friday meeting, but then some of the Justices got into an argument about the upcoming death penalty case. Lydia knew Stewart hadn't made up his mind yet about overturning the 1989 death penalty decision, but still, she couldn't help herself. She sniped at him. Then the meeting was over and I got busy and it dropped out of my mind." She turned to Callie. "I'm very sorry I didn't pursue it, my dear. Maybe he would have said something, but I just went about my business. I'm sorry."

"It's not your fault," Callie said.

Justice Xavier-Foxx bowed her head, but when she looked up, she was smiling. "Just smell those brioches. Let's have one before they get cold." She whisked off the napkin that covered the plate. "My husband makes them every Sunday morning, ever since he became a *cordon bleu* chef over fifteen years ago."

It was hard, but Ben didn't grab the plate itself and clutch it protectively to his chest. He took a bite of a brioche, felt it melt in his mouth, and began to wonder if Wheaties was the only breakfast option he should consider.

"Can you think of anyone who hated Justice Califano enough to hire someone to kill him?"

"Goodness, no! Why, there is no one I can imagine capable of such a brutal crime."

Callie said, "The Supreme Court is a very closed society, ma'am. Some have likened you to the nine princes and princesses. Three hundred-plus people spend hour upon hour together in that one building, seeing to the Justices' needs. Close proximity can lead to conflict. Can you think of anyone, ma'am, anyone at all you observed who might have disliked my stepfather, other than Justice Alto-Thorpe?"

"Stewart was a nice man, Callie. No one I ever saw or heard about disliked him."

Ben said, "Any spouses or other family members who might not have cared for Justice Califano?"

Justice Xavier-Foxx shook her head. "No. There is, however, one interesting spouse, Lydia Alto-Thorpe's second husband, Harry Thorpe. Her first husband died in a yachting accident, and Lydia, already nearing sixty, married Harry within six months. It was something of a scandal at the time, given she was a Supreme Court Justice, but soon forgotten. I have to tell you that I feel rather sorry for Harry even though he's a very successful businessman, owns Harry's. The flagship restaurant is in the Inner Harbor in Baltimore."

"I've eaten there. It's excellent," Callie said.

"I had no idea Justice Alto-Thorpe's husband owned it."

"Yes, well, Lydia overwhelms him when they're together in public. I've seen her occasionally put him down, or, more often, ignore him. But marriages work for a multitude of different reasons. The few times the Justices and their families have all been together, I've seen Harry Thorpe staring at Stewart with anger. Because of what Lydia had said? Probably. I'm sorry, this can't possibly have anything to do with Stewart's murder."

"I can't remember ever having too much information, ma'am," Ben said, then added without pause, "Was Justice Wallace ever inappropriate with any of the female employees in the Supreme Court?"

Justice Xavier-Foxx was unruffled. She said matter-of-factly, "There was occasional gossip to that effect, yes. Evidently this is an adult-long habit with Sumner."

Callie cleared her throat. "How about my stepfather, ma'am? Were there any female employees he liked more than he should?"

Ben kept his head down. He simply hadn't thought along those lines. He didn't think anyone had. He said nothing, waited.

To his astonishment, Justice Xavier-Foxx slowly nodded. "Perhaps not on Stewart's part, I don't know. Eliza Vickers, his senior law clerk, was in love with Stewart, if I'm not mistaken. A tough situation. She was more than thirty years his junior, in addition to Stewart being happily married to your mother, Callie. Eliza was in her second year with him, very unusual since most law clerks stay only a year. Did Stewart return her affection? All I can tell you is that Stewart was getting quite frantic that her second year was coming to an end in July. He didn't want to lose her. Very bright lawyer, is Eliza Vickers."

Callie hadn't expected to hear this, both Ben and Justice Xavier-Foxx saw it, but she kept it together. "You really think Eliza Vickers was in love with my stepfather? With Stewart? A man old enough to be her father?"

"I've learned over the years that a person's age becomes less and less important. It's the other things that matter, like respect, brains, kindness. Was she in love with him? I'd say so, yes. It's just my opinion, mind you, Callie."

Callie had to know. "Please, be honest with

me. Do you think Stewart was in love with her?"

"I can't say, Callie. I never saw any sort of inappropriate emotion when they were together. It's just that once I happened to look at Eliza when Stewart was speaking. It was crystal clear to me, another woman, that she loved him. Don't get me wrong. She never acted silly or smitten. She was tough, and those who didn't recognize her brilliance fell victim to it. I enjoyed watching her. By the time she hits thirty-five, she'll be formidable. She might be a Justice on the Supreme Court herself someday.

"I realize you all believe Stewart was killed by someone who knew him. That it was a personal act, not a terrorist act, and that is why I've told you this. I very much want you to catch Stewart's murderer. This information is more than likely a dead end, but I knew I had to tell you anything that might help."

Ben eyed another brioche but exercised control. "What do you think of Justice Califano's other two law clerks and his two secretaries, ma'am?"

Justice Xavier-Foxx smiled. "Stewart's law clerks, like all our law clerks, have their own beliefs, their own biases, their own core values. Sure they're young, still changing, evolving. You can hear arguments all over the Court. The lunchroom downstairs is a hotbed of controversy, argument, brutal insults. Do our law clerks sway us? Yes, sometimes. Young people are so passionate, so idealistic. It's difficult to resist them sometimes even when you know they don't have the ability to grasp the long view, the consequences of a decision."

Callie asked, "Do you think Justice Sumner Wallace could have behaved inappropriately with my mother?"

Again, Justice Xavier-Foxx was unruffled. "It wouldn't surprise me. He was always testing. As I said, everyone knows that Sumner has always had a roving eye. He'll never see himself as too old to follow through when he sees a woman he wants."

"Do you believe that Justice Wallace and my stepfather were best friends?"

"If Sumner did behave inappropriately with your mother and Stewart found out about it, I would certainly doubt it. However, I hope Sumner managed to hold himself in check with Margaret." She rose, looked at one, then the other of them. "Both of you are very young. Try to enjoy this special time. Detective, find the person who did this."

They left a few minutes later beneath a noon-high sun that shone brilliantly on the melting snow. Ben waved to the two federal marshals guarding the residence as he drove through the open gate. He said as he turned onto the highway, "Mr. Foxx stayed close throughout the interview, probably right outside the living room."

"How do you know that?"

"I smelled his aftershave. Old Spice."

"I wonder why he didn't come in, at least to meet us. We could have thanked him for the coffee and those marvelous brioches."

"Good question. That was well done of you, out of the blue asking her about, well, your stepfather messing around. I confess I never even thought of that."

"I certainly didn't get the answer I expected, that's for sure."

CHAPTER
14

45 Lawford Avenue N.E.
Georgetown, Washington, D.C.
Sunday morning

Savich and Sherlock stood a moment on
the icy front steps of Justice Lydia Alto-
Thorpe's house, staring at the recently
slammed door. The door was still shuddering.

Sherlock said, "Should I arrest her?"

"For rudeness? For telling us we're incompetent?"

"That's a start. Goodness, Dillon, I feel like
I've been bludgeoned. Can she harangue, or
what? She slammed the door right in our

faces," Sherlock said. Then she laughed. "She actually slammed the door in two FBI agents' faces. Isn't that a kick?"

"I'm still deciding what it was," Savich said.

The Justice had opened the door herself and blocked them, even though she knew who they were since they'd called out their names through the closed front door. She stood there, arms crossed over her chest. "Well, what have we here? More reporters?"

Sherlock had given her a sweet smile, pulled out her I.D., flipped it open, and said, "As you see, Justice Alto-Thorpe, we're FBI agents. May we come in?"

Justice Alto-Thorpe had said out of a mouth so tightly seamed they could barely see it, "This is ridiculous. I've already spoken to everyone. I know nothing about any of this except that you're all incompetent idiots. A madman invaded the Supreme Court of the United States of America and murdered a Supreme Court Justice! This is ludicrous, un-forgivable, and disgraceful! You allowed it to happen. All of you should be fired, beginning with the Marshal of the Supreme Court, Alice Halpern. The Attorney General should be shot. The President should resign."

And that had been only her opening salvo.

They walked back to Savich's Porsche. Savich waved to the two federal marshals who were sitting in their car across the street. He would swear there was a look of commiseration on their faces.

As they drove away, Sherlock said, "Well, even though I feel bruised all over, and we didn't learn a single thing except the Justice is extraordinarily pissed off, there is an upside to this."

"Yeah?"

"We have lots of time now for Eliza Vickers. She lives in McLean?"

Savich nodded, as he carefully negotiated a corner. "I guess you could say she is royally pissed."

"Bludgeoned, we've been bludgeoned by an expert." She sighed. "After we speak with Ms. Vickers we'll go home for lunch and see Sean and Lily. Hopefully everyone will be smiling and glad to see us. That will bolster our egos. Isn't Simon coming down from New York today to see Lily?"

"You bet. He's trying to talk my sister into marrying him sooner rather than later. What do you think?"

"I guess we'll see," Sherlock said, and settled back for the drive to McLean. "Simon's a pretty good talker."

Eliza Vickers opened the front door of her condo as soon as Savich's Porsche pulled into the driveway. The condo complex—The Oaks—looked lovely under a pristine blanket of snow. The individual condos were good-sized, modern, and well maintained. The grounds were nicely kept, the sidewalks well shoveled. The complex backed up against a maple and oak forest. Sherlock heard Dillon say, "Remind me to review the financials on her later. Nice buildings, nice setting. I wonder how much law clerks at the Supreme Court make?"

"Probably not all that much. It's such a prestige thing, I imagine. Sort of like being a Rhodes scholar."

Eliza Vickers was a surprise. She was tall, about five-foot-ten, full-figured, big-breasted, with long, straight dark brown hair. She wore white socks, jeans, and a huge creamy knit sweater. Big glasses distorted her eyes a bit, then she gave them a smile, and Sherlock saw a wealth of beauty on her face. The smile was brief, though, and it was clear she'd been crying. She rubbed her fists over her cheeks, trying to keep control, and whispered, "I'm sorry, I'm so sorry. Come in, let me get myself together."

The living room was good-sized, filled with light from a dozen windows that looked onto the woods, a modern fireplace, and a white sofa and chairs with a dozen accent pillows scattered artfully about. The carpet was white. Sherlock automatically took off her shoes, Savich followed suit.

"Yes, I know—why ever did I choose white? I guess it was during my off-guys phase, you know, back to virginal for a while. It's a pain now. Please come in. Can I get you coffee or tea?"

"Tea would be marvelous," Sherlock said. "Straight." That made Eliza smile a bit, that beautiful smile, and her eyes cleared behind those big glasses. "I'll be back in a moment."

"I smell him," Sherlock said.

"Who?"

"Justice Califano. I smell him. The same smell in his inner office at the Supreme Court Building."

"So it was an affair, then, not just Eliza Vickers worshiping Justice Califano from afar. He came here."

"Yes. And it was recent."

When Eliza Vickers walked back into the living room, she was carrying two mugs that each said UVA. "A good school," Savich said. "With one of the best law schools in the country, I understand. I thought you went to Harvard Law."

"I did. My younger brother goes to UVA." She gave them each a mug. "It's plain old Lipton. I hope you don't mind."

"It's excellent," Sherlock said, taking a sip.

Eliza wasn't a lightweight, nor was she fat. She was simply solid, statuesque. She took off her glasses a moment, and wiped them on the hem of her big sweater. Savich looked at her eyes. There was grief there, and confusion, but obvious intelligence as well. He felt immediate respect for her.

He said matter-of-factly, "Everyone tells us you're a real ball-buster, Ms. Vickers."

"Call me Eliza, please, Agent Savich. Goodness, yes, I suppose I am. Someone has to do it, or things don't get done quickly enough, and believe me, speed is of the essence. So much paperwork comes into a Justice's chambers, and all of it has to be reviewed, responded to. I keep things going, have from the day I walked into Stew—Justice Califano's chambers. I don't think any-one particularly dislikes me for it, but who knows? Who cares? We accomplish what needs to be accomplished."

"We understand that Justice Califano didn't want to lose you when your second year comes to a close in July, either as his law clerk or his lover." Savich paused a frac-tion of a second. "He was your lover, wasn't he, Eliza?"

Her mouth opened, shut, and then she sighed. "I don't know why I'm surprised you found out. It's just that I didn't think anyone knew. Actually I'm not certain that Stewart believed me as good a lover as a law clerk." She tried to smile, but this time she couldn't. "I didn't want to leave him and he certainly didn't want me to leave, but I was leaving, in July. I'd made up my mind. I would very much appreciate it if you wouldn't say any-thing about my relationship with Stewart to anyone, particularly to Margaret."

Sherlock said, "How long had you been lovers?"

"Four months now. Please, I don't want Margaret to know. Why hurt her needlessly? It would be cruel."

Sherlock said, "She'll have to know if it

turns out your affair had anything to do with Justice Califano's murder."

That knocked her back against the colorful pillows that lined the back of the white sofa. "How could I have anything to do with Stewart's murder? He was the finest man I've ever known in my life. He was brilliant, he was kind, he was gentle, he was unfailingly thoughtful. He loved being a Supreme Court Justice, and best of all, he was very good at it. We all needed him; the country needed him; justice needed him."

Such fine, idealistic words, Savich thought, and they came out of her so easily. Was she that good an actress? Or was she sincere? Fact was, she was a lawyer, a good one. Best not to forget that. He saw tears swimming in her eyes again and changed his direction for the moment. "Tell us about your law clerks, Eliza. What are their names?"

Sherlock didn't bat an eyelash. Of course Dillon knew everything about both the other clerks, how much they drank at parties, what sports they liked, but his look was very open and straightforward. She would have believed it instantly if she hadn't known better.

"There's Danny Boy, that's what we call him. Daniel O'Malley. I kid him about seeing him standing on the shores of Ireland, a bugle under his arm, ready to transport to France and join the Brits in the ditches. Daniel O'Malley, he's got that idealistic look, the burning fervor sort of thing. Fact is, though, that idealistic look isn't real. There isn't an idealistic bone in Danny's body. He doesn't come from money and he's grown up wanting it, desperately, and to him that means working for a big law firm in New York City. Danny is twenty-six, younger than his years should make him, eager to get his work done well because he wanted a glowing recommendation from Stewart to fire him off to the big time." She paused a moment, twisted the hem of her sweater. "I don't suppose he'll get one now." She cleared her throat. "I remember one time when I had to swat him down."

Savich said, "May I ask how you slapped him down?"

"I told him his grandmother, God rest her beloved soul, would turn over in her grave if she heard him advocate that 'under God' violates the separation of church and state in the Pledge of Allegiance. He tried to tell me she was Irish, not American, and she didn't really understand. I told him his grandmother was likely cheering when they added it in 1954, long before he was even born. Then I picked up the St. Christopher medal he always wears around his neck, pulled it tight, watched his face turn red, and laughed at him. He folded. End of story."

Since Savich agreed with her about that argument, he nodded. "Did Danny have a girlfriend?"

"Yes, only recently. He's very shy with women. She's a clerk over at the Department of the Interior, a computer geek, to tell you the truth, but it seems they are getting along, and that's good. Don't get the wrong idea here, Agents. Danny is law review, graduated Loyola with superior grades, and has a recommendation from a professor who was a former clerk, and still plugged into the clerk network. Naturally, this is true of just about every one of the thirty-six law clerks here. Danny never had enough money, which was par for the course with most of the law clerks, but he managed." She paused a moment, and this time she did manage to smile. "Do you know that in 1922 Congress first appropriated money for Justices to hire one law clerk each? Their salary was thirty-six hundred dollars a year. That's about a tenth of what the salaries are today. Given in-flation, I don't think we've made much progress." She smiled again, looked around her lovely living room. "My uncle owns a law firm in Boston. I worked for him before I came here."

Savich smiled back at her. "Thank you. And the other clerk?"

"Stewart elected to have only three law clerks this year instead of the typical four. Why, I don't know. I didn't ask him. So the other clerk is Elaine LaFleurette. A ridiculous name, and she hates it. She was consider-ing changing it, but she said her father would have a conniption fit and disown her, so she's sticking with it. But since she hates to be called Elaine, we all call her Fleurette. She went to Tulane, a big party school that she aced without really even trying, then went to Stanford where she found what she needed—more focus and less beer—and she did very well. She's not strong enough yet to take on the world, but she'll get there. She's a good woman, very good. She also admired Stew—Justice Califano. Actually, she worshiped the ground he walked on, like a substitute for her father, who is evidently something of a controlling son of a bitch.

Stewart always listened to her, always showed her respect, even when he wanted to put duct tape over her mouth. She came running into his office once when she heard us yelling at each other. She thought she needed to protect him from me. It was a close call."

She'd brought it back to her relationship with Justice Califano without them having to push her. Savich said, "What do you mean close?"

"Well, if she hadn't come bursting in, I'm afraid that Stewart and I might have been tearing each other's clothes off in the next five minutes. We liked arguing, it stimulated us, made us a little wild. We never made love in his office, but that time it would have been close, I'll admit it.

"And Stewart could argue, believe me. He could execute a 360 on the head of a pin just for fun, and argue the opposite side. He was that good. He had this ability to see both sides of an issue very clearly, and he could argue either side so well, he could talk nearly anyone over. It was a gift he had. But he was willing to change his mind as well. The good Lord knows even I made him change it sometimes. Don't get me wrong. He wouldn't change his mind about an issue or a case because he loved me, it was always about his sense of justice and the best way to achieve it without stomping on the Constitution. He believed our Constitution should serve our world today, but he always tried to get into the Old Ones' heads—that's what he called them.

"He had weaknesses, too. He could take a lawyer into dislike—and I know at least a couple of times that it colored his decisions. But he helped me form my own ideas about how to balance justice and the law in each individual situation. We'd disagree, we'd fight." Eliza stopped cold, looked down at her clenched hands. "And now he's dead, and we don't even know who killed him or why."

She started sobbing, and Sherlock went to her and pulled her into her arms and gently rocked her back and forth. She whispered against her hair, "I know, Eliza. We're so very sorry. We won't be telling Mrs. Califano anything, only if it's vital, which I can't imagine right now that it would be. It's all right, Eliza. Is there someone we can call for you?"

Eliza Vickers shook her head against Sherlock's shoulder, and slowly straightened.

"You're so small, but you're strong, aren't you?"

Sherlock gave her face a gentle pat. "Yes, I am. But I can't stand to see this pain. Listen to me now. It is right that you grieve, that you think of all you've lost, but you're young and smart, and you will get over this. You will move on, and you will marry and you might be lucky enough to have a child. Agent Savich and I have Sean, and we would give our lives for him. So you see, things can change, and they will, for the better. We'll be speaking to you again, Eliza."

Before they left, Savich made an appointment to see Eliza Vickers on Monday afternoon at the Supreme Court Building.

"I wonder," Savich said as he turned the ignition key, "if she expected to marry him."

"I sure hope she's too smart to have fallen into that trap."

"Next time we see her, let's be sure to ask. I want to hear what she has to say."

CHAPTER
15

Georgetown
Washington, D.C.
Sunday afternoon/evening

Lily Savich served homemade vegetable soup and polenta, an unlikely combination except that Sean adored it, and a warm baguette with strawberry preserves, which Sean also liked. Sean floated his polenta in the soup and hummed while he spooned most of it down his throat.

Sherlock said as she tucked Sean's napkin more firmly around his neck and wiped bits of polenta off his chin, "When's Simon coming, Lily?"

"Simon got hung up, and won't be here until this evening. Some big art acquisition for the Met. He's pretty impressed with himself. You guys got home sooner than expected."

"Yeah, well," Sherlock said as she spooned in a bit of soup, "Justice Alto-Thorpe blasted us out of the water for allowing murder to happen in the Supreme Court, wouldn't even let us in her house."

"She lambasted us all right," Savich said. "It was quite an experience."

"Somehow I can't imagine anyone lambasting either of you," Lily added, her voice wistful. "I wish I could have seen that. Okay, despite her, how's the case going?"

"We've got some interesting twists going." Savich's eyes nearly rolled back in his head at the taste of the soup. "You made the soup, Lily? It's wonderful."

And Lily said without missing a beat, "Sure, Sean and I sliced the veggies." She winked at Sherlock and mouthed "Balducci's," naming a high-end deli over on M Street. She continued, "After Justice Alto-Thorpe, you guys sure don't want to turn on the TV, it'll give you heartburn. Goodness, I had no idea there were so many experts on exactly what the FBI should be doing and isn't doing, on what the President should be doing and isn't doing. It shows no sign of stopping."

"The price of doing business in this town," Savich said. "Now, don't bother me, Lily. I've got a spiritual experience going with this soup. Sean? You liking it too?"

His boy sucked down a spoonful, most of it making its way down his throat, but some of the vegetables and broth dripping off his chin. He gave his father a huge grin and picked up a chunk of polenta out of his soup and squeezed it through his fingers.

"I was just waiting for him to do that," Lily said, watching him flatten his palm against his open mouth. "I think he likes the way it feels squishing between his fingers."

"Whatever works," Savich said. "Thanks so much for coming over, Lily. Graciella needed some time off, her mom's been ill."

"Believe me, it's my pleasure." Savich heard the hitch in her voice. She'd lost her own little girl over a year before, but now there was a nephew in her life, and he knew it mattered. He wondered if being with Sean was keeping her in Washington rather than marrying Simon Russo and moving to New York. On the other hand, *The Washington*

Post had picked up *No Wrinkles Remus,* her political cartoon series, and she was laughing more, looking better, happier.

"Yes, Lily, we really appreciate you feeding us and taking care of the little wild one here—" Sherlock was interrupted by her cell. "Excuse me," she said and turned away. "Sherlock."

"It's Jimmy Maitland, Sherlock. You guys are needed, now. There's been another murder."

"Who?"

"Daniel O'Malley, one of Justice Califano's law clerks."

"Oh no," Sherlock said. "Where did it happen?"

"His girlfriend found him in his apartment. Get over here as fast as you can. You got the address?"

"Oh yes. We'll be right there."

Both Savich and Lily were on their feet. "What is it, Sherlock?"

"Daniel O'Malley. Danny Boy. Someone killed him. Lily, can you—"

"If you're thinking about asking Mom, hang it up. Sean's mine. Go."

Sean wanted to go too. It took a couple of minutes to convince him that rolling his red ball over his Aunt Lily's stomach would be more fun.

Daniel O'Malley hadn't died easily. He'd fought, hard, but his killer had been stronger. He'd been strangled with his own St. Christopher medal.

He lay sprawled on his back in the narrow hallway that led from the living room to the bedroom of his apartment. His fingers were cut where he'd tried to get them beneath the heavy chain. The living room had been ripped apart—his one sofa, which looked like it had come from his parents, was turned facedown, a big TV chair ripped apart, the television smashed, all the dozen upon dozen of books pulled off the shelves, many of them ripped in two.

His apartment was on Biltmore Street N.E., near the middle of a long block in a blue-collar neighborhood that had undergone some recent gentrification. The apartment was small—a narrow living room, tiny kitchen, with everything in it smashed, the refrigerator open, milk pooled in the craters on the old linoleum floor. There was one bathroom, again with everything on the floor, a long skinny bedroom, three dead plants lined up on the windowsill, the only things that hadn't been destroyed. The mattress was turned over and slashed open. All the drawers in the small dresser were pulled out, shorts, undershirts, socks, pullovers thrown on the floor. Everything in the small closet was shredded, including two pairs of shoes.

They heard quiet weeping from the kitchen.

Jimmy Maitland and the medical examiner nodded to them in the hallway. Savich and Sherlock went down on their haunches beside Detective Ben Raven. He looked over at them. "You can thank Mr. Maitland for getting me here. He also called the dozen task force team leaders. This place is going to fill up pretty soon. He thought it would be more efficient than calling everyone together again at FBI headquarters."

"Is Callie with you, Ben?" Sherlock asked.

"Yes, she's downstairs in the car. I ordered her on pain of dismemberment to stay there."

Savich said, "Good, no one wants her to see this."

They studied Danny O'Malley's body. "It's like Justice Califano," Sherlock said. "He really fought, but in the end, the murderer toyed with him, let him think he could pull the chain free, but he couldn't, of course. The killer is strong, guys, he's very strong."

"And sadistic," Ben said. "He enjoyed this as much as he did strangling Justice Califano, got a real kick out of Danny's struggles, gave him a whiff of hope, then strangled him right through his fingers."

Sherlock said, "I wonder if he brought his own wire, then saw Danny's chain and decided that would do the job just as well."

Savich nodded slowly. "Yeah, that's probably right. He would have come prepared. He knew he was going to kill him, no doubt in my mind."

Jimmy Maitland crowded in beside them. "There's got to be some useful physical evidence this time. The guy was looking for something. Even the bathroom, it looks like a hurricane went through. The killer didn't care, just destroyed, even the mirror and the medicine cabinet, glass everywhere, all the pill bottles open, pills scattered on the floor. He even ripped up the shower curtain. Still, we'll go over this place thoroughly, just maybe he didn't find what he was looking for."

"Or maybe he wasn't looking for anything.

He was enraged and wanted to destroy everything," Ben said.

"That's possible," Maitland said. "But I hope you're wrong, and the murderer was looking for something." Jimmy Maitland rose and went off toward the kitchen.

Savich and Sherlock continued to examine Daniel O'Malley's body. "Do you smell that? It's like the Fantastik we use to clean the counters and bathrooms at home." She raised Daniel O'Malley's fingers and sniffed. "The bastard scrubbed under his nails, cleaned away any skin and blood, any evidence of a struggle."

Savich said, "Dr. Conrad is good. If there's anything to find, he and the forensic guys will find it."

They rose, stood looking down at the young man's body, the gray pallor, the bulging eyes, the smell of waste his body had expelled—no, Sherlock couldn't see him with a bugle now, uniform sharply pressed, standing on the shore of Ireland. Twenty-six years old and he was dead. "He was so young, so—new. Maybe Eliza was wrong, maybe he would have turned out to be Danny Boy, a bugle under his arm, fighting for justice, maybe he wouldn't have turned into a money-grubbing kind of lawyer. Why was he murdered?"

Savich said, "I don't know, but it doesn't feel good."

"No," Ben said. "It doesn't. Why was the place torn apart?"

Sherlock said, "The killer was looking for something. But what? What could a law clerk for Justice Califano have that was so important for him to find?"

Savich said, "There's lots to consider here, but like I said, I have a bad feeling about this. And about Danny. Let's speak to Danny's girlfriend. Hopefully she'll know what was going on with him."

Jimmy Maitland was looking both pale and furious when he walked back from the kitchen. "Damnation, this makes me mad, a young kid like this, why the hell did this maniac kill him?" He looked down at Danny O'Malley's body. "He was so damned young. It burns me to the ground."

Sherlock said, "You find out anything from the girlfriend?"

"His girlfriend—her name's Annie Harper—said she and Danny went to a movie Friday night, couldn't tell me what it was. She said Danny loved Italian flicks, the ones with subtitles. She spent the night with him. She said he was really upset about Justice Califano's murder when he heard it on the news Saturday morning. I'm going to shut up now. I want you guys to speak to her, form your own opinions, but I'll tell you, she's a mess right now, incoherent really. Came over here, had a key, let herself in and found him."

"It sounds like she belongs in the hospital right now," Sherlock said. "They'll probably want to sedate her. And we've got to call her family."

Jimmy Maitland nodded. "Yeah, I think that's the way to go. Hope to God she'll know what was on his mind. I don't mind telling you, I really don't like this.

"Okay, let me get Annie Harper to the hospital. I'm going to leave it to Dr. Conrad and the two forensic teams. We've got people out canvassing the neighborhood. The twelve team leaders are here. Come into the living room when you're done."

"Oh yeah, best to put a guard on her, just in case," Savich said.

Maitland nodded.

Five minutes later, twelve agents stood amidst the wreckage of the small living room. When Maitland spoke, everyone fell silent.

"We want every person who knew Danny O'Malley interviewed again as quickly as possible. Check alibis and phone records. The canvassing of Danny O'Malley's neighborhood hasn't turned up anything yet, but we'll continue pounding the pavement, speaking to every neighbor—and you can believe we'll get all the warrants we ask for.

"You all know the drill. Our murderer worked fast. What was he looking for when he tore up Danny's apartment? We need to find that out.

"Danny was killed within twenty-four hours of Justice Califano, according to Dr. Conrad's preliminary examination, which means he was killed early this morning or very late Saturday night. Annie Harper, his girlfriend, didn't spend the night on Saturday."

"That was her good luck," said Agent Ollie Hamish. "She'll realize that soon enough."

Maitland said, "Yes, she will, and then she'll have to live with it. Danny's murder brings us so close I can taste it. It's someone in this bloody loop, someone we've already met and interviewed, not some deranged stranger, not someone on the outside. Let's get it done, today, all of it."

Savich said, "We're going to focus on the

following scenarios. First, there's some connection between Danny O'Malley and Justice Califano, something in Danny's background that ties them together. If this is the case, we'll find out what it is."

Savich drew a deep breath. "The only other scenario that makes any sense is that when Danny found out about Justice Califano's murder, he either knew immediately who the killer was, or he'd seen or heard something he shouldn't have, probably in Justice Califano's office. And he acted on it."

Jimmy Maitland said, "I was hoping I was the only one thinking that."

Ollie Hamish said, "You hate it when young could go hand and glove with stupid. Well, we'll hope there was another reason, that maybe the two of them were tied together somehow in the killer's mind."

Savich nodded. "I simply can't think of another reason why the killer ransacked the apartment. He had to be looking for whatever it was that Danny was holding over his head. Danny could have also been involved in something with the killer, and not realized that part of the plan was to kill him as well. If it turns out that Danny did know something and tried his hand at blackmail, we've got to find out what he knew and how he knew it. So that means we've got to track every move Danny O'Malley made.

"We'll take his bills apart, strip his computer down to the hard drive. If he used them, we'll know. As to who's going to do what, Mr. Maitland's already made up assignments." He paused a moment, looked out over the devastation, then finally at the men and women who were packed into the small living room. "None of us want Danny O'Malley involved in some sort of blackmail, but the fact is that it's a possibility, and we've got to face it head-on." He turned to Agent Michaels. "When you interviewed him, Pete, did you get any impression he was keeping something back? Was there any hint that he wasn't being straightforward?"

Agent Michaels said immediately, "He acted like a choirboy, Savich, playing the hand-wringing innocent, tears in his eyes the entire interview. I should have realized—" Pete cursed under his breath.

Savich said, "Forget it, Pete. We'll hope it turns out he wasn't acting. We'll push harder on everyone else now. As Mr. Maitland said, we're close. Trust me on this, people. We will get this monster, and we'll get him soon.

First, we have to pin down exactly why he murdered one of Califano's law clerks."

Sherlock said, "If it turns out Danny was a blackmailer, what could he possibly have known? He wasn't anywhere near the Supreme Court Building on Friday night." She paused a moment, stared around at all the agents. "I hope Danny wasn't that stupid."

CHAPTER
16

After Savich told Ben Raven to meet them at Elaine LaFleurette's place in two hours, he and Sherlock drove again to Eliza Vickers's McLean condo.

Savich said, "I want to tell her myself, look her in the face and tell her about Danny. I want to see how she reacts for myself." She and Fleurette are our best leads now."

When Eliza answered the knock, he said without preamble, "Hello, Eliza. I'm sorry to tell you this, but Danny O'Malley is dead."

Eliza Vickers took the news like a body blow. She turned white, whispered, "No, no," and stumbled back from the front door. Savich grabbed her arm to keep her from crashing into the small side table in the entry hall.

"No," she said again, staring at them, shaking her head back and forth, rubbing her hands frantically over her arms. "This can't be true. It can't. Oh God. Not Danny, not him." She covered her face with her hands and stood there sobbing, rocking on her feet.

"Let's sit down, Eliza," Sherlock said. Together, they led her into the living room. Sherlock got her a glass of water. Eliza didn't seem to notice the glass at her mouth, but when she took a drink, it seemed to help.

It was several more minutes before Eliza raised her ravaged face. Her eyes were shocked, uncomprehending. "Has everyone gone mad? For God's sake, why would anyone want to kill Danny?"

"We're not certain yet," Sherlock said, "but Danny's apartment had been torn apart."

Eliza looked baffled. "But why? That doesn't make any sense. Danny didn't have any valuables hidden away."

Sherlock said, "It's possible Daniel O'Malley was trying his hand at blackmail and that's why his apartment was torn up. The killer was looking for whatever it was that

Danny was holding over his head. If Danny was attempting blackmail, it cost him his life.

"We're dealing with someone utterly ruthless, someone who doesn't hesitate when he sees something has to be done to save himself. And very possibly save the person who hired him to kill Justice Califano."

"You believe there are two people?"

"Yes. Someone hired the killer. He's very professional, Eliza, except for the risks he chooses to take, and I get the feeling that's how he likes it. He's an adrenaline junkie. The bigger the risk the better."

Eliza looked perfectly blank. "No, I can't believe Danny would do that. Besides, what could he have known? What? He was so sweet, but he worked hard because he saw this year as the servitude that would eventually land him the big bucks. He wasn't stupid. A blackmailer? Danny? I swear to you I never saw such a side to him—you know, actually making the decision to use what he knew to blackmail a killer? Why didn't he come to me? Why didn't he call you? I know money was important to him, but this? I just don't understand it." Her voice dropped off. "It's got to be another reason, it's got to be."

Sherlock said, "We're looking into everything, Eliza, but there aren't all that many ways to interpret this. It's possible that someone wants to kill everyone in Justice Califano's chambers. In case that's the goal, there'll be an agent here to guard you."

Eliza couldn't get her mind around this, they both saw it, and waited. "That's crazy."

"Yes, it is," Sherlock said.

Eliza sighed, paced from one end of her living room and back again. "Maybe the killer believed that Danny knew something, that Danny didn't try to blackmail him at all."

"That's possible," Sherlock said, "but not all that likely. Look, we're hoping that Danny's girlfriend will have information for us, but until then, let's assume Danny tried his hand at blackmail."

"It's tough, really tough. All right. If Danny was a blackmailer, then I was obviously wrong about him. Money was an obsession with him, and I never realized it. I wonder how long it takes to really know what's going on inside a person."

Sherlock said, "Do you know if Danny was in trouble financially?"

She shook her head. "Not that I know of. We're not paid princely wages at the Court, as you know, but he had his own apartment, though it was pretty spartan. I always got the impression that he was pretty careful with his money. He was just out of law school. And you know, he wanted desperately to have a year at the Supreme Court because he knew it would open doors for him. He told me he danced his mother around the room when he found out Justice Califano selected him."

"No gambling, nothing he was obsessed about having—cars, a boat, whatever? No expensive hobbies? Not a big clothes-horse?"

She shook her head.

"Then why would he do this, Eliza?" Sherlock asked.

"It doesn't say much for his morals, does it?" Eliza jumped up, began pacing, then whirled about. "Oh, Danny, you little pecker-head." And her eyes filmed with tears again. She began rubbing her face, not looking at either of them, probably looking inward to a young man she'd liked, a young man she'd believed she'd known, a young man she'd like to punch out, if only he wasn't already dead. She would never see him again to yell at him.

Sherlock said, "He was killed within

twenty-four hours of Justice Califano. That means that when he heard about the murder Saturday morning, he realized that what he knew was worth a lot of money. And he managed to notify the person who hired the killer. What could he have known, Eliza?"

"Oh God, I don't know. All right? How would I know what Danny knew and didn't know?"

"You knew Justice Califano," Savich said. "Danny must have overheard him talking with someone, or he may have read something Justice Califano left lying on his desk by accident. Something. Think back, Eliza."

She sat back down on the sofa, clasped her hands between her blue-jeaned knees, and rocked a bit.

Savich's voice deepened slowly, and he stretched his words out evenly. It was his interview voice, deep and soothing. "I want you to think back to Friday. You've just come in. I want you to tell us exactly what Danny did on Friday morning. Don't leave out a thing. Think particularly about when he had the opportunity to speak privately with Justice Califano. Just relax and think back, Eliza."

But she wasn't ready, and said instead,

"Danny's mom, dad, and three brothers live in New Jersey."

"Yes, they've been notified."

"You didn't tell them why you think he was murdered, did you?"

"No," Savich said. "They'd spoken to him yesterday when the news of Justice Califano's murder hit the airwaves. They wanted to make sure Danny was all right. He reassured them and told them not to worry. Now, it's time, Eliza. We need you. Danny needs you. You've been thinking about Friday for the last three hours. Talk to us."

"I have, yes," she said, still distracted. But Eliza Vickers was smart. She turned her eyes to Savich. Sherlock knew what she was seeing—dark fathomless eyes, eyes that held no threat at all, but an invitation to trust, and the unspoken promise of understanding. Sherlock recognized the concentration on Eliza's face. She sat forward a bit, all her own attention on Justice Califano's lover and senior law clerk, a woman she wished she could have met under different circumstances, a woman who could have been a friend.

Eliza spoke slowly, her voice cool and steady now. "Friday morning, all the Justices meet alone in the Chief Justice's conference room, at exactly ten-thirty. Like clockwork. But Stewart seemed to have forgotten about it. I reminded him. He went flying out of his chambers at exactly ten-thirty a.m."

"When did he arrive that morning?"

"At a quarter of eight. Always the same time. Stewart was very punctual. On Friday, we arrived at the same time, as usual, and had coffee together. He ate his morning sesame bagel while we reviewed several cases before the Eighth Circuit. Every Justice is responsible for supervising one or more of the thirteen Federal Appellate Courts. Stewart supervised the Eighth. We went over the majority opinion Fleurette had drafted for *Winters v. Kentucky,* reviewed several bench memos Danny had prepared and a post-oral argument memo I'd written. Stewart moved through all of this very quickly. Then he said he had some things he needed to do and wanted to be alone for a while."

"This was unusual?"

"No, not at all. That's why I didn't mention it to you this morning. I left him about a quarter to nine."

"What sort of things, in your experience, would occupy him in the mornings? Matters of the Court, personal things, outside business?"

Eliza's eyes remained locked on Savich's. "All of those things. The Court was revisiting the death penalty in the upcoming case on Tuesday. I knew he was chewing on that one, trying to determine if they should overturn the opinion they rendered in 1989.

"Now that I think of it, since we'd been talking about this case for several days, I don't think he needed more private thinking time about it. No, this had to be something else. Maybe it was about the party Margaret gives every year. She invites all the A-list people, and Stewart has to approve the list. The A-list gets turned on its head whenever there's a change of party after an election. As both of you know, it's a crazy town. Only the Justices get to be carried out in coffins, or choose to retire, depending on their personal political leanings, and who is in office at the time.

"Most of the Justices don't socialize much with politicians, or with the big society hostesses in Washington. They tend to be private. Those who are like-minded or enjoy each other's company spend some time together socially, but not all that often. They have such different interests, like Justice Xavier-Foxx's family horse farm. Justice Gutierrez has this incredible instinct for finance. Rich and very private, is Justice Gutierrez. Happily married, lots of kids and grandkids. Good man. Good brain. He loves sailing and crabbing, knows every square inch of the Chesapeake."

Savich drew her back. "So Justice Califano is in his office thinking about something. From a quarter of nine until ten-thirty a.m.— that's a long time for him to be alone, isn't it?"

"Yes, now that I think about it. Usually I'd be in and out, as would Danny and Fleurette, or the secretaries, but no, the door to his inner office was shut tight."

"Why, Eliza? You knew him well, what could it be?"

She paused, stared down at the thick gray socks on her feet, and said finally, "I would never mention such a private thing to anyone, but I suspect you already know. I think it could have involved Justice Sumner Wallace. Stewart wasn't happy about having Justice Wallace in his home, even though he knew Margaret had to invite both him and his wife to this party, but you see, Justice

Wallace hit on Margaret, and she finally told Stewart about it last week. It pissed Stewart off, which, when you think about it, is pretty ironic since he was sleeping with me." Eliza shrugged, looked away from Savich a moment—was it out of guilt, embarrassment, resentment? "The fact is that Stewart loved his wife, loved his stepdaughter, Callie Markham. I was in third place, and I knew it, but it didn't matter."

"You sound very philosophical about this, Eliza. You loved him, he loved you, but there was no future for you."

She shrugged, her eyes still on Savich's face. "I think he loved my brain as much as my youth, if you would know the truth. Did I love him? A man old enough to be my father? Well, there was an allure in sleeping with a Justice of the Supreme Court, at least I know myself well enough to have realized that from the beginning. He was a powerful man, it nearly came out of his pores. And confidence, he was loaded with it. But yes, I did love him. I tried to help him, to protect him, to smooth things out for him. Did he love me enough to leave Margaret? There was no way that would happen. No, it would have ended when I left. In my saner moments, I realized it, accepted it. I love the high-pressure life in the Court, and I loved learning from him. He helped me see the law as a tool of the nation. I hope to God that I gave him my best in return."

"Back up to Friday morning, Eliza. You haven't gotten him off to the meeting yet. Okay, his door was closed, and that was pretty rare, having the door closed that long, right?"

"Well, at some point he stuck his head out, asked Fleurette something. I know, it was an 'I Join' memo from Justice Spiros. It was a bussing issue in Alabama, and Justice Spiros wanted Stewart on board. Then he just nodded to us and went back into his inner office. He didn't close the door all the way this time. He must have left it cracked open, like he did most of the time, because I heard him speaking on the phone. It was after ten, must have been. I don't know who he was talking to. He didn't ask either of the secretaries to call anyone for him.

"The doors are pretty solid, so even if the door is open a bit, it's still private enough inside the office. Of course there are people all over the place outside. There are the tours, not that they come all that close, but you can usually hear people talking. And the Supreme Court Police are everywhere. Always noise, but in his inner office, with the door completely closed, you'd feel like you were in another world. Several dark leather sofas and chairs arranged in small groupings. Of course, there's a big conference table for himself and the three law clerks. Also, Margaret had given him a lovely Georgian silver set and he really got a kick out of serving coffee to any visitors. But you've seen his office, I'm sorry. You know exactly what it looks like."

Savich said, "True, but I didn't live there, not like you did. Now, Eliza, keep going. His door is nearly completely closed. What are you doing? What is Danny doing?"

"Agent Savich, part of my brain was always on Stewart, if he could possibly need me. I remember I was speaking to one of Justice Alto-Thorpe's law clerks—Bobby Fisher— yeah, like that chess player. Bobby was Justice Alto-Thorpe's clone, at least that's the image he projected. I suppose he was serious and not just kissing up, and that's why she loved him. It was really rather pathetic, and the other law clerks weren't shy about showing their contempt for him. Anyway,

Bobby was in our office, chewing the fat. Actually, he does that a lot, visits a good five minutes with the secretaries before coming to me, and all I could think about was how to get rid of the little jerk. He was usually after a date when he came visiting, but I always blew him off. I remember Danny was there, drafting a concurrence—that's an opinion that agrees with the result reached by the majority but for different reasons. He was hunched over his desk, concentrating. Then Bobby looked down at his watch, yelped, and bolted out of the chambers. He didn't bother to tell me why, the dork, probably because I turned him down again. But I looked up at our big clock right behind Fleurette's desk and saw it was one minute until ten-thirty—time for the Friday meeting in the Chief Justice's chambers. So I gave a fast knock on Stewart's door and opened it.

"He had the phone in his hand. He hung it up pretty fast when he looked at me and saw my urgency. 'What?' he asked, and I said in my usual shorthand to him, 'Friday meeting, conference room,' and he shook his head like who cared? He sat there, tapping his pen on the leather top of his beautiful desk, and he was frowning, looking off somewhere.

Then he shook his head again, as if he still couldn't decide on something, and got up. He didn't say another word, just gave this big sigh, and walked off to that meeting.

"I didn't see him until I was eating a sandwich at my desk at a little after noon. Danny and Fleurette went out to a café down the street, anything to get out of the pressure cooker for a while, they said, and Stewart walked in, nodded, and went right back into his office. He shut the door this time, all the way."

Savich said, "Why didn't you tell us this morning, Eliza?"

"I didn't think it was odd or out of character, just business as usual. When he was really thinking about something, he'd stay in his office by himself. When he wanted to discuss a topic, or he was ready for a good argument about it, he'd call me in.

"Sometimes we liked to leave the building to talk. Walk up into the residential neighborhood behind us. Check out the construction, just to be outside. It helped him to focus his mind."

"But on Friday, it's still lunchtime. What did he eat?"

"I brought him a pita sandwich, roast lamb, his favorite."

"He ate alone? In his office?"

She nodded.

"He didn't ask you to join him?"

She shook her head.

"Was this unusual?"

"No, not really."

"Where's Danny?"

"Danny got back about a quarter of one and Fleurette a little after one. Danny fritzed around a bit, not really doing anything useful that I could see, then he said he had to ask Justice Califano something. I was busy so I didn't ask him what it was, specifically, just tossed off something like, 'It better be important. He's got his brain wrapped around something.'"

"And what did Danny say to that?"

"He said, 'Oh, he'll make time for this, Eliza, he'll give me a few minutes.' Oh God, I'm sorry, I'm sorry, it seemed like business as usual, but now it looks so different. What did he mean by that? Danny already knew something, didn't he?"

Sherlock said, "Probably. You're doing great. Okay, Danny knocks on the door?"

"Yes."

"Did Justice Califano say anything you could hear?"

"Something like, 'Yes, Danny? Come on in, but not for long, I'm really busy.' Something like that."

"How long was Danny with Justice Califano?"

"I'm not sure, not long, maybe ten minutes. But I'm not sure. I got a call from a lawyer about procedure, then another call from the Solicitor General's office, more procedural questions. People were in and out, a good half-dozen.

"When Danny came out, he was quiet," Eliza continued. "He sat down at his desk, and he was quiet. I told you he wasn't stand-offish, maybe a little reserved with people he didn't know well, but with Fleurette and me, he'd usually yak up a storm. But Danny sat there, not saying a word. I remember that I started to ask him about a cert. Justice Cali-fano was concerned about. Oh, that's a for-mal request that the Supremes hear a case. I can see Danny sitting there, and now I can see something was on his mind. Then I got busy again, and ended up not saying any-thing. The rest of the day passed like all Fridays do. Everyone talked about their weekend plans. I think there was some sort of children's book festival going on over at Dupont Circle."

"Danny interested in books?"

"Yes. He said he was going to go see the storytellers with his girlfriend."

"Did he mention that he and his girlfriend were going to the movies Friday night?"

"I don't remember. I just don't."

Sherlock said, "When was the party Mrs. Califano was planning?"

"Not until next weekend. Poor Margaret."

"She'll be all right. She's got lots of friends with her, and her daughter."

"Yes, the famous five friends. I always thought that was wonderful—five women staying together all those years, sharing their lives, always there for each other."

Sherlock said, "Was Justice Califano carrying anything around with him on Friday— papers, anything like that?"

"He did have a habit of keeping some papers with him inside his breast pocket, usually whatever he was working on. Agent Sherlock, I can see him now, patting his chest to be sure he'd remembered, to be sure whatever he wanted was safe and sound with him. But I can't be sure if that meant he had any papers with him on Friday. Poor Danny, do you think he knew? Oh, Annie Harper. I've got to call her."

She was starting to lose focus, but that was all right. Savich rose. "You probably can't reach Ann Harper for a while, Eliza. After you've rested, I want you to go for a walk. I want you to review the day again, every moment of it, starting at the time you walked into your office. If you think of anything, doesn't matter if you think it has any importance at all, call me immediately."

Savich gave her his card with his cell number on it. "Keep Danny O'Malley at the front of your mind. Follow his footsteps. Sherlock and I are going to speak with Fleurette."

"So you'll tell her about Danny. Fleurette called me this morning, devastated, in shock really, about Justice Califano. At least her dad is flying in. He'll probably take her home, after Justice Califano's funeral. Now Danny's dead too. He'll be here for both funerals. Oh God. This is all so horrible."

"Yes, Eliza," Sherlock said, "yes, it is."

"Please prove Danny wasn't a blackmailer."

Neither Savich nor Sherlock said anything. It didn't look good.

CHAPTER
17

Elaine LaFleurette's daddy had money, Savich already knew that. Big Ed LaFleurette was a major player in commercial New Orleans real estate development. He was tight with the local police, not only for protection but also for enforcement, and was ensconced in the local political scene as well. Fleurette lacked motivation until she was accepted to law school, but now "driven" was the word usually used to describe her. She wanted to do things on her own, without her father's help. Well, except for where she lived. Why live like Danny when it wasn't necessary? She lived in a lovely quiet upper-class neighborhood, about as far removed from Danny O'Malley's digs as a dock bar from the Oak Room at the Plaza. It was a beautiful, well-tended brownstone, and it was hers, in her own name, a gift from Daddy after she passed the bar.

They found Ben Raven and Callie Markham in his Crown Vic parked down the block. The four of them walked together to the brownstone.

"Callie, I'm glad to see you," Sherlock said. "You twist Ben's arm here?"

"Actually, I had to threaten him again, you know, calling my editor at the *Post,* offering up goodies." She lowered her voice, close to Sherlock, "I really don't think he minds so much today. He's a tough guy, but I'm making inroads."

Sherlock patted her arm. "I'm just glad you stayed in the car at Danny O'Malley's apartment, like Ben told you to."

"Actually, I cuffed her to the door handle," Ben said. "All right, I didn't manhandle her. She obeyed me this time."

"Ben told me Danny and my stepfather were killed by the same man. I knew Danny, not well, mind you, but he always smiled when I visited. It's horrible."

"I agree," Sherlock said. "Now, I think it's good to have someone who knows Fleurette in on this interview, and your reporter's trained eye makes it even better."

Ben was looking at the two women. He didn't look very happy, more resigned. He'd found Callie on his doorstep when he'd gotten the call from Mr. Maitland about Danny O'Malley. He'd tried to get rid of her, but the woman was ruthless. Before they'd come here to Fleurette's house, she'd talked him into having lunch, said she really liked Chinese, spicy hot Szechuan, a good thing since it was a staple for him when he wasn't eating pizza, and she knew two places he hadn't eaten at before.

The four of them heard a man and a woman yelling at each other as they climbed up the six red brick front steps to the bright red front door with a lion-head knocker at its center.

They paused a moment, listening.

"You bastard! You used me because you wanted me to convince Justice Califano to vote to hear your damned case! You're despicable, you—"

"Get over it, Fleurette, it's all irrelevant. I'm a lawyer, you knew that going in. You knew there was a case I was involved in, so don't whine about it now. Hey, the old guy's dead, so we're not going anywhere, now are we?"

The four of them stepped back as the front door swung open and a man in his mid-thirties, with impeccably styled light brown hair, a handsome face, and a runner's body, came out, whistling, even as she continued to yell after him.

"I hope you rot and die! I hope your dick falls off!"

The guy looked at the four strangers, arched an eyebrow, gave them a cocky grin as he rolled his eyes back toward Elaine LaFleurette, and continued on his way to a dark green Jaguar parked in front of the house. He tossed his car keys in the air, caught them, and opened the door with the remote.

Savich flipped out his I.D. to the young woman standing in the doorway. "Agents Savich and Sherlock, Detectives Raven and Markham. Are you Elaine LaFleurette?"

"Yes. Look, I've already talked to you guys. I don't know anything. What now?"

Sherlock simply walked right up to her, pressing her back. "May we come in? It's sort of cold out here."

Fleurette stepped back automatically. She

was still flushed, her breath still hot with anger.

Sherlock pointed back to the man who was revving up the Jag. "I agree with you, he's a jerk," she said. "We couldn't help but over-hear. You want me to go punch out his lights?"

Fleurette stared at the lovely woman with her curly red hair who stood a good four inches shorter than she was, and laughed. "Nah, he's not worth you breaking a finger-nail. But you're right about him. He just dumped me because Justice Califano is dead, and so I can't help him now, not that I would have in any case. Thank God I didn't sleep with him.

"Callie? What are you doing with them? Oh God, I'm so sorry about your stepfather."

Callie said, "Thank you, Fleurette. I'm with them because I'm trying to help. About that jerk, you're lucky to be rid of him so quickly. Why'd you hook up with him in the first place?"

"Well, he is cute. And smart. But thank God it hadn't gotten serious."

Savich and Ben followed the two women into the living room, saying nothing at all. It was a gorgeous place, with highly buffed floors and an occasional Persian carpet. The living room was filled with high-quality Early American antiques, giving the living room a cozy feel. A fire blazed in the fireplace.

Fleurette obviously hadn't been expecting company. She was wearing old gray sweats, with only socks on her feet, and no make-up. Her blond hair was in a ponytail. Her features were sharp, her green eyes full of intelligence.

"The guy just showed up to kiss you off?" Sherlock asked.

"Yeah, you'd think he'd at least call first, give me a chance to do my face, but here he is, standing on my doorstep, wanting to tell me he's seeing another woman now. I wouldn't be surprised if it isn't Sonya Mc-Givens, Justice Wallace's clerk." Sonya Mc-Givens, Savich thought, unable to recall any specifics on her. But he would find out as soon as they got back to MAX and he opened his data port.

Sherlock said, "I'm sorry to tell you this, Miss LaFleurette—"

"Oh please, Agent Sherlock, you've heard me screaming at my former boyfriend, seen what a mess I am, please call me Fleurette, everyone does."

"Okay, Fleurette. I'm sorry to have to tell you this, but Daniel O'Malley was murdered, very likely by the same man who murdered Justice Califano."

Fleurette froze like a deer in the headlights. She stood there, staring at Sherlock, un-comprehending, her eyes blank, her face slack. Finally, she moistened her dry lips. "Danny—*our* Danny—is dead?"

"Yes, within the past twenty-four hours. Now, you're a smart person, Fleurette, you must see immediately that Justice Califano's murder and Danny's are somehow con-nected."

"But how?"

"We have to consider that Danny may have known something, maybe even tried to blackmail the murderer. We very much need your help, and we need it right now to find out who killed him."

"Why would you think Danny would do such a thing?"

Sherlock said, "His apartment was torn apart, Fleurette. Someone had been looking for something."

"And you think this something was some damning document that Danny had on the murderer?"

Sherlock shrugged. "Very possibly."

Fleurette looked over at Savich, who was standing leaning against the wall next to the fireplace, then at Detective Raven and Callie. She said, "I—I don't understand this. What could Danny possibly know about Justice Califano's killer?"

"Sit down, Fleurette. Let's talk about Friday."

Fleurette sat, took several deep breaths, and nodded. "I remember Danny going into Justice Califano's office. I remember he shut the door when he went in. None of us ever did that. If the door was cracked open, it stayed cracked open, but Danny closed it. Yes, that's what he did."

"So he wanted to speak to Justice Califano privately? With no one interrupting."

"Now that you put it that way, yes, okay."

"Who came in first Friday morning? You or Danny?"

"Me. It varied who was in first, depended on what each of us had to do on any given day. For the next couple of months things won't be so bad. It's the dog days—that's what they're called—April and May—when everyone puts in ninety-hour weeks. It's when the major decisions pile up and—"

Sherlock brought her back. "When did Danny get in on Friday?"

"Oh, I'm sorry. Around a quarter of nine, I think."

"What did he do?"

"He drank some coffee, ate one of those rolls from the downstairs cafeteria. He was reading something, jotting down notes. I didn't ask because I had my own stuff to do. I remember being a bit surprised that Eliza wasn't in with Justice Califano. They always met first thing every morning. The Justice always had his bagel. But Eliza was working at her desk that morning. When I came in, we had a bit of a chat, like usual, same with Danny."

"Do you know what Eliza was working on?"

"No, again, I had my own work to worry about. I was drafting a dissent."

"So you're all working. Then Bobby Fisher comes in to shoot the breeze?"

"Yeah, he's got a thing for Eliza, but she never gives him the time of day. He's kind of creepy, the way he worships Justice Alto-Thorpe. None of us like him. Then he left."

"And Eliza went into Justice Califano's office?"

"Yeah, it was time for the Friday morning

meeting in Chief Justice Abrams's chambers. Good ole Bobby had a stick up his—well, he hadn't said a word. He's awful, no manners, you know what I mean?"

Sherlock moved on. "So Eliza comes back out, followed by Justice Califano, who runs off to the meeting?"

"Yes, but it wasn't right away. She was in there maybe three, four minutes. I remember looking up at the clock, knowing how Chief Justice Abrams hated a meeting to start late."

"What time did Danny go into Justice Califano's office?"

Fleurette looked perfectly blank. "I don't remember that. No, wait, yes, I remember I had to go to the bathroom, but Danny still wasn't at his desk when I got back. Eliza waved toward the door when I asked where Danny was.

"I raised my eyebrows, but she just shrugged, then the phone began ringing. The secretaries always forward the calls to Eliza if the caller doesn't ask specifically for either Danny or me. Then both of us were tied up for a good half hour."

"So you don't know how long Danny was in the office?"

"Ten, maybe fifteen minutes. Oh God, poor Danny. Why would he do what you're suggesting? Why? It doesn't make any sense. He wasn't stupid. He wanted a recommendation from Justice Califano that would make the New York law firms sit up and beg for him. It didn't matter that both of us were second fiddle to Eliza. She's really brilliant, and even better, when Danny and I came last July, she knew the ropes since she'd already been there a year."

Fleurette looked toward the open drapes that gave onto the street in front of the brownstone. "Now it doesn't matter, does it?"

"No," Sherlock said. "No, it doesn't matter now. Did Danny give you any hint at all of what he'd spoken to Justice Califano about?"

Fleurette slowly shook her head. "No, but now that I picture his face in my mind, he looked—smug, yeah, that's it, Danny looked kind of smug. I hadn't seen that expression on his face before, so it struck me. I remember wondering, now what's going on here?"

"But he looked smug—like he'd found out something and rubbed Justice Califano's nose in it?"

"I didn't think that then, but it could have been something like that, I suppose. Oh goodness, it was only two days ago—and now Danny's dead."

"Do you remember seeing any papers on Justice Califano's desk, see him put any papers in his breast pocket, hear him on the phone?"

Fleurette slowly shook her head. "Wait— when he came out to run off to Chief Justice Abrams's meeting, he was sticking something in his breast pocket, and then patted the pocket. But he was always doing that."

"Any ideas about what the papers were?"

"No, not a clue."

"Did you ever hear of Justice Califano being involved with anyone at the Court?"

Fleurette rocked back with surprise. "Oh my, no, Agent Sherlock. He's old, and all sorts of proper and married, for God's sake." She paused a moment. "On the other hand, Justice Wallace has a reputation, if you know what I mean. He's a grandfather as well as a Justice of the Supreme Court. Isn't that disgusting?"

Sherlock patted her hand.

That was interesting, Savich thought. He looked over at Ben who'd taken Callie's hand to keep her still. Eliza Vickers and Justice Califano were indeed good actors if the law clerks hadn't known. But Justice Xavier-Foxx had noticed.

Sherlock rose, and everyone rose with her. She gave Fleurette her card and told her exactly what Savich had told Eliza Vickers. "Anything, doesn't matter if you think it's silly, you call me. We'll catch this guy, Fleurette, you can take that to the bank."

They drove six blocks over to Indiana, only a block from the Daly Building, to the Beau Monde Coffee Shop. Savich took his chances and ordered tea, the other three, coffee.

"So, Callie, tell me what you think of Fleurette," Sherlock said.

"She's really scared."

Ben slowly nodded. "You're right. I realize that now, but I didn't pick up on it when we were with her."

Savich said, "Do you think she was holding back?"

"She sure didn't seem like she was," Callie said. "I have to tell you, though, I'm surprised that she hadn't picked up on the affair Eliza was having with my stepfather. Such close quarters, in each other's faces every day. And yet Justice Xavier-Foxx, who's not around them that much, picked up on what Eliza felt for him."

"Yes, I was surprised, too," Ben said.

Callie sat back in the booth, fiddled with her fork. "I still can't come to grips with it. He wanted to marry my mom so much. I don't understand how that can be. My poor mother. Do you think she knew? Maybe guessed?"

"I hope not," Savich said. "Fleurette was scared," Savich continued as he selected a bag of Earl Grey tea from a box the waitress held out to him. "I wonder if she has something specific to be scared about."

"Justice Califano and Daniel O'Malley are dead," Ben said. "If I were Vickers or LaFleurette, I'd be scared on general principles."

"But Danny was acting strange, if they're telling the truth," Sherlock said. "You don't think either of those two women would be stupid enough to be in on it, do you, Dillon?"

"I wouldn't think so, no. The agents assigned to guard them, they'll keep an eye on them. They should be on the job pretty soon." Savich picked up his teacup, sipped cautiously, and sighed with pleasure. "Who knew I'd find good tea not a block from the Daly Building?"

Sherlock laughed, patted his arm. "Since Ben hangs out here, you can make it something of a hangout yourself. Callie, did you pick up anything else?"

Callie shook her head. "No, I don't believe so. Did Eliza Vickers think my stepfather would divorce my mom and marry her?"

"No. She seems philosophical about the future. I don't doubt her, Callie. She's a good woman, works hard, probably learns at a prodigious rate, but most of all, she enjoys being on the inside, close to power, which is one of the trimmings your stepfather provided her. But she knew that he loved your mother and you. She said so. You've got to let it go. It doesn't matter now."

But Callie couldn't let it go. "How could my mother not know? Not guess? I know if I were married to a man for as long as they were married, I'd know if he wasn't faithful."

"She's never given you any inkling that she had any suspicions at all?"

"No, she hasn't." Callie looked at Ben, whose expression surprised her. It was austere as a monk's, his eyes very cold. "What?"

Ben Raven said, "I don't approve of infidelity."

Savich raised his teacup and gave Sherlock's cup a tap. "Well, neither do we."

"But if Callie's right, why was Fleurette scared? Did you pick up on Eliza Vickers being scared as well?"

Both Savich and Sherlock shook their heads.

Savich said, "I need to get back and spend some time with MAX. We've got a whole crew inputting all the background information and interviews on all the players—the law clerks, the Justices, and your mother's and stepfather's friends and acquaintances, Callie. It's time for me to sort through some of that."

"Does that include financials? Bank stuff?"

Savich merely shrugged. "MAX went platinum a good while ago. He can find out almost anything at all. If he's in the mood, he can data-mine in Siberia."

"Okay, okay, I get it. You cut corners."

Ben said, "You aren't going to call that into your editor at the *Post,* are you, Ms. Markham? Do an exposé about misuse of federal power?"

Callie struck a pose that Sherlock thought

was very effective. It nearly put Ben Raven right under the Formica table. "I hadn't really thought about it, but now that you bring it up—ah, so many possibilities."

"To think I told this woman what an excellent butt she has," Ben remarked to the café at large.

Sherlock laughed and tapped Ben on the shoulder. Before she could say anything, Ben added, "She also thinks your husband is cute. What do you think of that, Sherlock?"

"A woman of excellent eyesight and taste," Sherlock said. "Hmm. Dillon, what do you think?"

"I'd be stupid to disagree with you," Savich said.

"You know what I think, Ms. Markham?"

"I'm sure you're going to tell me within the next three seconds, Detective Raven."

"I think I'll take you to the Tidal Basin and throw your black-belt ass in the snow. No one would hear your yells over the waterfalls at the Roosevelt Memorial."

"You could try, Detective Raven, you could try." She gave him a salute with her empty coffee mug.

"You guys put on a pretty good show," Savich said, peeling bills out of his wallet. "If you're through sniping, we're outta here. I want to stop off to talk to Dr. Conrad and to forensics again. Then it's back to headquarters and MAX."

"You'll want to see what MAX has turned up on Samantha Barrister's husband and son," Sherlock said.

"Who is Samantha Barrister?" Callie asked, her reporter's ears on alert.

"Oh," Sherlock said, and smiled at her. "She's a ghost who desperately needs Dillon to find out who killed her thirty years ago."

"Yeah, okay. Right. I got that." Callie stared from Savich back to Sherlock. But they were putting on their coats and gloves, and didn't say anything else. Callie touched Sherlock's sleeve. "Do you know what? I think I believe you."

Later that afternoon, the four of them drove in Ben's Crown Vic to Bobby Fisher's apartment on Hinton Avenue. "I wanted us to stay together today," Savich said. "Sorry about the Porsche, Ben, but it only holds me and Sherlock."

"I'm trying to be philosophical about this," Ben said. "A red Porsche classic 911. I'll bet your son's going to go nuts when he's old enough to drive it."

Savich grinned. "Possibly so, but thankfully, I can't imagine Sean doing anything right now but pulling spaghetti apart and wrapping it around his ears."

They found Bobby with three other Supreme Court law clerks in his apartment, part of a big complex near George Washington University, all eating pizza and drinking Heineken. The place wasn't a mess, but it wasn't all that large and there were four young bodies sprawled everywhere. There were nice pieces of furniture, and that surprised Savich.

The law clerks jumped to their feet when Bobby brought the four of them into the living room. They were all mid-twenties, dressed casually, and from their expressions it looked like they'd been talking nonstop about Justice Califano's murder. No surprise there. Bobby Fisher stood in the archway a moment, as if uncertain what he was supposed to do.

Savich said, "I'm Agent Savich and this is Agent Sherlock. We're FBI—this is Detective Ben Raven, Metro, and Callie Markham. Since all of you are here, it'll save us time."

"But, sir, we've already talked—"

"I don't know anything, Agent, I work for Justice Gutierrez who loved Justice Califano, loved him—"

"I've been in the bathroom all day with diarrhea."

Savich looked impartially at the group. They looked both scared and excited, and on the buzzed side. There were a good dozen beer cans on newspaper-littered surfaces. All those empty beer cans, well, that could work in his favor. Everyone was introduced, voices subdued. Savich said, "I know all of you have already spoken to the FBI, but we're here to tell you something you might not know yet."

All four of them, three men and one woman, leaned forward, their eyes glued on Savich's face.

He said, "Danny O'Malley is dead. He was murdered."

Savich, knowing that Sherlock, Ben, and Callie were watching them as closely as he was, saw the punch of surprise, then as his words sank in, the shock that showed clearly on their faces. None of them seemed particularly distraught yet, probably because of the unexpected blow they were absorbing.

"Okay," Ben Raven said, "let's all sit down and talk about this."

Tai Curtis, a law clerk for Justice Sumner Wallace, a tall, slender, good-looking young man, the one they'd been told disliked Eliza Vickers, looked like he'd been slapped. He streaked his fingers through his hair, standing it on end. "Oh, not Danny. That just can't be right, he's—oh shit, man. You aren't kidding us? Hey, you want one of us to confess?"

"Actually," Savich said, "spontaneous confessions don't happen all that often."

It was Bobby Fisher who asked, "Why would someone kill Danny, Detective Raven?"

Ben said, "Danny was murdered because he was somehow involved in this. Maybe he tried to blackmail the killer or the person who hired the killer. We're thinking Danny might have known something that he unfortunately didn't pass along to us. He was killed not twenty-four hours after Justice Califano."

There was more on the four faces now— fear, stark fear. Ben couldn't blame them. One of their own was dead, suddenly, violently. He said, looking at each face in turn, "He paid the ultimate price for a stupid decision." His voice sounded hard as nails, Callie thought. "We hope that none of you would now consider hiding anything from us, for your own personal gain, or for any other reason. If you know something, tell us now, for your own safety. I don't want to see any more dead bodies. If you've never seen a murdered body, come with me to the morgue and I'll let you see firsthand what could happen to you."

The three men looked ready to be sick.

Sonya McGivens, another law clerk to Justice Sumner Wallace, grabbed a slice of cold pizza out of a delivery box from Pizza Heaven and began chewing on it. A long string of cheese fell over her chin but she didn't seem to notice.

Savich noted that she was a knockout—a tall blond with classic features—and a bare midriff down to well below her navel. She was wearing bad-girl pants that barely covered her pelvic bones, and a lacy white top. Savich wondered if one of the reasons Justice Wallace had hired her was because of her looks. He also wondered if the Justice had ever lost his head with this young woman.

She said between frantic bites, "None of us know a thing, honest, Detective Raven."

Bobby picked up the last slice of pizza that looked nearly petrified. He held it out belatedly toward Callie. "No, thank you, you go ahead," she said, and tried not to shudder.

Ben said to Bobby, "I understand you were in Justice Califano's chambers Friday morning, shooting the breeze with Eliza Vickers until you remembered the Chief Justice's meeting, and took off."

Bobby Fisher slowly nodded. "Yeah. I wanted—" He stepped away from the other three law clerks, came close to Ben. "Okay, I don't want you to think I'm keeping anything back. The deal is I wanted to ask her out, but Eliza was playing hard to get. There was this show at the Kennedy Center I wanted to see. I wanted her to go with me."

"Did she accept?" Sherlock asked.

Bobby shook his head. "No, she never accepted. I guess that was maybe my last shot. Who cares? No tragedy. Usually she acts like a bitch to me, anyway."

"She was a bitch because?" This from Callie, who, if they believed she was a local cop like Ben Raven, was fine. Better yet, since she hadn't ever met these four, they didn't know her relationship to Justice Califano.

Bobby shrugged his narrow shoulders, looked away from her, not meeting her eyes. "She didn't like me. Called me Justice Alto-Thorpe's clone, and the way she said it wasn't nice. Sure, I usually agreed with my own Justice, she's brilliant, you know? Why wouldn't I want to be like her?"

Callie said, "So, you think Eliza was a bitch

because she wouldn't go out with you? Isn't that a bit over the top, Bobby?"

The other three law clerks were standing, all attention. Tai Curtis and Sonya McGivens nodded in agreement. Dennis Palmer looked blank, probably an expression he'd cultivated.

"Look, she wouldn't go out with me, and she wasn't very polite about it. It's not like I'm a pauper. I could take her nice places. And being a law clerk in the Supreme Court means I'm no run-of-the-mill law school graduate."

Ben said, "Yeah, I hear it's a great opportunity for all of you."

Bobby said, "Oh yes, it is. And when I met Justice Alto-Thorpe, I knew it would be a great year. I'm going into litigation, civil litigation in the entertainment industry, and I'm going to live in Malibu."

Ben Raven saw Tai Curtis and Dennis Palmer exchange looks that clearly said, *Can you believe this idiot?* Let them keep listening, Ben thought. When he got them each alone, there was no telling what would pop out of their mouths.

"Okay," Sherlock said, "she's a bitch because she wouldn't give you the time of day.

Most guys move on, Bobby, they don't get all hung up on it, don't insult the woman who rejected them. Did she dislike you because you respected Justice Califano less than Justice Alto-Thorpe?"

He flushed a bit. "The truth is I thought Justice Califano was pompous and overbearing, not at all like Justice Alto-Thorpe. Yeah, sure, Eliza knew what I thought. It's the truth." The other three law clerks were frowning, as if embarrassed to be in the same room with him.

Savich glanced over at Dennis Palmer, one of Justice Gutierrez's law clerks, a stocky young black man with a tough jaw and hard eyes. He was the best dressed of the four of them. He was drinking a can of Heineken, chugging it down. He wiped his mouth with the back of his hand and looked at Bobby with something like contempt.

Bobby picked up on it and hurried to say, "Hey, it's just that Justice Califano and Justice Alto-Thorpe usually disagreed, and I don't think either of them liked the other very much."

"How about Justice Bloomberg?" Callie asked, wanting to keep him talking. "How did he and Justice Califano get along?"

Bobby shrugged. "Justice Bloomberg isn't much of a talker. He sort of sits there like a big Buddha. Usually when court is in session, he nods maybe once an hour, says very little. However, he always votes with Justice Alto-Thorpe, and that's the right way, the just way."

Dennis Palmer said in a beautiful, deep voice, a voice that would very likely help him win over juries in the future, "Bobby's mainly right about Justice Bloomberg. But the fact is, he's the most junior Justice. That means he's the one who has to take all the notes, keep the records of all the proceedings. He doesn't have time to ask the lawyers questions. He's a deeply religious man, I do know that, but I've never seen him make any waves about it. As for my Justice—Justice Gutierrez—he and Justice Califano agreed a lot more often than they disagreed. They got along well. Actually, truth be told, the only Justice my Justice really didn't care for was Justice Alto-Thorpe, but of course he'd never say anything bad about anyone. Face it, Bobby, you suck up to her, you never see anything but what you want to see."

Bobby looked pissed off, but also resigned. "That's not true. You're all ganging up on me."

Sonya McGivens said, "We're not ganging up on you. Fact is you do suck up to her. If you saw her walking toward the bathroom, you'd probably rush down the hall in front of her to open the door. The stall door, too."

"She has her own bathroom, like all the Justices," said Bobby.

What he'd said was so absurd that the law clerks started shaking their heads and laughing. Sonya McGivens was laughing so hard she was holding her belly. She was hiccuping when she said, "I saw you once, following her, nearly into the bathroom, and yeah, you did open the door for her."

Bobby paused a moment, then said, frowning, "I wondered why she didn't use her own private bathroom."

The laughter grew louder.

Bobby looked like he wanted to hurl all of them out the front window, Sherlock thought, except it wouldn't be possible; it looked painted shut. "You're all laughing at me. Why the hell did all of you come over here today to drink my beer and scarf my pizza?"

"You begged us to come," Tai Curtis said.

"Look, we've got to straighten up here. We apologize, Bobby. Now, guys, Danny's dead, and these agents didn't come here to listen to us laughing about bathrooms."

Sherlock nodded to Tai. It was time to bring things back on track. "Let's continue, then. Now, Bobby, you spoke to Eliza, she blew you off, and you ran out. But you didn't remind her about the Friday meeting?"

"No, I guess I didn't," Bobby said, looking down at his banged-up Nikes. "I was upset at her, I'll admit it."

"Stop being a masochist, Bobby," Sonya said, not unkindly. "Stop asking her out. Eliza could eat you for breakfast."

Bobby turned a dull red and chugged down some beer.

This was going nowhere fast, Ben thought. "Did you see Justice Califano after the Friday meeting in the Chief Justice's chambers?"

"No. The Justices rarely ever hang around together when they're not in conference."

Callie said, "Do you know what Eliza had planned for Friday night?"

"Nah, she didn't say. I asked her, but she gave me this look, like what's it to you, jerk face? That's when I left."

"Fleurette heard you two arguing," Savich said. "What was that about?"

"The capital punishment case coming up. Eliza said I should consider trying to let some air into my brain, a little air couldn't hurt, and a new idea might find its way in. Can you believe she said that? Just because she didn't agree with me?"

Sonya rolled her eyes. "Oh no, Bobby, I simply can't imagine that."

Bobby said suddenly, "Wait, I do remember I saw Justice Califano and Justice Wallace talking on Friday afternoon, outside the gift shop on the basement level. The Justices were seldom down there, so it surprised me a little. I was on my way to get some soda from the cafeteria for Justice Alto-Thorpe, and there they were, standing there, real close, and neither of them looked happy."

CHAPTER
19

Now this was a kicker, if, that is, Bobby was telling the truth, Savich thought. "Did you hear anything they were saying to each other?"

Bobby shook his head. "No, but Justice Califano was intense. I remember he pulled some papers out of his jacket pocket, held them rolled up, and gestured with them in front of Justice Wallace's chest, as if he were punctuating each of his words."

"You heard nothing at all?" Sherlock said.

"I saw Justice Wallace rear back, like it was an attack and he looked surprised and indignant, but there were lots of tourists milling around, a big crowd of them, finishing up a tour in the gift shop to buy souvenirs, and I couldn't see them any longer. I wondered what it was about, but they disagreed sometimes, all of them. I didn't pay that much attention at the time."

"Okay," Sherlock said. "Let's get back to Eliza." From what Sherlock could tell, Eliza was well liked among the law clerks. Bobby Fisher would do well to watch his mouth. She said, "What do you think Eliza thought of Justice Califano?" She looked directly at Bobby, but the other three clerks knew the question was coming to each of them, and it set them to thinking. Too bad, but who knew what they'd say in response to another's comments?"

Bobby said, "Justice Alto-Thorpe thought Eliza and Justice Califano didn't get along all that well, but you know, I don't believe that. I know she admired the old guy. She tried to protect him and his time from anything she didn't think was important."

Sonya McGivens agreed. "Eliza practically worshiped him. The thing is, Justice Califano treated her like an equal in a way none of the other Justices do with their law clerks. Justice Wallace sure has never treated me or Tai like that. Justice Wal—" Her voice dropped off. She turned red, seemingly embarrassed, about what she'd almost said.

Dennis Palmer nodded in agreement. "That's true. It isn't at all like Justice Gutierrez treats me."

"And how does he treat you, Dennis?" Sherlock asked.

"He's always nice to me, don't get me wrong, always listens politely to what I have to say. But I always feel like he's ready to pat me on the back. I rarely feel he really wants to talk to me."

"So you think Justice Gutierrez treats you that way because you're black?" Sherlock asked.

He smiled at her. "No. I've never thought Justice Gutierrez is prejudiced. He hired me because I was law review, at the top of my class at Maryland, interviewed well, and presented him two top-flight recommendations. But I really do think it made him feel warm and fuzzy to hire a black man, because he's a minority himself, although I doubt he's ever thought of himself in that way."

"All right," Savich said. "Tell me about Danny O'Malley. Bobby, when you were in Eliza's office on Friday morning, what was Danny doing?"

"Okay. All right." Bobby took a deep breath. "Danny was at his desk, working on something, I don't know what. He looked up, saw me, and kind of winced. He did that whenever I came in. He never said anything nasty to me, not like Eliza did, he'd just sort of wince. Maybe he didn't like it that I'd ask Eliza out on dates. Maybe he wanted Eliza too, sort of a dominance thing."

"No," Sonya said. "Danny really liked Eliza, he looked up to her. He wasn't interested in her that way. He was going out with Annie Harper, you know, the girl he met over at the Department of the Interior."

Sherlock asked, "Bobby, did you see Danny go into Justice Califano's office?"

Bobby shook his head.

Tai Curtis said, "I wasn't anywhere close that day. You guys weren't either, were you?"

Dennis and Sonya shook their heads.

Ben said, "Bobby, did you see Danny at any other time on Friday?"

Bobby thought a moment, then nodded. "Yeah, I saw him and Fleurette go out to lunch. They had their heads together, talking real low, about what, I don't know. I didn't see Danny again. What did he have on the murderer, Agent Savich? What could he have possibly known, found out?"

"We don't know yet, but we will soon."

Callie said to Sonya McGivens, "Could I come with you to the kitchen, Ms. Mc-Givens? I need a glass of water."

"Sure." Sonya shrugged, tugged her lacy white top over her bare stomach, where it hovered for perhaps two seconds before slipping back up, and wandered out of the living room. She'd been here before, Callie thought. Why? Certainly not to hang out alone with Bobby.

"None of us are stupid, Detective—I'm sorry, I don't remember your name?"

"My name's Callie Markham."

Sonya stopped dead in her tracks, stared up and down at Callie. "I thought you looked familiar. You're Justice Califano's step-daughter. I was thinking maybe you'd given me a parking ticket or something, but that's not it at all. You've visited your stepfather before in his chambers, haven't you? And you're not a cop, you're a reporter—for *The Washington Post,* right?"

"Yes, I am. But I'm not here to do any story, Ms. McGivens. I'm on leave from the paper. I'm here because I think I can help with this

investigation, a sort of an inside eye, someone who knows many of the players. I really
want to find out who killed my stepfather.
Can you tell me what you nearly said out
there about Justice Wallace?"

Sonya rolled her eyes. "Please keep this
quiet, Callie. Can I call you Callie?"

"Of course."

"And call me Sonya. Okay, I'll tell you, not
that you'll believe it—Justice Wallace tried
to come on to me once, in a subtle sort of
way. I must have looked so horrified, he tried
to laugh it off as a joke. He looks at me
sometimes, I'll see him from the corner of
my eye, looking. I have a good figure and I
like to show it off, but to have a Supreme
Court Justice staring at you, well, it's enough
to put you off your feed. But who really
knows what old guys are thinking anyway?"

"I don't even know what young guys are
thinking most of the time," Callie said.

"That's easy. It's always sex. That detective
you're with, Ben Raven, now you look in
those sexy dark eyes of his, and he's trans-
parent as water. He might as well be wearing a neon sign: *Wanna have sex with me,
Callie?* He's a hunk. You guys dating, right?"

Ben the hunk wanted to have sex with her?

Nah, he barely liked her, although he had been looking at her butt. And he liked her butt, even if it was civilian. She cleared her throat, aware that Sonya was smirking at her. "No, we're not dating. I'm not lying, dammit. Listen, really, we're paired up on only this investigation. Since I'm not a cop, he isn't too pleased about me tagging along."

"Oh boy, are you ever blind. Polish up your eyesight, Callie. He likes you, I can tell. And you know what? He didn't look below my face once, not once. That's fortitude. Yeah, the man wants you."

Callie smiled, since this notion clearly astounded Sonya McGivens. "I'm curious, Sonya. You're not going to show off your body when you're out in the real world, are you?"

"Probably not, but it would be a temptation. Some guys on the jury wouldn't hear a single word out of the other lawyer's mouth. They'd be looking at me and agreeing with whatever I said." She sighed. "But professionalism has its place. I do wish guys and their libidos would remember that. Hey, since you're a reporter, you must have problems with men who think because you've got different equipment you shouldn't be allowed to play in their sandbox."

Callie grinned. "Tell you what. Let's go for drinks some evening and try to solve that problem. Right now, we've got to focus on this. Do you know if Justice Wallace may have behaved inappropriately with any other female law clerks?"

"There are only ten of us, but I think I'm the only one he ever tried anything with. I've heard some stories, everyone has, about Court secretaries that go back years. His poor wife. She seems nice, but downtrodden, like she knows too much and has no intention of doing anything about it. It's like her generation is hard-wired to protect their husbands even when they know the men have been unfaithful. Me, I can't stand women who let their husbands walk all over them, but I guess that's the way things were for them."

"So he never hit on Eliza?"

Sonya laughed, really laughed, and Callie saw her navel ring dance. She gasped out, "Justice Sumner Wallace hit on Eliza Vickers? Oh, that's a hilarious image. Oh no, he knew Eliza would have produced a spit right there, skewered him on it, and barbecued him. She'd have turned him into leather. No, he wasn't suicidal."

Callie liked Sonya and was tempted to ask if she thought Eliza had slept with her stepfather, but she couldn't get the words out of her mouth. She had a feeling that Sonya would have told her if she'd seen or heard anything.

Callie said, "Sonya, would you really be surprised if it turns out Danny O'Malley tried to blackmail whoever killed my stepfather?"

Sonya got a glass down from the cupboard, turned on the water at the sink, slid her fingers through it to make sure it was cold, and filled the glass, all without saying anything. When she handed the glass to Callie, she said, "Oh yes. You see, Danny always looked out for *numero uno.* He was a good law clerk, don't get me wrong, he worked hard, and he was smart, but he was after big money, wanted to make gobs of it, and unlike most of us, that's why he came to the Supreme Court. He believed it was his ticket to New York. He wanted to make his mark there, nowhere else, not like Bobby Fisher who obsesses about going to L.A. and defending the stars."

"Was Danny bright enough to succeed in the big time in New York, do you think?"

"The truth is we all have a ticket to just about anywhere, Callie. I don't know about Danny's future. He was really bright, but sometimes he'd talk and talk, and you'd know he hadn't read enough or thought enough about the topic to even give an opinion. He trusted his ability to bullshit. Maybe that's what he did here, only this time it didn't turn out well for him."

Sonya slammed her fist down on the counter. "Why the hell would he be so stupid as to get involved with a murderer? Didn't he care about Justice Califano's death? Did he really believe the guy who had the balls to kill a Supreme Court Justice in the Supreme Court library was going to pay him money because of any threat he made?" She shook her head, and paused. "Poor Eliza. She liked to think of Danny as an Irish lad filled with ideals. She was really wrong."

Callie took a drink of the water, placed the glass back on the kitchen counter. "What do you think about Dennis Palmer?"

"Dennis is okay. I just wish he'd get over this black thing. He likes to think of himself as Justice Gutierrez's token black boy, although he'd never admit it. I think he'd do better with one of the white Justices—conservative, liberal—it wouldn't matter. I swear none of them would give a damn if you were pink or black or green. Female, now, that's another matter. Isn't it ironic that you have sex discrimination in the Supreme Court?"

"Yes, it is. And Tai?"

"He works hard, puts in his two cents, but keeps his head down. He expends a lot of energy being careful about what he says and how he looks because he's gay, and hasn't advertised it outside our chambers. I have no clue if Justice Wallace has picked up on that."

"What does Tai think of Eliza Vickers?"

"He admitted to me once, after three beers on a Friday night at George's Pub, that he thought she was too smart for her own good, that it would get her into real trouble some day. She saw things she shouldn't see, he said, and she didn't know enough to look the other way."

Callie finally decided to ask. "Did he ever say anything about Eliza and my stepfather?"

Sonya looked genuinely surprised. "No, never. As I said, Tai keeps his head down, except around me and Justice Wallace's other law clerks. Then he'll mouth off, particularly if he thinks someone is attacking gays.

"As you can imagine, rumors abound in the Court. We're always in each other's chambers, gossiping, telling each other where our Justices stand on this or that issue and what we're working on." She paused a moment. "I'm really sorry about Danny. I'll tell you, Callie, if I had him here in the kitchen with me, I'd punch his lights out for being so damned stupid." She stood there, tears sliding down her cheeks. "Oh, poor Danny. It's scary. This is just too close to home, you know?"

CHAPTER 20

The Kettering home
Fairfax, Virginia
Sunday evening

Ben stopped off in Georgetown to let Savich get his Porsche, then led the way to the Kettering home in Fairfax. They pulled into the driveway just after seven o'clock that evening.

There weren't any reporters or TV vans hanging around. The media hadn't yet learned where the widow was stashed.

But there were four cars parked along the curb, two Mercedes, a Lexus, and a BMW.

Callie said to Ben, "It looks like Mom's friends are here."

Ben wasn't listening. He was staring at the display of automotive affluence, and grunted. He wasn't a snob, dammit, but couldn't any of them drive a plain old Ford? A truck, something useful, something that didn't smack you in the face with dollar signs and twelve cylinders, something like his? The Crown Vic had plenty of muscle, but that was different.

He realized Callie was staring at him, and grunted again. "I drive a Beemer too," she said, and gave him a shameless grin. "All right, so it's one of the cheaper models. You're a truck guy, right? Maybe you've got a dog hanging out the window?"

Savich and Sherlock joined them at that moment.

"I know it's late, Callie," Sherlock said, taking her arm, "but we'd like to see how your mom's holding up, see if she's remembered anything more. We won't keep her long. Looks like she's got lots of company in any case."

Callie nodded. "All her longtime friends are here. There's a couple of cars I don't recognize."

The snow was melting, the air was sweet and cold. The forecast predicted a dip below freezing tonight, turning what snow was left into ice. It was perfectly dark, not even a sliver of a moon. Callie felt colder than she should have, probably because she was stressed and tired, her stepfather was dead, and now Danny O'Malley was dead too. There was a monster out there, and she didn't have a clue if they were getting any closer. Savich kept stuff to himself, she'd realized that soon enough. So did Sherlock, for that matter. How odd that a husband-and-wife team worked together for the FBI. They were so in tune with each other. She wondered how long they'd been together. She looked over at Ben and wondered if she could ever be in tune with him like that. That stopped her in her tracks. Good grief, she was letting Sonya's remarks get to her.

She heard Savich laugh at something his wife said. Would they let her review all the interviews that Savich was putting on his laptop? She hoped so. She had a good eye. According to Savich, MAX was going to help highlight inconsistencies, red-flag interviews that were glaringly at odds with others, and do the analysis much more quickly than a person could. Evidently MAX was even going to suggest specific questions to ask. It sounded amazing, and she wanted to see it work.

She unlocked the front door and led them all in. When she went into the living room, she stopped cold.

In addition to Janette Weaverton, Juliette Trevor, Bitsy St. Pierre, and Anna Clifford, Justice Wallace and his wife were cozied up next to Justice Alto-Thorpe and her husband, both couples sitting on a sofa across from Margaret.

"This is an unexpected find," Savich whispered, and strode in, drawing all eyes to him immediately. He wondered for a moment how the two Justices had found out where Margaret Califano was squirreled away, then remembered the federal marshals assigned to them. They were probably parked discreetly outside.

Savich walked directly to Margaret Califano and took her hand. He smiled down at her. "I hope you're feeling better, ma'am."

"Callie called me about poor Danny O'Malley. I didn't know him well. It's unbelievable that he's dead too, just like

Stewart. What is happening here, Agent Savich?"

Savich said loud enough for everyone in the big living room to hear, "We don't know for sure, ma'am, but it would seem Danny O'Malley knew something and may have tried to blackmail the killer or the person who hired the killer."

A loud voice, anger simmering just below the surface said, "Given the general incompetence of the people who are supposed to protect us, I am not at all surprised. It is a disgrace, and I shall see to it that Congress does something about it."

He'd know that voice anywhere, Savich thought, and the words, and turned to Justice Alto-Thorpe, who was sitting on the edge of the sofa, mouth pinched, a cloud of disapproval hanging over her head. Her husband was looking off toward the windows, seemingly paying no attention.

Savich said easily, "I'm not surprised at your attitude, ma'am, given that you've already told Agent Sherlock and me your feelings on the subject at length."

"I shall see to it that new laws are passed. Murder done in the highest Court in the land!

It will go down as a disgraceful point in our history."

"Yes, indeed," Sherlock said. "As it should." She proceeded to introduce all of them to the Justices and their spouses. She got the distinct impression that neither Justice was pleased to see them.

Callie moved to sit beside her mother. Bitsy St. Pierre quickly scooted over to give her room.

Savich said to Harry Thorpe, "I had wanted to meet you, sir. I've been told that you own and operate Harry's."

Harry Thorpe looked up at Savich, his mouth opening to reply when Justice Alto-Thorpe said, "He sells fish. What are you doing here, Agents?"

Savich said, "We wanted to see how Mrs. Califano was doing. I assume that's why you are all here?" His question included Justice Wallace and his wife.

Justice Wallace said quickly, "Yes, of course. Beth and I are friends of the family, have been for many years. Naturally we'd want to see how Margaret is holding up."

Thankfully, Justice Alto-Thorpe remained silent, but she continued to look at Savich,

Sherlock, and Ben as if the murders were all their fault.

Savich said, "I assume your federal marshals brought you here?"

Justice Wallace nodded. "Fine fellows. We feel quite safe with them around." Beth Wallace didn't say a word. From her expression it was obvious she didn't want to be here. Sherlock saw her look directly at Margaret, and there was something in those faded eyes of hers, something that bothered Sherlock, something that wasn't quite right. Then it was clear. She knew, Sherlock realized, she knew very well that her husband had wanted to add another notch to his aging belt. Sherlock would wager she also knew that Stewart Califano knew about it as well and had been upset at her husband. But why was she looking at Margaret like that? Margaret wasn't the one in the wrong. Then Beth Wallace looked at her husband, saw that he was staring at Margaret. Sherlock saw her wince, look down at her clasped hands, slumping her shoulders, as if in defeat. She'd said everything she felt and knew without speaking a word. She was dressed in lovely black wool trousers, a pink cashmere sweater, and a matching black wool blazer. She looked good on the outside. But her insides?

Margaret said, "Would you like some coffee? Tea? No, not you, Anna, you've done enough."

"That would be lovely," Sherlock said. Janette Weaverton quickly rose. Did the women have a rotation schedule? Sherlock could easily picture Janette in tennis whites, skillfully wielding a racket. Yes, Janette looked like she'd be a winner at tennis. Sherlock smiled. "Why don't I help you fetch the goodies?"

The Kettering kitchen was large, the walls a pale yellow, the appliances sparkling new. A large pine table was set in the center, and Sherlock remembered the meal they'd had here with Miles and Katie and the children before they'd returned to Jessborough, Tennessee.

"This is a lovely home," Janette Weaverton said, and went efficiently to the coffeepot. Was she staying here with Margaret? Actually sleeping here? Were the other friends as well?

There was really nothing for Sherlock to do, which didn't surprise her. These women seemed so very organized. She leaned against the counter and said, "Margaret has more color in her cheeks. She's very lucky she has such good friends."

"She's still pretty bad, just sits there, staring off, and the rest of us sit there with her and worry and try to distract her. But she'll make it. Margaret's very strong."

"How did the five of you get together, Mrs. Weaverton?"

"Janette, please, Agent Sherlock. Incidentally, that's an interesting name. I bet you get lots of jokes about it since you're an FBI agent."

"Endless numbers of comments, yes. My father is a federal judge in San Francisco, and he gets the jokes too. But not in his courtroom—oh no. I think the 'Judge Sherlock' scares some of the defendants to their toes. Please call me Sherlock."

"Okay, Sherlock. The five of us got together in school. We all went to Bryn Mawr, outside Philadelphia, same place Callie went to school."

"You've known each other that long?"

"Well, we didn't all meet on the same day. I roomed with Margaret our freshman year, so I guess you'd call us the two originals.

Actually, we called ourselves the two Eves. Then we picked up Bitsy in biology the second year, Juliette shared an off-campus suite in the third year, and Anna Clifford, a math whiz, was tutoring one of our boyfriends in our senior year. We came together and stayed together."

"When did the duo set of Justices drop by? Were they unannounced?"

"They arrived maybe ten minutes before you did. And yes, neither couple called first. We've been talking about the Danny O'Malley murder."

Janette paused a moment with the silver tray and cups. "I've met Justice Alto-Thorpe twice. I wonder if she's always so disapproving of our federal police force?"

Sherlock smiled. "I imagine she hates law enforcement in general, and this sent her right over the top. I can tell you from firsthand experience she's been that way both times I've been near her."

"It's a wonder her lips don't disappear completely into her face."

Sherlock laughed, then sobered immediately. "I'm actually surprised that Justice Sumner Wallace came by, since he wanted to seduce Margaret and she told her husband about it. A lot of anger there. Why would he come?"

Sherlock calmly watched Janette Weaverton drop a coffee cup. Both women watched it hit the tile and shatter. That, Sherlock thought, was some payoff to the outrageous statement she'd just made.

"Oh dear, look what I've done. I'm so clumsy." Janette Weaverton quickly fetched a broom and dustpan from the walk-in pantry, and started in on the mess.

Sherlock said as she watched her sweep up the broken cup and dump it into the garbage can beneath the sink, "Surely you know what happened, Mrs. Weaverton. Surely you aren't at all surprised by this. Margaret told all of you about Justice Wallace and his unwanted antics."

Janette Weaverton washed her hands, dried them, and said as she turned back to Sherlock, "Margaret said very little about it to us. When Anna brought it up, Margaret laughed it off. I never got the impression it disturbed her very much. She thought he was an old fool. He's never hit on me." Janette began to arrange cups on their saucers on the big silver tray.

"Are there teabags?"

"What? Oh certainly."

She fetched a tea box, an early American piece divided into ten sections, each with a different tea. Sherlock picked out Earl Grey, Savich's favorite. "My husband rarely drinks coffee."

"Your husband is a lovely man. He obviously takes very good care of himself. You're a lucky woman."

Sherlock nodded in agreement. "Yes. We have a little boy, Sean is his name. Do you have children, Mrs. Weaverton?"

Janette shook her head as she poured cream into a small pitcher and set it on the tray. "No, my husband and I decided children weren't for us. Then we divorced." Ah, Sherlock thought, watching the woman, Janette Weaverton had wanted children, but why then hadn't she remarried?

"I've heard Mrs. Califano's boutiques are quite successful. I plan to buy my husband something for his birthday at the one in Georgetown. That's where we live."

A smooth eyebrow went up. "Georgetown?"

"My husband's grandmother was Sarah Elliott, the painter. She willed her beautiful home to my husband."

Janette Weaverton's jaw dropped. "Really? Sarah Elliott was your husband's grand-mother? *The* Sarah Elliott? How very incred-ible that must be."

Sherlock nodded, watched her put sugar packets and Equal in a small bowl, and set it next to the creamer.

Sherlock asked, "Do you work as well, Mrs. Weaverton?"

"No. I'm fortunate to have been born to very rich parents. I do, however, travel a lot. But things are different now with Stewart dead. Perhaps Margaret will need my help. I don't know yet."

"Would you want to join her in her busi-ness?"

"Unfortunately I have no business experi-ence. And, the sad fact is, I don't think I could sell a shoe addict a pair of Ferra-gamos."

Sherlock laughed. "Well, who knows? Shall I carry this for you?"

"Thank you. Imagine being an FBI agent, working with your husband. Does it cause problems for you at home?"

Sherlock smiled, lifted the heavy tray, and

said over her shoulder, "Not yet." People, she thought, you never knew what was in their minds, in their hearts, but bottom line, Janette Weaverton was a loyal friend to Margaret Califano, and that counted for a lot.

Conversation was strained in the living room. Margaret had fallen silent, despite everyone's best efforts, and sat clasping and unclasping her hands. Callie still sat beside her, her own hand on her mother's forearm, squeezing gently, every once in a while, so she'd know she wasn't alone.

Ben saw a strong resemblance between the two women, although Callie's eyes were bluer, her brows and hair darker. Callie had a sharper chin, but there was no doubt that the same intelligence burned brightly in both mother and daughter. It still bugged him that Margaret hadn't married Stewart Califano until Callie left for college. Being careful about protecting your daughter was one thing, but it seemed to Ben that Margaret had gone overboard.

Savich couldn't figure out Harry Thorpe. He sat there, silent and hunched over, saying not a word. He wasn't small or insignificant, he looked fit, he was a very successful businessman, rich in his own right, so why then did he look somehow beleaguered? Savich realized then that Harry had probably thrown in the towel long ago, had handed over the reins to this inflexible woman seated beside him with her intolerant spirit, her seamed lips, her extraordinary disapproval. How could he love her? What need could she possibly fulfill? A stupid question, Savich supposed. She was a Justice of the Supreme Court. She would be in the history books.

Savich said to Justice Alto-Thorpe, "Do you have children?"

The lips didn't unseam, but she finally nodded. "Yes, two girls. They're both lawyers, both practicing in Denver, Colorado. Harry is their stepfather. Their real father died eleven years ago in a boating accident."

Harry Thorpe didn't say anything.

"It's a lovely state," Justice Alto-Thorpe said.

Sherlock said, "I understand that a lot of Californians have moved to Colorado, driven up the home prices."

Bitsy St. Pierre said, "Everyone has signs that say 'Go west again.'"

Once everyone had coffee and Savich had his tea, Ben Raven said, "We spoke to

Bobby Fisher today, and three other law clerks as well at his apartment—Sonya Mc-Givens, Tai Curtis, Dennis Palmer. We told them about Danny O'Malley's murder."

The silence was sudden and acute.

"Bobby is a talented clerk," said Justice Alto-Thorpe. "As for Danny O'Malley, he was all right, too, despite being in a conservative Justice's chambers. You could change his mind. He had a good brain."

"Unfortunately, ma'am," Ben said, saluting her with his coffee cup, a cup so feminine and delicate he was afraid he was going to inadvertently crush the damned thing, "our working assumption is that his final decisions were stupid enough to get him killed."

Bitsy St. Pierre said, "I met Danny once. He was quite polite, actually insisted on taking the package I was hefting."

Savich settled into the dynamics of this strange group, knowing there were undercurrents he didn't understand, maybe secrets.

It was time, he thought. He looked over at Justice Sumner Wallace. "Sir, may I speak to you a moment, in private?"

Justice Wallace didn't particularly want to speak to Savich, it was clear on his face, but he rose and followed Savich into the front entrance hall. "What is it you wish to talk to me about, Agent Savich?"

"Please tell me about the argument you had with Justice Califano on Friday afternoon."

Two gray bushy eyebrows shot up. "Argument? I don't recall having an argument with Stewart on Friday. What is this all about, Agent?"

"You argued with Justice Califano in a public place, sir. Bobby Fisher saw you and told us about it. Since this argument occurred only hours before Justice Califano was murdered, I would really appreciate you telling me about it. It goes to his emotional state, might tell me what he was thinking or worrying about. You see?"

Justice Wallace no longer looked confused. "The *discussion* Stewart and I had on Friday," he said finally, "isn't at all pertinent to any of this. I will admit, however, that the timing was certainly unfortunate. Stewart was my friend. It is painful to remember it, Agent Savich."

"I understand that, sir, and I'm very sorry. What did you argue about, Justice Wallace?"

"As I said, it was a personal disagreement,

nothing more, and it had nothing to do with any of this."

"Sir, I must tell you that we know about the situation with Margaret Califano. We know that Justice Califano confronted you about it. Was that what the argument was about?"

"Do you realize who I am, Agent Savich?" Justice Wallace's voice was very soft, pitched low so there was no chance anyone else could hear him. Savich felt the very real threat of him, heard the absolute knowledge in his voice that he knew he was powerful, and nobody should screw with him.

Savich said in an equally soft voice, "Oh yes, I know. However, I hope you will understand that we must follow every lead we get, we must know every scrap of information even peripherally related to this. As a Justice of the Supreme Court, surely you must demand every pertinent fact from your law clerks on any given case. Surely you question all the lawyers who try cases before you as closely as you need to. Surely you must understand that I must operate in the same way."

Justice Wallace gave Savich a long look. Then he shrugged. "Very well. This will not go beyond the two of us, Agent. Do you understand me?"

"Yes, sir."

"Very well. It is painful, but I will tell you. Margaret had told Stewart I had tried to kiss her in the kitchen during a party some months ago. However, it was a lie on her part. The fact is Margaret wanted to sleep with me. I didn't want it, mind you, but she was insistent. Understand, everyone got a little drunk, so she really wasn't herself. She kissed me and I kissed her back. Stewart was understandably angry and confronted me outside the gift shop, as Bobby Fisher told you."

"What were the papers he was waving against your chest?"

"Papers? I don't remember any papers. Stewart always carried papers, his notes on whatever he was thinking about at any given time. Oh yes, I remember, he pulled them out of his pocket and began waving them around. I have no idea what they were, Agent Savich, no idea at all."

"Did you tell him the truth about Margaret?"

"Certainly not. I accepted his anger and apologized."

Savich thanked him. He wondered how much he'd just been told was the truth. It had been a very long day. He needed to go home and play with Sean before he went to bed. He wanted to give Lily a chance to be with Simon Russo and enjoy herself without having to worry about a little boy stuffing polenta in his nose.

They took their leave about five minutes later. Callie saw them to the front door.

"We'll do a very quick detour to headquarters," Savich said to Ben. "I'll give you some of MAX's data to look over tonight, then try to relax," Savich said. "I want your brain fresh in the morning. Oh yes, there's something else all of you need to hear." But he didn't tell them about his conversation with Justice Wallace until they were outside.

"Incredible," Callie said. "He actually accused my mom of coming on to him?"

"You don't believe him, do you?" Ben asked.

"At this point," Savich said, "I have no idea what to believe, but your mother, Callie, she seems gold-plated to me."

"She is."

When Savich pulled his Porsche into the garage at home at just after eight-thirty, he said, "After we play with Sean until he's snoring, I'm thinking some big fat hair rollers might be fun. What do you think?"

"You're teasing me. You know very well the moment Sean is down, you'll spend three hours with MAX."

"Hair rollers first," he said, kissed her again, and grinned.

She rolled her eyes and climbed out of his sexy Porsche.

CHAPTER
21

Savich lay on his back, staring up at the ceiling, Sherlock tucked against him, asleep, her leg sprawled over his belly, her soft curly hair brushing against his jaw. Her breath was warm and steady against his neck. He should have been asleep, but Danny O'Malley's girlfriend, Annie Harper, filled his mind. He wished there'd been time this evening to visit her at the hospital, to judge her state of mind, to see how coherent she was. To walk in and find your boyfriend's murdered body, it was a ghastly experience for anyone, particularly an innocent young woman.

Well, there hadn't been time. Tomorrow morning, first thing, he'd see to it. Savich knew that Annie had to know something, even if she didn't realize it, he was sure of it. But right now he had to slow his brain down, had to get some sleep. First thing in the morning, he'd call George Washington University Hospital—

He was suddenly aware he was dreaming. He was also very strongly aware of himself being in the dream. Sherlock was there with him, pressed against him, but it wasn't Sherlock he felt, it was a change in the air itself. It seemed suddenly heavier somehow, a bit more difficult to draw into his lungs. It wasn't particularly frightening, just different, something he'd never experienced in a dream before. That heavy air seeped slowly into him, and with it, something that should have been solid, but wasn't. He was no longer alone inside his mind; he was filled with something that stirred the hair on his arms, something he recognized because she was full-blown, right there with him.

It was Samantha Barrister.

How interesting that she was able to simply plug herself right into his brain. He still felt no particular fear, it was a dream, after all, nothing more. But he felt her fear, and her urgency, a dreadful urgency. She was waiting for him to acknowledge her, to let her know he was aware of her.

In that instant he saw her clearly. Her black hair, long and straight, nearly to her waist— an old hippie style from the early seventies when women parted their hair in the middle. She was wearing the same summer dress, the one she'd been wearing that night in the Poconos. She was very pretty, with dark blue eyes. Black Irish, that's what she was, although he didn't know how he knew. He'd been barely older than Sean when she'd been murdered.

He focused on Samantha's white face, and said in a whisper so as not to awaken Sherlock, "I'm here, Samantha. What's wrong? What's happened?"

She didn't answer him, just looked at him, afraid.

"You've got to know that I'm an FBI agent, Samantha," he said quietly. He spoke aloud because she seemed to understand him that way. "You've also got to know that my wife and I were called away from Blessed Creek when that Supreme Court Justice was murdered. I have to deal with that, no choice. But I haven't forgotten you. I've got my laptop—" Suddenly she looked perfectly blank,

and he very nearly smiled because her confusion was quite clear to him. "It's a computer, a really smart machine that can look
up old records, something that wasn't
around back in the early seventies. Computers are fast now, part of our daily lives. Well,
never mind that. I've gotten my computer
started to find out about you—as soon as I
can, I'll help you. I promise you that."

"My boy, my precious boy."

"Samantha, what is going to happen to
your boy?"

"Dillon?"

Savich jerked awake, opened his eyes
wide. He shook off the dream. There was a
sliver of streetlight coming through the bedroom window, not much, but he could see
that around the bed at least there was no
one there. Well of course she wasn't standing at the end of his bed, beckoning to him
with ghostly fingers he could see through.

"Dillon?" Sherlock's hair tickled his nose
as she raised her head, her eyes instantly focused on his face, but her voice still a bit
slurred from sleep. "Who are you talking to?
Were you dreaming? Are you okay?"

Then she stopped cold, her eyes alert, her

elbows locked over him. "Were you dreaming about Samantha again?"

"Yes. I'm okay, I'm awake now." The heaviness in the air was gone, and she wasn't in his brain anymore. He was awake, but oddly enough he sensed a sweet smell that lingered, jasmine, he thought. He smelled jasmine. He kissed Sherlock. "I can't let this go on any longer, Sherlock. In my dream, she was worried about her boy. I could be crazy, but I've got to deal with this. I've got to get up and go to MAX."

She kissed him quickly, let him go when he pulled away.

He paused in the doorway. "I was awake, thinking about what Annie Harper might know. I'm going to see her first thing in the morning. I'd like you to go to headquarters for me, coordinate all the information for MAX with Ollie."

He pulled on a pair of jeans, and then he was off to his study, top button open on his jeans, wearing nothing else. Sean liked the house warm, so jeans were all he needed.

Sherlock turned over and tried to go back to sleep—big fat chance of that happening. The strange thing was that she did just that, in only a couple of minutes, and her sleep was deep and dreamless.

Sherlock didn't know when Dillon came back to bed, only that he was holding her very tightly when the clock radio buzzed the following morning, and the early morning radio host began talking about a six-car pileup near the Tidal Basin.

George Washington University
Hospital Washington, D.C.
Monday morning

Annie Harper looked about twelve years old. Her face was clean of makeup, her light brown hair pulled back in a ponytail, and her hospital gown hung off her left shoulder. Even that thin shoulder looked twelve.

She was pale, her skin pulled taut over her cheekbones, as if something deep and vital had been sucked out of her. But it was her eyes that held him, dark eyes that seemed old, not twelve at all.

"Hello, Ms. Harper," Savich said, smiling as he walked to her bed, then immediately realized she wasn't alone. Her parents were standing close by, looking at him with their arms crossed over their chests, looking defensive and angry.

He wished for a moment they weren't here, but there was nothing to be done about it. She was, after all, only twenty-three, and it was good for her that her parents were with her, supporting her through this nightmare. "Do I know you?" Annie said, looking at him vacantly. She was probably still sedated to the gills.

"Not yet," Savich said. "I'm FBI Agent Dillon Savich. I was at Danny O'Malley's apartment." For a moment, he lightly clasped one of her pale hands. Then he turned to her parents, who were now crowding next to their daughter's bed, his hand extended. "Agent Dillon Savich." Mr. Harper finally uncrossed his arms and shook his hand, as did Mrs. Harper. Savich was patient, hoping to show them that he cared about their feelings, and indeed, he did feel compassion for these people. "Mr. and Mrs. Harper, I don't want to cause Annie any more pain than she's already experienced. Feel free to stay, but I do need to speak to her. I'm sure that you, as well as Annie, want us to find the man who killed Danny."

Mr. Harper opened his mouth, then shut it.

He studied Savich's face and slowly nodded. But when Mrs. Harper spoke, her tired voice was full of anger. "How could this have happened, Agent Savich? We knew Danny, we liked him. He was a fine young man—a law clerk for the United States Supreme Court for heaven's sake—and you let a Supreme Court Justice get murdered in the Supreme Court Building itself where there must be a hundred police, and what did they do? Nothing. And now everyone is saying that Danny was killed because he was involved somehow in Justice Califano's murder or knew something about it. I'm telling you, Danny liked Justice Califano, do you hear me? Liked him, respected him, and yet everyone is saying he did something wrong! This can't be true."

Annie Harper answered her mother, and Savich was pleased to hear some vitality in her voice. "Mom, I loved Danny, but the thing is, we don't know what's true. I want to know, don't you see? No matter how it turns out, I've got to know."

Savich said, "It's possible the murderer assumed Danny knew something."

Annie Harper shook her head, and looked down at her hands. "That's kind of you to say, Agent Savich, but I know you don't believe that." Her voice was tired. There was no anger in it, only infinite weariness.

Savich said, "I understand your frustration, Mrs. Harper. We will find out who did this and we will find out exactly why it was done." He held her eyes until finally Mrs. Harper sagged against her husband's shoulder. Mr. Harper put his arm around her and hugged her close to him. "Speak to Annie, Agent Savich. Her mother and I would feel better staying, if that's all right with you."

"That's not a problem." Savich turned back to Annie, who'd pulled the nightgown back up over her shoulder. Perhaps her eyes were a little brighter now. He wanted to take her mind off her parents, who were standing only six feet away, get her to focus on him, so he took her hand to give her comfort with the feel of human contact. He saw from the corner of his eye that her mother was watching his hand, holding her daughter's. He positioned himself between them and their daughter, and turned his back to them. There was another bed in the room. Thankfully it was empty.

"I understand you picked Danny up from the Supreme Court on Friday evening."

Annie nodded. "Yes, he was stuffing some things into his briefcase—it was a Gucci, I gave it to him for Christmas, just last month." Her breath hitched, and she fell silent. Savich wondered how many drugs were still in her system. But her words had seemed coherent, so he waited.

"Danny loved that briefcase, always carried it around with him even though usually he'd have nothing of any importance in it. We took my car, and he locked the briefcase in the trunk. We laughed about how he shouldn't take it into the movie theater with him—you know, a bomb, something like that."

Savich saw Mrs. Harper make a move toward her daughter, but Mr. Harper held her in place.

"We went to dinner first, at Angelo's over on Spreckels Street. Danny loved the olive, onion, and anchovy pizza there. Angelo's was his favorite restaurant in Washington."

"Where was the movie playing?"

"At the Consortium, over in Georgetown, you know, that arty theater that's usually half empty." She looked at her hands, and he felt hers move in his, burrow in a bit. "Whenever I said that, Danny would say no, it's half full."

Good, she'd given him a small joke, and that meant she was beginning to trust him. Her other hand lay open on her lap on top of the thin sheet that covered her, her fingers curved inward, a bit like claws. "I didn't want to see the film. I didn't share his enthusiasm for them, but—" She sighed. "Danny had been talking about it for a week and a half. I kept putting him off, hoping the thing would close, but it was still playing and I couldn't put him off any longer. We went to the nine o'clock show. The film was in Croatian, with subtitles, and the translation was so bad the dozen or so people in the theater were laughing. Danny didn't, though. It was like he was watching a different film, sitting forward, his eyes glued to the screen. It was filmed in Split, that city on the Dalmatian Coast where that Roman emperor built this huge palace that's still used today."

"When you were at Angelo's, did you talk about your day?"

"Not really. Danny didn't want to. He was always talking about Justice Califano, about Eliza and Fleurette, but Friday night, he just ate, listened to me talk mostly, or so I thought. You know what? I was jealous. I was thinking about Fleurette and how he thought she was so cool, and I was jealous. I wasn't very nice to him. I was going through the motions. I wanted to drive away with that Gucci briefcase I spent nearly a week's salary on, and throw it in a dumpster."

"But he wasn't thinking about Fleurette."

She shook her head. "No. When we got back to his apartment, he—" She looked over at her parents. Thankfully they were still six feet away, facing the window now, their backs to Savich and their daughter.

She lowered her voice and Savich had to lean down to hear her. "He jumped on me the instant we got through the door. Danny was always horny, but this time it was different. He was excited, not just about sex, but about something else. And it wasn't Fleurette. How could it be?"

Savich's heart began to pound slow steady beats.

"We made love on the living room floor." She said this in an even lower whisper, her eyes on her mother's back. "Then Danny got up and ran to the kitchen, opened a bottle of wine, and poured us each a glass. He toasted me, grinning like a loon. I'll never forget the look on his face. He said, 'Annie, I'm going to be rich.' And I said, well, sure,

Danny, you're smart and blah blah blah—I don't remember the rest of it. I said something about was he going to take a client on the side. Truth is, I was cold and wanted to put my clothes back on. But there he was, expecting me to drink the wine, and so I did."

She might be twenty-three, Savich thought, but she was still so very young, so insecure in her youth.

"Danny shook his head. 'No,' he said, 'this is something else entirely.' But he wouldn't say what. And he grabbed my hand and dragged me into the bedroom." Again, her voice was a whisper. "We did it again before he finally fell asleep."

"He said nothing about what this something else might be? No hints? Nothing else at all?"

Annie shook her head. "No, I was lying there listening to him snore. When I woke up the next morning, it was late. I put on one of his T-shirts and went into the kitchen. He was standing there, looking at the TV, and he was saying, 'My God, my God, my God'— over and over. We stood there and watched the news about Justice Califano's murder. I couldn't believe it. Danny looked like he'd been kicked in the gut, like his world had ended. But then everything changed on his face, and his posture became really straight. He got taller, I swear it, he stood there and got taller."

"You realize now that he'd come to a decision of some sort? That he realized he could use what he knew?"

"Yes, I can see that now. Poor Danny. It sure didn't take him long, did it?"

"Evidently not." Savich knew there was more, but not in her conscious mind, not yet.

"Then what did he say?"

"I asked him what the hell was going on with him, but he shook his head at me and said I had to leave, he had stuff to do, real important stuff."

"I was so mad. I yelled at him that I wasn't going to do his laundry for him anymore. I went in the bedroom, got dressed and left, didn't say another word to him."

"Where was he when you left?"

"I heard him moving around in the kitchen. I think he was on his cell phone."

"You didn't hear anything he said on his cell?"

She frowned, clasped his hand even harder, but slowly shook her head. "No. I remember how his voice fell, then it rose, but I was really so mad that I just slammed out of his apartment and went back to mine."

"But you went over again Sunday morning."

She was chewing on her lips. They were chapped. "Yeah, I did."

"Why?"

"I guess I wanted to know what was really happening with him. I suppose I was worried about Fleurette again. Have you ever seen Sonya McGivens, Justice Wallace's law clerk? Have you seen how she dresses when she's outside the Court?"

He was hard-pressed not to smile. "Yes, I have."

"She works out," Annie Harper said. "She really works out hard. Over at Interior, nobody works out." And she turned her face away from him, squeezed his hand until she was nearly cutting off the circulation, and began to weep.

Savich waited, trying to comfort her, when her mother turned toward them, the tortured look on the woman's face painful to see. He nodded to her and mouthed, "Annie will be all right."

When Annie quieted again, Savich said, "I would like to hypnotize you, Annie."

"No, there's no way you're going to do any hocus-pocus on my daughter! She's been through enough!"

Savich looked up at Mrs. Harper. "It's a very safe way for me to help her remember things she can't recall right now. Please remember, Mrs. Harper, Danny O'Malley was brutally murdered like Justice Califano. If Annie can remember more, it could help us immensely. You and your husband could be present, of course."

But again, it was Annie who answered. "That's fine with me, Agent Savich. I want to know who did this to Danny more than you do."

CHAPTER
22

Hoover Building
Fifth Floor
Late Monday morning

"I don't believe it," Frank Halley said, looking through the sheaf of papers in his hands. "MAX gives recommendations? You've got an alien inside that laptop, don't you, Savich?" Savich, who'd just slipped quietly into the big conference room, merely nodded at Sherlock, who was at the head of the room, in charge of the meeting.

Sherlock said, "Nope, Frank, Dillon programmed it. Maybe he's an alien. But I've never before met an alien that good in bed."

Savich grinned at his wife and felt his chest expand. He knew some of the agents had already seen him and were hooting and giving him high fives. When the laughter died down, Savich realized Sherlock had already handed out all the updated assignments five minutes before he'd gotten there. There was optimism in the air now, not the stark confusion that had reigned in yesterday's meeting. From listening to the other agents talk, Savich realized Sherlock had covered everything perfectly.

When the meeting broke up at last, Savich said, "Sherlock, you're coming with me."

"Where are you going, Savich?" Frank Halley still wasn't over his snit, given the aggression in his voice.

Savich said mildly, "We have a date with Dr. Emanuel Hicks out at Quantico. He's going to hypnotize Annie Harper for me."

"O'Malley's girlfriend?"

"The very same," Sherlock said. "You want to come along? You can deal with Annie's parents while Dr. Hicks and Dillon work with her."

"No, now that I think about it," Frank said quickly, "I've got more than enough to go over with my team."

"You do that so well," Savich said, kissed Sherlock's ear, and whispered, "I'm better in bed than any alien you've ever met?"

"So far," she said, and gave him a wicked smile over her shoulder as she walked out of the conference room.

Jefferson Dormitory
Quantico

Sherlock sat with Mr. and Mrs. Harper, having directed them to the farthest side of Savich's office. Savich heard her soothing low-pitched voice, the same voice she used when she was trying to talk Sean into doing something he really didn't want to do.

He turned when Dr. Hicks sauntered into the room. Dr. Emanuel Hicks always sauntered, it was one of his trademarks. His other trademark was the three very long hairs he combed from near his left ear over the top of his bald head. The three hairs didn't go all that well with the saunter, but since he was so gifted, Savich wouldn't have cared if he danced the salsa when he came into a room wearing a pink turban. He'd admired Dr.

Hicks since he'd been in the academy. He'd realized what a valuable resource he was.

He rose and shook hands. "Thank you for coming, Dr. Hicks. Anything else you need to know about this situation?"

"No, Savich, you covered it well." Dr. Hicks nodded toward the parents and without pause pulled a chair up to Annie's. He smiled at her. "I'm Dr. Hicks and I promise you that none of this is going to hurt. It was part of the oath I had to take to work for the FBI. How are you feeling, Ms. Harper?"

"Okay. Well, I really feel bad, like I want to cry all the time, but there aren't any more tears."

"No wonder, you've been through a terrible experience."

"I'm not the one dead, Dr. Hicks."

"The dead don't care anymore, Annie, only the living," Dr. Hicks said. "Now, you think you're ready?"

"I've never done this before. Don't you want me to lie down or something?"

"No, that's not necessary. Just get yourself comfortable in the chair. May I call you Annie?"

She nodded.

"Okay, now, I'd like you to look closely at

this silver dollar. It originally belonged to my great-grandfather. Look at it, nothing else. That's right, follow it with your eyes."

While he gently swung the silver dollar on its chain about four inches from Annie's face, he began talking about the people he knew who worked at the Department of the Interior—there were at least a dozen of them. His voice was soft, without inflection. Within four minutes, Savich thought she was under. Dr. Hicks slipped the silver dollar back in his vest pocket and said in his slow soft voice, "Annie, how do you feel?"

Annie was still looking at the place where the silver dollar had been swinging. "Cold. On the inside. Could Agent Savich hold my hand?"

Savich clasped both of her hands between his. The three of them were very close now. He saw from the corner of his eye that both the Harper parents were staring toward them, but thankfully, Sherlock was keeping them under control.

"Better now, Annie?"

"Yes," she said in a matter-of-fact voice. "I wish Danny could have been more like Agent Savich. This wouldn't have happened if he'd been like Agent Savich, but Danny was an opportunistic jerk."

Now this was interesting, Savich thought. He kept stroking her hands, which were becoming warmer by the minute.

He waited until Dr. Hicks nodded to him, then said, "Annie, did you realize Danny was an opportunistic jerk only yesterday, or some time before?"

"I guess I've always known, Agent Savich. He played a good game, what with his sweet Irish lad act. He liked me, don't get me wrong; I know he did. But he didn't love me, not like I talked myself into thinking I loved him. Can you believe I even did his laundry because he told me he loved the way I folded his clothes? What an idiot."

"What did Danny do to make you question his integrity?"

"Well, he lied to Eliza, told her he'd done stuff when he really hadn't, but not that much because Eliza's really smart, and he knew he couldn't get away with it. Then he'd kiss up to her big time because he knew she had real power over his life. She could get him fired if she wanted. Justice Califano really listened to her, at least that's what Danny was always telling me."

"Eliza never noticed when Danny didn't follow through? That he lied?"

"Not that he ever told me. He'd laugh about it, you know, like a little kid in grade school who'd pulled something over on the teacher. Eliza was always really nice to me. I think I could have been a close friend to her, only there wasn't time in her life, and I understood that. As for Fleurette, I don't think she knew Danny all that well, but I could be wrong."

"What about Justice Califano? Did he ever catch Danny in a lie that you know of? Catch him doing something he shouldn't have been doing?"

Slowly, Annie shook her head. "I don't know. I wasn't part of the inner circle. All my information came from Danny. If Justice Califano had caught him in a lie, he sure wouldn't tell me about it, would he? And the fact is, Danny wanted Justice Califano to like him. He wanted a great recommendation from him when the year was up. So it seems to me the last thing Danny would want to do is lie to Justice Califano."

"Okay, I want you to tell me about Friday. You picked Danny up at the Supreme Court Building. What sort of mood was he in?"

"The fact is I'd never know which Danny I'd see. The happy Danny or the brooding Danny. He wasn't either one on Friday. He was distracted, like there was really something on his mind. But he wouldn't talk about it, just kept eating those disgusting anchovies. I hate anchovies."

"Do you think he put something important in his briefcase?"

She looked thoughtful, then shook her head. "I don't know. Where is his briefcase?"

"We couldn't find it. It wasn't in his apartment."

"That's too bad. Danny would like to be buried with that briefcase. Oh, God, I didn't mean it like that."

"I understand. That's all right, Annie."

"I know he took it out of the trunk, I watched him carry it into his apartment. When I bought it for him I never thought the stupid thing would become some sort of icon to him."

"Let's move forward to Saturday morning. There wasn't any talk between you during the night, right?"

"No, he was snoring."

"You said he was saying 'Oh God, oh God,'

when he saw that Justice Califano was dead."

"Yes, over and over. I couldn't believe it either. It didn't seem real, like one of Danny's stupid foreign flicks that doesn't make any sense at all."

"But then he changed. Right before your eyes, he changed."

"Yes, completely."

"I want you to picture Danny in your mind, Annie. You're right there, watching the TV, then looking at him. What do you see?"

"He's acting like he just hit a really big jackpot in Las Vegas. He looks like he's conquered the world. Smug, that's it, he looks smug."

"So he might be thinking about what he knows? And that something could make him rich?"

"Yes, that's exactly it. It's so clear to me now. He thought about it for maybe three seconds, and then he decided to go for the money."

"What did he say?"

"He had stuff to do. I went to the bedroom, got dressed, and slammed out."

"But you heard him on his cell."

"Oh yes."

"Okay, Annie, you're standing there, you don't want to see him, but you hear him on the phone. Where are you standing?"

"In the front entrance."

"How far away is Danny?"

"The kitchen isn't more than fifteen feet away from where I'm standing."

"He's on a cell phone."

"Yes."

"Did the phone ring or did he initiate the call?"

"I never heard it ring, so he must have made the call."

"Just a moment, Annie. We checked his cell phone records and there was no outgoing call made on Saturday morning."

"I'm sure he was using a cell."

"Do you think it could have been a throwaway cell phone? Did he own one?"

"Yes, he had several of them, got them really cheap from a guy on the street."

Interesting, Savich thought, and dropped it. "Does he carry an address book in his pocket, along with his cell?"

"Yes, it's just a skinny little black book."

"So he pulled out the black book, looked up a number, and called it?" But not using his own cell phone, Savich thought, and realized Danny knew exactly what he was doing and wasn't about to take any chances on it coming back to bite him.

"Yes, that's what he would have done."

"Okay, you're standing there, angry, wanting to leave, but you pause. Because he's on the phone and you want to know what's going on, right?"

"Yes, that's exactly right. I wanted to know what he was planning on doing."

"You're listening. What is he saying?"

"I can't—"

He squeezed her hands, and began to lightly stroke his fingers over the now-warm flesh. "You're standing there, Annie. You're listening. What is he saying?"

She sucked in a deep breath, fell silent for a good minute. Savich didn't say a word, just kept holding her hands, waiting.

"He said 'I think we can come to some sort of agreement here.'"

There was a sharp cry of anguish from Mrs. Harper. Savich heard the soothing voices of both Mr. Harper and Sherlock.

"Anything else, Annie? You're still there, right?"

"No, I'm out the door."

"What were you thinking?"

"That I was pissed. That he was an idiot for thinking I loved him. Nothing, I don't know. Really, I didn't hear anything more. I didn't know what he even meant, but I knew in my gut he was doing something bad."

"But you didn't want to know what it was."

"Not then."

"Is that why you came back on Sunday?"

She nodded. "Yes. I wanted the truth. And, I'll admit it—I was worried about him. I thought he was going to do something, I didn't know what." She stopped and looked toward her parents. "I'm lying to myself. Yes, I knew he was doing something wrong, I didn't want to admit it to myself."

Savich nodded to Dr. Hicks. Slowly, Dr. Hicks brought her out of hypnosis. He told her she was a very brave woman, that what had happened was going to fade from her mind in time, and that she was strong enough to see things the way they'd really been, and would be able to put them in perspective. Savich smiled a bit as Dr. Hicks engaged in some therapy. He felt compassion for this waif, this young woman who'd fallen for a man who'd used her and then had died. Dr. Hicks went on to tell her that she would feel good about herself now, that she was hungry. A pepperoni pizza at the Quantico restaurant, The Boardroom, was what she wanted, and Savich would buy it for her. He looked over at her parents, who were listening to every word and nodding. He told Annie her parents would like the pepperoni pizza, too, that they were here for her, that they loved her and would stand by her.

Unfortunately, Savich thought, when he finally managed to get away from Quantico, Danny O'Malley's Gucci briefcase, his cell phone with its memory chip, a throwaway cell phone, and the skinny little black book were gone.

FBI Headquarters
Early Tuesday morning

Savich stood at the head of the conference table, looked out at the sea of faces.

"MAX has found an assassin who is a high-probability fit for our murderer. He has used the alias Günter Grass, middle name listed as Wilhelm. He has used the same M.O. as our killer on a number of victims—a garrote, up close and personal, and mostly in high-risk settings. The two have always gone together for him."

"Hey, that name sounds familiar," said another agent.

"Yes," Savich said. "The real Günter Wilhelm Grass won the Nobel Prize for Literature in 1999. Maybe some of you have read his first novel, *The Tin Drum.* He's also a poet, novelist, playwright, even a sculptor. He has described himself as a *'Spätaufklärer,'* a belated apostle of enlightenment in an era that has grown tired of reason.

"No one knows why the killer selected this name as his primary alias. I'd imagine he admires something about Günter Grass, or about something he wrote. Steve and the behavioral sciences group at Quantico will be telling us more about that. No one knows his real name. He only goes by the name Günter.

"Last night I spoke to our local Interpol guy here in Washington, Johnny Baines, to Jacques Ramie in Lyons, and to Hans Claus in Berlin. Günter Grass isn't on their current radar because he hasn't been active in well over ten years, at least not that anyone knows of. That's why it took MAX a little while to find him.

"The German and French authorities are certain that no such person or anyone similar is connected to any known terrorist cell.

"So the question is, where has the guy been? What's he been doing? Where is he now? Still in Washington or long gone? And how did the person behind the two murders even know about a guy like this, a professional assassin?"

Jimmy Maitland said, "Of course, there is no one by this name currently here in the U.S., no passports or visas issued in that name. Bottom line, we know who he is, but we have no clue where he is."

Ben Raven asked, "No old photos? Nothing?"

Savich nodded. "I'm passing out a grainy old photo that Jacques Ramie sent over. They tried to clean it up digitally, but it's still not good. You'll see that it's a photo of a much younger man. He's big, you can tell that much, and looking at the clothes, it would put the photo in the mid- to late eighties. Even though he's older now, he's still got to be pretty strong to take out Justice Califano and Danny O'Malley."

Jimmy Maitland shook his head. "The thing about picking high-risk places—it's very rare for a professional. A professional is in and out, clean and fast, gets the job done. But our guy's got to have this adrenaline shot. We've never run into anything like that before."

"Calling himself Günter Grass, that's just nuts," said another agent.

"He's giving everyone the finger," Jimmy Maitland said. "Done it for years; unfortunately, he's gotten away with it. He's still free. Estimates on how many people he's killed, Savich?"

"Jacques believes it to be around twenty. Günter was active until the late eighties, none of them high-profile killings—drug dealers, international mafia, those sorts of hits. Then nothing. Until Justice Califano."

"He probably made himself a big bundle and retired," said Jimmy Maitland. "Changed his name. He could be living anywhere in the world, or he could be living down the block from one of us, as far as we know."

"And that brings up another thing," Savich said, and sighed. "According to Interpol, the man is fluent in four languages—German, French, Italian, and, naturally, English."

"Does he sound American or English?"

"American, I'm told. The person behind

these murders knows Günter on a personal, business, or social level. And somehow, he found out exactly who and what Günter was and still is."

"Hey, Günter could be somebody's plumber," called out one agent.

"With what they charge, he wouldn't have had to take the job," said another agent.

CHAPTER
23

St. Luke's Episcopal Church
Washington, D.C.
Thursday morning

St. Luke's was far too small for the throng of mourners there to witness Justice Stewart Califano's funeral. The media were kept milling about outside the small Episcopal church, trying to catch a brief interview with all the notables who were invited.

There was room for only one hundred and fifty mourners inside St. Luke's. Friends and family only, other judges, members of Congress, and the President and Vice President

and their families. The President himself delivered the eulogy.

Margaret Califano sat with Callie, holding
her hand, both of them covered from head to
foot in black. Margaret's friends, their husbands and families flanked her. Like the
Swiss Guard protecting the kings of France,
Savich whispered to Sherlock.

Director Mueller, DAD Jimmy Maitland,
Sherlock, Savich, and Ben Raven sat two
pews behind Margaret Califano, and behind
them were several Supreme Court police
officers, including Henry Biggs, who still
looked frail, but at least was alive. Savich
wondered why Mrs. Califano had invited him.
She was, he decided, a class act.

When the service ended, the President and
First Lady were escorted out of St. Luke's,
surrounded by the Secret Service, then the
Vice President and Mrs. Chartly. Margaret
stood beside her husband's flag-draped coffin, shaking hands, speaking in her low quiet
voice, thanking people for coming. When it
was time, she looked toward the doors, saw
the media held back by the Metro police.
She drew a deep breath, squared her shoulders, and walked out with Callie to speak to
them, the coffin wheeled slowly after her by

the eight remaining Justices, an incredibly stirring sight Savich knew would be immortalized around the world.

The shouted questions stopped the instant she opened her mouth. Margaret spoke quietly, and graciously thanked everyone for their warmth and support for her family. Concerning the investigation, she said only that she was confident the FBI would find the man who had killed her husband. She also said that after her husband's interment at St. Martin of the Fields, she would speak to the media, at her own home. She politely declined to answer any questions, only repeated, "I will speak to you again later at my home."

The small, private interment went quickly and smoothly, with the media kept a good distance away from the gravesite by the same officers who had been at St. Luke's.

Savich, Sherlock, Ben, and a few more FBI agents accompanied Margaret Califano to the press conference she gave at her home on Beckhurst Lane. She answered every question patiently and politely.

"We hear *The Washington Post* has the inside track on this because of you, Ms. Markham," shouted one reporter. "Is that proper conduct for a major newspaper in an investigation of this stature?"

Callie stepped forward. "No, it certainly wouldn't be if such a thing were true, but it isn't. I'm on a leave of absence from the *Post.* I'm helping the authorities as much as I can, but only as Justice Califano's stepdaughter."

Jed Coombes, Callie's editor, called out, a mixture of sarcasm and bitterness clear in his voice. "It's true, she won't give us the time of day."

This brought more laughter.

"You're gonna fire her?"

A thoughtful frown. "Probably not."

When it was over, when finally all the TV vans and reporters had left, Sherlock went home to Sean, and Savich stopped in to see Jimmy Maitland at FBI headquarters.

FBI Headquarters
Thursday afternoon

It was winter, dark at five-thirty. A cold drizzle slapped against the window in Jimmy Maitland's office. Savich sat in front of his boss's desk, his hands clasped between his legs, staring at his shoes.

"MAX has come up dry, and so have we," Savich said. "Günter seems to have completely disappeared in 1988."

"Anything at all useful about Günter before 1988?"

Savich shook his head. "He could be an American, an Albanian, an Armenian. He left no clues. The guy's a pro.

"As for the rest of it, the local investigation—we haven't turned up a fingerprint, a footprint, usable DNA, not even a vague description by a witness. The garrote leaves no trace, one of its advantages.

"We've followed up on all the phone records, checked every deleted file on computers that could be connected to the Justice, but nothing has fallen out of that.

"Some of what we're looking at—further background checks on everyone who could be involved, review of both victims' financial records, interviews with felons Justice Califano convicted and white-collar criminals he bankrupted, going back many years—these will take more time, but as you know, they're a bit of a stab in the dark. So far, all we really have is the connection MAX gave us to

Günter, and the fact that whatever it was that triggered Justice Califano's murder, Danny O'Malley was somehow able to find out about it.

"Our interviews have been useful, but nothing seems to tie into anything substantial yet. All the inconsistencies, even the downright lies don't seem to matter. And Danny—the only person I can believe about Danny is Annie Harper, and that's because Dr. Hicks hypnotized her and I questioned her myself."

Jimmy Maitland said, "Danny O'Malley sounded like an opportunistic little prick."

"Yes, unfortunately he was. And deep down, Annie knew it, but she was too young and too in love to admit it. She does now."

"You sound like her father, Savich."

"I felt ancient when I was speaking to her."

"Nothing on the briefcase, the black book, or the cell phone." A statement, not a question.

Savich shook his head.

Jimmy Maitland said suddenly, "When was the last time you were at the gym?"

Savich's head whipped up. "Two, three days. Why?"

"That's your problem. You need to sweat this out of your system, have one of the guys bust your butt a little, let this slide off you for a while. Go, Savich, go work out, you need it."

Savich slowly rose. "Maybe you're right, sir." He grinned. "Then I can get Sherlock to rub me down with BenGay."

"Hey, that woman Valerie Rapper still at the gym? The one who came on to you?"

Savich was clearly startled. "How did you know about her?"

Jimmy Maitland, father of four sons, all of them built like bulls—like their father—and all firmly in the control of his wife, whom he could tuck under his armpit, said, "I know everything, and it's best you never forget that, boyo."

Savich was actually smiling when he left the Hoover Building to head to the gym. And when he walked through the front door of his house, so beat he could barely walk upright, Sherlock shoved him into the shower, then fed him a big plate of spinach lasagna. He fell asleep lying on his belly in the middle of the bed, Sean beside him, pressing his teddy bear's nose in the BenGay as he followed the path of his mother's massage.

Beckhurst Lane
Washington, D.C.
Thursday evening

Ben and Callie followed Margaret Califano into her house. Her friends were waiting inside the front door—Janette, Anna, Juliette, and Bitsy. Their families had evidently gone home.

Ben said, eyebrow up, "Are they going to move in?"

Callie said, "I'll assume that was an attempt at a joke. I guess they'll be here for her as long as they believe she needs them." Callie watched the women surround her mother as the group walked back into the living room. At least her mother was home again. Callie paused a moment more, watching them from the living room doorway. "They've always been around. For each other, and for all the kids. I grew up with these women. Each of them taught me something special—"

"Like what?" Ben asked.

Callie looked toward Janette Weaverton, who was laying the fire in the fireplace. "Janette taught me how to knit. Anna taught me how to play the piano. Juliette taught me tennis, and Bitsy, well, she taught me how to make the best pizza crust in the world. And that gives me a great idea."

She headed into the living room, Ben on her heels. She smiled as she clapped her hands. "Hey, everyone, I'm calling in for pizza. It's on me. Mom's home again, you're all here, we got through the day and the media. We've got champagne to celebrate Stewart's life and being here together, and we've got beer for our guy here. What does everyone think?"

For a moment, there was silence. Then Margaret smiled at her daughter. "Do you know, I think Stewart would like that."

"Good. It's done."

It was pretty clear to Ben that the women would as soon see the back of him, but they were all nodding and smiling, polite to their undoubtedly beautifully polished toenails. It was Bitsy who said, "Anchovies for me, Callie."

"As if I didn't know," Callie said.

Janette said, "I want double pepperoni."

Ben nodded. "A woman after my own heart—make that two."

Callie ended up ordering seven pizzas, including a large caper and olive for herself.

It was Margaret's first night home. Callie was going to stay with her for a while, but Ben got the distinct impression that her mother really didn't need her to stay or particularly wanted her to stay either. She had her four friends. Were her friends closer to her than her own daughter? They were all of an age, all of them had shared so many years of their lives together, each other's pain as well as happiness. He supposed they knew each other as well as old married couples must.

He turned to Janette Weaverton, who'd gone to open the drapes a bit to look out. "No more media," she said over her shoulder. "Margaret did an excellent job with them."

Ben joined her at the window. "Yes, she did. I understand from Callie that you taught her how to knit."

Janette didn't look at him. "She'd be quite good if she applied herself, but Callie's young, she's got so much stuff to do—and her career is really taking off. I think a Pulitzer might mean more to her than a knitted afghan." She turned to face him, her arms folded over her chest. "She knit me a sweater—her very first effort. I still have it."

"Does it look like a sweater, or is it one of those stereotypical things you see that goes on for yards and yards?"

"Nope, it's a sweater. She was good when she was twelve. Haven't you been to her apartment?"

He shook his head. "She's a civilian, ma'am. She was assigned to me. None of this is social."

"What a waste that seems, Detective. Callie's a special girl, always has been."

"So special that Mrs. Califano didn't marry Justice Califano until Callie went off to college?"

Janette Weaverton shrugged. "Maybe, maybe not. What happened to her sister's girl really affected her, affected all of us. None of us encouraged Margaret to change her mind about it. The thing is, though, Callie has gumption—she would have kicked her stepfather's ass if he'd ever tried anything with her. And she really liked Stewart, admired him tremendously."

Hearing a blueblood like Janette Weaverton talk about kicking ass made Ben choke. He coughed into his hand.

She laughed. "Oh, I see. You think I should

speak more demurely, to match my St. John suit?"

"What's a St. John's suit?"

Janette smiled. "That's what I'm wearing. It's a designer label. Did you know Callie has a black belt in karate?"

"Yeah, she might have mentioned it once when she wanted to boot me out the car window."

"The first thing Margaret did after her sister's daughter was molested was to enroll Callie with an excellent instructor, to be sure that Callie would never be a victim.

"You seem like a good man, Detective Raven. You're interesting, you're also an excellent listener. I'll bet you manage to get information out of the most obdurate of perpetrators, don't you?"

"I try, ma'am. Actually, I hear it's Agent Savich who's the master at it. They give lots of classes on interviewing at Quantico. One day I might go see what it's all about."

"You really think Agent Savich is all that good? It's been nearly a week since Stewart's murder and nearly four days since Danny O'Malley's murder, yet he doesn't seem to have turned up anything."

"He will. Justice Califano interacted with a

great many people, so many it makes your head ache, and everyone has something quite different to say. Lies? Just differences of perception? Sheer perversity?"

"I see what you mean. Well, you'd expect that, wouldn't you? It would be like Bitsy and me being married to the same man. We'd both experience him as very different men."

"I never thought of it like that. Do we change our behaviors so much with each different person we know?"

"I'd rather eat pizza than think about that," Janette said.

CHAPTER 24

The doorbell rang, and the delivery boy stood grinning from ear to ear with seven pizza boxes piled up to his nose. Callie, charmed by that grin, gave him a big tip.

Bitsy St. Pierre said between mouthfuls of her anchovy pizza, "This is delicious. Eat, Margaret, I don't want to have to tell you again." The other three women nodded. Ben watched them, his head cocked to the side. He was eating with six women, five of them his mother's age, something he couldn't remember ever doing before in his life. He decided he liked it.

Margaret took a small bite, chewed on it forever before finally swallowing it. Bitsy said matter-of-factly, "We buried Stewart today. It was a grand send-off. The President spoke, the Vice President spoke. You dealt magnificently with the media, Margaret. We've given Stewart a wonderful toast with his favorite champagne. He would have made one of his decision matrixes and concluded he was proud of you. Now, eat."

He'd heard them say such things to Margaret at least three or four times that evening. Did it help? Evidently so. Margaret Califano took a bigger bite of pizza and actually looked like she might be enjoying it.

Janette Weaverton appeared to be the quietest of the five women, although he hadn't found her reticent or shy at all. It was just that the others seemed more forceful in their opinions, bigger in their laughter. She seemed preoccupied. Yes, that was it.

Ben said, "Will you ladies be staying here tonight?"

Five sets of eyes turned to him. "Oh no," said Anna Clifford. "Our families are patient, they understand, but they want us back home. Since Callie's here now, we'll leave when it's time for Margaret to go to bed."

"Your husband, Mrs. Clifford, what does he do?"

"He used to be a banker, but now he's a

venture capitalist." She paused a moment, chewed some pizza. "Most people don't really understand what that means, exactly, but to me it sounds mysterious, maybe dangerous, like laundering Mafia money."

That drew a round of laughter, but Margaret said, in a serious voice, "There's nothing illegal in what Clayton does, Anna. He simply invests his own and other people's money in individual entrepreneurs or start-up companies that interest him. He's good at analyzing their growth potential, their planning skills, and deciding if they're worth the risk."

Anna smiled as she said, "Come on, Margaret, you know very well Clayton says it's like deciding whether or not to buy Boardwalk in Monopoly."

Bitsy said, "Eat more pizza, Margaret. Those chunks of pepper will bring back your sense of humor."

Margaret dropped her slice of pizza back on her paper plate. She looked like she was about to burst into tears. "You don't know what I did!"

"Mom, whatever it was—"

"Stewart wanted to be cremated. I didn't follow his wishes. It was the President, you see, and all the protocol experts. Everyone expected a big church service, Stewart in a coffin in front of celebrity mourners. I ignored his wishes and buried him." Margaret put her face in her hands and wept. "I buried him."

"Oh, Mom, don't." Callie put her arms around her mother and rocked her. The women gathered around, patting her hair, her shoulders, her arms. "It doesn't matter, Mom. Stewart wasn't there. That magnificent service was for all his friends, for the President, for all those people who admired him. It was for everyone there to say their farewells to him. And the burial itself was so beautifully done. He wouldn't have minded, truly."

Ben had never felt so useless in his life. If he could have disappeared in that instant, he would have.

Then the storm of tears was over. Margaret gave a small laugh. "Poor Detective Raven. I'm sorry for that. You poor boy, stuck among all us women, but you're doing very well, isn't he, Juliette?"

"Very well indeed."

Ben said, "You said that we hadn't gotten much done, ma'am. Well, actually that's not true. The FBI think they know who the assassin is. He calls himself Günter Grass, or just Günter."

Margaret said, puzzled, "The writer? The man who murdered Stewart is a German?"

"We don't know what nationality he is. Günter Grass is the name he uses. He's been inactive, supposedly for at least fifteen years now, until this. He's known to speak four languages fluently, including English. He could very well live among us. He could even be living locally, and the person who wanted Justice Califano murdered very possibly knew about Günter and his profession.

"This man killed twenty people in Europe in the seventies and eighties. We don't know why he stopped." Ben pulled two photos out of his shirt pocket. "Here's a grainy photo, digitally enhanced—Interpol is about ninety percent sure it's him—and here's one that's been aged to show how he'd probably look today, unless, of course, he's taken pains to change his appearance, which is possible." He handed both photos to the women and waited until each one had looked at them.

"Does this man look familiar to any of you?"

Juliette said, "He looks like a contractor my neighbor hired to gut her house."

Margaret said, "Detective Raven, if this Günter Grass hasn't killed anyone for at least fifteen years, doesn't that mean he made enough money to retire in style?"

"One could assume that, yes."

"Then why would he kill my husband and poor Danny O'Malley?"

"I don't know, Mrs. Califano."

Bitsy St. Pierre said, "Maybe the person who hired him found out about him, black-mailed him into doing this."

Janette said, "That's stupid, Bitsy. Look what he did to Danny O'Malley—killed him within twenty-four hours of a blackmail at-tempt."

"Yes," Margaret said. "It must be some-thing else. Maybe there's a tie between this Günter and the person who wanted Stewart dead."

"It's possible." Ben had watched each woman study the photos, watched for any sign of recognition on their faces. He hadn't seen any.

"Callie," Margaret said. "Does he look at all familiar to you?"

"Actually," Callie said, "I thought he looked a bit like one of our investigative reporters. No, no, just kidding."

Ben said, "If Günter's not an American, chances are he came here maybe fifteen years ago. He's physically strong, and he seems to like taking risks. Since he's well into his fifties, maybe even sixties, I doubt he's into any extreme sports, but he's still very strong and fit."

"But if he is an American," Anna Clifford said, "he could have lived here all his life and who would be the wiser for it?"

"That's true," Callie said. "And the thing with Danny, that was a big risk, right in the middle of the morning, anyone could have seen him go into Danny's apartment, heard him."

"But no one did, apparently," said Juliette Trevor.

Ben's eyes swung to her. She said, "There would have been some news about that, wouldn't there? A witness saying something, right? But there's been nothing reported at all."

"You're right. No one saw anything, and you can believe that everyone within a several block radius has been interviewed by experts." Ben put the photos in his pocket, and finished off his last slice of pizza. He looked from one woman to the next. All of them seemed to blur together, forming one image in his mind. They seemed united, and in that moment, he had no doubt they would pull Margaret Califano through this tragedy by sheer force of will.

He looked at his watch, saw that it was after ten o'clock. He rose, nodded to all the women. "Callie, I believe you and I are going to be having dinner with Savich and Sherlock tomorrow evening."

She rose to stand beside him. "Yes. I understand Savich is a great cook. Is that okay with you, Mom?" In her question she included all her mother's friends as well.

"Certainly," said Janette. "We'll all be here tomorrow night. We're going to have a potluck dinner; our families will be here as well. We're very pleased that you're working with the FBI and the local police, Callie." She patted her arm. "It also helps keep your mind occupied, doesn't it?"

"Actually, it helps me focus on who killed my stepfather and Danny. If it's Günter, I want him caught as badly as all of you do. Ben, I'll walk you out."

He shrugged on his black leather jacket, pulled on his black leather gloves. His hand was on the doorknob when he turned back.

"My mom has only one close woman friend. This is new to me. They're quite a unit, aren't they?"

"A unit—yes, that's a good word for them. All of them are incredible women."

"I'll pick you up tomorrow morning at ten o'clock. Savich wants us to see Fleurette. He said four other agents have already spoken with her, but he wants us to focus on her lunch with Danny on Friday. He says his gut is dancing, and tells him there's got to be something more there. He wants us to take a crack at it." Ben paused, grinned. "He wants to know exactly where they sat in the sandwich shop, what they ate, and the color of Fleurette's toenail polish, everything about that lunch until they got back to the Supreme Court."

"Sure, we can give it a shot. Do you know, it feels weird to be sleeping here. I never did very much since they bought the house after I went to college. I'd like to go back to my apartment, but I can't yet."

"Be patient, Callie. Now, tomorrow evening, dinner will be about six. Savich said he'll have Sean fed by then. I think his sister and her fiancé will be there too. Savich doesn't want to talk shop, but I'll just bet you we will." He reached out and lightly cupped her cheek in his gloved hand. "You okay?"

Callie didn't think, leaned into his hand, and stared up at him. "Sonya said you wanted to sleep with me."

He didn't move his hand. "That's what you two were talking about in the kitchen?"

"For just a couple of minutes."

"Sonya really said that?"

"Yes. She said you never looked below her face. She couldn't believe it."

Ben grinned at that. "The woman's built, but I wouldn't know anything about that."

"She said I was blind, she said you were interested."

"Is this a roundabout way to ask me if I am?"

"Truth is, I've never been very good at the man-woman thing. Yeah, tell me, I'd like to know."

"The answer's yes." Slowly, he moved his hand from her cheek. "I'll see you tomorrow."

"It'll be Friday. A week anniversary."

"Yes."

"Does Savich want to hypnotize Fleurette like he did Annie Harper?"

"He hasn't said. Let's take a crack at her first."

She smiled up at him. "Isn't it odd, Detective Raven? Here you are with this bird name, and you're not such a bad guy after all. You haven't bitched about taking me along with you in at least forty-eight hours."

"That long? Hmm. Well, the thing is," he said simply, "you've got a good brain."

Callie flushed. "I—thank you. Yes, thank you, Ben."

Georgetown
Washington, D.C.
Thursday evening

"I'm coming."

A few minutes later, Savich walked into their shared office, holding Sean over his shoulder, lightly rubbing his boy's back in light soothing circles. "He had a nightmare. What's going on?"

"I've got a surprise for you." She was grinning even as she patted Sean's cheek. "He okay now?"

"I think so. What are you up to? What surprise?"

"I know you wanted to get to work on Samantha Barrister, but you've been too busy to do much, so I contacted both the Boston and the Pittsburgh field offices on Tuesday. I massaged a few egos, and when that didn't work, I called in a couple of favors, convinced them this was important and required immediate attention."

"Why the Boston field office?"

"I'll tell you in a few minutes. I've had MAX working on everything too, but so far he hasn't found much since all this happened in the early seventies." Sherlock waved a nice thick folder at him. "But no matter, we're in business. Sit down, Dillon, just you listen, my man, to what I've found out."

Savich stared down at his wife. "Have I told you lately that my Porsche isn't in the same ballpark with you? You're amazing."

She stood up and hugged him and Sean to her. "I like hearing that. After you chew over what I've got, I'll bet you'll even agree to give me the Porsche if I ask you."

"That could be pushing it, sweetheart, but I'm open." He sat down next to her and settled Sean against his chest.

Sherlock sat next to him and opened the folder. "Let's begin with Blessed Creek, Pennsylvania, 1973, population of about three thousand seven hundred and eighty-five souls. The Barristers were the big cheeses, no one else remotely close to them in influence and wealth. They owned the only tourist facilities around Lake Klister, the six gas stations in the area, and Mr. Barrister was the mayor, had been for twenty years. He also owned the local bank and the two biggest grocery stores. It was the senior Barrister who built the big house on that knoll outside Blessed Creek.

"They had three sons. Townsend Barrister, the eldest, married a woman named Samantha Cooper, in 1964. It was a really big bash that included nearly all the townspeople. It was in the middle of the summer, a big barbecue at the house. The Barristers brought in all kinds of help. They really did it up right."

Savich, still rubbing Sean's back, said, "So they approved of their firstborn son's marriage?"

"It appears so, but I can't be sure. I'll need to go deeper. The couple moved into the big house with the two brothers and the parents."

"Ouch."

"Wasn't so bad. As you know from firsthand experience, that house is huge."

"You got any feel for how she got along with her brothers-in-law?"

Sherlock turned to see him rocking slightly in his chair, Sean held tightly against him. She smiled. Such a familiar sight, it made her want to grin like a loon. She cleared her throat. "I'm reading between the lines in all this stuff—articles on the family, biographical info on the brother, everything the Pittsburgh office could pull together. The second brother, Derek was his name, was two years older than Samantha. He unexpectedly left home three months after Townsend and Samantha married. He joined the army, went to Vietnam and was killed within three months. The family was devastated."

"Do you think he had the hots for his brother's wife?"

"There's no hint of anything like that, naturally, but it could explain his abrupt and un-expected departure. He was twenty-two, had just graduated from Penn State, was going to start training in his father's bank, but he up and left and joined the army."

"How about the youngest brother?"

"Jonathan. He was seventeen at the time, a senior in high school when Samantha and Townsend were married, and he remained living there until he went to Dartmouth that fall. He was a wild one, big into drugs—well, but a lot of people were back then."

Savich rose. "Give me a moment. Our boy is out. Let me go put him down."

When Savich came back, he leaned down and kissed the back of her neck. "What happened to Jonathan?"

"He lives in Boston now. He's very well-off, has three boys of his own, all married with children, and he's still married to his first wife. He seems fine financially and psychologically, as in no public fits or aberrant behavior."

"Okay, the parents. What happened to the senior Barristers?"

"Now that's really strange. Both of them drowned in a boating accident on Lake Klister. That was one year to the day after Townsend married Samantha."

"Was there any suspicion at all of foul play?"

"None that I've been able to see. One day they were there, hale and hearty, then the next day they were gone—there was no sudden storm or squall, nothing to explain why both of them fell out of their boat, other than talk of lots of booze. Evidently the senior

Barristers liked their martinis, and they liked to be on the lake fishing while they drank—so it could be that simple. The belief is that one of them went overboard, the other went in to make a save, and both drowned.

"Townsend took over everything. Problem is that Townsend wasn't the businessman his father was. But Samantha was. She began taking over very quickly. Then she got pregnant in 1966 and gave birth to Austin Douglas Barrister on August 14, 1967. Within a year she was running the whole show. It appears from the records that Townsend Barrister became something of a drunk, was arrested a couple of times on DUIs—out of the local area, so it couldn't be kept out of the regional press, but still he had enough influence to have the charges quashed.

"It wasn't in the local paper, naturally. Townsend also took up gambling, went to Las Vegas every two or three weeks.

"On August 14, 1973, on the very same day that they'd been married, the same day the senior Barristers drowned, the same day Austin Douglas Barrister was born, Samantha died as well. There was a huge party for Austin on the grounds of the house, a big barbecue for his sixth birthday. Samantha was running around seeing to everything. Townsend was manning the bar, probably drinking pretty steadily, and everyone seemed to be having a good old time, until they found Samantha. Here's a quote from the *Blessed Creek Weekly Journal:* 'Samantha Barrister's body was discovered on the floor of her second-floor bathroom at three o'clock in the afternoon by one of the guests, Mrs. Emmy Hodges, who said she'd wanted to use the facilities and thought that Samantha's bathroom would be free. "She was lying in blood," said Mrs. Hodges, "it was under her, seeping all around her. It was horrible. I knew she was dead, knew it right away." '

"Then there's the quote from newly elected Sheriff Doozer Harms, the sheriff we met in Blessed Creek just last Friday. He said, 'Mrs. Barrister was stabbed through the heart by a person unknown.' "

"You've got a gleam in your eye, Sherlock. What else did you find out?"

"First thing I did was locate the widower, Townsend Barrister, same as you did. He's in Boston. I managed to actually speak to him. He wasn't real happy to hear from the FBI, but I kept after him until he opened up. Turns out he's remarried to a woman who brought in lots of money that he hasn't managed to go through yet. He has a new family, two daughters.

"Now, here's why we couldn't find out anything about his son, Austin Douglas. When I asked him where his son was, he hemmed and hawed until I threatened to have agents on his doorstep. He finally said that Austin Douglas up and disappeared the day he graduated high school. He's never heard from him again, doesn't have a clue where he is."

Savich was surprised. "I didn't expect this when I set MAX on Samantha's murder. Well, it doesn't matter. We'll locate him, no problem. I'll give MAX the task of finding Austin."

"I already did. It turns out to be quite a problem, for MAX and for everyone. When Austin Barrister up and left Boston at eighteen, he must have latched on to a new identity, because I can't find him anywhere in the U.S.

"Boston field office is working on tracking him down, starting with interviewing the family and all his former high school friends."

"Sounds like he was escaping," Savich said. "I wonder why."

CHAPTER
25

Supreme Court Building
Washington, D.C.
Friday morning

Elaine LaFleurette wasn't in Justice Califano's chambers, only Eliza Vickers, who had a phone tucked under one ear, her finger poised above the button of another ringing line. She looked up, nodded at them, and began speaking more quickly into the phone. Ben and Callie moved to the visitors' chairs and sat down.

Two minutes later, Eliza laid the phone gently back into its cradle, leaned back in her chair, and closed her eyes. "Sorry for the delay. Detective Raven, Callie, it's good to see both of you." She ran her hand through her straight hair. "It hasn't stopped. We're having to review all of Justice Califano's unfinished work, decide which Justices and clerks will take over drafting majority and dissenting opinions on case votes already taken, and so much more—concurrences, join memos, bench memos, certs., but that's not your concern.

"I've been offered help, but somehow, I need to do it myself. I also need to speak to Mrs. Califano about all of Stewart's things." Her voice trembled a bit, but almost immediately she had herself in control again. She even smiled at them. "I haven't been able to reach her. Do you know where she is, Callie?"

"She went to the High Style Boutique at Tyson's Corner," Callie said. "Don't you have her cell phone?"

"Yes, but I didn't want to intrude like that, it's more personal." Eliza slowly rose and stretched. "I've been here since six o'clock this morning, trying to get all the stuff cleaned up. Now, would you like some coffee? I've made some in Stewart's office."

"No, thank you. Actually, we were looking

for Fleurette. Where is she? Why isn't she here helping you?"

"What time is it?"

Callie said, "It's nearly eleven."

"Her uncle was killed in Vietnam on this date in 1975. She visits the Wall every year at this time. She won't be back until noon."

Ben nodded, paused a moment, studying her face. "Are you okay? Is there anything we can do, Eliza?"

For a moment Ben thought she hesitated, but then the phone rang, she shrugged, and said over her shoulder, "No, everything is under control. Well, not really, but it will be. The funeral, it was very nice, Callie. The President was eloquent. Your mother and her friends all did very well."

"Yes, the President was eloquent, but then my stepfather was such a good man. It wouldn't be difficult for anyone to say wonderful things about him."

"No, it wouldn't," Eliza said, then again, looked as if she might say something more—but then she reached for the phone, gave them a small wave, and turned away. Callie heard her say, "Justice Califano's chambers. Eliza Vickers."

Ben said, "We're only about ten minutes

from the Vietnam Memorial. You ever been there?"

"Yes. It's always a two-handkerchief occasion, no matter how many times I go there. I think the Wall is the most moving memorial in all of Washington."

"Yes, I agree with you. Nearly everyone lost someone in Vietnam. One of my father's best friends managed to ship home with two shattered legs that healed in time, but his psychological wounds were more difficult. My father came here right after the Wall was finished. He saw his friend in a wheelchair in front of the Wall, looking for other friends who'd been lost over there. My father told me they spoke for some time, but he never saw him after that."

It took them eight minutes to get to Constitution Gardens, a beautiful open space that pointed east to the Washington Monument and west to the Lincoln Memorial. Callie looked around the vast empty space as they pulled into a parking place on the street. "Well, it is January, cold, and the only tourists likely to be here have to be from North Dakota."

They walked down the path toward the Wall. They saw Fleurette immediately, standing at the middle of the Wall, completely still except for a single finger she was tracing over a name.

Ben cleared his throat as they came down the walk so as not to startle her. There were only three other people scattered along the Wall, three older men who looked cold and determined. Even from ten feet, Ben could see a sheen of tears in their eyes and hear their low voices. He knew they were talking about young men who hadn't come home, but who'd left their names on a beautiful granite wall.

"Fleurette? It's Detective Raven and Callie Markham."

She seemed completely unaware of him for a moment. Then she slowly turned and straightened. "Is something wrong? What's happened now?"

"Nothing. We wanted to speak to you." He nodded to the Wall. Even though he knew, he asked, "Who is here for you?"

"My uncle, Bobby LaFleurette, my dad's younger brother. He'd be in his fifties now, not young anymore." She turned back, traced her fingers over his name. "He died in 1975, just months before the troop withdrawal. He was only twenty-one years old.

I'm twenty-six. Isn't that the strangest thing? He was so very young, and in many ways he'll be young forever."

Her finger traced again over the name, Robert R. LaFleurette. "His name comes right before Robert Petit and right after Douglas Mahoney. I've always wondered how they knew exactly who died in what order—that's how they're all listed, you know, in order of their death."

Callie said, "Why do you come here, Fleurette?"

"Because Bobby was so young, because my father never stopped talking about him, how fun and wild he was, how he would have been such a hotshot in the business world, if only he'd survived the war. My father brought me here when the Wall first opened, back in 1984. I was six years old, and I remember it so very clearly."

Callie said, "Fleurette, remember when we talked on Sunday? You said that Danny O'Malley had looked smug last Friday morning."

"Yes, I remember that."

"Smug how, exactly?"

"Like he knew something that neither I nor Eliza knew, and it tickled him. He looked—

pleased with himself. I remember he was nodding, like he was having this sort of internal conversation with himself, and he liked what he was hearing."

Ben said, "Think back, Fleurette. Do you remember if Danny looked at Justice Califano when he left his chambers to go to the meeting?"

She closed her eyes a moment, then they popped open. "Yes, Danny did do that. Yes, he did look at Justice Califano. It was a bit of a smirk, really. It all happened so fast it really didn't settle in when it happened. But when I close my eyes now, I can see Danny sitting there, tapping his pen against his desk pad, and a smirk passing over his face."

"Did Justice Califano notice? Did he look over at Danny?"

"I don't—"

"Close your eyes again, Fleurette. Think back."

Fleurette closed her eyes. She swayed a moment, leaned against the Wall for support. "Justice Califano's back was to me when he passed by Danny's desk, but he glanced at me before he left—and he looked suddenly tired."

"Tired?"

"Yes, he looked tired, like something was too much for him. There was something on his mind, something he knew he had to deal with, but he looked tired. Maybe I'm reading too much into it now. You want me to see something and so I'm trying too hard to co-operate with you."

"But you don't think so?" Ben asked.

Slowly, she shook her head. She looked up at the gray sky. "It's going to rain soon. I wonder if it will turn to snow again. I hope not. Everything becomes such a mess."

Callie said, "Fleurette, why are you scared?"

"Scared? Me? I'm not scared."

"Yes," Callie said slowly, "you are. On Sunday, I could see it very plainly. You are scared. Why?"

Fleurette looked off toward the Lincoln Memorial, then back again at Callie. "Look, two people close to me have been mur-dered. If you saw any fear in me, it's because of that."

"Nothing else?"

"No, nothing else. I'd sure tell you if there were."

Ben said, "Bobby Fisher—one of Justice Alto-Thorpe's law clerks—"

"Yeah, I know the little creep."

"He said you and Danny went out to lunch on Friday. You didn't mention that to us."

"That's because we only walked to the corner together. Danny was in a mood, preoccupied, snarly—I suppose it makes sense now—but then I thought, *Danny, you're such a pain sometimes.* I'd heard about a shoe sale at Maximillan's, not two blocks away. I dumped him and went shoe shopping."

"Bobby said you two had your heads together, a real chummy conversation," Ben said.

"No, that's Bobby being a creep again. He probably wanted you to focus your attention on someone else. He disliked Justice Califano, probably because he and Alto-Thorpe weren't on good terms."

"Bobby Fisher and Eliza—what did you think about that? You knew he wanted her to go out with him?"

Fleurette shrugged. "Oh that. Fact is, Eliza couldn't have cared less. Bobby didn't really come into her line of focus, you know what I mean? She put up with him. What she really wanted to do was drop-kick him out of the building."

"Do you think Eliza really disliked Bobby

that much? Do you think he hated her because she kept turning him down?"

"Who knows? When he finally ran out of there on Friday, she looked at me, rolled her eyes, and said, 'Well, maybe that's the last time I'll have to tell him to take a hike.'"

"So she never really took him all that seriously."

"No," Fleurette said. "The only person she took seriously was Justice Califano."

"So what did Danny say to you before you told him you were going shoe shopping?"

"Nothing really, just something like 'Women and shoes, that's all you think about.' Then he said he was going to see a foreign film with Annie that night, that he had something going—listen, Danny was always on the make. Usually whatever he said didn't mean anything."

"Except this time it did, didn't it?" Ben said.

Before Ben and Callie left her by the Vietnam Wall, next to her uncle's name, Ben remembered to ask Fleurette what color her toenail polish was last Friday. She looked startled, then laughed. "It's called 'I'm Not Really a Waitress Red.'"

Callie said to Ben as they drove away, "I

wonder if her father makes the pilgrimage here every year like Fleurette does."

"Somehow I don't think so. After all, he wasn't six years old when he first came here."

"She's scared, even though she denies it."

"Yes, I think you're right."

CHAPTER
26

Georgetown
Washington, D.C.
Friday evening

"Sean ate more spaghetti than you, Callie," Savich said, eyeing her plate. "You need more Parmesan? Garlic bread? How about more of Sherlock's Caesar salad? It's the best. I taught her how to make it myself."

"No, I'm fine, truly. It's so nice to go off our pizza diet. It's been a very long week."

"Your mom is having her potluck tonight with her friends?"

Callie nodded to Sherlock, who was cutting into a beautiful apple pie.

Simon Russo, Lily's art broker fiancé from New York, was sitting back in his chair, hands over his lean stomach. He was looking at Savich's sister, and there was such sweetness in his look that Callie gulped. She had listened to them talk about *No Wrinkles Remus,* Lily's political cartoon series that *The Washington Post* had picked up, about Sarah Elliott's paintings, one of which hung over the fireplace in the living room, but of course, the conversation always returned to Justice Califano and Danny O'Malley.

Savich served the warm apple pie with a big scoop of French vanilla ice cream on top. "Oh goodness," Callie said. "This is wonderful. Just smell that. Were you a chef in a former life, Dillon?"

"He was probably a sculptor and a chef," Sherlock said. "He's still both in this lifetime. When we go back into the living room I'll show you some of his work—"

Savich's cell phone rang. He answered, jumped to his feet. "Eliza? What is it, what's wrong?"

He listened, everyone else at the table focused on him.

Suddenly he yelled into the phone, "No! Eliza, fight him!"

He was already running for the front door.
"He's there, attacking her, right now! Lily,
Simon, stay here with Sean. Ben, get your
siren out, we're going to McLean. That bastard is there! Hurry!" He clamped the phone
back to his ear. "Eliza? Please, say something. Fight! You can do it, fight!"

Ben slammed the siren down on top of the
Crown Vic in a second, already on his radio
as he pulled out of the driveway, calling to
control to report a murder in progress at
Number 102, The Oaks condo complex in
McLean.

In the Porsche, Sherlock was on her cell to
Jimmy Maitland. "He's got Eliza Vickers right
now. Get the SWAT team out there, sir, a helicopter, the local police. We can't let him get
away. Oh God, Dillon heard him attacking
her!"

Savich was still holding his own cell phone
to his ear as the Porsche hit eighty miles an
hour, heading for the highway to McLean.
There were no voices now, no noise of any
kind, just silence.

Eighteen minutes later, they barreled into
the driveway, barely missing a squad car that
was parked halfway on the drive, halfway on
the front yard. There were a good dozen

blue-and-whites all over the block, cops everywhere. The front door of Eliza Vickers's condo was open, uniformed men and women streaming in and out.

Savich was at the door in an instant, his I.D. out. "Agent Savich. Where is she?"

A woman stepped forward. "I'm Detective Orinda Chamber, McLean PD, Agent Savich. We just got here. There was an initial charge into the place, so the scene's a mess. I've tried to keep everyone out after I saw she was dead. She's in the kitchen. I hear she was on the phone to you and you heard him attacking her?"

Savich nodded. "Please get all your people combing the woods, look for his car. Agents will be here very soon to help you, along with a helicopter and the Washington SWAT team. He's a big guy, probably in his fifties, white. He has to have had some sort of transportation, so let's get everyone on it." He paused a moment. "Detective Chamber, this is the man who murdered Justice Califano."

Orinda Chamber reeled back, then steadied and nodded. "Yes, sir. I'm on it."

Sherlock had run past him, pushed past the three men who were standing in the kitchen looking down at Eliza Vickers. She was lying on her side, her long straight hair tangled over her face, but Sherlock saw her eyes through the veil of hair, still bulging wide. Terror and surprise no longer filled them. They were empty now, empty even of the memory of life. Sherlock fell to her knees beside her, gently pulled her hair away from her face. "Eliza, I'm sorry. Oh, God, I'm so sorry."

"Hey, lady, who the hell are you? What is—"

Savich shoved his I.D. in the officer's face. "She's FBI. Back off. Go outside and help find this bastard."

"Yes, sir," one of the other officers said, and pulled the officer away.

Sherlock was leaning over Eliza, her hands shaking her shoulders, trying to awaken her, trying to make her empty eyes fill with life again. Tears streamed down her face. "Oh no, Eliza. I'm sorry, I'm so very sorry." Sherlock pressed her face against Eliza's hair, sobbing.

Savich came down on his haunches beside his wife. He rubbed her shoulders, didn't say anything, just gave her what comfort he could. He felt like crying himself. This bastard, this Günter freak, had killed her, knowing she was on the phone to him. Savich would never forget as long as he lived what the man said in the background after the phone had crashed to the kitchen floor: "Well, she's dead now, isn't she? You hear me, Agent Savich? This will be the only time. You've got *nada, rien, nichts.*" And he laughed. Savich had heard him still laughing as he'd picked the phone up off the kitchen floor and thrown it across the room, and walked out of there, the sound of his footsteps clear for Savich to hear. Savich had continued to listen, for the sound of a door opening, a window, anything. But there was only silence. And he'd known Eliza Vickers was dead and that he'd been helpless to do anything about it.

Günter had sounded as American as the apple pie they'd baked for dinner. American. No regional accent. Savich was aware of Ben and Callie standing in the kitchen doorway, keeping the other officers out.

Of course Günter was long gone. Savich knew in his gut they wouldn't find him, not this time. Too much cover in all the maples and oaks behind the condo complex, too many places to hide a car, a motorcycle, or even to run a mile to someplace near the highway.

He closed his eyes against the pain of Eliza's death, realizing he could hardly bear it either. He'd never seen Sherlock like this. She looked beaten down, crushed. Eliza Vickers, so smart, so very real, and he'd heard her die on his damned cell phone. He knew he would live with that forever. He lowered his head, holding both his sobbing wife and Eliza Vickers, who wasn't there anymore to care.

Suddenly, Savich reared up and yelled, "Ben, Callie, we've got to get over to Fleurette's house. Call her, tell her to hide. Call 911, have as many squad cars there as fast as possible to canvas the area, stop everyone who's alone in a car. Take her to my house. Hurry!"

Ben didn't hesitate. Both he and Callie were out the door. Ben tossed Callie his address book as he jumped into the car. "Fleurette's number, quick!"

She read it out, and he dialed. The phone rang once, twice, three times. Finally, Ben heard her voice. "Hello?"

"Fleurette?"

"Yes, who's this? It's after midnight, who—"

"This is Detective Ben Raven. No, be quiet and listen to me. Is your house alarm set?"

"Yes."

"Do you have a gun?"

A slight pause, then, "Yes, a twenty-two revolver."

"Loaded?"

"Yes."

"Good. Get the gun and come back to the phone."

After a short pause, she said, "Okay, I've got it."

"Now keep it close until Callie Markham and I get there. Find a place to hide where no one can surprise you, and stay there. If a man gets into your house, I want you to shoot to kill, you got me? Don't hesitate, shoot to kill. You'll be hearing sirens any minute. Keep inside. We're on our way. But don't let anyone in until you're sure it's me. Hurry!"

"But—but what's going on here, Detective Raven?"

"We'll tell you when we get there. Open your front door only to me, you got that? And don't shoot me. I'm going to be taking you over to Agent Savich's house in Georgetown. Do you understand?"

"No, and this is very frightening."

"It's good to be scared. Keep that gun close, and listen for any sound inside your house. We'll be there as soon as we can."

Ben punched off his cell phone, dialed 911, told the dispatcher he'd instructed the potential victim to keep her gun handy. The officers converging on the brownstone were not to go roaring in or she'd shoot them.

He punched off his cell phone again. "I sure hope they pay attention. I don't want her to kill anyone."

He slammed on the siren, and the Crown Vic roared onto the Beltway on-ramp. The roads were nearly empty, thank God. They were at Fleurette's brownstone in under twenty minutes. Several police cars had already arrived, their lights flashing, officers milling around the brownstone. Thank God none of them had gone up to the front door. "Stay in the car, Callie. I'll get Fleurette."

Ben ran up the walk, banged on the front door, calling out as he struck it with his fist. "Fleurette, it's me, Detective Ben Raven. You can let me in. Don't shoot me."

Fleurette opened the door immediately and

stepped back. She was holding a small .22 at her side. "So now will you tell me what's going on here, Detective?"

"Get inside, Fleurette." He turned to see Callie running up the walk, and waved her in. "Hurry."

Fleurette grabbed his arm. "All these cop cars. Detective Raven, what's happened?"

He searched her face as he said, "Eliza Vickers was just murdered."

Her face went utterly white. Her eyes went blank. Then she whimpered, deep in her throat, and sank to her knees on the floor.

Ben closed the door behind Callie and flipped off the light switch. It was completely dark inside the brownstone, not even a shadow for Günter to shoot at. He eased up the window a crack and yelled out, "We're okay in here. Spread out and check the neighborhood, we'll be leaving here soon."

"That you, Ben?"

"Yeah."

"Keep down. There's no sign of anyone here, but we're on it." He recognized Sergeant Teddy Russell's voice.

Ben held his gun at his side. "Fleurette, push your twenty-two over to me."

He heard the small gun slide across the

marble tile. It hit his boot. He put it in his belt holster.

"Detective—"

"No, no, stay quiet for a while longer." He pulled out his cell and called Captain Halloway, who answered like he'd been awake for hours. Ben quickly told him what was happening.

"Just keep the women safe, Ben. I'll handle everything else. Do you know the lead officer at Ms. LaFleurette's house?"

"It's Sergeant Teddy Russell."

"He's a good man. He'll get things done. Hang tight, Ben, hang tight and protect the women. We'll get you out of there soon enough."

Ben punched off his cell, then leaned back against the wall, closed his eyes a moment and let the events of the evening race through his brain. Incredible, all of it. At least Fleurette was alive. He said, "Let's stay down, and stay quiet. We don't know if the guy's out there yet. He's good at losing himself in the shadows."

Ben heard Callie moving toward Fleurette. "Stay down," he said. He opened his cell to call Savich while they waited. "We made it, Savich. Yes, I told her about Eliza. She's holding up. We'll be at your house as soon as I'm certain it's safe to take Fleurette outside." He heard Savich speaking to someone in the background, Sherlock, probably. "Okay, I hear the cops coming up the stairs. I'll see you at your house." Ben slowly rose. He went to the front door, stood to the side, and identified himself as he opened it. "Hey, Teddy, good to see you. Is it clear?"

"Not yet, Ben. Stay inside a few minutes longer until the rest of my men check in."

Ben nodded. "I spoke to Captain Halloway. He said he told you he was sending more squad cars."

"Yes, we're all spread out now, canvassing everything within a mile of the house, but it's tough, folks who live in this area like to party on Friday night."

"The guy we're looking for is American, probably in his fifties, white."

Sergeant Teddy Russell, a twenty-four-year veteran, put his beefy hand on the butt of the Smith & Wesson 1911 holstered at his belt, and looked from Ben to the two women. "Boy, you guys in Metro sure like to live on the edge."

CHAPTER
27

Georgetown
Washington, D.C.
Early Saturday morning

Fleurette sat at the kitchen table, a hot mug of coffee held between her hands, her head down, her blond hair straggling out of its ponytail. She was wearing an oversized cable knit navy sweater, blue jeans, and boots. An orange duffel bag and oversized purse lay at her feet.

"Thank you, Agent Savich," she said at last, still not looking up. "You probably saved my life."

"I'm just happy that Ben got there in time.

You'll be staying with my wife and me for a while, all right?"

Fleurette shuddered. "Thank you." She raised her head and looked from him to Sherlock. "Do you often have people like me staying with you?"

"No," Sherlock said, pouring more hot coffee into her mug, "not often. Here, drink this down, Fleurette, you need it."

Callie was leaning into Ben. She looked dazed and absolutely exhausted. She said, "I've got to call Mom, tell her what's happened."

Savich said, "No, not yet, Callie. She doesn't need to know right now. Let her rest, let her have a bit more recovery time before we hit her with Eliza's murder. We'll go over tomorrow." He watched Sherlock walk quietly out of the kitchen. He nodded to Ben, said to Fleurette, "Keep drinking that hot coffee."

He found his wife sitting on the bottom step of the staircase, her face in her hands. He sat beside her and pulled her into his arms.

In the kitchen, Lily and Simon were cutting slices of apple pie and heating them in the microwave. Lily said, "Fleurette, you need sugar, it will help calm you."

"I really don't want—"

"I know it's not chocolate," Simon Russo said, "but it's a good excuse to eat the best apple pie in the universe and not feel guilty about the calories."

Fleurette actually smiled. It fell off her face quickly enough, but it was a start. There was enough left for all of them to have a small slice. For a while, there was only the sound of chewing in the kitchen.

"Dillon?" Sherlock's voice was muffled against his shoulder. "I'm sorry I'm falling apart like this. It's just that—"

"If you weren't falling apart, then I would be," he said, and kissed her hair. "It's tough, sweetheart, really tough. I'm as sorry as you are. Eliza was special."

"Yes. Dillon, I liked her so very much and I'd only met her. Just twice and the funeral."

"But all three times were emotional, the kinds of meetings that draw people together. I really liked her, too, I really did." He drew a deep breath, kissed her again. "Why did he feel he had to kill her?"

"This time, we don't even know. Maybe she knew something after all, and he was afraid she was going to break. And she did break, she called you. Oh God, Mr. Maitland brought in the agents too soon."

"It was after Justice Califano's funeral, everyone believed it was over."

Ben stood alone in the archway of the living room. He cleared his throat. "I'm sorry to bother you, but there's something I forgot to tell you. When Callie and I went to see Fleurette at the Supreme Court Building this morning, only Eliza was there. She was cleaning out Justice Califano's stuff, and constantly answering the phone, really harried. We spoke for just a few moments. Before we left, I asked her if there was anything I could do. She hesitated, I'm sure of it. She looked sort of undecided, like there was something on her mind, but then the phone rang again and she waved us out. Damn, Savich, I didn't think anything about it."

"So maybe she did know something," Sherlock said. "But what? And he was there, in the condo, with her. Do you think he let her pick up the phone, dial you, speak to you?"

Savich said, "I wouldn't be surprised. Maybe he needed to take a risk again, and so when he heard her on the phone to me, that was it, this time. And then he garroted her, just like Justice Califano and Danny O'Malley."

Sherlock said against Dillon's neck, "And Fleurette was helpless, just like Eliza."

"Yes," Ben said. "She did have a gun, a twenty-two revolver, but he wouldn't have given her the chance to get to it."

Sherlock said, "Eliza was strong, probably stronger than Danny O'Malley. She must have fought him."

Both Ben and Savich were silent for a moment. Ben felt Callie come up behind him. He hadn't heard her, but somehow he knew she was there. She leaned against him, but said nothing.

Savich said, "Yes, I'll bet she did fight him, fought him as hard as she could. They took her to Quantico. Dr. Conrad went out there to do the autopsy. Since we were there so quickly, I doubt Günter took the time to remove all evidence of himself. Maybe we'll be lucky and she managed to scratch him. Something, all we need is something."

They sat together, listening to the low buzz of conversation coming from the kitchen.

Savich looked up to see that Ben and Callie had gone.

Suddenly, they heard a cry from Sean.

As one, they looked up. "Life goes on," Savich said as he slowly rose, bringing Sherlock with him. Sherlock straightened, scrubbed her hands over her face, and went up with him to see what had awakened Sean.

FBI Headquarters
Saturday morning

Dr. Conrad tacked up a blow-up photo of Eliza Vickers on the corkboard behind him. "Eliza Vickers fought hard. She was a big woman, one hundred fifty pounds, strong and very fit." He pointed to her hands. "She has defensive cuts, and she injured him at least once, scored some of his skin off. We can't be certain yet, but the skin was probably from his neck or face. It was under her nails along with some of his blood, and there had been no attempt to clean it off. You said he was laughing when he left, Agent Savich, but he had to be hurting, too, and bleeding.

He had to know he was leaving us evidence."

Savich said, "He was laughing because he knew I heard him killing her. He did that on purpose."

Dr. Conrad continued. "We have easily enough for DNA analysis, and as soon as that is complete, we will try to find a match, not just through domestic databases, but through Interpol."

Agent Frank Halley said, "Okay, he had to get the hell out of Dodge, so he didn't have time to clean up after himself. The profilers might be right, though, the guy is so damned arrogant, he might not have cared, just blew us off."

"That's possible," Jimmy Maitland said. "Anyone who uses Günter Grass as an alias is about as egotistical as any killer I've ever seen."

Savich heard Sherlock's cell phone play the beginning bars of *Bolero,* and looked up.

He watched her face as she listened, then said, her voice urgent, "We'll be there as soon as we can. Don't force his hand. Don't hurt him." He was stepping toward her as she jumped to her feet. "Dillon, we've got to go, now. It's Samantha's boy, they've found him, and there's trouble."

Jimmy Maitland didn't hesitate. "Samantha's son? Tell me later. Go, but you call me when you get back, okay?"

Savich nodded, even as he was running for the conference room door. "Ben, Callie, you're with us."

As they raced from the elevator toward their cars in the garage, Sherlock said, "I had the Boston field office put out an alert on the name Austin Douglas Barrister. If it turned up, I was to be called immediately. That was Chief Howard Gerber of the Petersboro, Maryland Police Department. He said they have a hostage situation, a man inside a house with his wife and two children. The Hostage Rescue Team was trying to talk him out when the guy yelled out that his name wasn't Martin Thornton, it was Austin Douglas Barrister. Chief Gerber realized he'd just read that name, looked it up, and called me. I told him we'd be there as soon as we could."

"Don't lose us," Savich shouted to Ben and gunned the Porsche out of the garage.

Savich headed the Porsche north on the Beltway. Sherlock said to him as well as to

Ben on her cell phone, "The siren is great, Ben. We want to get there as fast as possible. Until we got this break, we couldn't locate Austin Barrister. It was like he disappeared off the face of the earth. Neither the Boston field office nor MAX could track him down.

"Okay, now, it looks like Petersboro is about ten miles due west of Alston, Maryland, off 270. We're about forty-five minutes away, particularly with you, Ben, sitting on the siren. We'll probably get there with a four-car escort."

Ben said, "I'm with you. Tell Savich we're right behind him, at least I'm trying. That Porsche is something." Ben laughed as he shut down his cell.

Savich said to his wife, "You didn't tell me you'd put a tag in the system."

"Yep, I didn't really think it would result in anything, but who knew?"

Savich shook his head, amazed as always with her ingenuity, signaled, and passed a Beemer at one hundred miles per hour. "So he's been using the name Martin Thornton since he ran away from Boston."

"Yes. The Hostage Rescue Team was probably calling his name over and over, you know how they do—Martin, do you hear us, Martin?—and he must have cracked and shouted out his real name."

"Thank God for that."

"Thank God for a police chief who remembered the alert and acted quickly on it."

Inside the Crown Vic, Callie watched the traffic whiz by them, cars pulling over quickly as they neared, looking almost as if they were standing still. When they reached a clear stretch, all she could see of the Porsche was a flash of red.

"More pedal to the metal," Ben said, and soon the Porsche came back into sight.

"This is the strangest day of my life."

"You really think this is a strange day?"

"Don't arch that supercilious eyebrow at me, Ben Raven. First I'm allowed in a meeting on the sacred fifth floor of the FBI building, and the next thing I know, we're chasing Savich's Porsche to Maryland to find this guy who's the son of a woman who was murdered thirty years ago."

"That's why I went into law enforcement," Ben said, "the excitement. It's nonstop."

"Yeah, right, so you say. The cops I've

talked to usually whine about how boring it is—on the phone and the computer all day."

They rounded a bend and the Porsche accelerated forward out of a curve. "My oh my," Ben said. "Be still my heart. That car can go, just look at it."

Callie laughed at him. "So get yourself one—to go with your truck."

"Would you prefer I picked you up in a Porsche or a truck?"

"Now we're going on a date? You're asking me my car preference?"

He shrugged. "It might be fun in the truck. You and my dog could hang out the window, tongues lolling in the wind. Well, at least it could be fun in the summer. Now, about a Porsche—I'd probably get so many speeding tickets I'd get drummed off the force."

She laughed again, shook her head, and laughed some more. It felt great.

"Now, seriously, the thing about Porsches is that the minute your foot connects to the accelerator, it gains weight and pushes down harder and harder. Just look at Savich. You think he's got a clue how fast he's going?"

"Yes, I think he knows exactly how fast he's going."

"Well, maybe you're right, in this situation.

What do you think, one hundred and ten miles an hour?"

She shook her head, tapped her fingers to her chin. "No, more like one twenty." She paused, then turned to him. "Okay, I understand now. You've been distracting me. And you've done it very well. You've made me laugh. Thank you. Now, for our first date, I want to ride in the truck. I want to drive out in the wilds of Virginia to some country barbecue place where they don't have any tablecloths, just long wooden tables, and tubs filled with ice and beer. Hey, you're losing sight of him."

The Crown Vic leapt forward. One hundred miles an hour. Ben heard sirens behind him. Good, their escort was with them. He had to get closer to Savich, or the cops would go nuts at the sight of that speeding Porsche. He got on his radio, called dispatch. "This is Detective Ben Raven, on Highway 270. We're just past Rockville, Maryland. We're heading up to Alston, then ten miles west to Petersboro. FBI Agent Dillon Savich is in front of me, driving a red Porsche 911. My siren's on and I've got two cop cars behind me. Alert the highway patrol about our posi-

tion and the Porsche. This is an emergency."
He listened, said yes a couple of times, and
punched off.

"Okay, if we're lucky everything should be
all right. Let's hear it for a show of competence."

"An amazing thing, competence. I'm always pleasantly surprised when I trip over
it."

Ben caught sight of the Porsche. "He just
passed a patrol car coming off an exit onto
the freeway. I'm going to call dispatch again,
just to be sure." Ben memorized the patrol
car number and radioed dispatch again.

They watched the patrol car pull back a bit.
"Good."

Callie said suddenly, "Why would he go
after Fleurette?"

So much for distracting her, Ben thought,
and said, "I've been wondering the same
thing. Maybe she's another loose end. Like
Eliza."

"I don't think Eliza was just a loose end.
Don't forget, she was calling Savich, to tell
him something, maybe something she knew
but hadn't said anything about before. And
why not? Because she was afraid? Or be-

cause she was a part of something that led to my stepfather's murder?"

"Whoa—that's a giant leap. But you're a reporter, you're paid to make wild guesses, right?"

"Do you really think it's such a wild guess?"

"Maybe. Who knows? Hey, I'm trying to keep from killing us here. I'm now going one hundred and ten miles an hour. Keep an eye out for more patrol cars. Or any pedestrians who might be running across the highway." He laid a gloved hand on her leg as she laughed again. "You really want a down-home, hoe-down kind of country place where you get barbecue sauce all over your face and Billy Bob tries to make a pass at you?"

She laughed again. "That's it exactly. And just think, I'll be with such a guy's guy—truck, beer, testosterone, nice butt. What more could a girl ask? Look, Alton's coming up. I'll keep an eye out for Petersboro."

"Just watch the Porsche. Sherlock proba-bly has MAX on her lap and he's providing them directions."

"Nah, she's a real navigator. I'll bet she's using a plain old map."

Ben slowed to match the Porsche. The squad cars behind him kept thirty feet back.

Savich led them directly into a subdivision of ranch-style homes not far from the highway. A half-dozen squad cars were angled around one of them, a dozen or more police huddled behind them, using the cars for shields.

CHAPTER
28

Petersboro, Maryland

Neighbors were gathered, talking and pointing, looking both scared and excited, held behind a police line half a block away from the house. Savich pulled the Porsche behind a squad car three houses away from where Austin Douglas Barrister lived. Ben and the two highway patrol cars pulled in behind him.

He and Sherlock saw a man in a heavy jacket holding a bullhorn in his hand and ran toward him. Before they could get to him, an officer yelled, "Hey, buddy, get the hell back!"

Savich turned, pulled out I.D., and held it in the officer's face. "Where's Chief Gerber?"

Officer Ridley looked at the big guy in the black leather jacket who'd just climbed out of a sexy red Porsche that would cost him three years' salary and said, "So who gives a damn if you're FBI? Chief Gerber is busy. This is a local matter, *Agent,* we've got it covered."

"Let's try again, Officer. Where is Chief Gerber?"

Ridley took another step toward him, leaned right in his face now. "And why is that any of your freaking business?"

Savich grabbed Ridley by the collar and hoisted him off his feet. "I asked you where Chief Gerber is, Officer."

"Hey! What's going on here? Hey, you, let that officer down! Back away!"

The second officer reached for his gun. Sherlock grabbed his arm and stuck her I.D. in his face. "Don't you even think about drawing a gun on a federal officer. Back off, all of you."

"But—"

Sherlock said, "We're here because the man inside that house—his mother called me, frantic for help. The FBI has been looking for him. Now, where is Chief Gerber?"

"Right here, Agent Sherlock." A big beefy cop around fifty, with a baby face and a paunch starting to overflow his wide leather belt, approached them. "Calm down, guys. I was expecting these people. Lew, back off. Both of you get back to work."

Savich slowly let Officer Ridley down, but didn't turn his back on him. Testosterone filled the air, and adrenaline was pumping because of the uncertainty of what was going on inside that house, an explosive combination.

Sherlock stuck out her hand. "I'm Special Agent Sherlock, FBI. This is Special Agent Savich. You're Chief Howard Gerber?"

"That I am." He shook their hands. "You got here very quickly."

Sherlock said, "We've been looking for the man who lives in that house for several days. Thank you, Chief, for calling me so quickly. This is a personal matter for us, as well as professional. We think we can help."

Officer Ridley was still breathing hard, but Savich realized he now had himself under control. At least enough control so he wouldn't pull his gun and shoot him. Savich said, never raising his voice, never sounding anything but calm and in control, "Tell us what's happening here, Chief."

"As I told Agent Sherlock, the guy who lives here, his name's Martin Thornton. He's got a wife, Janet, two daughters, ages eight and ten, inside the house, and won't let them come out. We got a call from a neighbor about an hour and a half ago. They'd heard a gunshot and some screams. We think the husband went nuts. Why, we don't know. Joe Gaines, the one with the bullhorn, is from the Hostage Rescue Team. He's trying to get the guy to talk to him again, establish a dialogue. So far the guy hasn't talked much, except to yell out once that his name wasn't Martin Thornton, it was Austin Douglas Barrister. That's when we ran the name and found the alert to call you, Agent Sherlock." He paused a moment, eyeing Savich. "Okay, you said this is personal too. I've told you the facts as I know them, now it's your turn to fill me in."

Savich said, "We need him as a possible witness in a murder investigation, and I know a great deal about his life. Give me a vest. I've got to be the one to speak to him. I may be the only one who can get through to him.

His mother is the reason he cracked, and I'm the only one who knows her. She's extraordinarily important to him. You're going to have to trust me on this. It's the best chance for his wife and daughters. Austin too."

Chief Gerber had listened intently, listened to every inflection, then made a decision. "Under normal circumstances I wouldn't be inclined to let a hot dog who drives up in a red Porsche anywhere close to that house." He fell silent. Then he slowly nodded. "Guess these circumstances aren't all that normal though. Joe, give Agent Savich the bullhorn, he'll need it. Duncan, get Agent Savich a Kevlar vest. Keep your traps shut, I'll take responsibility." He studied Savich's face. "You're really sure about this?"

"As sure as I can be about anything."

"I recognize you now. You're the FBI guy heading the murder case at the Supreme Court, aren't you?"

"Yes."

Officer Duncan handed Savich a vest. Savich stripped off his leather jacket, peeled off his leather gloves, and tossed them to Sherlock. He pulled on the vest over his shirt. When he put on his leather jacket, he zipped it over his belt holster. He said low to Sherlock, taking her hands in his, "Another day in Paradise, right, sweetheart? Pray a little."

She wanted to wrap her arms around him and not let him go. She didn't want him to step anywhere near that harmless-looking house with a gun-wielding maniac inside. She said, "I will pray, you can count on that." Her mouth was dry with fear. She swallowed, but her voice still came out scratchy and hoarse. "Take care, Dillon." She stepped back. She felt someone against her back, felt a man's hand on her arm. It was Ben, with Callie beside him.

Savich took the bullhorn from Joe Gaines, and began his trek to the driveway. A large oak tree stood tall just off center in the front yard. He saw a basketball hoop set up over the double garage doors. The net was ripped, showing lots of use. There were a couple of girls' bikes leaning against the closed left garage door. He walked past dormant rosebushes lining the front of the house. The curtains were drawn over the single large front picture window. He was aware of the low murmur of cop voices behind him, and farther away, the worried and excited conversation of the neighbors. He wondered if there would be another shot and he'd be dead before he hit the ground.

He stopped just before he stepped off the driveway onto the sidewalk that led to the narrow front porch. He raised the bullhorn. "Martin, Austin—my name is Dillon Savich. I'm an FBI agent. I know your mother. It's because of her that I'm here. She's really worried about you. If you talk to me I can tell you all about it."

Dead silence.

"Your mother, Samantha Barrister, is worried about you, Austin. Let me come in and tell you what she said to me."

Savich didn't move, just held the bullhorn loosely at his side.

There was movement inside the house, then a woman's low voice. The wife was alive, thank God.

Savich stood still as a stone, the cold seeping through his boots and gloves. He finally saw the front door crack open, saw a flicker of movement, and knew it was Martin Thornton—Austin Douglas Barrister—standing close behind the partially open doorway, out of the line of fire from the police at the curb.

He didn't say another word, just waited.

"You're a liar," Austin said. "My mom's

been dead for thirty years. You hear me? Someone killed her! So who the hell are you? Why are you lying to me like this?"

The voice was low and scared, and there was something else, a loss of control, close to the surface. But he'd asked a question, and that was positive.

"I'm not lying, Austin," Savich said, and took another step up the short sidewalk.

"My name's Martin. Austin, that's someone else. Don't you move!"

"All right, I won't. But I'm not lying to you."

"Sure you are. Who told you about my mother?"

"Let me come closer and I'll tell you all about it."

A moment of silence, then, "All right, you can come up on the porch, but no closer."

Savich walked up the sidewalk, slow and easy, stepped up onto the porch and waited.

"Talk."

"I saw your mother a week ago Friday night, near Blessed Creek. I was driving to the cabin where my family and I were staying for the weekend when I had a blowout. I'd just finished changing the tire when a hysterical young woman ran out in front of my car, claiming someone was trying to kill her, and I had to take her home, right away. I couldn't get much else out of her. I followed her directions, and ended up at a huge house on top of a knoll. That was your old home, Aus—Martin. I had her sit on the sofa in the living room as I searched the house, but I didn't find anyone. When I went back to where I'd left your mom in the living room, she was gone."

Martin Thornton yelled, "She's dead, do you hear me? Dead for thirty years. You made this up, mister. Did my father send you? No, there's no way he could have found me."

Savich continued, keeping his voice calm. "I dreamed about Samantha the very next night after I was called back to Washington on an emergency. And again this past week. She mentioned you, her son, her precious boy. Since we couldn't locate you, we put out an alert, and Chief Gerber called us when you shouted out your real name just a little while ago. I'm not lying, Martin. Why would I?"

Savich knew that the cops couldn't hear either of them.

Martin Thornton's voice was hesitant. "I didn't mean to call out that other name, it just came out of my mouth. What are you saying? There's no such thing as ghosts. My mom couldn't come back—how could she?"

"I don't know, but she did come to me, then she was in my dreams. Martin, I'm here to help you, but I can't until I know what's changed in your life, what's happened to you to make you do this. Let me come inside. I'm not about to hurt you or your family. I'm here for you, but mainly I'm here for your mother, Samantha, and not as an FBI agent."

The door eased open and a man appeared in profile. Then he turned to face him. Savich knew Austin Douglas Barrister was only a couple of years older than he, about thirty-seven, but he appeared older. He had thinning black hair, a very pale face, and his mother's incredibly beautiful eyes. But his pupils were dilated, huge and black with fear, just as hers had been. He was thin, a bit stoop-shouldered, and wore dark brown corduroy trousers, sneakers, and a white shirt beneath a dark brown V-neck sweater. He heard his wife Janet say, "Let him in, Martin. I believe him. It sounds too crazy not to be true. Come, we'll work this out. Let him in."

Savich saw that Martin was holding a shotgun at his side, a weapon that could blow a hole through a man, Kevlar vest or not.

Martin slowly nodded. He looked out toward all the cops, shrank back a bit. "All right, you can come in, but I still think you're nuts." Then he laughed. "I said you're nuts? That makes both of us nuts. What did you say your name is?"

"Dillon Savich."

"Did the cops give you a gun?"

"I already told you I'm an FBI agent. Of course I have a gun. It's in the holster at my belt. Would you like me to drop it out here?"

Martin Thornton stared at him, the shotgun held tight in his right hand. Savich was close enough to see that it was an SKB model 785, a beautiful weapon, finely tooled with an automatic ejector, and with a silver nitrite finish. It was expensive, and it was deadly.

Martin Thornton said slowly, "No, leave it holstered. Come on in."

"Would you like to send Janet and the girls out?"

Suddenly a woman was standing at Martin's right shoulder. "No, I don't want to leave Martin. I'm fine right here. The girls are locked in a bedroom. They're all right too." She drew a deep breath. "This has happened twice before. We got through it. Come in, Agent Savich."

"Yeah, all right, come in," Martin said and stepped back, careful not to show himself fully in the doorway. Savich didn't blame him for that. Savich looked back to nod toward Chief Gerber before he stepped through the front door and waved his hand.

He stepped inside the house. It was dim and shadowy. He could barely see the woman standing beside Martin. He said, "Can we turn on some lights?"

Martin shut and locked the front door, then flicked on the light switch.

Savich looked into a good-sized living room, a long, narrow space with two thick carpets on the hardwood floor, comfortable furniture, a lot of chintz. Feminine, but inviting. It looked like a home, a happy contented home. This had happened twice before? And Janet had hung in there? That said something about her, about them. She was nearly as tall as her husband, plump, big-breasted, with long, naturally curly dark brown hair.

Savich saw the gaping hole in the living room wall where Martin had fired a blast at close range. So that's what the neighbors had heard, why they'd called the police.

Savich sincerely hoped Martin Thornton
didn't lose it like that again, and put the
same size hole through him. But suddenly,
he wasn't sure. Martin's eyes had gone hot
and dark.

CHAPTER 29

Savich didn't move. He nearly stopped breathing. He wondered in that instant what that SKB shotgun fired at this close range would do to his chest. Probably shred both the vest and him, and he'd be dead so fast he wouldn't even realize it. He smiled at Martin Thornton. "This hole in the wall. Do you know what it made me think about?"

Martin blinked, his eyes slowly focused. He looked over at the wall. "What?"

"I was thinking that this was the very first time I've seen what a shotgun blast could do to a wall, and I was wondering what it would do to a human body. I'm wearing a Kevlar vest, but even so, I think it would splatter me from here into the next block. It would make an awful mess."

Martin stared at him as if he'd lost his mind. Slowly, he shook his head. "No, I don't want to think what it would do to you."

"I hope you never have to see it. Now, I want you to listen to me carefully, Martin. Are you hearing me?"

Savich waited. Slowly, Martin nodded. Savich saw his fingers ease off the trigger, saw he was holding the shotgun more loosely now. Good, he had his attention.

"You've already done a very violent thing in firing that shotgun, but no one was hurt. Now concentrate, focus your mind. I want you to look inside yourself, Martin. Look at the powerful feelings that made you do that. Examine them, ruminate on each one of them. Look at them like you would something you want to eat, something you're not really sure of, but you're hungry, you have this compulsion to eat everything in front of you. I want you to ask yourself where those feelings are coming from."

Martin looked bewildered. "I don't know. I don't want to look at them. I want them to go away and stay away, but they won't. They get all heaped up in my head, and I can't see clearly, can't separate them out. They're there all of a sudden and make me crazy, they just—happen, like this morning, everything just popped. I knew it was happening, but I couldn't stop it, just couldn't."

"You're a strong person, Martin. You've survived what many men would never survive, so I know you can deal with this, too. I'm not a physician to give you drugs or tell you to meditate to stop the feelings from overwhelming you.

"What I know is this—you and I are standing right here, you've got a shotgun in your hand, the police are outside, and your family is frightened. This is real, Martin, and it could turn tragic. You have to deal with this right now. Without violence, without any more loss of control. I want you to focus your mind on the most real thing in the world to you—your wife, Janet, who's scared even though she's hiding it really well. You don't want her to be frightened any more, do you?"

"I—I, no, I don't. I hate it when this happens because I can see she's afraid, afraid of me. And she's afraid even more for the girls. Oh God, I love Janet."

"I can see why."

Martin shook his head, as if coming out of a fog. His voice was shaking as he said, "I'm sorry. I understand. I think I'm feeling better now. Those feelings seem to be backing off, I'm more in control again. Really, I'm not just saying that. Please, Agent Savich, sit down."

Martin paused, his hand loosening even more on the beautiful black walnut stock of the shotgun. He said, his voice curiously childlike, wistful, "I've never met an FBI agent before." He turned to his wife, and his voice was easier now, less frightened. "Janet, did you hear what he said?"

"Yes, and it makes a lot of sense to me, Martin. You didn't want to see a doctor before, but now that's what we must do." She glanced at Savich, and quickly again at the shotgun.

"Janet, did you hear what he said to me about my mother?"

She nodded. "Yes. He said your dead mother came to him, then she came to him again in his dreams. She spoke of you, her precious boy. She wants him to help you." She touched her husband's shoulder. "Martin, please put down that shotgun. I never want to see it again, ever. I want to throw it in the river."

He nodded and grinned at her, actually grinned. "It's going to cost us a fortune to repair the wall."

"Forget about the wall. Agent Savich is going to help us, Martin." She held out her hand. "Give me that thing. I know it's beautiful. I know you paid a bundle for it, but it frightens me. It destroys. I'm going to unload it and lay it beside the front door. Okay?"

"Here," was all he said, and handed her the shotgun. She paused a second, because she really didn't want to touch it, but she took it and did exactly what she'd said she would. She walked to the front door, unloaded the shotgun, and laid it on the floor.

Us, Savich thought, Janet had said *us,* not just her husband. And that may have been the right thing to say. When she returned, he said, "Please, both of you, call me Dillon." Odd how so few people called him by his first name, but somehow, in this circumstance, he knew it was right. He smiled at both of them.

"Thank you, Dillon," Janet said. "Sit down,

Martin. I'm going to go talk to the girls. They're scared and I want them to know everything is all right. I'll be right back."

Martin looked undecided, but for only a moment. "All right. I'm sorry, Janet, I didn't mean to—the girls, God, I scared them to death. I'm so sorry."

She hugged him, kissed his cheek. "It will be all right. I'll speak to the girls, make them understand, then I'll be back. I'm going to leave them in the bedroom, it'll make them feel safer, I think. Now, would you like some coffee, Dillon?"

He smiled at her. "Tea would be wonderful."

"A real live tea drinker. Goodness, we're coffee addicts in this house. I'll be right back. You talk to him, Martin. You talk to him, tell him everything, and then listen." She nodded, patted her husband's shoulder, and lightly shoved him down into a big easy chair with a remote control pocket holder on the side, obviously his chair.

Martin eased down into the chair like it was an old friend and stretched out his legs in front of him. As if by habit, he reached into the chair's side pocket, felt the remote control, brought his hand back up. He didn't face

Savich yet, just looked down at the remote for several moments. Then he splayed his palms on his legs, as if trying to relax. He said, still without looking up, "I lost it. I just lost it. Like Janet said, it's happened a couple of other times, but I never had a gun before." He shuddered, drew a deep breath, and at last met Savich's eyes. "I went out last week to a gun show in Baltimore, and I bought the SKB and a big box of shells."

"Why?"

"I don't know really. I felt I had to. Something was pushing me, like it had me by the throat. I felt like something bad was coming."

"Was it a memory, or dream, what?"

"A dream where everything is black, and I'm hiding, where, I don't know, but I do know to my soul I have to stay hidden. I know something horrible is happening, but I can't move."

"Do you think it had something to do with your mother's murder?"

Martin looked toward the hole in the living room wall. "Everything was black. I couldn't see anything, couldn't even tell where I was. I didn't even know my mother was murdered until I was eighteen."

"You didn't know or you didn't remember?"

"I don't really know which. All I knew was that she wasn't there anymore. Sheriff Harms—I remember him really well—he was younger then than I am now—I saw him in my dream when I was eighteen. I actually saw my hand in his. Mine was so small and his was like a giant's, I do remember that, and he was leading me downstairs and my father and a whole lot of people were there, looking very serious and sad. He handed me over to my father. Then I don't remember anything, except that we were living in Boston, though I don't remember moving there, or how or why. Mom was gone, and that was really hard, but my father said it wasn't our fault she died, that he expected me to be a good, strong, young man.

"After a while I didn't really ask about her anymore or think about her, accepted that my father and I were in Boston, and I went to school and made friends like any other kid.

"Like I said, I didn't know anything about how my mother died until I was eighteen. About two months before I graduated high school, I began having nightmares—really violent dreams about people having their throats cut, people being stabbed in the chest—horrible dreams, blood everywhere, and I'd wake up screaming." He paused, shuddering with memory. "I remember my father came in once. He didn't say anything, even when I gasped out the dream I'd had. He stood there, stared at me like I was a freak, like he was afraid of me. Then he left, and he didn't come back when I had the other dreams. I woke up alone and I stayed alone." Martin looked at Savich. "It was around that time I realized something was really wrong."

Martin's father hadn't said anything about this to Sherlock. Hadn't Townsend Barrister realized what the dreams meant? Of course he had.

Savich sat forward on the sofa, his hands clasped between his knees. "Later, did you talk to your father about the dreams?"

Martin shook his head. "I couldn't, and besides, I knew he didn't want to know. I'd look at him and my two little bratty and normal stepsisters at the dinner table, and I'd think, *I could dream tonight that someone is stabbing Cassie through her neck and cutting Tammy's throat.* And I could see their blood, their surprise, the looks on their faces and then they'd be dead.

"It wasn't something I could talk about. They wouldn't understand. My father be-haved as if he'd rather not even have me there, as if he'd rather I didn't even exist. It was like he was afraid of me."

"Then what happened? Did you tell your father anything?"

"Yes, I asked him one day how my mother died."

"Out of the blue? For the first time since she was murdered in 1973, you thought to ask him?"

Martin nodded slowly. "Yeah. It came to me, probably because of my dreams, I'm not sure. But it came out. Suddenly I had to know."

"What did your father say?"

"He told me there'd been a terrible acci-dent on the day of my sixth birthday. My mother had slipped and fallen on a kitchen knife, and she'd died. And he'd brought me here to Boston, so we could both recover, start over again. He called her death an ac-cident. Can you believe that?"

"I gather you didn't believe him?"

"No, I could see in his eyes he was keeping something back. I realize now he didn't want my half-sisters or my stepmother, Jenny, to find out, and be afraid, maybe be afraid of him.

"So I went off to search on my own. I looked up the Barristers in old newspaper files. Remember, this was before the Internet, back in 1984. But it was enough to point me back. I remembered a road sign clear as day—Blessed Creek. I knew it was a little hick town in the Poconos, in northeastern Pennsylvania. I drove out there. It didn't take me long looking through archives from that time to learn that she'd been murdered, that my father had taken me away to Boston right after the funeral."

"Is that why you disappeared after your high school graduation? Did you think your father had something to do with it?"

Martin wouldn't meet his eyes.

"Listen to me, Martin. You were only six years old when she was killed. Kids have an amazing ability to block things out that could harm them. And that's what you did. You saved yourself by repressing everything that happened until you were older, more ready to face up to what happened."

"I know, I know." He was twisting his hands together, and Savich knew that for the moment, they'd accomplished enough.

"Hey, don't worry about it, Martin. Show me how that remote works. It looks pretty fancy."

CHAPTER
30

Five minutes later, Janet Thornton came into the living room to see her husband showing the FBI agent how to work a remote that she hadn't yet figured out. She was carrying a colorful wooden tray, coffee, tea, and a small plate of cookies on top of it. She poured Savich some tea, arched a questioning eyebrow as she handed it to him.

"Straight is fine. Thank you."

The tea was delicious. He hadn't realized how cold he'd been. This was so mundane, so normal, sitting here learning about a remote, drinking tea, and knowing he'd find out soon enough why Martin had left the day after he'd graduated high school. For now, drinking tea was just fine. He drank, felt the warmth all the way to his belly, and thanked God he was still alive. "My wife, who's also an FBI agent, is outside with the police and your neighbors. I'd like to call her, tell her that everything's okay. Also, I don't want the cops to worry, maybe fire something in here. Okay by you, Martin?"

Martin drank his coffee, said nothing, only nodded.

"That's a very good idea," Janet said as she sat herself on the other end of the sofa, as close to her husband as she could get without climbing into his lap.

Sherlock answered before the second note sounded in *Bolero.*

"Sherlock, it's me. Martin is disarmed, we're talking, everything's under control. He's calm and rational, telling me what's happened to him. Please tell Chief Gerber and Joe Gaines, the hostage negotiator, they can stand down, at least put away their weapons. There's no reason for anyone to get hurt now."

He heard her speaking, then she was back on the cell. "Chief Gerber won't go for it. You need to tell him yourself, Dillon."

Savich did, slowly, easily, making certain

Chief Gerber knew he wasn't under any duress.

"Yes, I'm sure of it. In fact, I'm drinking an excellent cup of tea at this very moment. There's a plate of chocolate chip cookies in front of me. Janet Thornton is fine, as are the girls. I think it would be best if you dispersed the neighbors, told them that everything is all right. I don't want them looking at Martin like he's some sort of freak who will flip out when he walks out of here."

There was a long pause, then Chief Gerber said, "I'll do that, Agent Savich. Your wife said that if I don't believe you I might as well hang it up and sail to Fiji. Not a bad idea, really. But you've got to know that none of my people are leaving here until I see Martin Thornton in custody and everyone safely out of that house."

"Believe me, Chief Gerber, I appreciate that. Thank you for your cooperation. That will take some more time. Oh yes, would you please tell my wife it will be a little while longer?" He shut off the cell and slipped it back into his jacket pocket.

"You don't pull any punches, do you?" Janet Thornton said, a dark eyebrow arched up a good inch.

"No reason to. Both of you know exactly what the score is, what's going on outside. Chief Gerber is a good man. He'll deal with things. As for your neighbors, I'm thinking you guys should move away from here. People don't forget the sound of a shotgun, or police cars all over the neighborhood, not when they've got kids around."

"No, you don't pull any punches," Martin said. "Yes, we'll move. I hadn't thought that far ahead yet."

"Of course not," Savich said. "Do you feel like getting back to it, Martin?"

"Yes."

"Tell me why you disappeared right after you graduated, without saying a word to your father."

"When he looked me right in the eye and told me that my mother's death was an accident, something died inside. I simply couldn't accept who he was or what he was. I remember very clearly thinking my old man had lied to me, flat-out lied, not because of me, mind you, but because of his wife, Jenny, my stepmother, and their two daughters. I realized I had nothing to do with his new life. If he could, I think he would have swept me under the carpet or tossed me out with the trash."

"My wife, Agent Sherlock, said that isn't true at all. When she spoke to your father, he was frantic to know where you were."

Martin's clear brown eyes, very intelligent eyes, had no shadows or madness in them now, just disbelief. "It may have suited the moment. I really don't believe him."

Savich nodded. "You know him better than we. But tell me why you erased yourself."

"Erased myself," Martin repeated slowly, as if tasting the words. "Yes, I suppose I did that. I got a whole new identity. It's not hard to do if you live in Boston, and are willing to take some chances. I approached people on the street—fences, drug addicts—until I found the people who were willing to sell me an identity. I bought my name—Martin Thornton—got a social security number, a driver's license, everything I needed, and then I hitchhiked out of Boston, didn't tell a single person where I was going. Actually, I didn't know myself."

"Where did you go?"

"I went out to Seattle at first, got a job pumping gas, started working my way through school. The dreams stopped then. It seemed that when I found out about my mother's murder, I didn't need to dream about it anymore. The funny thing is, I wanted to remember my mother, I wanted to know what she was like. I wanted to know who murdered her and why. But the dreams never told me that." He stopped suddenly, stuck out his hand for Janet to take, and said, "I dated. I slept with my first girlfriend when I was nineteen. I felt like a man. I felt normal."

"You are normal," Janet said, and there was absolute conviction in her voice. "What happened to you, Martin—your mother's murder, being uprooted, not having your father tell you the truth—you dealt amazingly well with all of it. If I'd started having those dreams, I would have ended up in Boston Harbor or slitting my wrists. You didn't do either of those things. You survived.

"I don't blame you for leaving your father, for chucking all of it. The only thing is, I wish you had told me. We've been married eleven years, and you never told me. What Agent Savich said about the truth—he's right, only the truth will do. I wish you'd told me so I could have helped."

"I couldn't," he said, looking directly into

her eyes. "I never wanted to think about him again. I never wanted it to touch our lives. I didn't want it to hurt you, or us."

"Well, aren't you a bloody fool!?"

He actually grinned, squeezed his wife's hand. Savich held very still, knowing he was invisible to them in this moment.

A few moments later he brought them back.

"Martin, the first episode, when was that?"

Janet Thornton sucked in her breath. "What a horrible word."

Savich shrugged. "But I think it fits, more or less, don't you?"

"Yes," Martin said. "Now I can say that. Six months ago, it just hit me like a hammer. All sorts of wild things careened through my head. I thought I was going crazy. It lasted only a couple of hours, but I scared the hell out of Janet. She talked me down, thank God. The girls weren't here that time or the second time either. That was about two months ago, and that one lasted longer."

"You were here, at home?"

"Yes, Janet and I were having dinner—hot dogs and baked beans, potato chips—all my favorites. It was the day after my birthday. Janet thought we should have our own private celebration, without the girls. They were at a sleepover at a friend's house. I suddenly remembered this was exactly what I always loved to eat when I was little. I started crying. Janet held me, didn't stop talking to me, and finally, after a while, everything began to fade."

Savich looked thoughtful. "The day after your birthday. You nearly remembered something."

"You think so?"

"Maybe. Then what, Martin?"

"I—I was going to go to a doctor, really I was, to a shrink, but I didn't know anyone and I was, well, I was ashamed. No, I was afraid of what a shrink would say, afraid I'd end up in a padded cell and my life would be over, all except for those horrible dreams. Believe me, Janet's been on my case, but— I didn't go, just didn't."

"Doesn't matter now. If it's okay with you, Martin, I'm getting rid of that shotgun. I want you to promise me you'll never as long as you live have another gun in your home."

Martin looked over to where Janet had laid the shotgun on the floor beside the front door.

"All right. Yes, I promise, Dillon." He rose, but Savich held out his hand.

"Let me tell Chief Gerber that I'll be handing out the shotgun so they don't get nervous."

When Savich walked back into the living room a few minutes later, he said, "All done. Everything's fine now. We've got a lot of relieved people out there. Now, you guys got a good babysitter?"

They both stared at him. Janet nodded. "Well, yes, my mom. She lives in Rockville. She loves having the girls. When Martin had the second breakdown, I made an excuse and they stayed with her for three days."

"Good. Both of you are coming with me now, back to Washington. We'll drop the girls off at your mom's. You'll be staying tonight at the Jefferson Dormitory at Quantico. You'll be safe there, Martin. If something pops again in your brain, there'll be people there to control things.

"Where do you work, Martin?"

"I work in the IT section at the Giant corporate office."

"Really? I have some interest in computers myself. Maybe we can talk about that later.

Anyway, we can call your boss and get you some leave.

"After what's happened here, I'll have to take you into my own custody. We'll call it a temporary commitment. That should keep Chief Gerber from filing any charges.

"Tomorrow morning, you're going to meet Dr. Emanuel Hicks. I'd like him to try to hypnotize you, see if we can learn anything more about what happened to you when you were six years old. And he'll be recommending a psychiatrist to you who'll know all the facts. Sound okay?"

"It sounds like a miracle," Janet said.

Martin searched Savich's face, and slowly nodded. "Yes, it sounds okay to me, too."

Janet looked at Savich, held his eyes, and said simply, "Thank you so much for coming into our lives, Dillon. I'll go get us and the girls packed and call my mom."

Savich said, "Maybe the one to thank is Samantha Barrister. Yeah, I know how strange it all sounds, and maybe I dreamed some of it. But I'll tell you guys, she was as real to me as it gets. I'll tell you more about it after we get to Quantico.

"Right now, I'm going to bring in my wife—she's the one who found you, Martin—and

Detective Raven and Ms. Markham. They'll help get us on the road. The thing is, I'm heading up the investigation of Justice Stewart Califano's murder, and I've got to get back to Washington."

They both stared at him. Janet walked over to him and hugged him. "Bring on your wife. I can't wait to meet her."

CHAPTER
31

Georgetown
Washington, D.C.
Saturday night

It happened so fast that Sean, playing with Legos on the floor, didn't have time to react. Fleurette was sitting on the sofa, laughing at something Callie had said, when suddenly, one of the front windows shattered and a bullet slammed into the wall not six inches above Fleurette's head.

Savich was just coming through the kitchen door, carrying tea and coffee on a tray. "Everyone down! Sherlock, get Sean!" He dropped the tray, ran to Fleurette, and dragged her off the sofa. He fell on top of her, drawing his gun at the same time. He looked toward the shattered glass in the front window. Close, too close. He said, "Nobody move. Sherlock, you've got Sean. Ben, yeah, kill the lights, then pull all the drapes, call 911."

"Got it."

"Callie, get your nose pressed into the floor."

Callie was already down, in front of the sofa, not moving.

Sherlock had Sean beneath her. He was howling under her, but she didn't let him up, kept pressing him into the carpet, covering all of him. Ben crawled to the switch, went up on his knees, and punched off both light switches. There was still light arrowing in from the kitchen. He was crawling to the front windows to pull the heavy drapes when another shot rang out, shattering what was left of the front glass window, hitting low, then another and another.

Finally it was silent, except for the breathing in the living room. Savich said, "Everyone okay?"

Sean's yell was muffled from beneath his mother, "Daddy!"

"Sean is, but he sounds pissed," Ben said, and punched 911. They heard him give fast, terse instructions.

"They'll be here soon. Savich?"

"I'm dialing my boss right now." Jimmy Maitland answered on the first ring. Then another shot burst into the living room, ripping the back out of one of Savich's favorite chairs. "I heard that," Jimmy Maitland said. "What the hell is going on, Savich?"

"Günter's paying us a house call," Savich said.

"This guy crazy or what?"

"Bet on it," Savich said. "Hurry."

"Half the city will be there in a minute. Keep everyone safe."

Savich punched off his phone, and wrapped his arm around Fleurette's head again. "Okay, now, everyone stay as close to the floor as possible. Slow and easy, elbow your way out of the living room to the staircase. The kitchen light doesn't reach there. There aren't any windows near the staircase. It's the safest place in the house." He lifted most his weight off Fleurette. "You okay?"

"Yeah."

But she didn't sound okay. "I'm going to stay over you. Let's shimmy on our elbows together now. I'm right with you. Sherlock, you okay with Sean? You need any help?"

"Nope, got him." She nearly had to yell to be heard over Sean's howls. "We're okay. I'm dragging him beneath me. We're right behind you."

Ben said, "You guys stay down. Savich, Sherlock, you've got your guns. Callie, you sucking the floor?"

"I'm sucking," she said from outside the living room. "It won't need vacuuming for a week. I'm nearly to the staircase."

Another shot rang out, this one shattering a lamp next to a big sofa. Then another, blasting obliquely through a side window, going wild.

Ben said. "Okay, everyone stay down. I'm going out to see if I can find Günter. See if he'd like to dance with me."

"No!" Callie jumped to her feet and landed against him, knocking him back against the wall. She grabbed his shirt. "You're not going anywhere. Are you crazy? We're going to wait for help." She actually pulled him tight against her, hanging on for dear life. "Do you want to get yourself killed?"

"For God's sake, Callie, I'm a cop." He grabbed her hands, trying to pull her off him, but she held on tight. "Stop trying to strangle me. Listen to me, it's what I do for a living—serve and protect. Now get back down on the floor and crawl over to that staircase."

Her fingers dug into his shirt. "If you want to be a damned hero, I'm coming with you."

Sherlock gave Sean to her husband, and simply tackled Callie, took her down. Callie didn't stand a chance, black belt in karate or no, and now she was helpless, couldn't move. "I can't believe you're actually doing this to me," she gasped, her face in the carpet. "You really shouldn't be able to."

"I learned from the best. Be quiet, Callie, and don't move or I'll hurt you. Ben, go, and be careful. As soon as I get Callie to listen to me, I'll let her up. Dillon, you got Sean? Fleurette's down?"

"Yeah, we're fine. You keep Callie's face in the floor."

"Why did he try to kill me?" Fleurette whispered, coming up on her knees, clutching Savich, her breath hot against his neck, Sean trapped and crying between them. "I don't know anything, but he fired into your house. To kill me. Why? I really don't know anything that could harm him. Why would he come after me?"

"He obviously believes you do know something," Sherlock said over Sean's yells, "and it doesn't look like he's going to stop. Now, Callie, you got it together, or do you need to get more splinters in your face? Sean's crying, in case you hadn't noticed, and it really pisses me off that I'm not comforting him right now."

"I'm okay," Callie said, "or very nearly. I'm sorry. Ben's already out the door, the idiot. I swear I won't go after him. Go get Sean, Sherlock."

"Fleurette and I have him," Savich said. "Get yourself together, Callie. Don't make me regret bringing you into this investigation."

Callie drew a deep breath, hiccuped, and said, "I'm sorry, it's just that Ben—"

"I know. But it's his job. Let it go. Get yourself together."

"Okay, okay, I'm trying but, he's such a macho moron, saying he's going to go out there and dance with that monster."

"That particular macho moron is an excellent cop," Sherlock said.

"That was just a touch of cop humor," Savich said.

"He knows what he's doing. Now, Callie, we're going to glide slowly across the floor to sit next to Dillon and Fleurette. I'm going to hug Sean. We're going to wait for the cavalry. You just stay down, you got that? Ready?"

They were both breathing hard by the time they could lean against the staircase. Sherlock pulled Sean from between Fleurette and Dillon, and pressed his small face against her shoulder. "It's okay now, champ," she whispered against his wet cheek, "don't worry, it's okay. Mommy's right here. It was just a loud noise. You can yell louder than that."

Not even a minute later sirens sounded loud, at least a half dozen of them. When the front door opened, both Sherlock and Savich had their guns aimed at it. Ben called out before he showed his face, "Jimmy Maitland is here along with lots of my guys and FBI agents. They're already spreading out, searching for Günter, talking to every neighbor who'll answer the door. You guys okay?"

"Yeah, we're fine," Sherlock said.

Ben made his way over to one of the living room side windows, pulled the drapes tight. Once the room was shrouded, Ben turned on the light switches. Everyone blinked. Savich said, "All of you, stay away from the windows. No telling what that maniac might try. Thing is, after that first shot, he knew he was shooting blind, knew we wouldn't just stand in the middle of the living room. So why did he keep firing?"

"He thought he might get lucky," Ben said.

"But the chance he'd hit Fleurette?"

Sherlock said, "You know, I don't think he cared. I think he wanted to terrify us, let us know he was close. I don't know about the rest of you, but it worked for me."

Callie came up on her hands and knees, and stared at Ben. Then she was on her feet, running at him. She grabbed him close and held on, her face buried in his shoulder. "I should kill you, you macho asshole, running out there like that and this madman with a gun, shooting like crazy. He's a good shot, and he would be really happy to see you dead, even if you aren't Fleurette. Dillon is right, he didn't care who he hit, and here you were making that lame joke about dancing with him—if that's an example of cop humor, you need a new writer."

He holstered his gun in his belt, put his arms around her and hugged her. "Well, he wasn't all that good a shot this time, was he? And he tried six times. If you start crying, I'm going to throw you out the front door."

"I'm not crying, you jerk."

Ben grinned down at her. "Good. I'm all right. He's long gone. One thing Günter isn't, is stupid. He knew cops would swarm here within minutes after he fired those shots. He had to know too that it would be a miracle if he got to Fleurette after the first miss. Maybe they'll find his car, or one of the people who lives a couple of blocks over saw him running to his car, got the make. Maybe someone actually got a look at him."

Sherlock said, looking around the shattered living room and at each of them in turn, "Günter took his shot, missed, but all of you know he'll be back. He wants Fleurette dead and he's not going to stop until it's done or we get him first."

Savich said, "We were lucky your parents weren't here, Fleurette."

Fleurette, still plastered against him, shuddered. "If they'd still been here, he might have shot one of them. I can't stand this. I don't understand why he's doing this. I don't know anything!"

Sean began humming, the sound very loud in the entrance hall. It made everyone smile, which was a good thing. Sherlock was standing to the side, close to the staircase, rocking him from one leg to the other. She said, between kisses on Sean's cheek, "We're all okay, but this was way too close. I'm thinking that to keep you completely safe, Fleurette, we need to take you to Quantico. No one could get near you there. Security could catch a runaway flea there. Little sucker could end up on the firing range."

Fleurette looked shell-shocked, but she straightened, her eyes blinking as if waking from a dream. She looked toward Sherlock. "That was funny. You guys are so amazing, so—what if he'd hit Sean? I couldn't take that. It would have been my fault."

Sherlock's voice was calm. "You know something, Fleurette? You're right about one thing. I'm thinking about our boy too. He'll be safer with you out at Quantico. This is the second time violence has come into our home. If it were just Dillon and me, that would be different, but Sean's the important one, and we're supposed to protect him. Now, no more angst from any of you. It's done. I've got to clean up that coffee before it stains the floor, and then you're going to Quantico, Fleurette. You can call your parents from there. They can visit you there for as long as they're in town."

Savich rose, took Sean from Sherlock, and began rocking him in exactly the same way she had, one large hand going up and down on his son's back. "I really wish we didn't have to tell your parents about this, Fleurette."

"No choice, Dillon," Callie said. "It was on the police radio, and soon it will be all over the news. I don't see any choice. The media will descend any moment. And they'll be all over us if we're still here."

Sherlock muttered under her breath at the coffee and tea spreading over the floor. She walked into the kitchen to get paper towels to clean it up. "Callie's right, Dillon," she said as she came back into the living room. "This is Georgetown. If the chef at Pamplona's cuts his thumb chopping a carrot, it's front page in the *Post*. Worse, this is an FBI agent's house, who also happens to be the lead investigator on Justice Califano and Danny O'Malley and Eliza—" Her voice caught in her throat and she dropped to her knees and viciously wiped up the coffee and tea, in wide, heavy strokes, her pain palpable to Savich. Savich handed Sean to Ben, who nestled him into the crook of his arm, gathered up some more paper towels and helped her.

Fleurette and Callie stood silent, watching Ben rock Sean, and Savich and Sherlock clean up the spreading spill. The creamer ran into the seam where the wide oak planks met. "It's a beautiful oak floor," Fleurette said, and grabbed some paper towels and went after the creamer. "My mom said it was the prettiest floor she'd ever seen and she wondered how you kept it so nice what with Sean running all over the place. Will it stain?"

"No, it'll be fine," Sherlock said, took a final swipe and rose to her feet. "Callie, we don't need you down here on your knees too. Thank you, Fleurette. There, all done. Hey, Ben, you're a natural. Sean's nearly out."

Ben paused in his rocking and looked at her. Sherlock wanted to laugh, the expression on his face was so priceless. Then he said slowly, "Yeah, I guess I am a natural. Thing is, I'd be a natural too with a red Porsche."

Callie laughed, got up, and walked to him. She punched him in the arm. "You are such a guy." Then she cocked her head to one side as she looked at Sean, asleep in his arms. "Yeah, I guess you are a natural."

A moment later there was pounding on the door. "Let's get it over with," Savich said and went to let in Jimmy Maitland and a half dozen FBI agents and Metro cops.

CHAPTER
32

Jefferson Dormitory
Quantico
Sunday morning

Dr. Hicks was flummoxed, and Savich knew why. Martin Thornton wasn't going under. Something inside him was fighting the loss of control. Martin wasn't going anywhere.

Savich wondered if this was Dr. Hicks's first failure. It was just the three of them in Dr. Hicks's small office; Janet was in the Quantico gym, working out with some students, who'd been assigned to keep an eye on her.

Dr. Hicks tried again. "Martin, listen to me

carefully. I want you to relax, I want you to let yourself go. You're safe, you do understand that, don't you?"

"Yes, of course."

"No one's going to hurt you. I know you want to remember. I know you want to know the truth about what happened on your sixth birthday. I'm here to help you do it, but you have to help me, you have to let go. Now, let's try again. Concentrate on this bright silver dollar, keep your eyes on it, watch it swing back and forth and try to focus that brain of yours."

Martin stared at the blur of silver as it swung back and forth several dozen times, until his eyes nearly glazed over. He finally shook his head, rubbed his temples with his fingertips. "I'm sorry, Dr. Hicks. Nothing's happening and believe me, you're right, I want it to. I want to remember. I want to know what happened to my mother that day. You know what else? I want to remember what she looked like, what she smelled like. I know she wore a perfume like flowers, but I can't smell it anymore. I'm beginning to believe I do know what happened that day. I want to see the man who killed my mom."

"I agree you might have seen your mother

murdered," Savich said. "Martin, do you remember hiding in the attic? Martin—Austin.
Which do you prefer?"

"I'm Martin Thornton now, Dillon, have
been for more years than I was Austin."

"All right, then, Martin. I've described the
house to you, described the attic, described
your mother. Do you remember the attic?
Can you see it in your mind at all? Do you remember ever being in an attic?"

"No, I don't. There's nothing there."

Dr. Hicks put the watch away, sat back in
his leather chair, and crossed his hands over
his skinny belly. "I'm thinking that when
Agent Savich is through with this current
case, you need to go back to Blessed Creek,
see the house where you spent the first six
years of your life. You need to climb up that
ladder into the attic, go into the bathroom
where they found your mom. I'm thinking
that might break that dam in your memory,
help everything flood back."

Martin's eyes lit up. "I could go back now,
with Janet."

"No way are you going anywhere, Martin,"
Savich said, his voice sharp. "You're going to
promise me that you'll stay right here.
Promise me."

"But—"

"Promise me."

"All right, I promise."

"I don't want you going anywhere. You're in a safe place, and right now, that's exactly what you need—to feel safe. You need to know that if something happens in your brain, you'll have help to deal with it. Forget the frustration of not remembering. It will all come back when it's ready to. Now, Dr. Hicks has the name of an excellent psychiatrist, and you'll want to tell him or her everything you know, everything you've felt, in great detail. Who do you have in mind, Dr. Hicks?"

"Dr. Lynette Foster. She works regularly with the FBI. She's very good with memory issues, cases of trauma. You can trust her, Martin."

Slowly, Martin Thornton nodded.

Savich said, "I've already spoken to Janet. Believe me, she's not worried about your girls or anyone but you. You're here for the near future. Hey, the food in The Boardroom is pretty good, and you have the PX with plenty of FBI souvenirs to buy, pretty cool stuff you can give for presents. Best of all, you can spend some time with Janet. You're staying, Martin, until I'm through with this case."

Dr. Hicks smiled when Martin nodded.

"Excellent. Now, Janet's in the gym, getting started on losing fifteen pounds she said, and it's been over an hour. Dr. Hicks will show you the gym, then you and Janet can have lunch, wander the grounds if you like.

"I'm going to head out to the Hoover Building. By the way, can you do any of your work remotely if you have access to a computer?"

"Yeah, sure. I spend most of my time on the computer."

When Savich left, he saw Martin standing tall, his shoulders no longer slumped. He heard him say to Dr. Hicks, "I've got lots of work to do. You said this Boardroom place has some good food?"

Savich would swear as he walked down the hall of the Jefferson Dormitory that he heard Martin Thornton whistling.

FBI Headquarters
Washington, D.C.
Early Sunday afternoon

Savich looked out over the thirty-plus agents and cops in the conference room. "Last night, as most of you already know,

Günter fired six shots into my living room, his primary target Fleurette. His performance last night shows he's becoming increasingly less controlled, more desperate, but given what he did in the middle of Georgetown, I certainly can't say he's any less daring. So long as he continues, our chances of finding him improve. So far the only physical evidence we have are ballistics from the recovered bullets—probably a plain old thirty-eight. We've located Günter's approximate range and position, but apart from a few broken branches, some partial footprints in the snow, he left nothing behind.

"But we may have a lead. Two Metro policemen found a witness, an older man who was walking his dog two blocks over. They're not convinced he's reliable, but let me report what Mr. Avery told them. He said he saw a man running toward a car. He thinks it was a light gray, or maybe white, late-model Toyota. Said the guy was fast, ran easily, was tall and well-built. He was wearing a Burberry coat, black gloves on his hands.

"Now the thing is, the two policemen had major doubts about Mr. Avery's mental acuity. They thought he might be embellishing, even creating, all these excellent details to impress them. Evidently Mr. Avery also told him that the car fishtailed as it drove away, headed east. He thinks it was a Virginia plate, the first two letters RT or BT. There's no match for that plate to a late model Toyota, so we're checking for recently stolen Toyotas and reports of stolen plates with those letters. Mr. Avery did not hear any shots.

"As I said, the police weren't sure we could believe much of anything he said, that he wandered all over the lot—even asked his dog's opinion—seemed a little too, well, old and odd is how they put it. Oh yeah, the police officers said when he asked his dog's opinion, the little sucker actually barked.

"It's clear we have no unified, specific theory for these latest crimes, the murder of Eliza Vickers and the attempted murder of Elaine LaFleurette last night. In Danny O'Malley's case, there are strong indications he made contact with the perpetrators. For the two women, the connection to Justice Califano is of course clear, but the killer's specific motives are not."

He paused, looking out over the group. "All right, I want every idea, every speculation you've come up with on why Eliza Vickers was murdered, and why Fleurette was shot at. Ollie, you're nearly busting out of your vest, so you lead off."

Ollie Hamish, Savich's second-in-command in the Criminal Apprehension Unit, cleared his throat. "Okay," Ollie said, "let's start with Eliza Vickers." He sat forward, his hands clasped in front of him on the conference table. "Ben told us about last Friday when he and Callie were in Justice Califano's office looking for Fleurette, but only Eliza was there, cleaning up things. He said that when he asked her if there was anything he could do, she hesitated. I can't get that out of my mind." He paused a moment, focusing his thoughts. "She knew something. Maybe she didn't realize how important it was, but you know, that's not very likely. What was it? Was she involved in Justice Califano's murder? Did she turn on him because he wasn't about to leave his wife for her?" Ollie shot an apologetic look at Callie. "Rage can do terrible things to people, we've all seen it. Eliza Vickers could have found out who Günter was, maybe she'd dated him or met him some other way and hired him or persuaded him to murder Justice Califano—"

Sherlock shot to her feet. She bent over the table, her hands flat on the piles of paper on front of her. "No, that can't be right, Ollie. Eliza was solid. Listen to me, it's true I only met Eliza Vickers twice, then spoke to her briefly at Justice Califano's funeral, but I felt I knew her in all the important ways. I even admired her. Eliza couldn't have had Justice Califano killed, she was devoted to him, loved and respected him as both a man and as a Justice. Did she have him killed out of jealousy? No way. She knew there was no future for them. That isn't it, Ollie. It's got to be something else.

"Say you did believe she was responsible, then the logical follow-up would be that Günter then killed her because she was cracking under the pressure. It doesn't fly. No, this hesitation Ben and Callie saw, it was about something else entirely."

"Okay, Sherlock, if it wasn't about this, then what do you think she hesitated about?"

Dillon's calm voice always cooled her down. She said, the emotional edge gone from her voice, "Maybe she wanted to say something about Danny O'Malley, or she was worried about Fleurette, thinking maybe Fleurette could be a target too."

Agent Foley said, "All right, let's go with

that. So if Eliza was thinking about Danny O'Malley or worrying about Fleurette, then why wouldn't she say something to Detective Raven? Why wouldn't she warn him that Fleurette might be in danger, and why would she think that? Why?"

Ben said, "The thing is, the place was a madhouse. She was the only one there. The phone rang, and she waved us out. That's what happened. What was she thinking?" Ben shrugged, then turned to Callie. "You got any thoughts on this? You were there, you saw exactly what I saw."

Callie said, "Yes, she hesitated. I saw it. Wondered about it, but just for a moment. Unfortunately, I was focused on finding Fleurette, we both were."

Ben said, "I'm thinking that maybe Eliza wondered if Fleurette knew something, but then again, why wouldn't she tell us?" Ben saw that Sherlock was ready to break in, gave her a half-smile, and added, "No, I don't think Eliza herself knew anything about Justice Califano's murder. And I don't think she'd want Justice Califano dead, for any reason. I think Eliza could have walked in and found Justice Califano making out with Sonya McGivens or Fleurette or Tai Curtis on his big mahogany desk, and still not have re-acted with violence. Like Sherlock said, she was too together and on-track with herself. She was too accepting of who and what Justice Califano was."

Ollie Hamish said, "All right, I'm hearing you guys. So her hesitation has got to mean that she found out something, or heard something, but she wasn't quite sure what it meant, maybe didn't want to say anything to Ben until she was sure, one way or the other—"

Ben said, "So whatever she heard was from someone she trusted or liked or simply couldn't conceive of having anything to do with Justice Califano's murder."

Jimmy Maitland spoke for the first time. "Let's say Eliza Vickers did find out something. In any case, it was the real deal. It got her murdered. And that means, people, that we're back to tracing her movements. We need to know where she went, who she saw, or talked to, everything, since Justice Califano's murder. And as far back as we can. Jagger, you and Brewer put your teams on it."

Savich said, "We already checked her phone records, no go there. Maybe we'll get lucky and she actually visited whoever it was. Maybe she asked too many questions, made this person nervous, and that signed her death warrant."

Jimmy Maitland said, "The person knew she wasn't going to let it go, knew she was smart, knew she'd gnaw on it until she figured it out, so the person called Günter. Like you said, Savich, it signed her death warrant."

Frank Halley said, "But what did she hear? And where was she? In Justice Califano's office? Or maybe someone called her, warned her, but she wouldn't believe it. Maybe there's someone else here, someone else in the Supreme Court Building, another law clerk."

Savich nodded. "Good. Keep going."

Another FBI agent said, "But why wouldn't this other law clerk, or whoever it was, tell us? We've been all over them, at least three, four interviews of everyone who works there. And why Fleurette?"

Savich said, "Okay, we've got some good solid ideas on Eliza, but still nothing definitive. Why Fleurette? I'm thinking now the reason Günter wants Fleurette dead is pretty straightforward—he saw her speaking with

Danny O'Malley last Friday, and he believed Danny was confiding in her."

Callie said, "She walked with him for a block or so when they left the Supreme Court to go to lunch."

"And Günter saw them together," Savich said. "Okay, we need to get back to the law clerks again just in case one of them knows more than they've told us. Also, we need to go back to my neighborhood today to canvass a wider radius. When you have your assignments, we'll head out again."

When the conference room cleared, Savich approached Mr. Maitland and Director Mueller. "Thank you for staying. I'd like your permission to let the world know that Elaine LaFleurette isn't at our house any longer. Two reasons: first, for Sean's safety, and second"—Savich searched the faces—"I think it's time we became proactive. We may be able to flush Günter out. We can select a volunteer to impersonate Fleurette, make her visible on the grounds at Quantico. Most assassins would never risk a kill at Quantico, but Günter?"

Ben said, "For Günter, it would be the ultimate high for him. Trying to kill Fleurette on the grounds of the safest compound in the world? I don't think he could pass that up."

"He couldn't," Savich said. "He'd have to use a rifle. Let's say he's got only average skill as a sniper. With a good sniper rifle, say a gas-operated semiautomatic, he could hit his target at about twenty-four hundred feet. If he's an expert, that goes up to three thousand feet. That's a very long distance, well off the grounds.

"The new sniper rifles are even more accurate than those we used five years ago. For example, the Yugoslavian M-76 has a longer, heavier barrel and a modified stock that's more ergonomic. It's chambered in a much better long-range caliber than the calibers of the rifles it's derived from. I'd wager he'd use one as good as that. Could he hit a person at three thousand feet? I wouldn't want to bet against it."

Director Mueller said slowly, "We'd be putting agents' lives at risk. And to have agents and SWAT teams trying to cover that huge area twenty-four/seven, the necessary manpower boggles the mind. There's lots of egress, roads and trails both. We have to assume Günter is an expert. Have you mapped out the terrain where he'd have his best shot, Savich?"

Savich nodded. "Yes, we have. Unfortunately there's more than just one."

Director Mueller looked toward Jimmy Maitland, who nodded. "It's a big risk, Jimmy. But I'd bet on our snipers over just about anyone. Can we have enough of our guys out there to keep a reasonable guard over our agents?"

"We can try," Jimmy Maitland said. "I can get the Washington, D.C., SWAT team and the Hostage Rescue Team at Quantico. Also, we can enlist SWAT teams from all the local cop shops. No doubt everyone wants to bring this asshole down. But there's no way to keep it secret—we can't expect to hide that many men from view. Günter will know it's a trap. I don't think there's anything we can do about that."

Savich grinned at them. "We're not even going to worry about it. I want him to find out. Don't you see? Günter will see it as a direct challenge. He'll want to spend time out at Quantico finding the firing spot he wants, locating the positions of our snipers, figuring out how to get away. Oh yes, I'm counting on Günter to thumb his nose at us.

"Okay, the first step is to let Günter know exactly where Fleurette will be. Callie, you want to be a turncoat and reveal Fleurette's hideout to the *Post*?"

Callie laughed. "My editor will wet himself. It'll be in the evening paper." She punched Ben in the arm. "Hey, you think this might mean a Pulitzer?"

"Nah, this'll probably just save your job," Ben said.

They all laughed. Director Mueller stood up. He looked at all of them in turn. "I wish us all luck with this."

When the conference room door closed behind the director, Savich said, "Okay, we've got a plan. We're finally acting, not just reacting."

"Let's get it done, boyos," said Jimmy Maitland.

CHAPTER 33

Quantico
Late Monday afternoon

Some dead leaves moved, three fingers gave a little wave. Dave Dempsey heard Joe Boyle's low-pitched voice. "Hey, did you tell your wife you might tangle with Günter?"

Dave whispered back, "I wanted to, but she isn't speaking to me right now, said I was a pig."

A low chuckle. "Yeah, so what else is new? Hey, do you think this Günter character will really show?"

Dave said, "Agent Savich told us he's betting on it. Says this guy loves to take the big risks, and what bigger risk could he take than coming to Quantico to kill Elaine LaFleurette? He said Günter will know it's a trap and he won't care. It'll make him even more determined to come out and play with us. What do you think, Joe?"

"I'm not as sure as Savich is. I mean, this Günter guy's survived a lot of years, and that's gotta mean that he isn't stupid."

Dave whispered, "On the other hand, he went right to Savich's house in Georgetown and shot it up—is that nuts or what? And he got away. Sounds like he's got bigger guavas than my mother-in-law."

Joe said, "Take a look around. There are lots of low hills, lots of trees and bushes, true, but everything's bare now. That makes it really tough for him."

"But there are still some places to hide. Look at us, nearly thirty of us and we've managed it."

Joe said, "Okay, agreed, but Quantico itself is safer than the fricking Mint. How can this goon imagine he'd actually get in here, no matter how crazy he is?" He was silent a moment. "I'll bet he'll leave us lying out here for a week, just laugh and watch us. I wonder how long Giffey Talbot is going to wander

around outside the Jefferson Dormitory before Savich finally calls this off.

"I was thinking about Giffey—quite a thing,
offering yourself up as bait."

Dave shifted a bit more underneath a bush
that barely covered him, and swept his eyes
westward. "Hey, we're bait too, we're just
armed with sniper rifles. Savich said he could
be an expert sniper, who the hell knows?"

Joe was listening to Dave shifting in the
bushes when he heard some branches
snapping off to the side. "Did you hear that,
Dave? Hey, look at three o'clock. I saw
something moving. All of our people are supposed to stay down, but I saw something
move. Just beyond those pine trees."

Dave Dempsey squinted in the watery sun-
light toward the hillock, didn't see anything.
"Who do we have over there?"

"Luther Lindsay."

"I don't see anything, but call him now,
Joe. This isn't the time for second-guess-
ing."

Dave heard Joe whisper urgently into his
radio, "Luther, movement in your area. What
have you got over there? Luther? Dammit,
talk to me. Luther!"

Both Dave and Joe could hear their own

breathing. Luther was a fifteen-year man, married with two teenage girls, solid as a rock, and he could hear footsteps on a carpet. Günter couldn't have gotten to Luther.

Joe repeated, "Luther? Dammit, talk to me, Luther."

Dave Dempsey was on his own walkie-talkie, calling command. "Captain Ramsey, possible situation. Lindsay isn't answering. Joe swears he saw some movement over there where Luther's supposed to be. He can't raise Luther. We're moving out."

Within seconds six SWAT team members were moving fast, bent over, with only the sound of the branches crunching underfoot as they converged on Lindsay's location.

A shot rang out, then another.

As they climbed the knoll, Joe Boyle could see down into the Quantico quadrangle. Giffey Talbot, her two FBI agent guards behind her, was standing in front of the entrance to the Jefferson Dormitory. She was weaving, looking down at her bloody hands over her chest, the agents behind her were shouting, their guns drawn, jumping in front of her. He watched Giffey fall, one agent catching her before she hit the ground. They both covered her with their bodies as shouts filled the air.

Joe yelled, "Oh Jesus, Dave, he's near Luther's location, and he shot Giffey! Get him!"

"Luther!" Dave Dempsey dropped to his knees beside Luther, one of the best of the best, a dead shrub half covering him. He was shaking as he pressed his fingers to the pulse in Luther's neck. His fingers sank into his flesh to touch the silver wire embedded deep in his neck. Luther was dead.

Within moments, using a general mayday to every SWAT team member, Chief Ramsey deployed them all in twos and threes, to close in on where the shot had been fired. He prayed as he barked out orders that they wouldn't find any more men dead.

Six minutes later, Dr. Clyde Peterson, the surgeon stationed at Quantico for the duration of Operation Flower Girl, came out of the small exam room, peeling off his blood-covered surgical gloves, and said to Savich, "Agent Talbot is alive. We're stabilizing her, then getting her to Bethesda. I won't lie to you, Agent Savich. It's a large caliber bullet, slowed down some by her vest, but still real close to her heart. She's actively bleeding and it's going to be close. It'll depend on exactly what it hit. So pray. I'll keep in touch."

Pray, Dr. Peterson wanted him to pray. Savich watched two men roll Giffey by on a gurney on a dead run. She as white as the sheet pulled up to her neck, an oxygen mask over her nose and mouth, blood running into IVs in her arms. Her own blood was everywhere, surely more blood than a body could lose. If Giffey died, it would be his fault, because he'd been arrogant enough to assume three SWAT teams could control the perimeter, could protect Fleurette—Giffey—from this monster. Dear God, not Giffey. She was a good agent, he'd watched her volunteer for a myriad of assignments, always eager, ready to take on the world.

Savich stood with his back against a brick wall, aware of all the activity going on around him as the helicopter lifted off the pad right outside the Jefferson Dormitory. He knew that Captain Ramsey was searching methodically, that the captain knew a lot more than he did about how to cover the grounds as quickly and efficiently as possible to find Günter. There was nothing he could do to help out there. All he could do was stand here like a dolt and know that he'd been the one to bring it all about.

Jimmy Maitland came striding up to him. "I just spoke to Chip Ramsey. Dammit, Luther Lindsay is dead, but thankfully, everyone else is accounted for. Günter penetrated the lines all the way to Luther without being spotted. That means he was in a camouflage uniform, just like the SWAT guys, his face blackened. He obviously knew the terrain well enough to pick a rise he could shoot from.

"Chip doesn't know how long he waited there before he took out Luther, but he's thinking it wasn't long at all. Someone would have noticed. Günter saw Fleurette flanked by two bodyguards, standing right in front of the Jefferson Dormitory, took Luther out, and took his shot. Dave and Joe heard the struggle and headed to Luther's location. Günter heard them, and that's probably what saved Giffey's life—threw his aim off.

"The thing is, Savich, why would he think that we'd actually put Fleurette out there in harm's way? He knew we'd set a trap for him."

Savich said, "I saw Fleurette and Giffey standing side-by-side after Fleurette had finished Giffey's makeup, done her hair this morning, given her one of her dresses and her coat. I swear I couldn't tell them apart. Could be twins."

"Well, Günter must have believed it was her, too. I'm willing to bet he was ready to spend a couple of hours watching, may have been surprised anything could come of it this quickly. The bastard."

"How did he get Luther?"

"Chip says Luther was on his belly, looking toward Giffey sweeping the area, and Günter jumped on his back, looped the wire around his neck, and that was it. Luther probably managed to fight, and that's what Joe Boyle and Dave Dempsey saw—the bit of noise, the shadow of movement was Luther trying to save himself. But he couldn't. Then Günter sighted in on Giffey— he actually used Luther's own rifle—but before he could shoot, he heard Joe and Dave and that, thankfully, pulled his aim off a bit. He fired, saw her fall, saw it was a chest shot, and he was out of there.

"This is a tough one, Savich. I've known Luther for more than a dozen years. Chip and I will speak to his family as soon as I can get away. Amanda Lindsay is a great lady, and their teenage girls are terrific. Dammit, dammit."

Savich nodded, swallowed. He'd met Luther about six years before, admired his skill, his humor, his love for his family. But his skills hadn't saved him. He tried to think of something to say, but couldn't. All he saw was Giffey on that stretcher, lying in her own blood, and he couldn't stand it. He said then, "Giffey might die, and I know it's my fault if she does."

"We all knew the risks, Savich, Giffey, too. We all went along with this plan as our best opportunity. It may have been the only way we had to get Günter."

It was in that moment Savich realized they still had a chance to pull it off, to protect Fleurette and get Günter. "Sir, I've got another plan, although since this one was such a spectacular failure, I wouldn't blame you for telling me to shove it."

"Lay it on me, Savich, let's see."

When Savich finished, Jimmy Maitland sucked in a deep breath. "I like it, and it might work. Your brain is good, Savich, keep using it. You need to go see Fleurette. She's with her parents and Sherlock, and she's really shaken. I'll keep in touch with Bethesda, have Dr. Peterson call you as soon as he knows Giffey's status.

"Yeah, this might work. You can bet Günter will be glued to the TV, waiting to hear the breaking news that Fleurette is dead so he can celebrate."

Savich said, "We've got to outthink him. That's why we can't come out and announce she's dead, and that's why we'll delay announcing who was taken to Bethesda in the helicopter."

"Director Mueller sure won't like holding back like this, dancing around the truth, but I think he'll agree. Then we have Callie. You think you can convince her to go along with this?"

"In a heartbeat."

"Maybe we're being premature. There's still a chance we can get our hands on him today. Chip has the SWAT people spread out all over. Since we don't have anything more reliable, we're looking particularly hard at any late-model cars, Toyotas, you know, like Mr. Avery described last night, and anyone fitting Mr. Avery's description. We might get this guy."

He stopped talking, saw that Savich looked

frozen, as if stuck to the wall he was leaning against.

"Savich, stop blaming yourself. I need you sharp and focused on getting this plan of yours to work."

"Dr. Peterson told me to pray."

"I'll wager a lot of people at Quantico are praying. Do your job, Savich. Where's Sherlock when I need her here to punch your lights out?"

"You told me she's with Fleurette and her parents."

"Yeah, so I did. And look at what else I forgot—it must be senility that I clean forgot that you're God and you make all the decisions around here. Well, you're not, so get over it. Do your job. Get Günter." Jimmy Maitland turned, his cell phone already in his big hand. He turned back, frowned. "Hey, what's Giffey's name short for?"

"Gifford. She told me her mom named her after Frank Gifford, lived near him in New York City, at One Lincoln Plaza. Her dad liked Gifford too, he's a real football nut. Giffey told me once it was the only thing she could ever remember her parents agreeing about."

"I'll talk to her parents too. They need to get to Bethesda." Mr. Maitland looked down at his watch. "I've got to speak to Director Mueller right away, tell him about your plan. I'll bet the media are calling already."

Savich was grateful to his boss for dealing with Giffey's parents and Luther's family. One phone call, and your world, as you knew it, was gone. Just gone. He thought that if he had to speak to them, he'd start crying.

CHAPTER
34

Savich found Fleurette in his office, sobbing in her father's arms, her mother standing by looking helpless. Sherlock was watching them, sitting on the edge of the desk.

Sherlock looked up. "Giffey?"

"She's on her way by helicopter to Bethesda." And then he saw Fleurette's white face and lied clean. "She'll be all right. She's fit and strong. Giffey will be all right. They're going to be in touch with us constantly. I'll let you know immediately if something happens. Okay?"

Mr. Malcolm LaFleurette, a tall, handsome man dressed like a diplomat in a gray cashmere Italian suit, looked up over his daughter's head. "How did this happen, Agent Savich?"

"It shouldn't have, Mr. LaFleurette. It shouldn't have."

"The shot the guy made—I can't imagine shooting that far and actually hitting someone."

"It was over three thousand feet." Savich paused a moment, saw that they were all trying to make sense of the distance, and said, "That's more than ten football fields."

Elaine's head snapped up. "Ten football fields? I don't think I can even see that far."

"He had a very powerful scope, the very best of everything." Savich looked toward Sherlock, even managed a small smile. "Excuse me a moment," he said to Fleurette, nodding solemnly to her mother, Norma Lee, who was looking at him as if he were their savior, and how could that be? He took Sherlock outside and leaned his forehead against hers.

Sherlock smiled up at him, gave him a hug, and cupped his face between her palms. "Giffey will make it, Dillon. No, don't shake your head at me. Stop looking like you're going to fold in on yourself with guilt. You made the right decision based on what you knew. She'll pull through this."

At that moment, Savich simply couldn't believe how very lucky he was that she'd come into his life. "You know, for the first time, I think she just might." He hugged her again. "Where's Sean?"

"Lily took him over to your mom's. Your mom, Lily told me, begged so pathetically that she had simply no choice. I think Simon wanted to score points, so he went with them. You know Simon always charms your mom's socks off."

"He'll ooze charm. He wants Lily powerfully bad. Listen now, and tell me what you think of this."

When he walked back into his office, Savich felt like a hundred pounds had been lifted off his back. "Fleurette, let me tell you what's going to happen. I'm going to ask Callie Markham to release to the press that you were actually the one shot, not an FBI agent. It will help us keep you safe. But you're staying right here, inside at least for a few days. You can go to classes, work out in the gym, stuff pizza down your gullet, but you'll have to remain indoors. There'll always be two agents with you."

"What are you going to do, Agent Savich?"
Savich gave Mr. LaFleurette a big smile. "I'm going to get Günter, but believe me, my first priority is to keep Fleurette safe. What do you say, Fleurette? Will you do as I ask?"

Fleurette pulled herself together, straightened her shoulders, and, for the first time since Savich had come into his office, she turned back into an adult. She stepped away from her father, hugged her arms around herself, and nodded at her mother. "Yes, Agent Savich, I'll do exactly what you say. You know something? I'm finally thinking straight, and I realize that Günter must have seen Danny talking to me, and believed he was telling me secrets. Obviously, he didn't see me ditch Danny after a block or so. What I don't understand is why he didn't kill me right away."

Savich said, "For whatever reason, the person who hired him believed Danny O'Malley and Eliza Vickers were greater and more immediate threats."

"All of this is quite terrifying, Agent Savich," said Mrs. LaFleurette. She looked young enough to be Fleurette's older sister, with the same hair, the same eyes, same tilt of the head. "You know as well as we do that Elaine won't be safe until the assassin is caught or dead."

Sherlock said, "That's right. And we have a lot of people hunting him right now. There are witnesses, there always are. We'll find them, just like we found Mr. Avery last night. But you're right, Fleurette isn't safe until we take him down, and that's why she's staying right here. Inside."

Sherlock paused a moment, then pulled two photos out of her shirt pocket. "I know we already showed you these photos, Fleurette, but would you look at them again?"

Fleurette took the photos, walked over to the window, and studied them in the bright light, for a very long time. Finally, she shook her head. "No, I'm sorry."

"Think back to Friday when you were walking with Danny. Did you see anyone looking at you?"

Again, she shook her head. "No, if he was there, I wasn't aware of him at all."

Sherlock said, "Okay, why don't we go downstairs to a conference room where there's a TV. Dillon, it's been thirty minutes. Okay, let's all go see if Director Mueller is on yet."

Director Mueller was just coming on. Fox TV had mobilized fast. Director Mueller looked stoic, grave and solemn. His eyes sheened with tears when he spoke of Luther Lindsay, the dead SWAT team member from the Washington, D.C., field office. He was tremendously apologetic to everyone. As for any other casualties, and who was behind the assault, he promised full disclosure as the information became available. Even though he took responsibility, he managed to convey the impression that he was doing his best under trying circumstances. He took no questions. As far as Savich could see, it was a flawless performance of bureaucratic cover-up. There wasn't a word about Fleurette. And Günter would start to wonder why.

As for Savich, he wondered whether Director Mueller's mother would be on the phone to him right after the press conference demanding to know what was really going on. He wondered if Director Mueller would tell her.

Savich's cell phone rang. His first thought was Giffey. But it was Callie, who said immediately, "How is Giffey?"

"I don't know anything yet. Did you do it?"

"Oh yeah. I just faxed Coombes a note about how badly the FBI screwed up in trying to protect Fleurette, how Director Mueller was trying to keep it all quiet. I told him I thought Fleurette was the one shot and they'd taken her to Bethesda. Old Jed will eat it up, bet he's claiming he knew Director Mueller was covering his ass by not admitting she'd been shot at Quantico. Made me sick to give that slant, but I did it, as you asked. Jed will write it up as a scoop and make it really contemptuous of the FBI. He and I will both be in trouble when Fleurette shows herself safe and in one piece. So I hope this was worth it to you."

"I hope so too. I owe you one, Callie."

Not three minutes later, his cell rang again, and this time he knew it was about Giffey. He didn't want to answer it. He stared down at it like it was a snake about to bite him. Sherlock's hand suddenly covered his. She didn't say anything, smiled up at him, and nodded.

"Savich here." He listened for some time, then said, "Great news. Thank you, Dr. Peterson. We'll be here."

There was silence in the conference room,

only the movement on TV, muted now, by Sherlock.

Savich said, "That was Dr. Peterson. He said that Giffey's got Dr. Edward Bricker operating on her. He's one of the best thoracic surgeons in the world. They've got the bleeding stopped, and Giffey's hanging in there. Dr. Peterson thinks she's going to make it. She still has to pull through surgery, and the next twenty-four hours will be critical, but I could hear the optimism in his voice. She's got a good chance."

"Thank God," Fleurette said. "Oh, thank you, God."

An hour later, Savich walked back into his office to see Ben and Callie in close conversation. When they saw him, they stepped quickly apart, and looked embarrassed. Well, well, Savich thought, and smiled at them. He could think fast on his feet, and he did so now. "I've got a favor to ask of you guys, that is, if you're both free tonight."

"Sure, no problem," Ben said. Callie nodded.

Savich studied his thumbnail a moment, then said, "I'd like you and Callie to go to a pretty nice restaurant in Georgetown this evening—how about Filomena's on Wisconsin?"

"That's a real fancy place, Dillon," Callie said. "It's one of my mom's favorite restaurants. I can't imagine we could get in on such short notice."

"Who's paying?" Ben asked.

Savich laughed. "The FBI will reimburse you. When you call, mention my name to the maître d'. He knew my grandmother, Sarah Elliott, and he's still impressed that I'm her grandson. He'll get you two a table, probably a really good one.

"Spend some time at the bar first. All I want you to do is listen to what's being said. I want your opinions on whether or not people saw through Director Mueller's fancy excuses. And if they've read the *Post,* does everyone believe that Fleurette is at Bethesda. Talk to people, see what they think. What you don't want to hear is that Fleurette isn't the one who was shot here at Quantico, or that she's dead. We want speculation on that. What do you guys think?"

Callie shot a look at Ben, but nodded. "All right."

When Savich met Sherlock a few minutes later, she said, "I ran into Ben and Callie.

They said something about dining out on the FBI this evening, and then Callie sort of looked confused and said she really didn't understand why this was so important to you."

He grinned at her. "Yeah, well, we'll see what comes of it. Now, I need to deal with Bethesda."

Filomena's
Wisconsin Avenue, N.W.
Georgetown, Washington, D.C.
Sunday evening

Callie took a bite of her beautifully pre-pared swordfish, looked up, and saw Ben staring at her. "What?"

He shook his head, but didn't look away. The fact was she didn't look like he was used to seeing her, and he couldn't quite get him-self used to the transformation. She was wearing a little black dress that had long sleeves and no back to speak of, and high heels that put her nearly at six feet tall. He'd picked her up earlier at her mother's house, she'd waltzed down the stairs, looking the way women always look when they're going to drive a man crazy. He couldn't stop staring at her. And she was wearing her hair differently, pulled back and up on her head with dangly little curls hanging over her ears. He said, "I was thinking you look pretty good tonight."

"Why, thank you, sir. Your suit looks pretty good, too."

"What? This old thing?"

She laughed. "Yes, that old thing—Italian, right? And you think my mom's friends are snobs."

"I picked you up in my Crown Vic. You can't get more pedestrian than that."

"Yes, you did. I wanted the truck, but I probably couldn't have climbed in it anyway, not in these heels. You know, Ben, actually, I think you look hot."

He stirred around the little pile of potato fritters, and kept his mouth shut.

"This dress does wonders for my butt, don't you think?"

"Well, it sure is short. I've only seen you in pants, boots, and sweaters big enough to fit me. And your hair's always stuffed under a cap."

"No hat hair tonight." Callie pulled off a piece of her dinner roll, and decided that what she really wanted to do was jump over the table and kiss him stupid. Instead, she cleared her throat and said, "I'm still wondering why Dillon sent us here. Does he think Günter is the type to eat at fancy restaurants?"

And in that instant, Ben saw the light. He and Callie had been maneuvered by an expert. It gave him a jolt to realize he probably wouldn't have thought of it himself, although he should have. Regardless of how this lovely candlelit dinner had come about, he was sitting across from a beautiful woman who was wearing a short black dress, eating swordfish. What had she said? Oh yes, Günter. Ben said, "Who knows if this is Günter's kind of place?"

"For all we know, he could own the joint."

"That's depressing and true. I think after dinner, we should walk to Barnes and Noble, it's a good place to hang out and listen to people talk."

As they walked down M Street, the frigid January air seeping under their collars and up Callie's dress, Ben said, "In those stilts you're wearing, you're nearly to the bridge of my nose."

"Nah, I'm above your eyebrows, admit it."

It seemed natural to take her hand, even more natural for her to move closer.

In every Barnes & Noble aisle, like at Filomena's, nearly everyone had believed Director Mueller was covering up the shooting of another law clerk, read the *Post,* that's where the real scoop was.

Callie said, "Jed was fast, as well as going the extra ten yards beyond what I told him."

They heard a man say, "I sure wouldn't apply there if I was fresh out of law school. I wonder if there'll be a shortage next year."

"All three of the law clerks who worked for Justice Califano—dead in a week."

"The *Post* didn't say she was dead. She's in Bethesda."

"Who knows?"

They walked through the aisles, pausing to listen when they hit a new group of people.

"I sure hope they protect that poor law clerk this time. If she's still alive."

"Bingo," Ben said.

When Ben and Callie left, he found himself driving back toward Savich's house. He said, "I spoke to Savich when you went to the bathroom. I told him what we'd heard, and he said okay, good, that was what he'd hoped. I got the impression that he feels like shit about Giffey. I heard it in his voice. He blames himself."

"Yes, he would. And given what happened, I'd blame myself too. Where are we going?"

Ben slowed down in front of the house, then pulled to the curb and put the car in park. "I wanted to check on them. Everything looks quiet. I know Savich has a state-of-the-art security system, protection for his grandmother's painting, of course. But still—"

"You wanted to make sure. No problem."

"One more stop?" Ben pressed the turn signal, went right toward the house where old Mr. Avery lived. "I remember it being 2371 Lombard Street. It's not too late. Let's stop in and talk to him. You game?"

CHAPTER 35

Nathaniel Avery answered the door almost immediately. He was decked out in a tatty pale blue chenille bathrobe that fell nearly to his bony feet. It looked like it belonged to his wife. Ben felt his optimism sinking fast. Truth was, Mr. Avery looked like a batty old codger who wouldn't know a Toyota if it had its name printed across the windshield.

At least Mr. Avery wasn't wearing fuzzy house slippers, or Ben might have turned right back around and left. No, his house slippers were a manly dark brown leather.

"Who're you, sonny?"

Ben pulled out his badge, held it out for

Mr. Avery to study, which he did, pushing his glasses up on his nose and looking at Ben's badge for a long time, silent the whole while. He finally looked up. "Okay, you're really a cop. And you?"

"I'm Callie Markham. I'm with him."

"What are you two doing here all duded up?"

"We had dinner at Filomena's," Ben said smoothly. "The swordfish was excellent."

"I never cared none for swordfish."

Callie said, "Do you think we could speak to you about last night, and the man you saw jump into that car and drive off?"

"I already spoke to a good half-dozen local cops. I was hoping maybe the FBI would call, but they haven't checked in yet. You think they might?"

"Nah. I think we're the best you're going to get," Ben said. "It's been twenty-four hours since you spoke to anyone, and I'll bet that you, Mr. Avery, have thought and thought about it, replayed the scene a lot in your mind."

"Well, yeah, that's true enough. I know all about that agent's house getting shot up— we haven't ever had anything that exciting happen in this neighborhood."

"Maybe, sir, if we all discuss it together, you might remember something new that could help us."

Mr. Avery's glasses were sliding down his nose as he waved them into a dark living room where the TV was on, but there was no sound. "Marylee, don't worry, it's the cops!"

An old woman with lots of beautiful silver hair, wearing an identical pale pink chenille bathrobe and fluffy pale pink slippers, was sitting in a La-Z-Boy chair, feet up, staring at them. "What did you say, dear?"

Mr. Avery raised his own voice to a yell. "It's the police! Go back to your knitting, Marylee. Everything's okay. Where's Luciano?"

There was a surprisingly robust bark, and then a tiny black dog pranced out, tail wagging like a fast metronome. "That's Luciano, my little boy. He's only two, my happy little camper, always on the go. I have to walk him six times a day. He loves to waggle around, walks right up to big dogs and barks at them, tries to lick them." Mr. Avery leaned over, knees creaking, and picked up Luciano, who licked him all over his face, barked, and then paused, cocked his little head, and stared at Ben and Callie.

"Now Luciano is a seriously cute dog," Callie said. "What's his breed?"

Mr. Avery leaned close, whispered, "He's a miniature poodle, but he doesn't know it. If you asked him, he'd say he's human." He patted the dog, raised his voice, and waved them in. "All right, you come in and sit down. Marylee doesn't use the sound on the TV, couldn't hear it unless it was loud enough to blast out the neighbors, but she likes it on while she knits. Good lip-reader, Marylee."

Mr. Avery settled himself in a matching La-Z-Boy, settled Luciano on his bony legs, and waved Ben and Callie to a very lovely brocade sofa opposite him.

"All right. Ask your questions, Detective Raven."

"Let's go over exactly where you were when you saw this man, Mr. Avery."

"I was maybe twenty feet south of my house."

"There was a half-moon last night, so that means light. Were you wearing your glasses?"

"Yep, have to when Luciano does his business because I gotta scoop it up. And I don't want a car to run me down when Luciano wants to walk over to Madison Avenue, that's one of his favorite areas around here."

"Okay, so you saw a man. How old was he? What did you think when you saw him?"

"He wasn't old, but gawldarn, Detective Raven, a guy'd have to be seventy before I wouldn't think he was a kid. Okay, let's say he was getting up there, middle age, fifties, I'd say. He was big, looked fit, no fat that I could tell. He was wearing a Burberry coat. I know Burberrys because that's all my brother wears, the affected dufuss. I only noticed him because he was running. You don't see that very often on a Saturday night in this neighborhood. No druggies hang out here, just good solid folks, like Marylee and me and Luciano. We've been here for forty-five years."

"Where was his car parked?"

"About twenty feet north of my house, on this side, it was the only car out on the street. Like I said, this is a homey neighborhood, folks have garages and use them. No punks with cars up on blocks in their driveways or on the street."

"You said it was a white car, maybe a pale gray?"

"I think now it was white."

Callie beamed at him. "So you remember that now."

"Yep, thought about it a lot, like Detective Raven said I'd do. I told the other cops it was a gray or white Toyota, late model, maybe a 2000 or a 2001, but I wasn't all that sure at the time. Guess they had good reason not to take me seriously about it. I saw a couple of Toyotas today, and that's what it was. The Toyota had two doors, not four. It was clean, even the radial tires."

Ben said, "So the guy runs up to the driver's side, pulls open the door, jumps in, starts the car, and peels away from the curb."

Mr. Avery was shaking his head. "You know what—hey, Luciano, come back to Daddy—don't chew on Marylee's slipper!—good boy, that's a good boy. Now, what was I saying? Oh yeah, the thing is, now that I think about it, the car was already running."

Ben didn't move a muscle.

"That's something else I remember now. You see, Detective Raven, there wasn't time for this guy to run to the car, open the door, stick the key in the ignition, turn over the engine, and take off. Nope, he jumped in the driver's side." Mr. Avery snapped his fingers.

"Yeah, I remember that clearly now. The car had to be running. And he didn't have to open that door, it was already ajar."

Ben, doubtful now, and hating it, hoping the cops weren't right about Mr. Avery making things up, nonetheless said, "Were you going to call the FBI about remembering this, Mr. Avery?"

Mr. Avery was shaking his head. "Well, maybe, if they'd asked again, but I knew they were thinking I was just an old buzzard with pudding for brains and probably blind and deaf as a post, like poor Marylee. They sort of acted that way last night. I mean, they were respectful, and they nodded a lot, but you know, I saw them looking at each other when they didn't think I'd notice. Why waste my time?" Mr. Avery paused a moment, then cursed. "Yeah, I would have called tomorrow, anyway. My pa was a cop, taught me what was right."

"Good for you," Callie said.

Ben sat forward, hands flexing on his knees. His eyes were bright, and he felt his heart begin to pound. "Well, I'm here, Mr. Avery, and it seems to me you're as sound as I am, sir. Okay, then, were you saying there was someone else in the car?"

Both Callie and Ben waited to the sound of Marylee humming to the theme song of a television show no one could hear, her knitting needles clacking loud in the silence. Luciano was standing on his hind legs, his front paws on Mr. Avery's knee, tail wagging, as if waiting to hear what his master was going to say, too.

"You know, I don't remember hearing the car running, but then, I wasn't really paying any attention, until I saw this guy heading toward that car on a dead run, that Burberry coat flapping around his legs. I guess someone in the car saw him coming, and that someone had to turn on the ignition key. The driver's side door wasn't shut, yeah, it had to be partly open, that's it, because, like I told you, that guy comes running up—he wasn't even out of breath, I remember that too— and he pulls the door open, jumps in, his foot slams down hard on the gas, and he fishtails it away from the curb."

Callie's foot was tapping. She was sitting forward.

Mr. Avery pulled Luciano back up on his lap. "Jeez, yeah, now I see it, you know what else? Someone moved inside the car, in the passenger seat. I remember when he floored the gas and the car fishtailed a little bit, someone's head jerked back. It had to be a woman because her hair sort of fanned out. Yeah, it was a woman waiting for him, a woman who turned on that car. That or some sort of weird hippie guy with long hair."

It was close, but Ben avoided picking up Mr. Avery and Luciano and waltzing them around the living room.

Ten minutes later, Ben was on his cell to Savich, telling him how smart old Mr. Avery turned out to be.

Savich said, "You're sure the old man has it together and he wasn't spinning a good story for you?"

Ben said, "He's a piece of work, I'll grant you that. Initially he comes across on the flaky side, but his brain is intact, Savich. I'm as sure of that as I am that my mother found my stash of *Playboy* magazines when I was eleven years old."

"Okay. You're right, Ben, this could be big. Well done. Tell Callie she's a princess. Oh yeah, did you guys enjoy Filomena's?"

"Probably as much as you intended us to."

"Well, that's good."

When Ben hung up, he turned to Callie.

"Savich said you were a princess. Does that make you proud?"

Callie laughed, then sobered quickly. "All right. What are we going to do now?"

"I'm taking you home. I think we've got enough for tonight."

"I agree. So there was a woman in Günter's car. I suppose now Savich will find out where every woman involved in the case was last night. Oh, Ben, you will call me the minute you find out anything about Giffey?"

"You got it."

He turned the Crown Vic around and headed toward Margaret Califano's house on Beckhurst Lane.

After about five minutes of staring straight ahead through the windshield, Callie said, "You know, you did look like a natural."

"What? A natural what?"

"When you were holding Sean last night. You looked like a natural."

"Oh yeah, well, I got four nieces and nephews, two of each. I've changed a couple of diapers in my time."

Now she did turn to face him. "Really? You've really changed diapers yourself?"

"It isn't rocket science, Callie. What with

the Velcro tapes, I'd bet you a baby could do his own diaper. Where's this coming from?"

She shrugged. "We did have a lovely dinner, didn't we?"

"I was salivating more over that dress of yours than I was the swordfish."

"It's been just over a week. It doesn't seem real."

He nodded, turned smoothly onto Caledonia Street and continued west. He wanted to ask if she'd like to neck with him, but managed to hold his tongue.

"Hey," she said, "Mr. Avery is something else, isn't he?"

"Yes, he is, and that little dog is a ridiculous little bit of fluff, but you know what? I liked him. Happy little critter. Can't believe I'd say that about a poodle. A miniature poodle, for God's sake. Thing is, I can see him crawling all over me at six in the morning, licking my face off."

As a matter of fact, Callie could picture it too, and that was a surprise. What wasn't a surprise was that she could also see herself, lying next to Ben Raven, laughing, waiting for Luciano to leap over on her. Why did feelings and attachments have to sprout like weeds at a time like this?

Ben shot her a look, but didn't say a word. When they got to Margaret's house, he walked Callie to the front door. The lights were all off except for the porch light.

"Looks like your mom's friends have gone for the evening." He waited until she'd unlocked the door and stepped inside.

"Callie, about this natural thing."

"Yes?"

"Ah, forget it. Never mind. I'll call you when I find out anything about Giffey." She was bundled up in her black wool coat, a bright red scarf wrapped around her neck, but he could clearly picture that sexy little black dress beneath. No, it wasn't the time, dammit. "Sleep well. I'll see you in the morning." He turned to leave when she grabbed his arm and yanked him back. Then she looked up at him and said, "Don't go. Oh dear, am I an idiot or what? I forgot that my mom told me she wanted me to move back to my own place this evening. She said she was fine now, that she needed to be by herself for a while. I told her I would, that I'd see her for dinner tomorrow night. I forgot. I wonder what I should do."

"Check on her, make sure she's okay, then I'll take you to your apartment."

She nodded. "Okay. What will we be doing tomorrow?"

"I have a meeting with Captain Halloway and Police Commissioner Holt at the Daly Building at eight-thirty, but I'll call, let you know when I'll be coming by to get you. Savich will have something for us to do, count on it."

"Come in with me. I'll check on Mom, then we can have some of her fancy French roast coffee. Anything I'd have at home would be stale, probably growing mold. And Mom always keeps some croissants in the freezer. What do you think?"

Ben wasn't tired either. He was hyped. He could take on the world. The fact was he wanted to take her to bed, and that made everything even more intense. "Okay, a croissant sounds good. You got real butter?"

"Maybe Mom does. You'll have to take your chances."

She took him to the ultra-modern stainless-steel kitchen, gave him a bag of gourmet coffee, and pointed him to the coffee machine, a European thing that looked like you'd need a degree in French engineering to figure it out.

Callie said, her voice dropping to a whisper, "Let me go upstairs and check on Mom. Thing is, I'm still worried about her. I'll be back in a minute."

"Yeah, go on up, make sure she's really asleep. If she wakes up, hears us moving around down here, it might scare her since she's expecting to be alone."

"I'll be right back."

"I'm right here," Margaret said, smiling at both of them as she walked into the kitchen. She looked pretty good, Ben thought, as he nodded to her.

"You having any problems with the coffeemaker, Ben?"

"He's a guy, Mom. It's in his genes."

Margaret laughed. "Stewart never had that particular gene." Her voice dropped off, but she didn't start crying. She walked to the cabinet and reached for coffee mugs.

Ben's cell phone rang. "Raven here."

Both women watched him as he listened for several moments. When he punched off, he said, "I'm sorry, but something's come up. Mrs. Califano, Callie, I'll see you tomorrow."

And he was gone.

Callie started to go after him, then stopped. "I wonder what's going on?"

"He'll tell you tomorrow."

"Yeah, but in the meantime I'll miss all the fun."

Margaret said, "I think I'd rather have tea. Will you join me?"

CHAPTER
36

Bethesda Naval Hospital
Surgical Intensive Care Unit

The large room was filled with shadows except for the semicircular workstation where six nurses and three clerks manned computers and monitoring equipment, filed reports, and wrote notes in the patients' charts in the muted light of their individual desk lamps. Conversation within the group was low but frequent, just above the hum and repetitive beeping of the monitoring equipment.

Only the curtain to cubicle twelve was pulled back slightly.

At eleven-thirty, an X-ray technician slid her I.D. badge through the slot reader in the SICU door and maneuvered in, pushing the portable X-ray unit in front of her. She was wearing rubber-soled shoes and made no sound when she walked over to the dry erase board to find the cubicle of her patient. She nodded to one of the nurses, who looked at her from behind the console, nodded toward cubicle twelve, and looked back down at the chart she was checking. The X-ray tech located the patient, and disappeared inside uncurtained cubicle number five. There was a soft murmur of voices, the sound of a machine being positioned, then silence.

The X-ray tech emerged from the cubicle five minutes later, gave a small wave to the staff behind the large workstation, and wheeled out her equipment. Minutes later, another I.D. badge slid through the door slot. A tall older man walked in silently, wearing a white lab coat over green scrubs, carrying a plastic tray with blood-drawing paraphernalia. He was whistling under his breath. The nurse gave only an infinitesimal start, then shook her head at the obvious black dye job on his hair and mustache. Her fingers moved away from a small button at her side.

The lab tech smiled at her, and then, like the x-ray tech, checked the dry erase board for his patient. "You'd think," he said, "that docs would try to schedule these nonemergent blood draws when the patient has a chance of being awake."

"Nah," one of the nurses said, "better to catch them half asleep, they don't worry as much."

The lab tech carried his tray to cubicle number four and quietly pushed the door open, disappeared inside.

After the lab tech left, it was silent again in the large room, and in fact hardly anything seemed to happen in the SICU for the next two hours. The monitors continued their repetitive low-hum vigil, and the patients' heart rates and blood pressures read out as curiously stable for an intensive care unit. None of the nurses left the central workstation.

At a quarter to one in the morning, the door to cubicle twelve opened. Agents Savich and Sherlock came out stretching.

Savich said, "It's time for a shift change. Are all the new patients ready?"

"I got a buzz from Agent Brady. He says

all's clear, and they should be arriving as a group just about now."

In the next moment, the door to the SICU swung open and three men and two women dressed in hospital nightgowns came walking in, behind them a score of new nurses, clerks, and techs.

"Hurry," said one of the patients. "Brady said they just spotted a guy coming this way from the pathology lab."

A patient with a huge bandage wrapped turban-style around his head waved an IV line toward his assigned nurse, who rolled her eyes at him.

Within two minutes, new patients were lying in beds in five of the cubicles. The nurses and staff were settled in behind the workstation, and the machines and monitors resumed their low buzz, the sign all was normal once again.

Savich paused a moment in the doorway to check over the SICU once more. "Let's go home, Sherlock."

Forty-five minutes later, Savich pulled the Porsche into his garage. Sherlock punched in the code to disarm the security system, saying over her shoulder, "I'm bushed. Nothing's as tiring as waiting for someone who doesn't show."

Savich rubbed her shoulders as they walked into the kitchen. She turned on the overhead light.

"Bed never sounded so good," Savich said as he pulled a bottle of water from the refrigerator, unscrewed the lid, and took a long drink. He wiped his hand across his mouth and said to his wife, who was leaning against the counter, "Günter is crazy, no doubt in my mind about that. Given the risks he's taken to date, I was betting he'd take this one too. But he fooled me."

"Maybe he'll show in the middle of the night."

Savich shook his head. "Too quiet. Too empty. He's crazy, but he's not stupid."

He drank deeply again.

His fingers tightened slightly around the bottle when he heard a whisper of movement not ten feet away from the dark dining room.

Sherlock caught his eye. She picked up a dishcloth, wiped down the island surface, and turned to face him, looking relaxed, her arms crossed over her chest. "Even though

Günter's crazy, he must have realized his luck couldn't hold out. He's an old man, Dillon, old and used up. Quantico was his last hurrah. He's got no more in him. So why is he here now?"

A man's deep voice came out of the shadows, a bit of a slow Southern pace to his words. "Because I knew you flat-footed morons were setting another obvious trap at Bethesda, just like at Quantico. I've been waiting for you here, Savich, for quite some time. And now you'll tell me where you've hidden Elaine LaFleurette."

"I believe we have a guest, Sherlock. Günter, come into the light, no need to be shy."

A tall barrel-chested man walked into the doorway, a SIG-Sauer held in his left hand. As soon as Savich saw he wasn't hiding his face, he knew Günter intended to kill them. He was dressed in black, even his hands were gloved in black leather, a black cap pulled down to his ears. He looked fit and strong, but his face was deeply seamed, his mouth small and deeply grooved. He looked old, like he'd lived through too many long nights planning too much death. Did he look crazy? His eyes did, Savich thought, cold and empty.

"Günter Grass," he said, savoring the sounds. "You found out that name very quickly. I haven't used it for years."

Savich asked as he walked slowly toward the man, "You came here even though Fleurette is in Bethesda?"

"Keep your distance, Savich, don't try to rush me. I know you can fight." Günter backed up so that he kept ten feet between them. "Both of you, drop the SIGs now and kick them over here."

Savich and Sherlock both eased their guns from their belt holsters, laid them on the kitchen floor, and kicked them over to where Günter stood.

Günter pointed his SIG directly at Sherlock. "Both of you, come into the living room. Savich, keep her between us." When they were in the living room, Günter motioned them to sit on the sofa. He walked to the living room archway, his SIG still pointed at Sherlock's chest. "Enough now. Where's Elaine LaFleurette?"

"At Bethesda," Sherlock said. "In the surgical ICU. Don't you remember? You shot her."

Günter fired. The shot was deafening in the quiet living room. Sherlock sucked in her breath as the bullet grazed the outside of her arm and buried itself in the wall behind her. She jerked at the shock of it, but didn't cry out. She clapped her hand to her arm. Savich was on his feet, in motion.

"Stop or I'll kill her!"

Savich was breathing hard, adrenaline and rage pumping through him. He wanted to kill Günter, but he had his gun on Sherlock. He reined himself in and sat back down, heart thudding hard against his chest, afraid now. "Are you all right?"

"Yes, I'm all right, Dillon. I'm all right."

Günter was smiling. "You don't screw with me, you hear? I am as much a professional as you are. When I ask you a question, you don't smart-mouth me, you got that?"

"Yes, I've got that." Sherlock knew the numbness would fade soon and her arm would be on fire. But the wound wasn't bad, he'd just wanted to scare her. His quiet threat of more violence scared her more than the bullet that had already torn through her flesh.

Savich said, "Put the gun down now, Günter. There are a dozen more FBI agents surrounding the house. It stops here, now. There's no way out for you."

Günter stared at him. "You set me up at Bethesda? And here in your own house?"

"Yes, that's right. I underestimated you once. I wasn't about to do it a second time. Put down the gun and we can end this without any more killing."

Savich saw the instant Günter believed him, the instant he knew it was over for him. Something in his eyes went dead and flat. He was suddenly afraid that Günter would shoot both of them before he could be stopped. He had to keep him talking. "Tell us why you murdered Justice Califano, Günter. Why you murdered Danny O'Malley and Eliza Vickers. Why you still want to kill Elaine LaFleurette. This is your chance to tell us and the world. Tell us who was working with you, it doesn't matter now, does it?"

Günter continued to hold his gun locked on Sherlock's chest. "You want the truth? All right, I'll tell you a bit of truth."

He paused, his eyes calm now, resigned, and Sherlock would swear she saw relief there as well. He continued in a slow voice. "I am actually impressed with you, Agent Savich, as one professional to another. But the end must come for all of us, me, Califano, you—the difference is that while you have chosen it for me, you did not choose this ending for yourself. But I have. I knew some time ago my life was coming to an end. The only question was, how to end the drama, how to make the exit?

"Do you know why I chose the name Günter Grass? Because my father was born in Danzig, as Grass was, and Grass wrote *The Tin Drum,* the story about where, and what, I came from. His Oskar's world crumbled, and he built a life for himself with what skills he had, as I did. The Nazis literally sacked my parents' home, destroying everything. Near the end of the war, it was a Polish judge who condemned my father to death. To save herself and me, still in her womb, my mother degraded herself, and slept with that judge, and so I am here. After my father's death in front of a firing squad, my mother moved in with that judge. And then she married him, married the man who'd killed my father. She betrayed my father and slept with that monster. I never forgot. When I was seventeen, I became the judge and the executioner and avenged my father. I garroted both of them, just as I did that whore Eliza Vickers and her confidant Daniel O'Malley.

"I called myself Günter in a long-ago life.

Let me tell you about that Günter. For a very long time he killed to earn his bread. It was the only thing at which he was truly skilled, the only thing he had a taste for. All of his targets deserved to die—they were evil people, drug dealers, revolutionaries, fanatics, terrorists, or just simply criminals who'd corrupted those around them. And of course there were the dishonest judges who accepted payoffs, who kept mistresses. But he tired of cleaning up society's mess and being hunted for it all the while. And so Günter ceased to exist, and I came here and became an American.

"I thought it an act of fate—the complete turning of the wheel, if you will—when I saw Justice Califano kissing a young woman in the middle of the day in a small park, the two of them standing in the shade of an oak tree. There was no one else around. Except for me. She was laughing, kissing that old man's mouth, her hands pressed against him, between them. This man was not just any corrupt judge like my stepfather—he was a Justice of the Supreme Court!

"I watched them, and felt my rage build until I wanted to kill both of them right there in the park, but I knew that would be foolish and dangerous for me, and because I must be sure. And so I followed them to a condominium. I found out the young woman he was taking advantage of was one of his law clerks. I saw soon enough that he had obviously turned this young woman into a whore, just like my mother. I loved killing her, loved her futile struggles, knowing you were hearing it all. And I saw my mother's face when the life went out of her. Killing her was almost as gratifying as choking the life out of that corrupt justice. He disgusted me. He was a filthy, common little man, as bad as any of the garbage I killed in Europe. I savored the instant when Califano realized he was dying, realized he was paying the ultimate price. It was my destiny to end his life, or die trying.

"You want a bit more truth, Agent Savich? It surprised me that I actually succeeded, both at the Supreme Court and at Quantico. You really did a very poor job of damage control, don't you think?"

Savich said, "And so you killed three people because two of them were having an affair?"

"You know as well as I do that evil is always banal and common, if you look at it closely, and it must find other evil, and feed. And so I will go down in history as the man who killed a Justice of the Supreme Court and two of his law clerks—those young acolytes who supped and slept with him, and drank in his words, and knew what he was, and reveled in it."

Savich said, "You garroted Danny O'Malley and tried to kill Elaine LaFleurette because you believed they sanctioned Califano's affair with Eliza Vickers?"

"They all knew what he was doing, and they did nothing. Just as no one did anything when my mother slept with that judge. They enjoyed his power, lusted after such power for themselves. They deserved to die."

He was breathing hard, the gun jerking slightly in his hand. He was near the edge. Savich said quickly, his voice low and steady, "Why haven't you told the world why you killed these three people? Don't you want everyone to know why you made an example of Justice Califano?"

For the barest moment, Günter simply stared at him. Then he shrugged, and his voice was as empty as the still air itself. "I destroyed him. That is all I need. Whatever the world thinks, it doesn't concern me."

Savich said, "What makes you think I won't tell the world?"

Günter smiled. "Because you'll be dead, as dead as I will be. Three corpses know the truth. It is enough."

Sherlock said, "But you weren't alone in this, were you? Who was the woman with you the night you fired into our house?"

Günter laughed, but his gun never wavered from her chest. "Who cares anyway? That woman in my car was just a drunk I picked up at a bar. She was good camouflage, to help me get through roadblocks."

"But you know it stops here, Günter," Sherlock said. "It stops now."

Günter laughed. "It doesn't stop until I say it does. I've spent enough time with you. I'm going to die, but you're going to hell with me."

Ben shouted from behind Günter, "Don't you even think of shooting or I'll blow your head off!"

Günter whirled, fired, and kicked out all in the space of a moment. The bullet slammed into the wall not two inches from Ben's head as Günter's left foot struck his arm, numbing it instantly, and sending the gun crashing to the floor, skidding toward the front door.

Ben dived at Günter, slamming him onto his back to the hall floor, but Günter's locked fisted hands smashed hard into Ben's throat, just as his legs kicked up against his back, throwing him off. Ben fell against the areca palm, gagging, trying to get his breath. Günter fired into the living room, sending Savich and Sherlock diving behind the sofa. Then he fired toward Ben as he rolled away, shattering a beautiful Chinese vase, and sending the palm tree crashing to the entrance hall floor. It was the palm tree that saved Ben's life. The next bullet shot through fronds, striking so close he could smell the singed material from his jacket sleeve. Günter burst through the front door, slamming it behind him, and leaped down the front steps.

Ben heard Savich shout at him, but he didn't stop. He grabbed his gun up in his left hand, threw open the front door, and raced after him, Savich three feet behind him.

From the darkness, Jimmy Maitland yelled, "No, hold your fire!"

"There's no escape, Günter," Savich shouted. "Agents are everywhere. Stop where you are and drop the gun."

Savich switched on the front lights, held his SIG in front of him as he looked at Günter. Ben was just to his left, behind a large urn that held an Italian cypress tree. For an instant, their eyes met.

Günter didn't drop his gun, he shot from the hip, missing Savich by inches. Before he could fire again, a single loud rifle shot pierced the air. Günter whirled about, thrown forward as he slapped one palm against his neck. The last thing he saw was Dave Dempsey stepping from out behind a car at the curb, a sniper rifle aimed at him.

A half-dozen agents came running from their positions, guns aimed at the unmoving body. They walked to where the man who'd wreaked so much devastation lay, unmoving.

There was absolutely no sound for a good thirty seconds. Finally Jimmy Maitland said, "Jesus, am I glad that's over."

Ben nodded, stood up. "Sherlock, are you okay?"

"Yes, fine. Don't worry about me."

Jimmy Maitland said, "He doesn't look all that scary now, does he? He just looks like a dead old man with a slack jaw. Nice shot,

Dave. And thank you, Ben. You shaved it a little close, but you got him out to us."

He turned to Savich, who had Sherlock pressed against his chest. "I was watching through the living room window, Savich. When he put that bullet through Sherlock's arm, I nearly shot him myself then. Okay, I guess it's time to call Dr. Conrad and get the trash taken away."

Two paramedics came quickly forward, stepping over Günter to see to Sherlock. Ben looked at Savich, but Savich was focused on his wife.

He turned back and smiled at Dave Dempsey. "That was a good shot, Dave."

"I guess it's something for Luther's family. But not enough. It's never enough."

"Ben," Savich called out, "check him for I.D. Find out who he is."

Günter lay on the sidewalk on his back, his gun still in his hand. Both Jimmy Maitland and Ben went through all his pockets. They came up with nothing at all, not even a fake driver's license. Slowly, they both rose. Ben called out, "Nothing, Savich. Nothing at all."

"It's not a surprise," Jimmy Maitland said, staring down at Günter. "He lived with another man's name and died with no name at all."

Savich had bared Sherlock's arm. "The bullet came real close to your knife scar."

"I'll be fine. Dillon, before you turn the paramedics loose on me, I think you, Ben, and I should talk. You know we do."

"Yes," he said slowly. "Yes, of course you're right. Ben, could you come into the house for a minute?"

Ben nodded.

Savich picked her up and carried her inside over her protests, leaving the paramedics to wait in the ambulance for another ten minutes before Savich called them in.

Jimmy Maitland wondered if Savich would ever tell him what the three of them discussed.

CHAPTER
37

Tuesday night

It was just after eleven o'clock when Ben pulled his truck into Margaret Califano's driveway.

"I can't believe it's over," Callie said. "And you never said a word to me. I could have stayed outside with the other agents."

"I couldn't, direct orders from Savich. You've been saying that all evening. I guess that means I'll never hear the end of it, will I?"

"Probably not. But I'll forgive you since Savich gave me that great inside interview for the *Post* this morning. Coombes is dancing on the file cabinets, high-fiving everyone he runs into, an idiot grin on his face. You said you liked my story, but what do you really think? Did you notice it was above the fold on the front page? Right there with my own byline?"

She was so proud, he smiled. "Yes, I really did like your story. It was excellent. Congratulations. So this means your job is safe?"

"Oh yes. Suddenly I'm valuable to him again. I was relieved to see Sherlock looking back to normal, well, nearly so. Dillon kept going on about the sling."

"He told me it reminded him of a night he didn't want to remember. He wouldn't tell me about it."

"Maybe I can get it out of Sherlock." Callie settled back against the seat and closed her eyes. "It's all happened so fast, I still can't quite process it, even after writing my story. I'm glad Günter's dead, but the fact that he picked my stepfather by chance? It didn't matter which Justice he murdered? Stewart was such a fine man—" She stopped and drew a deep breath.

Ben repeated what he'd been saying over and over to her that evening, "He was crazy, Callie, just plain crazy. He wanted to go out in a blaze of glory. How better to get attention than to murder a Supreme Court Justice, any Supreme Court Justice, and all his law clerks?

"You want to know something else? When he realized that Savich had set a trap for him, he wasn't about to die ignominiously in an FBI agent's living room. He wanted to continue his blaze of glory last night, and that meant getting outside Savich's house to take on a dozen FBI agents trying to bring him down. It was very much in character for him."

Callie said after a moment, "And you believe he picked up a woman in a bar as camouflage?"

"Being crazy didn't make him stupid. That was real smart of him. Who'd be looking for a couple?"

"He'd been Günter Grass for so many years," she said. "I guess he never even knew who he actually was."

"As Jimmy Maitland said, he used another man's name in life and died with no name at all. Callie, before you go in, I want to say something. I sure liked that black dress you wore the other night. Can I see you wear it again sometime?"

She gave him a small smile. "I'm moving

back to my apartment tomorrow. My mom says now that it's over, she doesn't need me with her anymore."

"Ah."

"Ah good or Ah bad?"

"Do you know it's only a thirty-eight-foot walk from my front door to my king-size bed?"

She laughed, leaned over, kissed him on the mouth, and was out of the door of the Crown Vic. "Tomorrow, Ben?"

"Sure. Great. You know, that little black dress of yours would look even better hanging on my bedroom doorknob."

"What a guy-type visual. Be still my racing heart." She gave him a little wave and walked up the sidewalk to her mother's house. He waited until she unlocked the front door and disappeared inside before he drove away.

Callie turned to set the house alarm, wondering why her mother hadn't armed it when she'd gone to bed. She walked upstairs, and paused a moment by her mother's bedroom door, listening. Slowly, she pushed the door open and stepped into her mother's lovely bedroom. The white spread shone stark and cold in the moonlight pouring through the window.

She walked to the bed to make sure her mother was all right.

The bed was empty.

She turned on the lights, searched for a note, then walked to her own bedroom to look for one.

She picked up the bedroom phone to call Bitsy when she saw the blinking message light. She pushed the play button. There was a call from her mother's manager at the Tyson's Corner store, one from the dry cleaner, a message to call her lawyer about Stewart's will, and finally, the last message. "Margaret, this is Anna. Come to Janette's house right away. It's an emergency."

Anna had called an hour and twelve minutes before.

What emergency? Callie started to call, then slowly laid the phone back in its cradle. It was no surprise they were meeting at Janette's house because there was no family to juggle around at her house since her divorce some ten years before. The five friends frequently met there.

What emergency? Callie didn't pause, bundled back up in her coat and gloves, and headed out to her car.

Janette Weaverton lived in Emmittsville, Maryland, not more than a twenty-minute drive this late at night.

There weren't many people on the road, and she made good time. She pulled into Janette's driveway behind her mother's Mercedes nineteen minutes later.

Besides her mother's Mercedes, Callie saw four familiar cars parked in Janette's driveway.

There were a lot of lights on in the house. Callie walked to the front door, quietly opened it, and stepped into the warm front entrance hall. She eased the door shut behind her. Janette was a minimalist, everything spare, utilitarian. She remembered as a child that Janette had loved girlie-girl stuff, but that had changed after her husband had left.

Callie heard women's voices as she walked toward the living room. She paused just outside the open door when she heard Juliette's voice: "And just what are you proposing to do now?"

Callie heard her mother say, "Calm down, Juliette. It won't help if we all fall apart. It's been a shock, but we'll deal with it. Let's talk about this. We'll figure out what's best."

"But Stewart was your husband, Margaret," Bitsy said. "How can you be so damned calm about it?"

"What do you want me to do? Shoot her for stupidity? Poor judgment in men? That's nothing new, is it?"

Anna said, "How can we be certain the FBI are convinced that he acted on his own? Don't forget he wasn't alone in that car—"

Margaret said patiently, "Agent Savich said Günter told him it was a woman he'd picked up in a bar, for camouflage. That was the last door and he closed it. He never implicated any of us in any way." She paused a moment, then said, "Günter told his grand lie to protect you, to protect all of us. It's all in Callie's headline story for the *Post*. He committed the murders to show how skilled and fearless he was, that he could even kill a Justice of the Supreme Court in the library itself."

Janette said, tears thick in her voice, "But he was crazy, deranged, just look at what he did—he should have been killed at the Supreme Court, at Quantico. He was completely out of control."

Callie stepped into the living room.

Five pair of eyes stared at her.

"Callie!"

"Hello, Mother," Callie said, then nodded at the four women. Anna, Janette, and Bitsy had been crying. Her mother hadn't, though she was the one of them who had lost the most. Juliette looked to be in shock. Callie said slowly, "I guess there was a woman involved after all. Which one of you was it?"

It was subtle and automatic. The five women all moved to stand together. For a moment, they all blended, standing shoulder to shoulder, as if they'd closed ranks against her. "Do you want to tell me what's going on here?"

"Nothing that need concern you, Callie," Margaret said. "Like everyone else in the country, we were just discussing that murderer, Günter Grass."

"He protected one of you, thus protecting all of you when he lied about being alone in this rampage?"

Margaret shot a look at the other four women, watched each of them nod, then turned back to face her daughter. "Listen to me, Callie, because this is the most important thing I will ever say to you in your life."

Not my mother, please, not my mother. "I'm listening."

"One of us was involved with Günter. Naturally she didn't know he was Günter. He told her his name was John Davis, probably another lie. She had no reason not to believe him when he told her he'd been born and raised in Maryland." Margaret paused a moment, saw that Callie was closely studying all their faces. "Do you want to know the why of all this tragedy, Callie? All right, I'll tell you. Did you know that it was Eliza Vickers herself who called me to tell me she was sleeping with Stewart?"

Callie shook her head. "No, I didn't know that."

"Oh yes. That bitch really wanted my husband. She wondered if I'd sensed he was having an affair, and of course I had. A wife always knows, they say, and it's true. But I hadn't asked Stewart for a divorce and she didn't understand that. So she told me that Stewart had admitted to her that he'd married me because he wanted to be close to you, Callie. Ridiculous, of course, and naturally, I laughed at her."

"Why didn't you ask Stewart for a divorce if you knew he was unfaithful to you?"

"I probably would have, eventually. To punish Stewart I came on to Sumner Wallace. It was small of me, but I wanted to break up their friendship. But that's not important now."

"I can't believe—Eliza really told you that?"

"Oh yes. She was getting desperate. She had only six more months in Stewart's chambers, then she was gone.

"Naturally, I told my friends. And one of them told her boyfriend. Günter. He was enraged that a Justice of the Supreme Court would sleep with a law clerk, that he would invite scandal and dishonor like that, hurt his wife and, in turn, her friends. She was angry as well, but she remembers now that he really seemed over the top about it. But then he didn't say anything more.

"Günter made his decision to kill Stewart. He didn't tell her what he'd done, and naturally, none of us imagined it was he who had killed Stewart.

"Then Danny O'Malley called me, saying he was going to tell the world about how Stewart had married me just to get at you if I didn't pay him off. Evidently he'd overheard Eliza's phone call to me. That was careless of her."

Callie said, "I don't understand. Danny went into my stepfather's office that Friday morning. Was he trying to blackmail Stewart as well?"

"Oh no. He was warning Stewart that all of it was going to hit the fan. He did this not because he worshiped Stewart, but because he knew that he could give him recommendations that would get him into the finest law offices in the country. But after Stewart was killed, Danny immediately realized what he knew was valuable. He told me he was also going to call Eliza, get money from her as well. Of course I told my friends about it, and without hesitation she told her boyfriend. Then Danny was garroted, just like Stewart."

"And no one considered this murderer just might be close to home?"

"Callie, you must understand. Günter never said another word about any of it to her. She had no idea if he'd even really paid any attention to her. Would you suspect your boyfriend of murder? Of course not.

"I will be honest with you. My friends suspected I was behind Stewart's death, though they loved me too much to openly accuse me. No, Bitsy, be quiet. It's true and you know it. Didn't I have the best reason?

"The evening of Stewart's funeral, your Detective Raven showed us all the photo of Günter, taken many years before. None of us recognized him, except the one who was seeing him, and even she wasn't certain, she was more disbelieving than anything.

"But she confronted him Friday morning. He changed, Callie, even as he told her it was the truth, she watched him change into a man she didn't know. He made her believe that if she told anyone, he had friends who would kill not only her, but the rest of us. She should have called the FBI, but she didn't, and it's too late now.

"He didn't tell her he was going to kill Eliza, but when Eliza's murder hit the news on Saturday, she knew. Oh yes, she knew, and she realized she was dealing with a madman.

"She was terrified, for herself and for us, and so she kept quiet. He kept telling her he was doing all this for her, for us, for me."

Callie said, "One of you was with him the night he shot up Agent Savich's house trying to kill Fleurette."

Margaret said, "She was an accessory to Fleurette's attempted murder, no denying that since she was in the car, waiting for him. Günter forced her to go with him. Again, he threatened to kill her if she didn't do exactly what he told her to do. You can't for one minute believe she knew what he planned, or that you were there, Callie."

"But she heard the shots. She knew something bad had happened."

"Oh yes, she knew, but she was also terrified. When she heard he'd been killed by the FBI, she called us. That's why we're all here. We didn't realize until after reading your story in the *Post,* Callie, that Günter had lied about all of it, to protect us."

"She knew, but she told no one."

"If she had, that crazy man might have killed her. He was crazy, Callie, you know that, regardless of why he did anything, he was crazy. He figured he had nothing to lose. What would you have done, Callie?"

I would have killed him myself, but she held herself quiet. "I don't know."

"No, no one could ever guess what she would do in such a situation. But the fact remains, crazy as he was, he protected her and the rest of us last night before he was killed. He lied to Savich and Sherlock and Ben, and they unwittingly lied to you and the world."

"You can't expect me to keep quiet about this, Mother."

"Yes, I can and I do, Callie. Think a moment. She didn't know what he planned, none of us did. She didn't know what he'd done until after she saw that photo and began to wonder, and then he killed Eliza. She was terrified, nearly over the edge herself.

"And she was terribly worried about me. I was a basket case, and she had to pretend that everything was all right, she had to protect me. As I said, it wasn't until we got word that Günter had been killed by the FBI that she told us the truth.

"What good would it do if you told your friend, Detective Raven, about this? What good? She might be prosecuted though she committed no crime. What would be the point of that? It could only result in the truth coming out. I loved your stepfather, Callie. I don't want his name going down in history as the Supreme Court Justice who screwed a law clerk and was murdered for it, along with two other law clerks. I know that you cared for him too. It's not much of a stretch to believe I would be implicated as well.

"She has suffered enough. All of us have.

Leave it alone, Callie. I'm asking you to leave it alone."

"I'm very sorry about the affair between Stewart and Eliza, Mother. I'm sorry you knew about it. I'm very sorry Eliza wasn't the fine woman Sherlock believed she was."

Margaret shrugged. "As I told you, a wife always knows."

Callie said, "Would all of you like to know something? Günter was dead wrong. Fleurette didn't know a thing about Stewart and Eliza. Regardless, one of you aided and abetted a murderer."

Margaret said, "Not knowingly, not willingly. She couldn't control him. He kept her a prisoner. She was as much a victim as the others."

"No, she's still alive, isn't she?"

Margaret said, "Günter was a madman when all was said and done. She was not responsible!"

Callie looked at each of them in turn. She'd known them all her life, loved and respected them. They were always there for each other. Even though one of them had kept quiet about her stepfather's murder, her mother had no intention of exposing her. None of them did. To tell the police would mean exposing her mother as well as the others.

"I don't know," Callie said. "I've got to think about this, Mother."

"While you're thinking, remind yourself what your own newspaper would do with this story. I want Stewart's name protected."

"I understand that."

He mother stepped back into the circle of women. "Think hard, Callie."

Four of them had hair long enough to fan out. Any of the four could have been in the car with Günter. Any could fit Mr. Avery's description.

Except for her mother. Thank God.

Callie looked at them one last time, wondering which one had slept with Günter, which one had been threatened by him, which one had lived with his madness, with the knowledge of what he was doing. And had done nothing to stop him in the end.

CHAPTER 38

Blessed Creek, Pennsylvania
The following Tuesday afternoon

Martin Thornton walked into Sheriff Doozer Harms's office. No one was inside except Doozer, sitting behind his big wooden desk, working the *New York Times* crossword. He looked up when the door opened. "How can I help you?" He laid down his pencil, but didn't rise.

Martin said, "I guess you don't remember me, do you, Sheriff Harms? Actually, I remember you even though the last time I saw you I was only six years old."

Sheriff Doozer Harms grew very still. He

looked behind the man standing in front of him out the glass windows that gave onto Main Street. He saw no one. He smiled and kicked back, put his booted feet up on his desk. "Well, well, if it isn't Austin Barrister. Imagine you of all people turning up on my doorstep this beautiful, snowy day. It is you, isn't it? It's hard to tell, you haven't aged well. Fancy you showing up here, after so many years."

"I came to see you because I remember now, Sheriff. I've been out to the house. It all came back to me when I stepped into the bathroom."

"So," Sheriff Harms said slowly, his fingers caressing the pistol butt on his belt, "you finally remember stabbing your mama, do you, boy?"

Martin smiled. "Nice try, Sheriff. But that isn't what happened. As I said, I remember, all of it. Clear as a bell."

Sheriff Harms rose, spread his palms on the desktop. "You were six years old when your mama died, Austin, a hysterical little boy who couldn't even say who he was or where he was. What you think you remember, Austin, it's all from your child's imagination."

"That's another good try, Sheriff."

"Nope, there's nothing for you to remember, but here you are, standing here in front of me in my office, all straight and defiant. Sometimes there's just no rhyme nor reason to life, is there? Hey, sometimes there is no big, bad wolf."

"And sometimes there is. That's what you are, Sheriff. You murdered my mother."

Sheriff Harms pulled the gun out of its holster. "You're not threatening an officer of the law, are you, Austin? Now, it isn't that I'm not glad to see you, but it's time for you to go away now. Don't come back."

"I saw you plunge the knife into her chest. It's as clear as anything now."

"What do you want, Austin?"

"The truth. That's all."

"You want the truth, do you? I wonder, are you devious enough to be wearing a wire, you little pissant?"

He laid his gun on the desktop, walked to Martin, jerked open his coat, and patted him down. No wire. And no gun. "Why are you really here, boy?"

"I want the truth, just like I said. I want to know why you did it."

Sheriff Harms stepped back, picked up his gun, and held it loosely in his hand.

Martin said, "I know you won't kill me, at least not here. In case you're tempted, though, my wife is down at the Blue Bird Café, expecting me in an hour. Nope, you can't kill me here, right in your office."

"Me kill you? Nah, I like to have my gun handy when I'm with people I don't trust, keeps them honest. No matter what you think you remember, I didn't do anything wrong. Now, why don't you get out of here."

Martin said, "I know you killed my mother. I also know there's nothing I can do about it. I'm not stupid. A little boy's testimony about something that happened over thirty years ago against the revered Sheriff of Blessed Creek—who would pay any attention?"

"There you go again, making accusations." He brought his gun up, aimed it at Martin's head. "You know, I could take you out and your wife too, if you screwed with me."

"I have no intention of screwing with you, Sheriff."

Sheriff Harms took a step back, leaned against his desk, the gun still in his hand. "Like you said, Austin, no one would pay any attention to you if you shot off your mouth.

But if you did, it would really piss me off. I'll bet you it'd piss me off enough to come after you and kill you dead. You know that, don't you, Austin?"

"Is there anything you'd flinch from doing, Sheriff?"

"I'm a lawman, and I've had the guts for thirty years to keep myself and this town safe from people like you. Don't you think to fuck with that, Austin."

"I'm asking you to tell me why you killed my mother."

Sheriff Harms walked to the door, opened it, looked up and down Main Street. A few people he'd known for years, but not a stranger in sight. He turned, shut the door, locked it. He leaned once more against his desk and grinned. "You know, it's just the two of us here. All my deputies are out patrolling. Grace is having her lunch."

"Then tell me the truth. You said it wouldn't matter."

"You want the truth? All right. Why the hell not? You really surprised your daddy."

"My father? Don't you try to bring my father into this. It was you I saw."

The sheriff laughed. "You really believe that? You lived another twelve years with your mama's murderer, at least with the guy who paid for it. Don't be stupid, Austin, of course your daddy was in on it. You know what else? After he left, Townsend called me once a week, told me how you didn't have a clue, not even an inkling of what had happened, didn't even seem to remember your mother, didn't seem to care. I stewed over it, worried about it, but after a few years, ended up letting it go.

"Then he called me, what was it—oh yeah, must have been nearly twenty years ago, scared out of his gourd that you were suddenly asking questions, and he worried you were going to remember. Your daddy was always a pathetic excuse for a man. He knew what had to be done, but he didn't have the guts to do it." Sheriff Harms shrugged. "I knew I should go right up to Boston and shoot your ass. I was planning my trip, didn't tell your daddy, of course, no telling what he'd have done, but then you just up and disappeared right after you graduated high school. I couldn't believe you did that, neither could your father. But you were gone. Poof, gone. I thought maybe you'd come back, but you didn't. I thought I'd find you. After all, you were only a kid, eighteen years old, and what did you know? I'll tell you, I checked you out as if you were a fugitive, looked all over for you, but there wasn't a single sign of you. No credit cards, no licenses, nothing at all.

"Then here came the Internet, every year better and better. It should have been a piece of cake, but it wasn't. I still couldn't find hide nor hair of you. How did you do it, Austin?"

"Actually, I bought an entire new identity, not all that hard when you hit the streets in Boston."

"Not bad for a puling little rich kid."

"Do you know I kept trying to make myself remember, but I couldn't? Just shadows, voices, until this afternoon when I finally went into the house, and walked into the bathroom where you murdered my mother, and then I climbed up into the attic.

"All right, Sheriff, tell me you're making this up about my father being involved. Tell me what happened."

Sheriff Harms laughed, stroked his fingers over the barrel of his gun, and began to toss it from his right to his left hand, again and again, knowing that Austin was looking at it. He wanted to scare him, make him worry that he might not live through this little drama, at least not for long. Maybe a nice car accident off the cliff road into Long's Quarry, with his wife in the car beside him.

Martin said, "There's no reason for you not to tell me, no reason for you to keep saying that my father was a part of it. You're just too chicken to tell the truth, aren't you, Sheriff? All you can do is throw the blame on someone else."

"Nah, why would I even care what you thought? Hey, I know Townsend's your dad, that you believed in him for eighteen years, but the fact is you must have known way down in your gut there was something wrong about your daddy, why else would you have skipped Boston, disappeared, never contacted him again?

"Yep, it was your daddy who wanted your mama murdered. He offered me a whole lot of money to off her. But you know, Austin, I was worried about keeping the money coming in since it was your mama who ran the business, and wasn't that a funny thing back then, particularly thirty years ago? But your daddy promised me it wouldn't be a problem, there was lots and lots of money, and he'd be in control again once she was out of the way. Your daddy liked to gamble, went off to Las Vegas at least once a month, and Sam was giving him grief about all his losses. Maybe he thought about divorcing her, I don't know. But what happened was that your mama figured out he was cheating on her. She had him followed, and a private investigator caught him catting around with a couple of local women. He documented it with lovely big black-and-white photos. Your mama was going to divorce him, and he couldn't have that. She'd take all his money, and you. I guess he figured he didn't have any choice but to have me kill her, so your daddy promised he'd get me elected sheriff of Blessed Creek for life, if that's what I wanted, and that's what I did want. I'd just been elected by a real narrow margin with his help, and I knew I'd need really big bucks to keep this job come the next election. It's amazing how well people treat you if you've got some money to spend, and your old man has paid me well over the years. It was sure a blessing for both of us that he married a rich woman in Boston, since he has no talent with money. His folks were right about that.

"You know something else, Austin? Your grandparents drowned in the lake, so drunk they couldn't even swim back to the frigging boat. I've wondered if maybe your daddy made their martinis really strong, or maybe added a little something extra. You know, I think they were about ready to acknowledge to the world that he wasn't quite right, that he was a real loser with money. But who cares when all's said and done?"

"So you two planned to murder her the day of my sixth birthday party."

"Everybody was there. It was a really big deal. There were so many people there, laughing, eating. After I made sure your daddy was surrounded by a dozen people so he'd have an alibi, I followed your mama to the bathroom and stabbed her in the heart. It was real easy.

"Only thing is, I looked up, and there you were, standing there, eyes wide as an owl's."

Martin said slowly, "And then you took my hands, told me Mommy would be all right, and you took me up to the attic."

"Fancy you remembering that. Your daddy was really pissed that you'd witnessed the murder, didn't know how you'd managed to slip away from all those kids you were play-ing with. That's when I put you in the attic, told you to stay there or something really bad would happen to you. We decided to leave you up there in the attic, in a nice dark corner, let you think about things. We left you there for a good hour, until Old Emily found your mother's body. That's when I had to get you down, before people started looking for you. You were so freaked out I nearly had to drag you out of the attic. You didn't say a word, just gave me this blank look.

"Your daddy got you out of there fast, right after the funeral. I think he was afraid I was planning how to kill you, and he was right about that. I hate loose ends. Another accident, I would have come up with something. You didn't speak for a month, and when you did, it was obvious you didn't remember anything, you had amnesia and your daddy didn't think you'd ever remember. And after a while I thought, Who'd believe a little kid anyway, without any proof? Why take the chance of another killing? So there's your truth, but don't ever think you can do anything with it. There wasn't ever a lick of proof, I made sure of that since I was the sheriff, responsible for investigating Samantha's murder. No murder weapon, no witnesses, no suspects. Well, the husband, there's always the husband, but he was pouring drinks for a dozen party guests, a great alibi. Who killed her? Hey, I tried my best, but I couldn't find the killer."

Martin's hands were tight fists at his sides. "I hope you got an ulcer worrying about me over the years."

"Nah, you became ancient history. So you've found out what you wanted to know. Why not do us both a favor, get lost, and get over it. You've been someone else for nearly twenty years anyway. If I were you, I'd stay that person, and I'd stay away from your daddy. No telling what he'd do if you confronted him now he's got that nice, rich wife and two daughters. He'd want to protect them from you. Hell, he might even kill you himself if you went to him and told him that you knew what he'd done."

"Are you planning to kill me, Sheriff Harms? Not here, you wouldn't be that stupid. But you're afraid I'll tell someone, aren't you? You wouldn't like that, it would mean a scandal, wouldn't it, open everything up again? And there's my father. You think I'd let him off the hook? Because of my half-sisters?" Martin walked up, grabbed the sheriff's shirt collar in his fists, and shouted right in his face,

"For the love of God, you crazy hick, he hired you to kill my mother! My mother!"

Sheriff Harms said very quietly, "Step away from me, boy, or I'll heave you out the door. Believe me now. If you do ever say anything, ever lay your hands on me again, I'll kill you and your wife. Count on it. Now get out, Austin."

Martin stepped back, lifted his right arm, and unbuttoned his cuff. He shook his wrist, and Sheriff Harms saw the small gold medical alert bracelet. "This is my wire, Sheriff. Things have progressed, haven't they? Everything you've said is crystal clear, for the future jury, on a tiny recorder in here. You've been had, Sheriff."

"I see you think you've been pretty smart about this, don't you," Sheriff Harms said, eyes hot and dark. "But it won't do you any good, you fucker. Your little wife either, if there even is a wife." He looked again into the deserted street outside and raised his gun. "Okay, Austin, I don't want to do it here, but it looks like I have to. What could I do, what with you coming in here and going crazy on me?"

A man's deep voice said from behind him, "I don't think so, Sheriff Harms."

The sheriff whirled around to face the man he'd worried himself nearly sick over since that snowy night two and a half weeks before, the man who'd claimed to have seen Samantha Barrister. "You!" He started to raise the pistol, but Savich was faster. He turned, kicked out his leg so fast it was a blur, and sent the pistol flying into the front window with such force it shattered the glass and skidded on the sidewalk in front of the sheriff's office.

Sheriff Harms yelled from the pain in his wrist, at the unfairness of it all, and lunged toward Savich.

Martin grabbed the sheriff's injured arm, jerked him around, and sent his fist into his jaw. The sheriff staggered, but didn't go down. Martin hit him against the side of his head, then landed a punch in his belly. The sheriff fell hard against his desk, landing facedown on the floor.

Savich stepped over him and tapped Martin's shoulder. "Looks like you laid him right out. Good job." He was grinning as he shook Martin's hand. "Well done, Martin. Do you feel you got everything we came for?"

Martin grinned back as he rubbed his knuckles. "Yeah, I do."

A Pennsylvania state trooper, Sergeant Ellis Wilkes, stepped in from the back of the office where a door led to three jail cells, then three more state troopers crowded in behind him. He stared down at the sheriff. "Imagine," he said, "this man has been the sheriff of Blessed Creek for more than half of his life, and all of it because of a vicious, cold-blooded murder."

Martin said, "Are you sure we've got enough on him?" He handed the small gold bracelet to Sergeant Wilkes.

"With the witnesses we have here today and that recorder, Sheriff Harms is toast. Oh yeah, he's going down big time."

"Good," Martin said. "Good." There was more relief in his voice than satisfaction. Finally, for him, it was over. Except for his dad.

He and Savich watched the state troopers haul out Sheriff Harms's unconscious body. When they were alone, Savich laid his hand on Martin's shoulder. "Your father, Martin. I spoke to the Boston police yesterday. In addition to everything else, they also have the evidence of over twenty years of payments to the sheriff. You can bet that Sheriff Harms will roll hard on him.

"The Boston police are waiting for me to call again before they pick him up."

"You knew my father had to be in on it, didn't you, Dillon?"

"Yes, it was the only thing that made sense. I have to call them, Martin."

"But you didn't say anything about it to me."

"No."

"Because you didn't think I could handle it."

"No, I didn't tell you because I knew you'd have doubts. It had to come from Sheriff Harms."

Martin Thornton nodded as he said without hesitation, "He paid this man to murder my mother. Make the call, Agent Savich." Martin heard Janet's voice, and turned to see her running ahead of Sherlock into the sheriff's office. He was smiling as he caught her up in his arms.

EPILOGUE

Georgetown
Washington, D.C.
End of January

Savich said, "Who was that on the phone?"

"Lily. She and Simon have decided to get married in March."

"Why March, for heaven's sake?"

Sherlock shook her head, smiling. "She said it just felt right and besides, she's made him suffer enough. She laughed, said Simon's agreed they'll live here in Washington for six months and New York for six months. We'll see how long that lasts. Oh yes, *No Wrinkles Remus* has been picked up by *Newsday*."

"Good. Someone there's got a brain. It's one of the best political cartoons I've ever seen. And what a relief. She's finally picked the right man, thank the good Lord."

Sherlock handed him a sleeping Sean, who gave a little snort when he felt his father's big hand stroke his back.

"I heard from Janet and Martin Thornton today. They're doing fine. Martin's on some meds, as you know, but he said his shrink doesn't think he'll need them for much longer, given what's happened. I think he's smart and insightful. Best of all, he's got Janet. She's working on getting him to contact his stepmother and his two half-sisters. Maybe they can help each other. Hey, sweetheart, you ready for bed?"

"Well," Sherlock said, "Sean certainly is. I was thinking about a nice hot shower. You know, I haven't scrubbed your back in a while. Not since Wednesday night when you came in all sweaty from the gym. What do you think?"

Savich kissed her ear. He was whistling quietly as they walked upstairs. In the shower, Sherlock soaped up her hands and washed his back. He was leaning against the tiled wall, feeling almost relaxed enough to collapse and drown, when she said, "Are you satisfied we did the right thing about Günter?"

Savich stilled a moment. "Yes. I'm very glad you suggested we discuss what happened before we talked to anyone else. We saved Margaret Califano and Callie endless pain, and protected Justice Califano from a scandal that would have destroyed his name and harmed the Supreme Court itself."

She nodded against his shoulder. "I still wonder, though, if Günter acted alone."

"Remember Günter said he'd tell us a bit of truth? And so, I think, he did. Let it go, sweetheart. I have."

He turned around to face her. Hot water cascaded down over them. "I decided to label that file Pandora's box to remind me that Mr. Maitland is satisfied that Günter acted alone. So, yes, I'm going to keep that box tightly closed."

She let the water pulse against her back as she lathered her hands to scrub down his chest. She raised her face. "I sure don't want the key to that box. Let's forget there is one, Dillon, okay?"

.   .   .

It was late, deep in the night, when Savich shook his wife's shoulder. "Wake up, Sherlock, wake up. You're dreaming."

Sherlock jerked awake, blinked at his face above hers. "What? Dillon? What's the matter?"

"You were moving around, dreaming. A nightmare?"

Sherlock shook her head back and forth on the pillow. "No, no nightmare. Actually, for the very first time, I dreamed about Samantha."

He pulled her tightly against him, and said against her hair, "I dreamed about her as well. Did she say or do anything in your dream?"

"No, she was there, in my line of sight, and she was smiling. What was your dream about, Dillon?"

He turned over on his back, his arms crossed under his head. "She gave me a beautiful smile, too, and then nodded to me and patted my arm. I felt this wonderful feeling of warmth and contentment come over me. Then she was gone, and I woke up to hear you thrashing about."

"Do you think you'll tell Sean about her someday?"

Savich laughed. "Doubtful, but who knows?"

"I wonder if there were things your father never told you that happened to him."

"I'd bet the bank on it."

Sherlock settled back down for sleep, her head on her husband's shoulder. "The oddest thing, Dillon, I think I smell jasmine."

Savich didn't say anything. He wasn't about to say the words out loud. He breathed in the subtle scent, and closed his eyes.

Callie Markham's apartment
Georgetown
That same evening

Ben rang the doorbell.

A good three minutes later the front door opened and Callie stood there, wearing old sweats and thick socks on her feet. Her hair was uncombed, and her face was scrubbed clean. She squeaked. "I should have known you'd catch me looking like the rag queen.

You're early. I haven't put on the little black dress yet."

He stepped in, pulled her against him, and kissed her. "I don't care. I wrapped up a case early and I wanted to see you, maybe celebrate with a good-quality beer."

"I've got some Coors stashed in the fridge for our Super Bowl party."

As he followed her through the living room and into the kitchen, he was struck, as he usually was, by the number of books. They were everywhere, on every surface, overflowing every bookshelf, even though three entire walls of the living room were covered with built-ins. And there were flowers, three vases of them, Christmas cacti blooming wildly, and at least half a dozen different kinds of ivy, all trailing happily over surfaces to the floor. A good dozen bright pillows were tossed on every chair and sofa. Even the rugs that covered the wooden floor were bright, each a different style. It was warm and inviting. He liked being in the room, watching TV, reading, making love with Callie. It felt like home. He lightly touched his hand to her shoulder. "Have I told you how much I like your apartment?"

"Sounds to me like you're laying down some pretty broad hints here, Ben."

"It's bigger than my place. You've got a guestroom, and your office is really too big for you. You need another body in there to make it feel like home."

"You mean like Dillon and Sherlock's?"

"Something like that. Remember you told me I was a natural?"

"Yes, I remember."

"What did you mean by that?"

She looked at the white curtains splotched with red poppies covering the kitchen windows that Janette had sewn for her. She closed her eyes a moment, drew a deep breath, and looked down at her nails. She needed a manicure.

"Well? What do you say? You want to marry me?"

Very slowly, she turned back and stepped against him, wrapped her arms around his back. She said against his neck, "For such a guy, that wasn't a bad proposal at all. I'll think about it."

"Fair enough. Then I'll tell you I love you if you'll say it at the same time. On three?"

"I'm counting," she said, and clicked off her fingers. They were both laughing when they shouted out at the same time, "I love you!"

Later, when they were sitting on the sofa, Callie on his lap, leaning against his shoulder, Ben said, "I know you're grieving for your stepfather, but I was wondering if there was something else, Callie."

"What do you mean—?"

He talked right over her. "Sometimes you look a million miles away, like you're thinking about something that's taking you else-where."

She was silent.

"I hope you feel you can tell me anything, Callie."

She raised her head and looked him squarely in the eyes. "What happened, Ben—Günter dying like he did—it was for the best. I know that."

He nodded, waited.

"I guess I mean that it's over. All of it, and there's only the aftermath to deal with and I'm doing that." She kissed him on the cheek. "Did I tell you that I am very happy you're in my life?"

She watched his expression lighten, saw humor come back into his eyes. He was grinning as he said, "Tell me every day, okay. You want to know something?"

"Since I'm maybe even practically engaged to you, I guess I can handle anything you want to tell me."

"I think you're a natural too."